THE ROSE CODE

Kate Quinn is the *New York Times* and *USA Today* bestselling author of historical fiction. A native of southern California, she attended Boston University where she earned a Bachelor's and Master's degree in Classical Voice. She has written four novels in the Empress of Rome Saga, and two books set in the Italian Renaissance, before turning to the 20th century with *The Alice Network*, *The Huntress*, and *The Rose Code*. All have been translated into multiple languages. Kate and her husband now live in San Diego with three rescue dogs.

ALSO BY KATE QUINN

The Alice Network
The Huntress

THE EMPRESS OF ROME SERIES

Lady of the Eternal City
The Three Fates (novella)
Empress of the Seven Hills
Daughters of Rome
Mistress of Rome

THE BORGIA CHRONICLES

The Lion and the Rose
The Serpent and the Pearl

COLLABORATIVE WORKS

A Day of Fire: A Novel of Pompeii
A Year of Ravens: A Novel of Boudica's Rebellion
A Song of War: A Novel of Troy
Ribbons of Scarlet: A Novel of the French Revolution's Women

THE ROSE CODE

KATE QUINN

HarperCollins*Publishers*

HarperCollins*Publishers* Ltd
1 London Bridge Street
London SE1 9GF

www.harpercollins.co.uk

HarperCollins*Publishers*
1st Floor, Watermarque Building, Ringsend Road
Dublin 4, Ireland

First published in the United States by William Morrow,
an imprint of HarperCollins*Publishers* 2021

This edition published by HarperCollins*Publishers* 2021

1

A catalogue record for this book
is available from the British Library

ISBN: 978-0-00-845584-2 (HB)
ISBN: 978-0-00-845585-9 (TPB)

Printed and bound in Great Britain by
CPI Group (UK) Ltd, Croydon CR0 4YY

MIX
Paper from
responsible sources
FSC C007454

This book is produced from independently certified FSC™ paper
to ensure responsible forest management.

For more information visit: www.harpercollins.co.uk/green

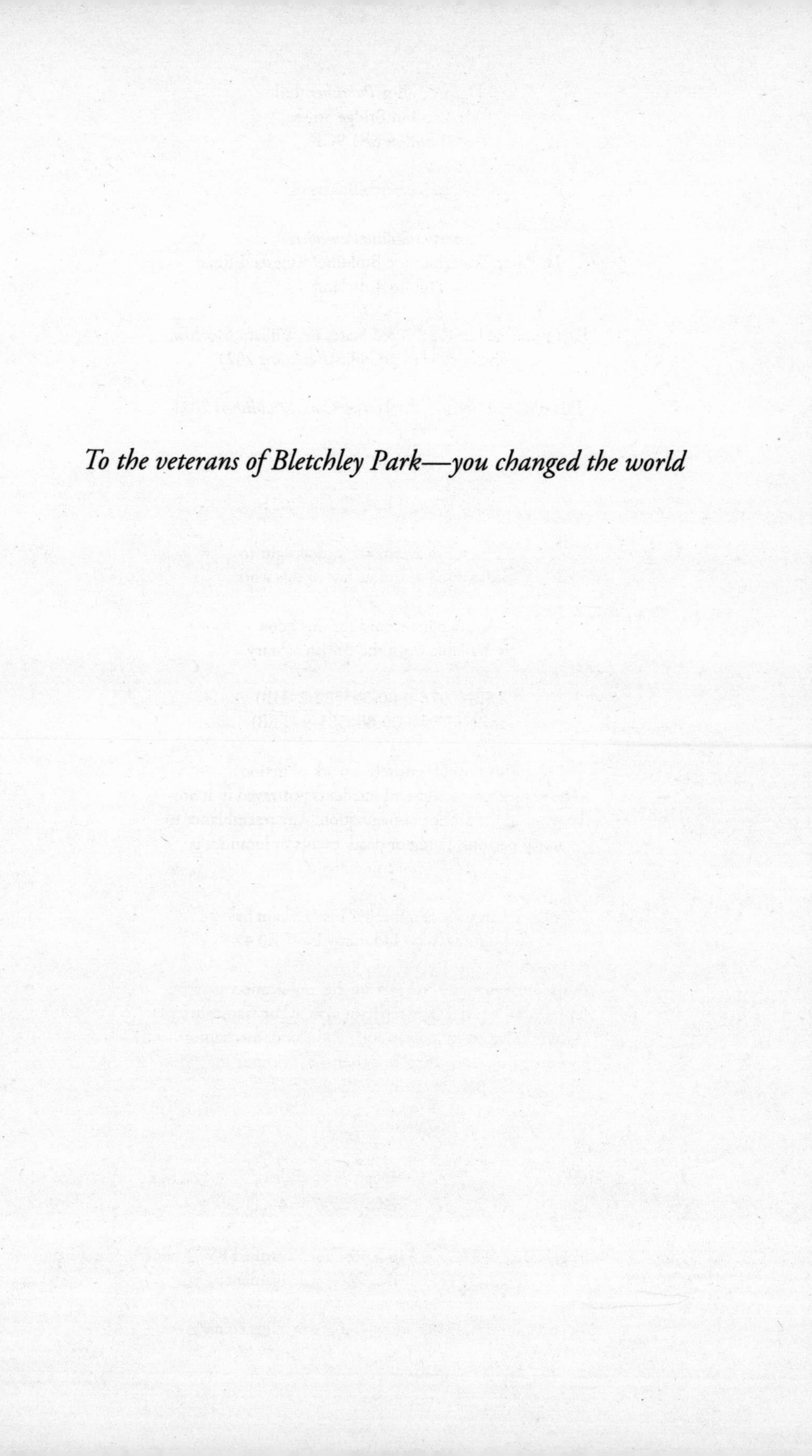

To the veterans of Bletchley Park—you changed the world

INTRODUCTION

In the autumn of 1939, Hitler's advance seemed unstoppable.

German military communications were relayed using hand ciphers, teleprinter codes, and above all Enigma machines—portable cipher devices that scrambled orders into nonsense so they could be relayed via Morse code over radio transmitters, then unscrambled in the field.

Even if the scrambled orders were intercepted by the Allies, no one could break the encryption. Germany thought Enigma was unbreakable.

They were wrong.

PROLOGUE

November 8, 1947
London

The enigma arrived in the afternoon post, sealed, smudged, and devastating.

Osla Kendall stood, twenty-six years old, dark haired, dimpled, and scowling, in the middle of a tiny Knightsbridge flat that looked as if it had been bombed by Junkers, wearing nothing but a French lace slip and a foul mood as she looked at the piles of silk and satin exploding over every surface. *Twelve Days Until the Wedding of the Century!* this morning's *Tatler* had gushed. Osla worked for the *Tatler;* she'd had to write the whole ghastly column. *What are YOU going to wear?*

Osla picked up a rose satin gown whorled with crystal beading. "What about you?" she asked it. "Do you say 'I look simply smashing and I couldn't care less that he's marrying someone else'?" Etiquette lessons at finishing school never touched *that* one. Whatever the dress, everyone in the congregation would know that before the bride came along, Osla and the bridegroom were—

A knock sounded. Osla flung on a robe to answer it. Her flat was tiny, all she could afford on her *Tatler* salary if she wanted to live alone *and* be close to the center of things. "Darling, no maid?

No doorman?" Her mother had been appalled. "Move in with me until you find a husband. You don't need a *job*." But after sharing bedrooms with billet-mates all through the war, Osla would have lived in a boot cupboard as long as she could call it her own.

"Post's come, Miss Kendall." The landlady's spotty daughter greeted her at the door, eyes going at once to the rose gown slung over Osla's arm. "Oooh, are you wearing that to the royal wedding? You look scrummy in pink!"

It's not enough to look scrummy, Osla thought, taking her bundle of letters. *I want to outshine a princess, an actual born-to-the-tiara princess, and the fact is, I can't.*

"Stop that," she told herself as soon as she'd shut the door on the landlady's daughter. "Do *not* fall in the dismals, Osla Kendall." All over Britain, women were planning what they'd wear for the most festive occasion since V-E Day. Londoners would queue for hours to see the flower-decked wedding carriages roll past—and Osla had an invitation to Westminster Abbey itself. If she wasn't grateful for that, she'd be just like those ghastly Mayfair moaners blithering on about how *tiresome* it was attending the social event of the century; what a *bother* getting the diamonds out of the bank, oh, woe is me to be so tediously *privileged*.

"It'll be topping," Osla said through gritted teeth, coming back to her bedroom and chucking the rose dress over a lamp. "Simply topping." Seeing London swanning about in banners and confetti, wedding fever whisking away November chill and postwar gloom . . . the fairy-tale union of Princess Elizabeth Alexandra Mary and her handsome Lieutenant Philip Mountbatten (formerly Prince Philip of Greece) would mark the dawn of a new age, hopefully one where ration laws were finally swatted down and you could slather all the butter you wanted on your scones. Osla was all in favor of ushering this new era in with a slap-up celebration—after all, she'd achieved her own fairy-tale ending by any woman's standards. An honorable term of service during the war, even if she could never, *ever* talk about it; a flat in Knightsbridge paid for by her own salary; a wardrobe crammed with gowns all in the latest go; a job writing entertaining fluff for the *Tatler*. And a fiancé who had put a sparkling emerald on her finger; don't forget him. No, Osla Kendall had no excuse to get in a blue funk. All the business with Philip had been years ago, after all.

But if she could have cooked up an excuse to get out of London—found some way to be geographically elsewhere (the Sahara desert, the wastes of the North Pole, *anywhere*)—during the moment Philip bent his golden head and made his vows to England's future queen, Osla would have taken it in a jiff.

Ruffling a hand through disordered dark curls, she flipped through the post. Invitations, bills . . . and one square, smudged envelope. No letter inside, just a torn sheet of paper with a block of scribbled nonsense letters.

The world tilted for a moment, and Osla was back: the smell of coke stoves and wet wool jumpers instead of furniture polish and tissue paper; the scratch of pencils rather than the hoot of London traffic. *What does* Klappenschrank *mean, Os? Who's got their German dictionary?*

Osla didn't stop to wonder who'd sent the paper—the old pathways in her mind fired up without a hitch, the ones that said, *Don't ask questions, just get on with it.* She was already running her fingers along the square of scribbled letters. *Vigenère cipher,* a woman's soft voice said in her memory. *Here's how to crack it using a key. Though it can be done without . . .*

"Not by me," Osla muttered. She hadn't been one of the boffins who could crack ciphers with a pencil stub and a little sideways thinking.

The envelope bore a postmark she didn't recognize. No signature. No address. The letters of the cipher message were so hastily slashed, it could have been anyone's handwriting. But Osla turned the paper scrap over and saw a letterhead block, as though the page had been torn from an official pad.

CLOCKWELL SANITARIUM

"No," Osla whispered, "no—" But she was already fishing a pencil stub from the nearest drawer. Another memory, a laughing voice intoning, *These have knelled your fall and ruin, but your ears were far away—English lassies rustling papers through the sodden Bletchley day!*

Osla knew what the message's key would be: LASSIES.

She bent over the paper, pencil scratching, and slowly the cryptogram gave up its secrets.

"STONEGROVE 7602."

Osla drew a breath in as the words crackled along the telephone wires all the way from Yorkshire. Astounding how you could recognize a voice in two words, even when you hadn't heard it in years. "It's me," Osla finally said. "Did you get it?"

Pause. "Goodbye, Osla," her old friend said coolly. No *who is this*—she knew, too.

"Do not hang up on me, Mrs.—well, whatever your name *is* now."

"Temper, Os. Feeling out of sorts because you're not the one marrying a prince in two weeks?"

Osla caught her lip in her teeth before she could snap back. "I'm not faffing about here. Did you get the letter or not?"

"The what?"

"The Vigenère. Mine mentions you."

"I'm just home from a seaside weekend. I haven't looked through the post yet." There was a distant rustle of paper. "Look, why are you ringing me? I don't—"

"It's from *her,* you understand me? From the *asylum.*"

A flat, stunned silence.

"It can't be," the reply came at last. Osla knew they were both thinking of their former friend. The third point in their shining wartime trio.

More rustling, a tearing sound, then Osla heard a breath and knew that far away in Yorkshire, another block of code had come out of its envelope. "Break it, the way she showed us. The key is *lassies.*"

"'*English lassies rustling papers through the sodden—*'" Breaking off before the next word. Secrecy was too much a habit with them both to say anything significant over a telephone line. Live seven years with the Official Secrets Act round your neck like a noose, and you got used to curbing every word and thought. Osla heard a pencil working on the other end and found herself pacing, three steps across the room, three steps back. The heaps of gowns across the bedroom looked like cheap pirate's loot, gaudy and half-submerged in the wreckage of tissue and cardboard, memories and time. Three girls laughing, doing up each other's buttons in a cramped spare bedroom: *Did you hear there's a dance in Bedford? An American band, they've got all the new Glenn Miller tunes . . .*

The voice came at last from Yorkshire, uneasy and mulish. "We don't know it's her."

"Don't be daft, of course it's her. The stationery, it's from where she—" Osla chose her words carefully. "Who else would demand our help?"

Pure fury in the words that came spitting back. "I don't owe her one bloody thing."

"She clearly thinks differently."

"Who knows what she thinks? She's *insane,* remember?"

"She had a breakdown. That doesn't mean she went loony."

"She's been in an asylum nearly three and a half years." Flatly. "We have no idea what she's like now. She certainly *sounds* loony—these things she's alleging . . ."

There was no way they could voice, on a public line, what their former friend was alleging.

Osla pressed her fingertips to her eyes. "We've got to meet. We can't discuss this any other way."

Her former friend's voice was full of broken glass. "Go to hell, Osla Kendall."

"We served there together, remember?"

On the other end of Britain, the handset slammed down. Osla lowered her own with shaky calm. *Three girls during a war,* she thought. Once the best of friends.

Until D-Day, the fatal day, when they had splintered apart and become two girls who couldn't stand the sight of each other, and one who had disappeared into a madhouse.

Inside the Clock

Far away, a gaunt woman stared out the window of her cell and prayed to be believed. She had very little hope. She lived in a house of the mad, where truth became madness and madness, truth.

Welcome to Clockwell.

Life here was like a riddle—a riddle she'd heard during the war, in a wonderland called Bletchley Park: "If I was to ask what direction a clock's hands go, what would *you* say?"

"Um," she had answered, flustered. "Clockwise?"

"Not if you're inside the clock."

I'm inside the clock now, she thought. *Where everything runs backward and no one will ever believe a word I say.*

Except—maybe—the two women she had betrayed, who had betrayed her, who had once been her friends.

Please, the woman in the asylum prayed, looking south, where her ciphered messages had flown like fragile paper birds. *Believe me.*

EIGHT YEARS AGO

December 1939

CHAPTER 1

"*I wish I was a woman of about thirty-six, dressed in black satin with a string of pearls,*'" Mab Churt read aloud. "That's the first sensible thing you've said, you silly twit."

"What are you reading?" her mother asked, flipping through an old magazine.

"*Rebecca,* Daphne du Maurier." Mab turned a page. She was taking a break from her dog-eared list of "100 Classic Literary Works for the Well-Read Lady"—not that Mab was a lady, or particularly well-read, but she intended to be both. After plowing through number 56, *The Return of the Native* (ugh, Thomas Hardy), Mab figured she'd earned a dip into something enjoyable like *Rebecca*. "The heroine's a drip and the hero's one of those broody men who bullies you and it's supposed to be appealing. But I can't put it down, somehow." Maybe just the fact that when Mab envisioned herself at thirty-six, she was definitely wearing black satin and pearls. There was also a Labrador lying at her feet, in this dream, and a room lined with books she actually *owned,* rather than dog-eared copies from the library. Lucy was in this dream too, rosy in a plum-colored gym slip, the kind girls wore when they went to some expensive day school and rode ponies.

Mab looked up from *Rebecca* to watch her little sister canter her fingers over imaginary fences: Lucy, nearly four years old and too skinny for Mab's liking, dressed in a grubby jumper and skirt, forever pulling off her socks. "Lucy, stop that." Tugging the sock back up over Lucy's foot. "It's too cold to be running around barefoot like a Dickens orphan." Mab had done Dickens last year, numbers 26 through 33, plowing through chapters on her tea breaks. Blech, *Martin Chuzzlewit.*

"Ponies don't wear socks," Lucy said severely. She was mad for horses; every Sunday Mab took her to Hyde Park to watch the riders. Oh, Lucy's eyes when she saw those burnished little girls trotting past in their jodhpurs and boots. Mab yearned to see Lucy perched on a well-groomed Shetland.

"Ponies don't wear socks, but little girls do," she said. "Or they catch cold."

"You played barefoot all your life, and you never caught cold." Mab's mother shook her head. She'd given Mab her height, an inch shy of six feet, but Mab stretched into her height with lifted chin and squared shoulders, and Mrs. Churt always slouched. The cigarette between her lips waggled as she murmured aloud from an old issue of the *Bystander.* "'*Two 1939 debs, Osla Kendall and the Honorable Guinevere Brodrick, had Ian Farquhar to chat to them between races.*' Look at that mink on the Kendall girl . . ."

Mab cast an eye over the page. Her mother found it all enthralling—which daughter of Lord X curtsied to the queen, which sister of Lady Y appeared at Ascot in violet taffeta—but Mab studied the society pages like an instruction manual: what ensembles could be copied on a shopgirl budget? "I wonder if there'll be a Season next year, what with the war."

"Most debs'll be joining the Wrens, I reckon. It's the Land Army or the ATS for folks like us, but posh girls all go for the Women's Royal Naval Service. They say they got the uniform designed by Molyneux, him who dresses Greta Garbo and the Duchess of Kent . . ."

Mab frowned. There were uniforms everywhere these days—so

far, the only sign there even *was* a war. She'd been standing in this same East London flat, smoking tensely alongside her mother as they listened to the radio announcement from Downing Street, feeling chilly and strange as Chamberlain's weary voice intoned, "This country is at war with Germany." But since then, there'd hardly been a peep from the Huns.

Her mother was reading aloud again. "'*The Honorable Deborah Mitford on a paddock seat with Lord Andrew Cavendish.*' Look at that lace, Mabel . . ."

"It's Mab, Mum." If she was stuck with *Churt,* she wasn't ruddy well putting up with *Mabel.* Plowing her way through *Romeo and Juliet* (number 23 on Mab's list), she had run across Mercutio's "*I see Queen Mab hath been with you!*" and plucked it out on the spot. "Queen Mab." That sounded like a girl who wore pearls, bought her little sister a pony, and married a gentleman.

Not that Mab had any fantasies about dukes in disguise or millionaires with Mediterranean yachts—life wasn't a novel like *Rebecca.* No mysterious moneyed hero was going to swoop a Shoreditch girl off her feet, no matter how well-read. But a *gentleman,* some nice, comfortable man with a decent education and a good profession—yes, a husband like that was within reach. He was out there. Mab just had to meet him.

"Mab!" Her mother shook her head, amused. "Who d'you think you are, then?"

"Someone who can do better than *Mabel.*"

"You and your *better.* What's good enough for the rest of us isn't good enough for you?"

No, Mab thought, knowing better than to say so, because she'd come to learn that people didn't like your wanting more than you had. She'd grown up fifth of six children all crammed together in this cramped flat that smelled of fried onions and regret, a toilet that had to be shared with two other families—she'd be damned if she'd ever be ashamed of it, but she'd be doubly damned if it was *enough.* Was it such a terrible thing, wanting to do more than work in a factory until you got married? Wanting more in a husband than one of the local factory workers, who would probably drink too much and eventually run out altogether like Mab's dad? Mab never tried to tell her family they could make more of themselves; it was fine with her if they were happy with what they had, so why couldn't they leave *her* alone?

"You think you're too good to work?" Mum had demanded when Mab protested leaving school at fourteen. "All these kids around and your father gone—"

"I'm not too good to work," Mab had flashed back. "But I'm going to work *for* something." Even at fourteen, laboring at the grocer's and dodging the clerks who pinched her bum, she'd been looking ahead. She got a clerk's post and studied how the better customers talked and dressed. She learned how to carry herself, how to look people in the eye. After a year's scrutiny of the girls who worked the counters at Selfridges, she walked through those double doors on Oxford Street in a cheap suit and good shoes that had taken half a year's wages, and landed herself a job selling powder compacts and scent. "Aren't you lucky," Mum had said, as if it hadn't taken any work at all.

And Mab wasn't done yet, not by a long shot. She'd just finished a scrimped-for secretarial course, and by the time she turned twenty-two early next year she intended to be sitting behind some shiny desk, taking dictation and surrounded by people who said "Good morning, Miss Churt" instead of "Oi, Mabel!"

"What are you going to do with all that planning?" her mother asked. "Get yourself a fancy boyfriend to pick up the tab for a few dinners?"

"I've no interest in fancy boyfriends." As far as Mab was concerned, love stories were for novels. Love wasn't the point—even marriage wasn't the point, not really. A good husband might have been the fastest way up the ladder toward safety and prosperity, but it wasn't the only way. Better to live an old maid with a shiny desk and a salary in the bank, proudly achieved through the sweat of her own efforts, than end up disappointed and old before her time thanks to long factory hours and too much childbirth.

Anything was better than that.

Mab glanced at the clock. Time for work. "Give me a kiss, Luce. How's that finger?" Mab examined the upheld knuckle where Lucy had run a splinter yesterday. "Good as new. Goodness, you're grubby . . ." Wiping Lucy's cheeks with a fresh handkerchief.

"A little dirt never hurt anyone," Mrs. Churt said.

"I'll draw you a bath when I get home." Mab kissed Lucy, fighting irritation at her mother. *She's tired, that's all.* Mab still winced to remember how furious Mum had been, enduring such a late addition to a family that already boasted five children. "I'm too old to be chasing after babies," Mum had sighed, watching Lucy crawl about the floor like a crab. Still, there hadn't exactly been anything they could do about it except manage.

For a little while longer, anyway, Mab thought. If she landed a good husband she'd wheedle him into helping her sister, so Lucy would never have to leave school for a job at fourteen. If he'd give her that, Mab would never ask for anything else.

Cold slapped her cheeks as she hurried out of the flat into the street. Five days until Christmas, but no snow yet. Two girls in Auxiliary Territorial Service uniforms hurried past, and Mab wondered where she'd sign up if service became compulsory . . .

"Fancy a walk, darling?" A fellow in RAF uniform fell into step beside her. "I'm on leave, show a fellow a good time."

Mab shot him the glance she'd perfected at fourteen, a ferocious stare leveled from below very straight, very black brows, then sped her pace. *You could join the WAAF,* she thought, reminded by the fellow's uniform that the Royal Air Force had a Women's Auxiliary branch. Better than being a Land Girl, stuck shoveling cow shit in Yorkshire.

"Come on, that's no way to treat a man going to war. Let's have a kiss . . ."

He sneaked an arm around her waist, squeezing. Mab smelled beer, hair cream, and an ugly flicker of memory pushed upward. She shoved it down, fast, and her voice came out more of a snarl than she intended. "Bugger off—" And she kicked the pilot in the shins with swift, hard efficiency. He yelped, staggering on the icy cobbles. Mab pried his hand off her hip and headed for the Tube, ignoring the things he called after her, shaking off the shiver of memory. Silver linings—the streets might have been full of handsy soldiers, but plenty of soldiers wanted to take a girl to the altar, not just to bed. If there was anything war brought in its wake, it was hasty weddings. Mab had already seen it in Shoreditch: brides saying their vows without even waiting for a secondhand wedding dress, anything to get that ring on their finger before their fiancés went off to fight. And well-read gentlemen rushed off to war every bit as fast as Shoreditch men. Mab certainly wasn't going to call the war a good thing—she'd read her Wilfred Owen and Francis Gray, even if war poetry had been deemed too indelicate for "100 Classic Literary Works for the Well-Read Lady." But she'd have had to be an idiot not to realize that war was going to change her world beyond rationing.

Maybe she wouldn't need to get a secretarial post after all. Could there be war work somewhere in London for a girl who'd come tops in typing and shorthand, some post where Mab could do her part for king and country, meet a nice man or two, and look after her family?

A shop door banged open, releasing brief strains of "The Holly and the Ivy" from a radio inside. By Christmas of 1940, Mab thought, things might be entirely different. This year, things had to change.

War meant change.

CHAPTER 2

I need a job. It had been Osla's first thought, returning to England at the end of '39.

"Darling, aren't you supposed to be in Montreal?" her friend Sally Norton had exclaimed. Osla and the Honorable Sarah Norton shared a godfather and had been presented at court a Season apart; Sally had been the first person Osla telephoned when she stepped back on English soil. "I thought your mother shipped you off to the cousins when war broke out."

"Sal, do you think *anything* was going to keep me from finagling my way home?" It had taken Osla six weeks, seething and furious, to scheme an escape after her mother had shipped her to Montreal. Some shameless flirtation with a few influential men for travel permits, some creative fibbing to her Canadian cousins, a tiny bit of fraud—that air ticket from Montreal to Lisbon had been *much* better off with Osla than its original owner—and a boat ride out of Portugal later, *voilà*. "Goodbye, Canada!" Osla sang, tossing her traveling case into the taxi. Osla might have been born in Montreal, but she didn't remember anything before arriving in England at the age of four, trailing behind a recently divorced mother along with the trunks and the scandal. Canada was beautiful, but England was home. Better to be bombed at home among friends than be safe and corroding in exile.

"I need a job," Osla told Sally. "Well, first I need a hairdresser because that horrid boat from Lisbon gave me lice, and I look like a dog's dinner. *Then* I need a job. Mamma's in such a pelter she's cut off my allowance, for which I don't blame her. Besides, we've got to poker up, as the Yanks might say, and do our bit for the war." The old sceptred isle in her hour of need, and so forth. You couldn't be booted out of as many boarding schools as Osla Kendall without picking up a good bit of Shakespeare.

"The Wrens—"

"Don't talk slush, Sal, everyone expects girls like us to join the WRNS." Osla had been called a *silly deb* enough times for it to sting—a burbling belle, a champagne Shirley, a mindless Mayfair muffin. Well, this Mayfair muffin was going to show everyone a society girl could get her hands dirty. "Let's join the Land Army. Or make airplanes, how about that?"

"Do you know anything about making airplanes?" Sally had laughed, echoing the dubious labor superintendent at the Hawker Siddeley factory in Colnbrook, where they applied several days later.

"I know how to take the rotor arm off an automobile to save it being stolen by Huns if we get invaded," Osla retorted pertly. And in no time at all she was clapped into a boiler suit, drilling eight hours a day in the factory training room beside fifteen other girls. Maybe it was dull work but she was earning a wage, living independently for the first time in her life.

"I thought we'd be working on Spitfires and flirting with pilots," Sally complained across the workbench on New Year's Eve. "Not just drilling, drilling, drilling."

"No grousing," the instructor warned, overhearing. "There's a war on, you know!"

Everyone was saying that now, Osla had observed. Milk run out? *There's a war on!* Ladder in your stockings? *There's a war on!*

"Don't tell me you don't despise this stuff," Sally muttered, banging her Dural sheet, and Osla eyed her own with loathing. Dural made the outer skins for the Hurricanes flown by RAF squadrons (if RAF squadrons actually flew any missions in this war where nothing yet was happening), and Osla had spent the last two months learning to drill it, file it, and pot-rivet it. The metal fought and spat and gave off shavings that clogged her hair and nose so thickly her bathwater turned gray. She hadn't known it was possible to cherish a hatred this profound for a metal alloy, but there you were.

"You'd better save some swoony RAF pilot's life when you're finally slapped onto the side of a Hurricane," she told the sheet, leveling her drill at it like a gunslinger in a cowboy film.

"Thank God we got tonight off for New Year's," Sally said when the clock finally ticked over to six in the evening and everyone streamed for the doors. "What dress did you bring?"

"The green satin. I can slither into it at my mother's suite at Claridge's."

"She's forgiven you for bunking out of Montreal?"

"More or less. She's chuffed about everything these days because she's got a new beau." Osla just hoped he wouldn't be stepfather number four.

"Speaking of admirers, there's a gorgeous fellow I promised to introduce you to." Sally threw Osla an arch look. "He's the goods."

"He'd better be dark. Blond men simply aren't to be trusted."

They pelted laughing through the factory gate toward the road. With only twenty-four hours off every eighth day, there was no point wasting a minute of those precious hours heading back to their digs; they hitched a ride straight into London in an ancient Alvis, its headlights fitted with slotted masks to meet blackout regulations, driven by a pair of lieutenants who were already absolutely kippered. They were all singing "Anything Goes" by the time the Alvis pulled up at Claridge's, and as Sally lingered to flirt, Osla skipped up the front steps toward the hall porter who for years had been a sort of butler, uncle, and social secretary combined. "Hello, Mr. Gibbs."

"Good evening, Miss Kendall. You're in town with Miss Norton? Lord Hartington was asking after her."

Osla lowered her voice. "Sally's fixing me up with someone. Did she give you a hint?"

"She did indeed. He's inside—Main Lounge, Royal Navy cadet uniform." Mr. Gibbs looked judicious. "Shall I tell him you'll be down in an hour, once you've changed?"

"If he doesn't love me in a boiler suit, he's not worth dressing up for in the first place." Sally came dashing up and started interrogating Gibbs about Billy Hartington, and Osla sauntered inside. She rather enjoyed the stuffy looks from men in their evening tails and women in their satin gowns as she breezed over the art deco floors in a grubby boiler suit. *Look at me!* she wanted to shout. *I've just finished an eight-hour day in an airplane factory and now I'm going to do the conga round the Café de Paris until dawn. Look at me, Osla Kendall, eighteen years old and finally* useful.

She spotted him at the bar in his cadet uniform, turned away so she couldn't see his face. "You wouldn't happen to be my date, would you?" Osla asked that set of rather splendid shoulders. "Mr. Gibbs says you are, and anybody who's ever been to Claridge's knows Mr. Gibbs is never wrong."

He turned, and Osla's first thought was, *Sally, you rat, you might have* warned *me!* Actually, that was her second thought. Osla's first thought was that even though she'd never met him, she knew exactly who he was. She'd seen his name in the *Tatler* and the *Bystander;* she knew who his family was and the degree to which he was related to the king. She knew he was exactly her age, was a cadet at Dartmouth, and had returned from Athens at the king's request when war broke out.

"You must be Osla Kendall," said Prince Philip of Greece.

"Must I?" She repressed the urge to pat at her hair. If she'd known she had a date with a prince, she would have taken a moment to brush the Dural shavings out of her curls.

"Mr. Gibbs said you'd be along right about now, and Mr. Gibbs is never wrong." The prince leaned against the bar, tanned golden, hair glinting like a coin, eyes very blue and direct. He took in her dirty boiler suit and gave a slow grin. *Oh, my,* Osla thought. *That's a smile.* "Absolutely smashing getup," he said. "Is that what all the girls are wearing this season?"

"It's what Osla Kendall is wearing this season." She struck a magazine pose, refusing to regret the green satin gown in her bag. "I will not be confined within the weak lists of a country's fashions—"

"*Henry V,*" he said promptly.

"Oooh, you know your Shakespeare."

"They crammed a bit into me at Gordonstoun." He nodded at the bartender, and a wide-brimmed coupe frothing with champagne materialized at Osla's elbow. "In between all the hiking and sailing."

"Of course you sail—"

"Why 'of course'?"

"You look like a Viking; you must have put some time in on an oar or two. Have you got a longship parked round the corner?"

"My uncle Dickie's Vauxhall. Sorry to disappoint."

"I see you two are getting along," Sally laughed, slipping up beside them. "Os, our godfather"—Lord Mountbatten—"is Phil's uncle, so that's the connection. Uncle Dickie said Phil didn't know *anyone* in London, and did I know a nice girl who could squire him around—"

"A *nice* girl," Osla groaned, taking a slug of champagne. "There's nothing more deadly than being called *nice*."

"I don't think you're nice," the prince said.

"Don't you say the sweetest things?" Tipping her head back. "What am I, then?"

"The prettiest thing I've ever seen in a boiler suit."

"You should see me pot-rivet a seam."

"Anytime, princess."

"Are we going dancing or not?" Sally complained. "Come upstairs and change, Os!"

Prince Philip looked speculative. "If I made you a dare—"

"Careful," Osla warned. "I don't back down from dares."

"She's famous for it," Sally agreed. "At Miss Fenton's, the upper-form girls dared her to put itching powder in the headmistress's knickers."

Philip looked down at Osla from his full six feet, grinning again. "Did you do it?"

"Of course. Then I stole her suspender belt, climbed the chapel roof, and hung it from the cross. She kicked up *quite* a shindy over that. What's your dare?"

"Come out dancing as you are," the prince challenged. "Don't change into whatever satin thing you've got in that bag."

"You're on." Osla tossed down the rest of her champagne, and they piled laughing out of the Main Lounge. Mr. Gibbs gave Osla a wink as he opened the doors. She took one gulp of the icy, starry night outside—you could see *stars* all over London now, with the blackout—and looked over her shoulder at Prince Philip, who had paused to tilt his head up, too. She felt the champagne fizzing in her blood and reached into her pack. "Am I allowed to wear these?" She pulled out her dancing shoes: green satin sandals with glitters of diamanté. "A princess can't conga without her glass slippers."

"I'll allow it." Prince Philip tugged the sandals away, then picked up her hand and placed it on his shoulder. "Steady . . ." And he knelt down right there on the front steps of Claridge's to undo Osla's boots, waiting for her to step out of them, then peeling off her wool socks. He slid her satin sandals on, tanned fingers dark against her white ankles in the faint moonlight. He looked up then, eyes shadowed.

"Oh, *seriously.*" Osla grinned down at him. "How many girls have you tried this on, sailor?"

He was laughing too, unable to hold his intent expression. He laughed so hard he nearly toppled over, forehead coming for a moment against Osla's knee, and she touched his bright hair. His fingers were still braceleted around her ankle, warm in the cold night. She saw how passersby were staring at the girl in the boiler suit on the front steps of Mayfair's best hotel, the man in naval uniform on one knee before her, and gave Philip's shoulder a playful smack. "Enough swooning."

He rose. "As you wish."

They danced the New Year in at the Café de Paris, tripping down the lush carpeted stairs to the underground club. "I didn't know they did the foxtrot in Greece!" Osla shouted over the blare of trombones, whirling through Philip's hands. He was a fast, fierce dancer.

"I'm no Greek . . ." He spun her, and Osla was too out of breath to continue until the music relaxed to a dreamy waltz. Philip slowed, raking his disordered hair back into place before gathering Osla up with one arm about her waist. Osla put her hand in his, and they fell easily in rhythm.

"What do you mean, you're no Greek?" she asked as couples

bumped and laughed all around them. The Café de Paris had a warm intimacy that no other nightclub in London could match, maybe because it was twenty feet belowground. Music always seemed louder here, champagne colder, blood warmer, whispers more immediate.

Philip shrugged. "I was carried out of Corfu in a fruit box when I wasn't even a year old, steps ahead of a horde of revolutionaries. I've not spent much time there, don't speak much of the language, and won't have any cause to."

He meant he wouldn't be king, Osla knew. She had some vague knowledge that the Greek royals had regained their throne, but Philip was far down the line of succession, and with his English grandfather and English uncle, he looked and sounded like any royal cousin. "You sound more English than I do."

"You're Canadian—"

"—and none of the girls I came to court with would ever let me forget it. But until I was ten, I had a German accent."

"Are you a Hun spy?" He raised an eyebrow. "I don't know any military secrets worth seducing me for, but I hope that doesn't put you off."

"You're very ill behaved for a prince. A positive menace."

"All the best ones are. Why the German accent?"

"My mother divorced my father and came to England when I was small." Osla revolved under his hand in a spin, came back into the curve of his arm again. "She stuck me in the country with a German governess, where I spoke only German Mondays-Wednesdays-Fridays, and only French Tuesdays-Thursdays-Saturdays. Until I went to boarding school, I only spoke English one day a week, and *everything* with a German accent."

"A Canadian who sounds like a German and lives in England." Philip switched to German himself. "Which country really has a claim on the heart of Osla Kendall?"

"*England für immer, mein Prinz,*" Osla replied, and switched back before they really *could* be accused of being Hun spies in this room full of tipsy, patriotic Londoners. "Your German's perfect. Did you speak it at home?"

He laughed, but the laugh had a sharp edge. "What do you mean, 'home'? Right now I'm on a camp bed in Uncle Dickie's dining room. Home is where there's an invitation or a cousin."

"I know something about that."

He looked skeptical.

"Right now I share digs with Sally. Before that, there were some dreadful cousins in Montreal who didn't want me. Before that, my godfather let me stay with him while I did the Season." Osla shrugged. "My mother has a permanent suite in Claridge's, where I'm de trop if I stay longer than a night, and my father died years ago. I couldn't tell you where home is." She smiled, very bright. "I'm certainly not going to get in a flap about it! All my friends who still live at home are dying to get away, so who's the lucky one?"

"Right now?" Philip's hand curled against her waist. "Me."

They waltzed in silence for a while, bodies moving in perfect ease. The dance floor was sticky with spilled champagne; the band dragged. It was near four in the morning, but the floor was still packed. No one wanted to stop, and that included Osla. She looked over Philip's shoulder and saw a poster pinned to the wall, one of the ubiquitous victory posters that had sprouted like mushrooms all over London: *WE BEAT 'EM BEFORE, WE'LL BEAT 'EM AGAIN!*

"I wish the war would get going," Osla said. "This waiting . . . we know they're going to come at us. Part of me wishes they'd just *do* it. The sooner it's begun, the sooner it's over."

"I suppose," he said shortly, and moved so his cheek was at her hair and they weren't eye to eye anymore. Osla could have kicked herself. All well and good to say you wished the war would kick off when *you,* being one of the gentler sex, wouldn't be the one fighting it. Osla believed everyone should fight for king and country, but she was also aware that this was a very theoretical position when you were female.

"I do want to fight," Philip said into Osla's hair as though reading her mind. "Go to sea, do my bit. Mainly so people will stop wondering if I'm secretly a Hun."

"What?"

"Three of my sisters married Nazis. Not that they were Nazis when they first . . . Well. I'd like to shut up the fellows who think I'm slightly suspect because of the family sympathies."

"I'd like to shut up the ones who think a dizzy debutante can't possibly do anything useful. Do you go to sea soon?"

"I don't know. If I had my way, I'd be on a battleship tomorrow. Uncle Dickie's seeing what he can do. It could be next week, it could be a year."

Make it a year, Osla thought, feeling his shoulder firm and angular under her hand. "So, you'll be at sea hunting U-boats, and I'll be banging rivets in Slough—not too shabby for a silly socialite and a slightly suspect prince."

"You could do more than bang rivets." He gathered her closer, not taking his cheek from her hair. "Have you asked Uncle Dickie if there's anything at the War Office for a girl with your language skills?"

"I'd rather build Hurricanes, get my hands dirty. Do something more important for the fight than bang typewriter keys."

"The fight—is that why you finagled your way back from Montreal?"

"If your country is in danger and you're of age to stand and defend it, you do so," Osla stated. "You don't cash in on your Canadian passport—"

"Or your Greek passport—"

"—and bunk out for a safer port of call. It's just not on."

"Couldn't agree more."

The waltz ended. Osla stepped back, looked up at the prince. "I should get back to my digs," she said regretfully. "I'm knackered."

Philip motored Osla and the yawning Sally back to Old Windsor, driving as ferociously as he danced. He helped Sally out of the backseat; she gave his cheek a sleepy peck and negotiated her way across the dark street. Osla heard a splash and a yelp, then Sally's voice called back sourly: "Mind your shoes, Os, there's a lake in front of our door . . ."

"Better put my boots back on," Osla laughed, reaching for her diamanté buckles, but Philip swung her up into his arms.

"Can't risk the glass slippers, princess."

"Oh, *really,* now," Osla hooted, settling her arms about his neck. "How slick can you get, sailor?"

She could almost feel his grin as he carried her through the dark. Osla's boots and evening bag dangled against his back, hanging from her elbow, and he smelled of aftershave and champagne. Philip's hair was mussed and sweat-damp from dancing, curling softly against her fingers where her hands linked at the back of his neck. He splashed through the puddle, and before he could set Osla down on the step, she brushed her lips against his.

"Gets it out of the way," she said, flippant. "So there's none of that terribly awkward *will-we-won't-we* on the step."

"I've never had a girl kiss me just to get it out of the way." His mouth smiled against hers. "At least do it properly . . ."

He kissed her again, long and leisurely, still holding her off the step. He tasted like a blue, sun-warmed sea, and at some point Osla dropped her boots into the puddle.

At last he set her down, and they stood a moment in the darkness, Osla getting her breath back.

"I don't know when I'll go to sea," he said at last. "Before I do, I'd like to see you again."

"Nothing much to do around here. When we aren't banging Dural, Sal and I eat porridge and muck about with gramophone records. Very dull."

"I don't imagine you're as dull as that. In fact, I'll wager the opposite. I'll lay odds you're hard to get over, Osla Kendall."

Any number of light, flirtatious replies sprang to her lips. She had flirted all her life, instinctively, defensively. *You play that same game,* she thought, looking at Philip. *Be charming to all, so no one gets too close.* There were always people angling to get close to a pretty brunette whose godfather was Lord Mountbatten and whose father had bequeathed her a massive chunk of Canadian National Railway shares. And Osla was willing to bet there were many more people angling to get close to a handsome prince, even one tarnished by Nazi brothers-in-law.

"Come see me any night, Philip," Osla said simply, playing no games at all, and felt her heart thumping as he touched his fingers to his hat and walked back to the Vauxhall. It was the dawn of 1940, and she had danced in the New Year in a boiler suit and satin sandals with a prince. She wondered what else the year would bring.

CHAPTER 3

June 1940

Mab was doing her best to disappear into her library copy of *Vanity Fair,* but even Becky Sharp flinging a dictionary out a coach window couldn't hold her attention when the train leaving London was so crowded, and when the man in the seat opposite was fondling himself through his trouser pocket.

"What's your name?" he'd crooned when Mab dragged her brown cardboard suitcase aboard, and she'd shot him her iciest glare. He'd been forced off to one side when the compartment filled up with men in uniform, most of them trailing hopefully after a stunning brunette in a fur-trimmed coat. But as the train chugged north out of London, the compartment emptied of soldiers stop by stop, and when it was just Mab and the brunette, the fondler began crooning again. "Give us a smile, luv!" Mab ignored him. There was a newspaper on the compartment floor, tracked with muddy boot prints, and she was trying to ignore that too—the headline screamed Dunkirk and disaster.

"We're next," Mab's mother had said as Denmark fell, Norway fell, Belgium fell, Holland fell, one after another like boulders rolling inexorably off a cliff. Then ruddy *France* fell, and Mrs. Churt gave even bleaker shakes of the head. "We're next," she said to everyone who would listen, and Mab nearly bit her head off. *Mum, would you mind not talking about murdering, raping Huns and what they're going to do to us?* It had been a terrible row, the first of many once Mab had tried to persuade Mum to leave London with Lucy. *Just for a while,* she said, and Mum retorted, *I leave Shoreditch feetfirst, in a box.*

And *that* row had been so bad, it was just as well that Mab had received this odd summons a week ago about a post in Buckinghamshire. Lucy didn't really understand she was going away; when Mab had hugged her tight that morning before departing, she'd just put her head on one side and said "'Night!" which meant *See you tonight!*

I won't be seeing you tonight, Luce. Mab had never been away from Lucy overnight, not once.

Well, Mab would take the train back to London the first day she had off. Whatever this post was, there had to be days off, even in wartime. And maybe her living situation in—what was this town called again?—would be decent enough she could see about moving her family here to the country. Better the middle of nowhere among green fields than soon-to-be-bombed London . . . Mab shuddered and went back to *Vanity Fair,* where Becky Sharp was headed for a new job in the country too, not appearing to worry much about *her* homeland's being invaded. But in Becky's day it had been Napoléon, and Napoléon didn't have bloody Messerschmitts, did he?

"What's *your* name, lovely?" The fondler had switched his attentions to the little brunette in the fur-trimmed coat, who was now the only other passenger in the compartment. His hand began to work away in his pocket. "Just one smile, gorgeous—"

The brunette looked up from her own book, flushing pink, and Mab wondered if she'd have to intervene. Normally she abided by a Londoner's strict rule of *keep your nose out of other folks' business,* but the brunette looked like an absolute lamb in the woods. Just the sort of female Mab both slightly resented and also envied—expensively dressed, pampered skin that a gushy novel would describe as *alabaster,* the sort of pocket-sized figure all women wanted and all men wanted to take a bite out of. The kind of silly overbred debutante, in short, who had grown up riding ponies and wouldn't have to lift a finger to bag herself a husband of means and education, but was otherwise completely useless. Any Shoreditch girl could handle a train compartment lothario, but this little bit of crumpet was going to get munched right up.

Mab laid down *Vanity Fair* with a thump, irritated with the fondler and rather irritated with the brunette too for needing rescuing. But before she could even snap *Look here, you . . .* the brunette spoke up.

"My goodness, *look* at the tent in your trousers. I can't say I've ever seen anything quite so obvious. Most fellows do something incredibly creative with their hats at this stage."

The man's hand froze. The brunette put her head to one side, eyes widening innocently. "Is something wrong? You aren't in pain, are you? Chaps always act like they're in such *pain* at this point, I'm nobbled if I know why . . ."

The fondler, Mab observed, was red as a beet and had withdrawn his hand from his pocket.

". . . Really, do you need a doctor? You're looking absolutely in the basket—"

The man fled the compartment with a mutter. "Feel better soon!" the little brunette called after him, then looked over at Mab, eyes sparkling. "That fixed him." She flung one silk-stockinged leg over the other with evident satisfaction.

"Nice work," Mab couldn't help but say. Not such an easily munched bit of crumpet after all, even if the girl didn't look a day over eighteen. "If I have to get rid of a fellow like that, I rely on a good icy stare or a kick in the shins."

"I can't do an icy stare to save my life. This face simply won't glower. If I try, fellows tell me I look *adorable,* and there's nothing to make you flip your wicket like being told you're *adorable* when you're furious. Now, you're clearly tall, and you've got eyebrows like an empress, so I'm sure you have a very impressive glare?" Tilting her head in invitation.

Mab had been about to retreat into her book, but she couldn't resist. Arching one brow, she looked down her nose and let her lip curl.

"Now that's a slap-up stare to freeze the marrow!" The brunette put out a hand. "Osla Kendall."

Mab shook it, surprised to feel calluses. "Mab Churt."

"*Mab,* that's topping," Osla approved. "I was going to guess Boadicea or Scarlett O'Hara; someone who could drive a chariot with knives or shoot Yankees on staircases. I got stuck with *Osla* because my mother went to Oslo and said it was too too utterly divine. What she meant was that I was conceived there. So now I'm named after a city that is being crawled over by Germans, and I'm trying not to take it as a prediction."

"Could be worse. What if you'd been conceived in Birmingham?" Mab was still trying to make sense of the girl's work-roughened hands in contrast to her Mayfair drawl. "Surely those calluses didn't come from finishing school."

"From building Hurricanes at the Hawker Siddeley factory in Colnbrook." Osla saluted. "Who knows what I'll be doing now. I was called to interview in London, and then the strangest summons arrived telling me to go to Bletchley station—"

"But that's where I'm going." Startled, Mab dug out the letter in her handbag, much puzzled over when it had arrived in Shoreditch. Turning, she saw an identical letter in Osla's hand. They held the sheets side by side. Osla's letter read:

> Please report to Station X at Bletchley station, Buckinghamshire, in seven days' time. Your postal address is Box 111, c/o the Foreign Office. That is all you need to know.
>
> Commander Denniston

Mab's was more official—*I am desired by the Chief Clerk to inform you that you have been selected for the appointment of Temporary Clerk . . . you should attend for duty in four days' time, traveling by the 10:40* a.m. *train from London (Euston) to the third stop (Bletchley)*—but the destination was clearly the same.

"Curiouser and curiouser." Osla looked thoughtful. "Well, I'm dished—never so much as heard of Bletchley *or* Station X."

"Me either," said Mab, and wished she'd said "Nor I." Osla's polished voice and breezy slang were making her self-conscious. "I had an interview in London, too—they asked me about my typing and shorthand. They must've got my name from the secretarial course I took last year."

"They didn't ask me about typing at all. This hatchet of a woman tested my German and my French, then told me to run along home. About two weeks later, this." Osla tapped the letter. "What can they want us for?"

Mab shrugged. "I'll put my hours in for the war doing whatever they want. What matters to me is earning a wage to send home, and being close enough to London to visit every day off."

"Don't be so prosy! We could be walking right into our own Agatha Christie novel here, *The Mystery of Station X . . .*"

Mab adored Agatha Christie. "*Murder at Station X: A Hercule Poirot Mystery . . .*"

"I prefer Miss Marple," Osla said decidedly. "She's exactly like every spinster governess I ever had. Just with arsenic instead of chalk."

"I like Poirot." Mab crossed her legs, aware that her shoes, no matter how carefully she'd shined them, looked cheap next to Osla's hand-stitched pumps. *At least my legs are just as good as hers,* Mab couldn't help thinking. *Better.* That felt rather petty and mean-spirited, but Osla Kendall was so clearly a girl who had everything . . . "Hercule Poirot would give a girl like me a fair hearing," she went on. "The Miss Marples of the world take one look and decide I'm a tart."

When the train drew to the third stop at last, Osla whooped "Tallyho!" but Mab's hopes soon waned.

Half a mile of suitcase dragging from the dreary, crowded station led them to an eight-foot chained fence topped by rolls of barbed wire. The gates were manned by two bored-looking guardsmen. "Can't come in here," one said as Mab rummaged for her papers. "Got no pass."

Mab brushed her hair out of her face. This morning she'd set it into perfect waves with kirby grips, and now she was sweaty and annoyed and her waves were falling out. "Look here, we don't know what we're supposed to—"

"Come to the right place, then," said the guard in a country accent she could barely understand. "Most of 'em here look as if they didn't know where they was, and God knows what they'm doing."

Mab gave him the icy stare, but Osla stepped forward, all wide eyes and trembling lips, and the older guard took pity. "I'll escort you up to the main house. If you want to know where you are," he added, "you're at Bletchley Park."

"What *is* that?" Mab demanded.

The younger guard sniggered. "It's the biggest bloody lunatic asylum in Britain."

THE MANSION LOOKED out over a rolling green expanse of lawn and a small lake—redbrick Victorian with a green copper dome, stuck all over with windows and gables like a Christmas pudding studded with glacé cherries. "Lavatory Gothic," Osla shuddered, but Mab stared enchanted, unable to keep herself from wandering off the path toward the lake. A proper country house and grounds like Thornfield Hall or Manderley, the kind of house that eligible bachelors were always renting in novels. But even here, war had placed its ugly mass-produced boot firmly on both mansion and personnel. Hideous prefabricated huts dotted the grounds, and people rushed haphazardly across the paths—fewer men in uniform than Mab was used to seeing in London, and certainly more women than she was expecting. They hurried between the huts and mansion in tweeds, knits, and abstracted expressions.

"They all look like they strayed into a labyrinth with no exit," Osla observed, following Mab toward the lake as the guard stood looking impatient on the path.

"Exactly. Where do you think we—"

They both halted. Crawling out of the lake, soaking wet, plastered with reeds, and clutching a tea mug, was a naked man.

"Oh, hullo," he called cheerfully. "New recruits? About bally time. You go on back, David," he called up to the waiting guard. "I'll take 'em up to the mansion."

Mab saw with some relief that the man wasn't entirely naked, just stripped down to his drawers. Above them he had a freckled, concave chest; a face like an amiable gargoyle's; and hair that even soaking wet was clearly as red as a telephone box. "I'm Talbot, Giles Talbot," he explained in an Oxbridge drawl, wandering over to a heap of clothes on the bank as Osla and Mab murmured their introductions and tried not to stare. "Took a jump in the lake after Josh Cooper's tea mug. He chucked it into the reeds, working through some problem or other. Trousers," Giles Talbot muttered, shaking out his clothes. "If those buggers in Hut 4 hid them again—"

"Can you tell us where we're supposed to go?" Mab interrupted, irritated. "There has to be *someone* in charge of this madhouse."

"You'd think, wouldn't you?" Giles Talbot buttoned his shirt, then shrugged into an old checked jacket. "Commander Denniston is the closest we've got to a warden. Right-ho, follow me."

Hopping first on one foot and then on the other to pull his shoes over bare feet, he set off toward the mansion, shirttails flapping over wet drawers and bare white legs. Mab and Osla looked at each other. "It's all a front," Osla whispered. "We're going to be drugged as soon as we set foot into that hideous house and then sold into durance vile, just you wait."

"If they were trying to lure us into durance vile, they'd send someone more appetizing than a half-naked stork," Mab said. "What *is* durance vile, anyway . . ."

The mansion's entrance hall was oak-paneled and spacious, with rooms branching off each side. There was a pegboard with a copy of the London *Times* pinned up, a Gothic-looking lounge, a grand staircase visible through a pink marble arcade . . . Giles whisked them upstairs into what looked like a bay-windowed bedroom turned private office, bed replaced by cabinets, everything reeking of cigarette smoke. A small harassed-looking man with a professorial forehead looked up from the desk. He didn't sputter at the sight of Giles's naked legs, just remarked, "You found Cooper's tea mug?"

"And some new recruits, fresh off the London train. Aren't they getting prettier? Miss Kendall here could whistle a chap off a branch any day of the week." Giles beamed at Osla, then looked up at Mab, who topped him by half a head. "Lord, I love a tall woman. You're not pining for some RAF pilot, are you? Don't break my heart!"

Mab pondered getting out the icy stare but put it away unworn. This entire atmosphere was simply too strange to offend.

"You're a fine one to talk about looks, Talbot. I've never seen anything as unappetizing as you lot of skinny Cambridge boffins." Commander Denniston—at least, that's who Mab presumed it was—shook his head at Giles's bare white legs, then looked at Osla and Mab's identification and letters. "Kendall . . . Churt . . ."

"My godfather might have been the one who put my name forward," Osla prompted. "Lord Mountbatten."

He brightened. "Then Miss Churt will be the one from the London secretarial pool." He gave back their papers, rising. "Right. You have both been recruited to Bletchley Park, the headquarters of GC & CS."

What's that? Mab wondered.

As if reading her mind, Giles volunteered, "Golf, Cheese, and Chess Society."

Commander Denniston looked pained but plowed on. "You'll be assigned a hut, and your head of hut will fill you in on your duties. Before that happens, my job is to impress upon you that you will be working in the most secret place in Britain, and all activities here are crucial to the outcome of the war."

He paused. Mab stood frozen, and she could feel Osla at her side equally motionless. *Bloody hell,* Mab thought. *What* is *this place?*

He continued. "The work here is so secret that you will be told only what it is necessary for you to know, and you will never seek to find out more. Besides respecting internal security, you will be mindful of external security. You will never mention the name of this place, not to your family or friends. You will find that your colleagues refer to it as BP, and you will do the same. Above all, you will never disclose to anyone the nature of the work that you do here. To reveal the least hint might jeopardize the whole progress of the war."

Another pause. *Are they training us to be spies?* Mab wondered, astonished.

"Should anyone ask, you are doing ordinary clerical work. Make it sound dull, the duller the better."

Osla piped up, "What work *will* we be doing, sir?"

"Good God, girl, have you listened to a single word I've said?" Impatience crept into Denniston's voice. "I don't know what you will be doing, in any specific way, and I don't want to know." He opened a desk drawer and took out two sheets of yellowish paper, laying one in front of each of them. "This is the Official Secrets Act. It clearly states that if you do any of the things I have warned you against, if you disclose the slightest information which could be of use to the enemy, you will be guilty of treason."

The silence was absolute.

"And treason," Commander Denniston finished mildly, "makes you liable to the most extreme penalties of the law. I'm not sure at the moment whether that's hanging or firing squad."

It couldn't get any quieter, but Mab felt the silence congeal. She took a deep breath. "Sir, are we allowed to—refuse this post?"

He looked startled. "There's no pistol to your head; this isn't Berlin. Refuse, and you will simply be ushered off the premises with strict instructions never to mention this place again."

. . . *And I'll never know what really goes on here,* Mab thought.

He laid two pens before them. "Sign, please. Or not."

Mab took another breath and signed across the bottom. She saw Osla doing the same.

"Welcome to BP," Commander Denniston said with the first smile of the exchange. Just like that, the interview was over. Giles Talbot, still with his damp shirttails flapping, steered them out into the hall. Osla gripped Mab's hand once the door shut behind them, and Mab wasn't too proud to grip back.

"Wouldn't take it too seriously if I were you." Incredibly, Giles was chuckling. "That speech is a knee-weakener the first time you hear it—Denniston was out when it was my turn, and I got the whole harangue from a wing commander who pulled a pistol out of his drawer and said he'd shoot me if I broke the sacred secrecy of et cetera, et cetera. But you get used to it. Come along, let's get your billets sorted—"

Mab halted at the staircase, folding her arms. "Look here, can't we get a hint now about what this place actually *does*?"

"Isn't it obvious?" He looked surprised. "GC & CS—we call it Golf, Cheese, and Chess Society because the place is packed with Oxford dons and Cambridge chess champions, but it stands for Government Code & Cypher School."

Mab and Osla must have looked baffled, because he grinned. "We're breaking German codes."

CHAPTER 4

The day the Bletchley Park boarders were due to arrive, Beth Finch lost half an hour down the center of a rose.

"Really, Bethan, I've been calling and calling. How long have you been sniffing that flower?"

I wasn't sniffing it, Beth thought, but didn't correct her mother. Sniffing a rose was at least normal—roses smelled nice; everybody agreed on that. Not everybody looked at a rose and got entranced not by the scent but by the pattern of it, the way the petals overlapped like stairs winding inward . . . inward . . . she'd run her finger gently along the spiral, moving toward the center, only in her mind there wasn't a center with stamens. There was just the spiral, going on and on toward infinity. It sounded very poetic—"What lies at the center of a rose?"—but it wasn't the poetry that entranced Beth, or the scent. It was the *pattern*.

And before she knew it she'd lost half an hour, and her mother was standing there looking cross.

"They'll be here soon, and look at this room!" Mrs. Finch took the bud vase from Beth, placing it on the mantel. "Wipe down the mirror, now. Whoever these girls are, they won't have anything to complain about in this house. Though who knows what kind of girls are boarding away from home, anyway? Leaving their families for a *job*—"

"There's a war on," Beth murmured, but Mrs. Finch had been

on a tear since learning that, being in possession of a spare bedroom with two narrow beds, they would be required to billet two females working at nearby Bletchley Park.

"Don't tell me it's the war. It's flighty girls taking any excuse to bolt out on their families and get into trouble." Mrs. Finch moved about the room in small quick motions, straightening the bedside-table doily, tweaking the pillowcase. She and Beth had the same mouse-fair hair, the same nearly invisible brows and lashes, but Beth stood round-shouldered and slight while her mother was imposing, handsome, her bust like a prow. "What kind of war work are they going to be doing in the middle of *Bletchley*?"

"Who knows?" The war had sent such ripples through their sleepy little village: blackout preparations, the call for Air Raid Precautions wardens, Bletchley Park just down the road suddenly a hub of mysterious activity . . . everyone was curious, especially with *women* coming to work there as well as men. Women were flinging themselves into all sorts of new ventures these days, according to the papers—joining the FANYs to be nurses or shipping overseas with the women's Royal Navy. Every time Beth tried to think herself patriotically into one of those roles, she broke out in a cold sweat. She knew she'd be expected to do her bit, but she'd volunteer for something behind the scenes, something even utter idiots couldn't muck up. ARP First Aid, maybe, rolling bandages and making tea. Beth was hopeless at most things. She'd been hearing that all her life, and it was true.

"These boarders had better be decent girls," Mrs. Finch was fretting. "What if we end up with two tarts from Wapping?"

"I'm sure not," Beth soothed. She didn't even really know what a tart was; it was her mother's all-purpose condemnation for any female who wore lipstick, smelled of French scent, or read novels . . . Guiltily, Beth felt the weight of her latest library paperback in her pocket. *Vanity Fair.*

"Run out to the post office, Bethan." Mrs. Finch was the only one to call Beth by her full name. "I can feel one of my headaches coming on . . ." Massaging her temples. "Rinse out a cloth for me first. Then after the post office, the corner store."

"Yes, Mother."

Mrs. Finch patted her shoulder fondly. "Mother's little helper."

Beth had been hearing that all her life, too. "Bethan is so helpful," Mrs. Finch loved to tell her friends. "What a comfort to think she'll be with me when I'm old."

"She might still marry," the widow down the street had said at the last Women's Institute meeting. Beth had been making tea in the kitchen, but the old woman's whisper carried. "Twenty-four years old—that's not *utterly* hopeless. She hardly has two words to say to anyone, but that doesn't bother most men. Someone might still take her off your hands, Muriel."

"I don't want her taken *off my hands,*" Mrs. Finch had said with that brisk finality that made everything seem preordained.

At least I'm not a burden, Beth reminded herself. Most old maids were just a drain on their families. She was a comfort, she had a place, she was Mother's little helper. She was lucky.

Tugging at the thin mouse-fair plait hanging over one shoulder, Beth went to put the kettle on, then wrung out a cloth in cold water the way her mother liked. Bringing it upstairs, she darted back down and set off on errands. All Beth's siblings had settled out of town when they married, but not an afternoon passed when Beth wasn't dispatched to post a letter full of maternal advice or a package with a maternal decree. Today Beth posted a square package to her oldest sister, who'd just delivered a baby: one of Mother's samplers, a wreath of pink roses round the words *A Place for Everything and Everything in Its Place.* An identical sampler hung over Beth's bed and over the bed of every new baby born to the Finch family. It was never too early, Mother said, to instill proper notions about one's place.

"Have your boarders arrived yet?" the postmaster inquired. "They're peculiar fellows, some of them. Mrs. Bowden at the Shoulder of Mutton inn, she's got a pack of Cambridge dons coming and going at all hours! That won't please your mother, eh?" He waited for a response, but Beth just nodded, tongue-tied. "Something not right with that last Finch girl," the postmaster whispered to his clerk as she turned away, and Beth felt herself flushing crimson. Why couldn't she manage ordinary small talk? It was bad enough being slow-witted (and Beth knew she was), but did she have to be so flustered and awkward as well? Other girls, even the dimmest, seemed able to look people in the eyes when spoken to. It was one thing to be quiet, another thing to freeze in every social gathering like a frightened rabbit. But Beth couldn't help it.

She dashed home just in time to lift the kettle off the heat. At least the Finch household had been assured it would be *girls* boarding, not men. If life were a novel, the mystery boarders would have been dashing young bachelors who would then immediately have vied for Beth's hand, and Beth couldn't imagine anything more terrifying.

"Beth," Mr. Finch called absently from his armchair, doing the crossword. "'A freshwater fish of the carp family,' five letters."

Beth flipped her braid back over one shoulder, laying out the tea things. "*Tench.*"

"I thought *bream*—"

"*Bream* puts a B into Seventeen Down." Beth reached for the teapot, perfectly able to envision the crossword, glimpsed this morning when she'd set the paper by her father's breakfast plate. "And Seventeen Down is *codify.*"

"Seventeen Down—'to organize into a system, as in a body

of law,' six letters—right, *codify*." Her dad smiled. "I don't know how you do that."

My one talent, Beth thought, rueful. She couldn't cook, she couldn't knit, she couldn't make conversation, but by God, she could finish the Sunday crossword in eight minutes flat without a single mistake!

"'Unlucky or ill-fated,' seven letters—" Beth's dad began, but before she could say *hapless,* footsteps sounded outside, and their boarders were being ushered in with a clatter of suitcases. Mr. Finch held the door, Mrs. Finch shot downstairs like a ferret into a rabbit's burrow, and by the time Beth had taken care of the kettle, introductions were flying. Two girls, both clearly younger than Beth, entered the spotless kitchen and immediately seemed to take up all the air. Both were brunettes, but that was where the similarity ended. One was dimpled and beautiful and wrapped in a fur-trimmed coat, chattering in a very posh accent. The other was about six feet tall with severe features, perfect red lipstick, and black eyebrows arching like cavalry sabers. Beth's heart sank into her shoes. These girls were just the sort who made her feel clumsy, slow, and, well, *hapless*.

"So pleased," Mrs. Finch managed to say through pursed lips, "to welcome you to my home." Her gaze traveled up and down the tall brunette, who returned the stare coolly. *Tart,* Beth knew her mother was thinking. Who knew about the dimply girl, but the one with the eyebrows had without a doubt been classified as a tart before she spoke a single word.

"We are *so* chuffed to be sent here," the dimply girl gushed, curly lashes working up a breeze of enthusiasm. "One can always tell *nice* people, can't one? I knew the moment I saw your absolutely topping vegetable garden . . ."

Beth could see her mother thawing at those polished Mayfair vowels. "We hope you'll be teddibly comfortable here," she said, her own accent hitching north. "You'll share the room beside my daughter, first floor. The toilet—the loo, that is—can be found at the bottom of the garden."

"Outside?" The smaller brunette looked startled. The tall one shot her an amused look.

"You'll get used to it, Osla Kendall. I've never lived in a single flat with a loo inside."

"Oh, shut up, Queen Mab!"

Mrs. Finch frowned. "What is it you young ladies will be doing over at Bletchley Park?"

"Clerical work," Osla said breezily. "Such a snore."

Another frown, but Beth's mother left it for now. "Lights out at ten. Hot baths every Monday, no dawdling in the tub. We have a *telephone*"—proudly; few homes in the village did—"but it is for important calls only. If you'll come upstairs . . ."

The kitchen seemed to echo when the newest additions to the household swept out. Dad, who hadn't said a word after shaking hands, sat back down with his newspaper. Beth looked at the tea tray, scrubbing her hands up and down her apron.

"Bethan . . ." Mrs. Finch swept back into the kitchen. "Don't just stand there, take up the tea."

Beth made her escape, glad to be spared the dissecting of the two lodgers she was certain her mother was about to deliver. She paused outside the spare room door, mustering the nerve to knock, and heard the rustling of suitcases being unpacked.

". . . one bath a *week*?" Mab's voice, crisp and scornful. "I call that stingy. I'm not demanding hot water; I don't mind a cold-water scrub, but I want clean hair however I can get it."

"We've a washstand at least—hello again!" Osla Kendall exclaimed as Beth came in. "Tea, how scrummy. You're a darling."

Beth couldn't remember ever being called a darling. "I'll leave you," she muttered, but she saw a copy of *Vanity Fair* unpacked from one of the bags and exclaimed despite herself, "Oh! That's a good one."

"You've read it?"

Beth flushed to the roots of her hair. "Don't tell Mother."

"Wouldn't dream of it!" Osla plucked a scone off Mrs. Finch's second-best china. "No one should tell their mother more than one-third of anything they get up to. Curl up with us and have a chin-wag . . ."

Without knowing how it happened, Beth found herself perched on the end of Osla's bed. It wasn't much of a conversation; she hardly said two words as the other girls nipped back and forth about Thackeray and whether they should start a literary society. But they both smiled at her periodically, all encouraging glances.

Maybe they weren't *quite* so intimidating after all.

Are not there little chapters in everybody's life, Beth had read in *Vanity Fair* only that morning, *that seem to be nothing, and yet affect all the rest of history?*

Too soon to tell . . . but perhaps this was, in fact, going to be one of them.

TWELVE DAYS UNTIL THE ROYAL WEDDING

November 8, 1947

CHAPTER 5

Inside the Clock

Three girls and a book—that was how it all began. Or so it seemed to the woman in the asylum, lying in her cell, fighting the cocktail of lethargy that had been pumped into her veins.

"Our institution is very progressive," a balding doctor had said when she first arrived, spitting and struggling, at Clockwell Sanitarium. Nearly three and a half years ago—6 June, the day of the Normandy invasions, the day that began Europe's liberation, and her own imprisonment. "You may have heard horror stories about patients chained to walls, hosed with ice water, and so forth. We believe in gentle handling here, mild activity, sedatives to calm the nerves, Miss Liddell."

"That is not my name," she had snarled.

He ignored her. "Take your pills like a good girl." Pills in the morning, pills at night, pills that filled her veins with smoke and her skull with cotton wool—who cared then about *mild activity*? There were blunted tools for working in the rose garden around the big gray stone house; there was basket-weaving in the common hall; there were novels with missing pages—but very few patients made use of these things. Clockwell's inmates dozed in armchairs or sat outside blinking at the sun, eyes dulled and dreamy from the fog they swallowed every morning in tablet form.

Progressive treatment. This place didn't need chains or electrical shocks; it didn't need beatings or ice baths. It was still a killing bottle, an eater of souls.

Her first week here, she'd refused to swallow anything the doctors gave her. She got the syringe instead, orderlies holding her down for the needle prick. Afterward she stumbled back to her cell—they could call it a room, but any room with locks on only the outside was a cell: window barred with mesh, bed bolted to the floor, a high ceiling so she couldn't reach the light fixture to hang herself.

She thought of hanging herself that first week. But that would have been giving in.

"Looking well today!" The doctor beamed, popping in on his daily rounds. "Still a bit of a cough from that springtime bout of pneumonia, eh, Miss Liddell?"

The woman registered under the name *Alice Liddell* no longer bothered to correct him. She swallowed her pills obediently, then as soon as he left went to the plastic basin that served as a chamber pot at night. Forcing her fingers down her throat, she threw the tablets up in a wash of bile, then reached an indifferent thumb into the mess and ground everything together so the nurses wouldn't guess. She'd learned a few things in three and a half years. How to vomit up her medicine. How to fool the doctors. How to slide past the orderlies who were spiteful and cultivate the ones who were kind. How to keep her sanity in the midst of madness . . . because it would be easy, so easy, to go authentically mad here.

Not me, thought the woman from Bletchley Park. She might have been sitting gray-faced and coughing in a madhouse cell, but she had not always been *this.*

I will survive. I will get out.

Not that it would be easy. The walls circling Clockwell were high and barbed; she'd walked them a thousand times. Every entrance—the big gates at the front, the smaller access doors used by the grounds crew—was locked, the keys kept under guard. And even if she could get past that wall, the nearest town was miles away across barren Yorkshire moors. A slippered woman in an institutional smock stood no chance; she'd merely wander the gorse until she was recaptured.

She'd known from her second week here that if she was to get out, she would need help.

She'd smuggled her ciphered messages out last week. Two desperate missives launched into the void like messages in bottles, sent to two women who had no reason to help her.

They betrayed me, the thought whispered.

You betrayed them, the whisper said back.

Had they received the letters yet?

If they had, would they listen?

London

Osla stood in her lace slip and robe, looking at the message that had thrown such a spanner into her day. The echo of the telephone's furious slam on the other end of the line in Yorkshire still reverberated, along with her former friend's choked voice. *Go to hell, Osla Kendall.*

A clock ticked in the corner, and a blue satin dress slid off the heap on the bed. What she would wear to watch Princess Elizabeth marry her own former boyfriend now seemed the stupidest bit of bobbery in the world. Osla flung down the cipher message, and sunlight bounced green sparks across the lines of code, reflected off the big emerald ring her fiancé had put on her left hand four months ago.

Any other woman, Osla reflected, would have run to her husband-to-be if she got menacing letters from a madhouse inmate. It was the sort of thing fiancés liked to know, if the women they loved were being threatened by lunatics. But Osla knew she was not going to tell a soul. A few years at Bletchley Park turned any woman into a real clam.

Osla sometimes wondered how many women there were in Britain like her, lying to their families all day, every day, about what they'd done in the war. Never once saying the words *I may just be a housewife now, but I used to break German ciphers in Hut 6* or *I may look like a brainless socialite, but I translated naval orders in Hut 4.* So many women . . . by the end of the war in Europe, Bletchley Park and its outstations had four women to every man, or so it seemed when you saw the swarm of Victory-rolled hair and Utility frocks come spilling out at shift change. Where were all those women now? How many men who had fought in the war now sat reading their morning newspapers without realizing the woman sitting across the jam-pots from them had fought, too? Maybe the ladies of BP hadn't faced bullets or bombs, but they'd fought—oh, yes, they'd fought. And now they were labeled simply housewives, or schoolteachers, or *silly debs,* and they probably bit their tongues and hid their wounds, just like Osla. Because the ladies of BP had certainly taken their share of war wounds.

The woman who had sent Osla the Vigenère square wasn't the only one to crock up and end in a madhouse, gibbering under the strain.

Get me out of here, the ciphered message read. *You owe me.*

The cipher message said a lot of other things, too . . .

The telephone shrieked, and Osla nearly jumped out of her skin. She snatched up the handset. "Did you change your mind about meeting?" It surprised her, the thrum of relief that went through her. No love lost between herself and her old friend, but if she had someone to face this problem with—

"Meeting whom, Miss Kendall?" The voice was male, insinuating, oilier than Brylcreem on a Cheapside shoe salesman. "Where are you off to? Private rendezvous with the royal fiancé, perhaps?"

Osla straightened, jangling nerves subsiding in a rush of straightforward loathing. "I don't remember which scandal rag you write for, but stop talking slush and bugger off." She banged down the handset. The sheet sniffers had been haunting her doorstep ever since the royal engagement had been announced. It didn't matter that there wasn't anything to find; they wanted dirt. One hour ago, she'd been looking for any excuse to get away from them, from the wedding hysteria, out of London altogether . . .

She heard the furious voice through the telephone again: *Go to hell, Osla Kendall.*

"Oh, plug it," Osla said aloud, making a sudden decision. "I'm coming to talk to you whether you like it or not."

Because nothing about the woman in the madhouse could be discussed by telephone, and the only person she could talk to about it lived in York now. A long, *long* way from London.

Two birds, one stone.

SEVEN YEARS AGO

June 1940

CHAPTER 6

Dear Philip: I work in a blinking madhouse, Osla imagined scribbling to her fair-haired prince—not that she could give him details about her new job in those letters posted to Philip's ship, but she'd got into the habit of talking to him in her head, spinning the straw of daily life into entertaining gold anecdotes. *It's a small madhouse tucked inside a larger one. The large one is Bletchley Park, the small one is Hut 4. Hut 4 simply defies description.*

She'd turned up for her first shift promptly at nine the morning after signing the Official Secrets Act, thrilled to her bones to be doing something more important than pot-riveting seams. All she wanted in this world was to *prove* herself, prove once and for all that a Mayfair giggler who'd curtsied to the king in pearls and plumes could poker up in wartime and serve as well as anyone else. Could do something important, even . . .

Well, banging Hurricanes together might have been useful, but this was in a different class. Osla had already vowed she'd stick it out here, no matter how hard it was. She was only sorry she and Mab wouldn't be working together. *Dear Philip: The girl I'm billeted with is simply divine, and I forbid you to ever meet her because you would probably fall in love on the spot and then I would have to hate her. Not you—you wouldn't be able to help yourself; Mab would wing a superb eyebrow at you and that would be that—but I can't afford to hate her because it's clear I will need allies if I am to survive in the house of the Dread Mrs. Finch. More about* her *later.*

Osla and Mab had sauntered to the gates of Bletchley Park in the bright June morning, where Mab was shunted to Hut 6 and Osla to Hut 4. "Well then . . ." Mab perched her little chip hat at an aggressively chic angle. "Show me just one eligible bachelor, Hut 6, and we'll get along fine."

Osla hoped Mab was met by a more appetizing specimen than the fellow who answered her own knock: a stocky balding fellow in a Fair Isle jumper. "German naval section," he greeted Osla as she stepped into the long green-painted building squatting next to the mansion like a frog. "You've got the German, then?"

"You mean have I got a German tucked in my handbag?" Osla quipped. "'Fraid not, darling."

He looked blank. She sighed, spouting some Schiller in her impeccable *Hochdeutsch.* He waved for her to stop. "Good, good. You'll assist with the registration, the W/T sorting, the teleprinted traffic . . ."

He whisked her inside the hut and showed her through: two large rooms separated by a door, a small room at the end, another little room after that which had been subdivided even smaller. Long tables heaped with papers and atlases, swivel chairs, pigeonholes, green steel filing cabinets . . . it was stiflingly hot, the men in shirtsleeves while the women patted perspiring faces with handkerchiefs. With a distracted "Have a go!" he passed Osla over to a motherly middle-aged woman who took in the new arrival's evident confusion with a smile.

"It wouldn't be any clearer if he tried to explain. These Oxbridge types are hopeless at explaining *anything.*"

Dear Philip: My entire introduction to the world of codebreaking was "Have a go!"

The middle-aged woman introduced herself as Miss Senyard

and made introductions to the others—a few girls like Osla, all Mayfair diction and pearls; a few girls with "university" stamped all over them, all efficient and friendly as they showed the new girl the ropes. Some were sorting wireless telegraphy forms; some were collecting unknown German naval codes and identifying call signs and frequencies with slashes of a pencil. Osla received a towering stack of loose papers and a punching machine—"Take these signals and bind them up properly, dear. It's the early naval Enigma traffic; poor Mr. Birch's cupboards are positively overflowing and we've got to get it filed."

Osla studied a sheet: a report of some kind, translated German broken and patchy as if parts of the sentence hadn't come through. "Why is this in German and not that?" she asked the girl next to her, nodding at the cards with their keys and call signs, much of it gibberish.

"This is the undeciphered stuff. We log it, register it, then it goes out to the naval section boffins to be broken. The boffins are the brainy ones." Admiringly. "Who knows what they do or how they do it, but the undeciphered stuff comes back to us broken into readable German."

"Oh." That was where the important work was done, then. Osla wrestled with the punching machine, fighting a sense of deflation. Punching holes to bind papers together and stick them in cupboards—was this really the best use of her language skills? Had she managed yet again to land in a place where the real work was being done by someone else? Not that she was going to get in a wax about needing to be important, she just wanted to be used *well* . . .

Never mind that, she scolded herself. *It's all important. And it's only your first day.* "What do we do with all these reports and signals, then? Once they come back broken into German."

"It's all translated, logged, analyzed. Miss Senyard's box files have copies of every German naval and naval air signal—periodically we get someone in a tearing hurry, requesting a copy of this report or that one. And we send the raw decrypts to the Admiralty, as well as reporting by telephone. We've got a direct line; Hinsley rings since he's liaison, then they give him the brush-off and he goes about muttering insults for the next hour."

"Why do they brush him off?"

"Would *you* believe it if some reedy Cambridge student from the middle of nowhere called to tell you where the U-boat wolf packs were, and when you asked how that information was obtained, his reply was *You don't need to know*?"

Dear Philip: The Admiralty currently making decisions for your beloved navy lurches along on shrugs, shoeboxes, and ignorance. Is this entire war run by idiots? That would explain why we're on the verge of being invaded. Not that she ever would have written Philip anything so defeatist. Osla kept her letters cheerful; the last thing a man at war needed was gloom from the home front. But to herself, in her own head, she didn't mind being pessimistic. It got difficult keeping your chin up, all the while imagining what London would look like once the Jerries had nailed German street names over the signs to Piccadilly and St. John's Wood. It could happen. Not that anyone said it, but everyone was in a pelter worrying that it *would* happen.

The Americans weren't coming to the rescue. Most of Europe had fallen. England was next. That was the bleak reality.

I might see the news here first, Osla thought, reaching for a new report. She might know before anyone else in the country—before Churchill, before the king—when they were being invaded, because the next decoded German report might be orders for a pack of destroyers to sail for Dover. Just because the brainy boys here could decode what the Nazis said to each other, that didn't mean they could stop it.

I don't know what you're doing in there, Osla thought to the boffins breaking codes for the U-boat packs that hunted ships like Philip's, *but do it faster.*

That made her wonder. "If this is naval section, can we look up our own ships in the decrypted reports? See if the Germans have flagged them in their radio traffic?" Like HMS *Kent,* currently bearing a certain fair-haired royal midshipman toward Bombay . . . "Or are we not allowed to ask about such things?" The orders had been no talking to anyone outside Bletchley, and no talking to anyone outside or inside about one's work, but those instructions still left quite a few gray areas. Osla had no intention of breaking the Official Secrets Act on her very first day. *Dear Philip: I'm going to be hanged for treason, or possibly shot by firing squad.*

"We all talk in-hut," the reassuring answer came. "It's all right as long as everything you learn *stays* in-hut. You can try looking up a ship if you've got a fellow on board, but you can't pass on anything you find to his mum."

That wouldn't be a problem, Osla reflected. Philip never mentioned his mother. He'd talk about his sisters, the ones who had married Nazis and to whom he could no longer write; he'd talk about the sister who died in a plane crash with her entire family a few years ago; he'd even mention his long-estranged father—but never his mother.

"So, your shipboard friend—" A nudge. "Fiancé?"

"Oh, just a boyfriend," Osla murmured, banging away at the punching machine. She'd had boyfriends since she was sixteen, casual crushes conducted over late-night dancing and the occasional kiss in the back of a taxi. Nothing serious. Philip had gone to sea in February; they'd barely known each other six weeks—dancing at the Café de Paris when Osla got a night off from the Hurricane factory; long evenings when he'd drive to her shared digs and lie with his head in her lap as they listened to gramophone records and chatted the night away. "Are you falling for your handsome prince?" Sally Norton teased one evening after Philip ambled out after midnight.

"He's not *my* prince," Osla retorted. "He's looking for a girl to splash out with before going to war, that's all. For me, he's just another boyfriend."

Except Philip was the only one who made her bones burn. The first kisses of her life that felt dangerous. The last night before he'd shipped out, he'd gripped her hand tighter than usual and said abruptly, "Write to me, Os? If you do, I'll write to you. I haven't anyone to write to, really."

"I'll write," Osla had said, no jokes, no teasing.

He leaned in for another of those long, heated doorstep kisses, the ones that went on and on, his hands moving across her back, her fingers deep in his hair. Before he pulled away, he pressed something into her hand and then leaned down and crushed his lips to her folded fingers for a long moment. "So long, princess."

She'd opened her hand and seen the cool glitter of his naval insignia like a little jeweled pin. As she fastened it to her lapel like a brooch, she warned herself again, *Careful*. Her mother spent all her time making a mug of herself over unsuitable men, and Osla was determined to be the apple who fell a *long* way from that tree.

Someone came over, a scholarly type in an unraveling jumper, interrupting Osla's musings. "Give me a hand, girls? I need this report . . ." And he rattled off a series of numbers.

"Make him out a copy, dear," Miss Senyard directed, pulling the report, and Osla obeyed as the man nearly danced on his toes with impatience. Osla remembered red-haired Giles saying the Park was stuffed with Oxford dons and Cambridge chess champions, and wondered where *he* worked—if he was one of the brainy ones working the middle stage of this process: taking the raw gibberish from German radio traffic, the stuff they were registering and logging, and breaking it apart until it was something that could be read, translated, analyzed, and filed in sections like this one.

"Thanks." The man flew off with his copied report, leaving Osla feeling both pleased and deflated, and she went back to binding and filing signals. She had absolutely no idea what had just happened, why that one report had been needed, and she never *would* know. That was all right; it was important to someone, and she'd played her part . . . but there wasn't any doubt this job was a lot simpler than she'd hoped for. The pace might have been frenetic, but anyone with a teaspoon of brains and a little attention to detail could bind and file.

Dear Philip: Am I an ungrateful cow if I've gone from wishing I could do more for the war than bang sheets of Dural, to wishing I could do more for the war than wield a punching machine?

"My job's a yawn, so let's hear about yours," Osla told her billet-mate that night. Mab had just slipped in from the outdoor loo, and Osla lay across her narrow bed in slip and knickers, trying to get in a chapter of *Vanity Fair* before lights-out. "Day one—how was it?"

"Not bad." Mab stripped out of the robe she'd donned to go downstairs, standing in her own slip and knickers. "Can't say much more than that, can I? All this secrecy; are we even allowed to ask each other 'How's work?'" Mab's slip was nylon and very worn. Osla, in peach silk with French lace inserts, remembered the girls of her deb season tittering about the *poor* girls, by which they meant the ones who wore the same frock twice in one week . . . she'd watched Mab unpack exactly four dresses from her suitcase into their shared wardrobe, all perfectly pressed, and felt self-conscious unpacking more than four of her own.

"Mind you," Mab went on, picking up her hairbrush, "I don't think our nosy landlady cares about secrecy. Did you see her pursing her lips over supper when we wouldn't answer every question?"

"And good luck to anyone else trying to get a word in." Osla had tried to ask the washed-out daughter a thing or two, but the poor mouse hadn't uttered a peep around her mother's peppering questions. Osla still wasn't sure if the girl's name was Beth or Bess. She wondered if she could get by with *darling* through the entire war.

"I'll tell you one thing about my hut." Mab's hair crackled as she stroked the brush vigorously through it. "It's got my future husband in it somewhere. I've never seen so many eligible bachelors in my life."

"Oooh. Glamour boys?"

"I said eligible, not glamorous." Mab gave that grin of hers, the one that cracked the cool, guarded expression on her rather severe face and made her look like a pirate who had spotted a Spanish treasure galleon on the horizon. *HMS* Queen Mab, *out to chase and board the unsuspecting bachelors of Bletchley Park,* thought Osla. "Anyone in your hut catch your eye?"

"Oh, I'm not looking for a fellow," Osla said airily.

Dear Philip: It's a madhouse, and maybe my job's a touch undemanding . . . but I think I like it here.

CHAPTER 7

June 1940

If Bletchley Park had a motto, Mab thought, it would be *You dinnae need to know.*

"Are the other huts set up like this one?" Mab asked as she was whisked through the central corridor of Hut 6.

"You dinnae need to know," said her new supervisor, a middle-aged woman with a crisp Scottish voice. "You're assigned to the Decoding Room . . ." And she ushered Mab into a box of a place, all lino and blackout curtains, filing cabinets and wooden trestle tables. But it was the two machines that made Mab stare: awkward composite things bristling with three rows of keys, a set of wheels on one side, big spools of tape somehow attached. Mab thought they looked like a cross between a typewriter, a shop till, and a telephone switchboard. A woman sat hammering at one of the machines, hunched like Quasimodo (*The Hunchback of Notre Dame* had been number 34 on "100 Classic Literary Works for the Well-Read Lady").

"Miss Churt, is it?" The Scotswoman led Mab to the unoccupied machine. "Most of our girls are Newnham College or Girton College; where did you graduate?"

"Claybourn secretarial course, top of my class." *Take that, Girton College.* Mab wasn't going to be embarrassed by her lack of schooling any more than she was going to be embarrassed by her nylon underwear in the face of Osla's French lace slips.

"I suppose it disnae matter," the Scotswoman said dubiously. "This is your Typex machine. It's mocked up to decipher the encrypted messages the Germans send by radio to their officers in the field. Each service of the German armed forces sends those messages using a service-specific key, over their own wireless networks, and the settings of that key are changed daily. Our listening stations across Britain and abroad intercept these messages, transcribe them, and send them to BP. By the time they make their way to the Decoding Room, they are given to you as coded messages." She held up one finger. "You will be given settings, a different setting for each key"—a second finger—"you will align your machine to those settings"—a third finger—"and you will punch the coded messages into the machine so they can be decoded into German. Do you understand?"

Not really. "Yes, of course."

"You'll get an hour at noon for dinner, and there is a toilet block outside. This hut works round the clock, Miss Churt. Fourteen days on the nine-to-four, then fourteen days on the four-to-midnight, then twelve days on the midnight-to-nine."

The Scotswoman bustled off to some other compartment of Hut 6. The girl at the other Typex machine, snail-hunched in a pebbly jumper, slid a stack of papers over as Mab took her seat. "That's the rest of the day's Red," she said without preamble. "Bit late today. The boys in Hut 3 get tetchy if we haven't got it for them by breakfast. Here's the setting." She showed Mab how to fix up her Typex machine for decoding Red traffic: the order for the three wheels; then something she called the *Ringstellung,* rattling off numbers that each equated to a letter of the alphabet . . . Mab followed along, head swimming. "Then a check to be sure the setup's correct; set each of your three wheels to A and type out a keyboard alphabet. If it corresponds exactly letter for letter, you're ready to start. See?"

Not really. "Yes, of course."

"Now you just bang through each message as fast as you can." Indicating the big spools of tape attached to the Typex. "Type in the encrypted stuff, and it'll feed out in plain-text letters. If it looks like German, pass it on. If it looks like rubbish, put it aside and one of the more experienced girls will take a second crack at it."

"I don't speak German—"

"You don't have to. Just recognize it. The tricky part is looking past the five-letter clumps everything is sorted into, but you'll get the knack."

Mab stared at the stack. "We'll never get through all of this."

"Up to a thousand messages a day in Red since France was overrun," the girl said, which made Mab feel no more confident. Slowly she picked up the first message. Blocks of letters: ACDOU LMNRS TDOPS—on like that for a whole page. Mab looked at her partner, hunched over her own identical sheet of nonsensical five-letter groups, and wondered what Lucy was doing, back home. *I shouldn't have left you for this, Luce. You're alone with Mum in a city that's going to get bombed any day, and I'm stuck in a hut typing ruddy nonsense.*

But there wasn't any use whining about it, so Mab squared her shoulders, typed a few letter groups that the other girl had said were the introduction and signatory, then began on the main message: ACDOU LMNRS TDOPS FCQPN YHXPZ . . . To her surprise, the letters came out different: KEINE BESON DEREN EREIG NISSE.

"*Keine besonderen Ereignisse,*" said the girl to Mab's left. "You'll see that one now and then. I know a bit of German by now—it means 'no special developments.'"

Mab stared at the message. *No special developments.* So this message wasn't too important, then . . . or maybe it was. Maybe it came from an area where developments were expected. Maybe that was critical news. She kept typing, and the machine kept spitting out five-letter clumps of German until the end. "What do we do with these when—"

"Write the final position of the wheels under the message setting, sign it, stick the original decrypt to it, and put it in that tray. Keep going through your stack—things will get slow later, but we're in a rush now to get all the Red decoded."

"What *is* Red? If I can ask."

"Red's the key for German air force communications."

"Why Red?" Mab asked, fascinated.

A shrug. "It was the colored pencil the boffins were using when they were first figuring out how to crack it. We've also got Green, Blue, Yellow—all different keys for different traffic."

"Who are the boffins?"

"The brainy boys who make the initial breaks. They work out the setting for each cipher—if they didn't, we wouldn't know how to set our machines to decode all the messages." Patting the Typex's three wheels. "The Jerries change the settings every day, so every night shift as midnight ticks over, the boffins start all over again, figuring out the new setting for every—single—key."

"How?"

"Who knows? However they do it, we decode it and then it moves off to Hut 3 for translating and analysis."

Mab supposed that was what the German-speaking girls like Osla did: take this mess of German in five-letter blocks and turn it into nice legible English reports. Air force communications, army communications, intercepted at distant listening stations (whatever those were—Mab imagined men in headphones listening in on German radio channels, jotting Morse madly), then whirled through the various Bletchley huts so university boys could crack them open, so typing-pool girls like Mab could decode them, so bilingual girls like Osla could translate them. Like a conveyor belt at a factory. *We're reading your post,* Mab thought, picking up the next report. *Take that, Herr Hitler.*

She hammered another message out on the Typex, taped and processed it, reached for another. By noon she had the knack of scanning those five-letter clumps, seeing which were rubbish and which were German. Her back hurt from curling into a C, her fingers were sore from hammering the stiff keys, but she was smiling. *Look at me,* she thought. *Mabel from Shoreditch, decoding ruddy Nazi intelligence.* Mum would never have believed it, even if Mab had been able to tell her.

It was two more days before Mab got a look at the men her seatmate called the boffins.

"This box of pencils and supplies is for the boys in the next room. Miss Churt, take it over." Mab obeyed, dying for a look at the other denizens of Hut 6.

Stalky, red-haired Giles Talbot answered her knock.

"Oh, it's you! 'Divinely tall goddess—'"

"Tennyson," she said, pleased to recognize the quote.

He grinned up at her. "Don't tell me you ended up in our ring of the Inferno, Miss Churt?"

"Decoding Room," Mab answered, reflecting that it was strange to see Giles in trousers, not just white legs stuck all over with duckweed. "Do make it *Mab,* not *Miss Churt.*"

"If you'll make it *Giles,* O faerie queene—"

"Spenser! And yes, I will." Mab handed the box of supplies over, looking around. Another stuffy room crammed with men hunched over desks, every surface heaped with scraps of paper, pencil stubs, and jumbled strips of letters. The fog of concentration in the room was as thick as the fug of cigarette smoke as the men muttered and scribbled. They looked like they were at the absolute end of their tether, like they'd fallen off another planet. But Mab would eat her hat if these weren't the brainy boys who cracked the keys . . . and she'd bet they were all Cambridge or Oxford boys, too. Her hopes rose. University degrees weren't exactly thick on the ground in Shoreditch.

Of course, a good university didn't mean a good man. Mab of all people knew that. She shoved that particular memory away before it could curdle her stomach into an icy ball, down, down, *bloody go away*—and smiled at the roomful of potential husbands. *Just let one of you be* nice *as well as educated and gentlemanly, and I will make you the best bloody wife you ever dreamed of.*

"What's a girl to do for fun round here when shift's over?" Mab asked Giles with a dazzling smile.

"There are more recreation clubs here than you can shake a stick at. Highland dancing, chess—"

"I'm not one for reels or game boards. Do you like books? Osla Kendall and I are starting a literary society—"

"Love a good yarn. I'm your man."

Maybe you are, thought Mab, who had made up the literary society on the spot. Not the lure she'd have used for the lads back home, but in this crowd . . . "First meeting Sunday next. Bring the boys." She aimed another smile round the room and went back to her Typex.

"I'm knackered," Osla groaned when Sunday next finally arrived. "The work's not hard, but every day it feels like the pace doubles."

"My hut, too." If it had been peacetime, the frenetic rate of the work would have given Mab thoughts of transferring elsewhere, but with a war on, all you could do was grit your teeth. She reached up to fluff her hair. "Forget the work for a night. It's time for fun." The Shoulder of Mutton inn was to host the first meeting of the Bletchley Park Literary Society—Giles said their fish and chips weren't to be missed, and after Mrs. Finch's leaden stews, fish and chips sounded like heaven.

"I nabbed a fellow for tonight's meeting, by the way—just for you." Osla too sounded like she was determinedly putting her very long week behind her, along with the war and everything else unpleasant. "He's Hut 8, simply scrumptious. The tallest thing you've ever seen; positively made for a six-foot wife. You won't be stuck in flats your entire life."

"I don't mind men who are shorter than me. I mind men who are touchy about being shorter than me."

"What about Giles, then? He's too much the jester to get in a wax about anything, much less tall women."

"Something tells me he's the bachelor type . . . we'll see after tonight." Mab grinned. "The nice thing about meeting men here is that they can't drone about what they do. They actually *have* to talk about books or the weather—"

"Or, God forbid, ask you a question or two about yourself." Osla grinned back, swinging her crocodile handbag. "Are you heading *chez Finch* first to change?"

"Yes, red print frock."

"You'll look slap-up. I don't think I'll bother changing, just nip straight there all scruffy and ink stained, and no one will look at me when you swan in."

Osla could roll in a gutter and still everyone would look at her, Mab thought. Even at the end of a very long shift, she looked rumpled and adorable rather than frazzled and exhausted. It should have been easy to resent Osla, but Mab couldn't quite manage it. How could you resent a girl who scouted men over six feet tall for another girl's husband pool?

"There you are," Mrs. Finch greeted Mab as she came into the scrubbed kitchen. "Working on a Sunday, I see."

"No rest when there's a war on, Mrs. F." Mab tried to slide past, but Mrs. Finch blocked her way.

"Now why won't you just give us a hint what you do?" she said with a little laugh. "What do you all get up to behind those gates, my goodness—"

"Really, it's too boring to talk about."

"You can trust me!" Mrs. Finch was clearly not giving up. Her voice was cozy, but her eyes had a certain gleam. "Just a hint. I'll dole you a bit extra from the sugar ration."

"No, thank you," Mab said coldly.

"Such a careful one." Mrs. Finch patted her arm, gleam in the eye hardening, but she moved out of the way. Mab rolled her eyes at the retreating back, not realizing until she heard the nearly inaudible voice that Mrs. Finch's colorless daughter was sitting in the corner of the kitchen, shelling peas.

"You should just tell Mother something. She won't be satisfied till she knows."

Mab looked at the other girl. Hardly a girl; she was twenty-four and she volunteered with the Women's Voluntary Services when she wasn't being run off her feet by her mother—but she gave the impression of a girl, with that colorless skin that showed every wash of emotion and those eyes that never rose from the floor. Mab couldn't help a flash of annoyance. "I'm not here to satisfy your mother's curiosity, Bess."

The girl flushed dull red. "Beth," she said almost inaudibly. She sat shoulders rounded, like a puppy whose cringing practically invited a certain kind of person to give a good kick. As she carried the shelled peas to the counter, Mab could see the outline of a paperback hidden in her skirt pocket.

"Done with *Vanity Fair* yet?"

Beth flinched, fiddling with her plait's stringy ends. "You didn't tell Mother, did you?"

"Oh, for—" Mab swallowed some less than polite words. A woman of twenty-four should not be apologizing to her mother about a library habit. *Grow a spine,* Mab wanted to say. *While you're at it, put a lemon rinse on that hair and try looking people in the eye.* If there was anything Mab couldn't stand, it was limp women. The women in her own family were hardly perfect—in fact, most of them were flint-hard cows—but at least they weren't *limp.*

Beth sat back down at the kitchen table. She'd probably sit here the rest of the night until her mother told her to go to bed.

"Get your coat, Beth," Mab heard herself saying.

"W-what?"

"Get your coat while I change. You're coming to the first meeting of the Bletchley Park Literary Society."

CHAPTER 8

The Shoulder of Mutton reared its thatched head at Buckingham and Newton roads, the bar cozy and bright, the private sitting room low beamed and inviting. It was everything Beth feared about social gatherings: tight quarters, loud noises, cigarette smoke, fast conversation, strange people, and men. Anxiety choked her throat, and she couldn't stop fiddling with the end of her plait like it was a lifeline.

"—you billet here, Giles?" someone was asking the lanky red-haired man. "Blimey, you got lucky."

"Don't I know it, Mrs. Bowden's a gem. Not much bothered by rationing; I swear she's queen of the local black market. We've got the private room, get your drinks . . ."

Beth found herself clutching a sherry she didn't dare sip. What if her mother smelled liquor on her breath?

"Swig that down," Mab advised.

"W-what?" Beth was eyeing the group piling around the table. Osla, laughing as an army lieutenant lit her cigarette . . . several gangling academic sorts gawping at Mab like puppies . . . red-haired Giles and a truly massive black-haired man who had to duck under the rafter . . . all of them worked at the mysterious Bletchley Park, so what was *Beth* doing here? She didn't know what to make of these people—some looked so shabby in their patched tweeds that her mother might have taken them for tramps, but they talked in such overeducated drawls she could hardly understand a word they said.

"Relax," Mab said. She had a glass of beer, and she'd thrown one leg over the other in casually elegant fashion. "We're only here to talk books."

"I shouldn't be here," Beth whispered.

"It's a literary society, not a bordello."

"I can't stay." Beth set her sherry down. "My mother will pitch a fit."

"So?"

"It's her house, her rules, and I—"

"It's *your* house, too. And really, it's your father's house!"

Beth's words dried up. Impossible to explain how slight a presence her father really *was* in the Finch household. He never put his foot down. He wasn't that kind of husband, that kind of father. *The finest of men,* Beth's mother always said smugly when other women in the village complained of overbearing husbands.

"I can't stay," Beth repeated.

"'*The greatest tyrants over women are women,*'" Mab quoted. "Have you read that far in *Vanity Fair*?" She arched one brow, then addressed the men across the table. "So, shall we vote on a book every month? How shall we tally up—"

"Popular vote," one of the skinny academics was saying. "Or the ladies will have us all reading romantic tosh—"

"Romantic tosh?" Osla demanded, squashing in on Beth's left. "The last thing I read was *Vanity Fair*!"

"That's about girls, isn't it?" Giles objected.

"It's written by a man, so that's all right," Mab said tartly.

"Why do you men get the swithers if you have to read anything written by a female?" Osla wondered. "Aren't we a century out from poor Charlotte Brontë signing herself *Currer Bell* to get published?"

Fish and chips arrived, leaking grease. Beth didn't dare touch hers, any more than the sherry. Nice girls did not eat in public houses; nice girls did not smoke or drink or argue with men . . .

Osla's a nice girl, Beth thought, marshaling arguments for later. Nothing Mab did was going to find approval with Mrs. Finch, but Osla was another story. *She's been presented at court; you can't say she isn't a lady, Mother!* And here Osla was crunching up chunks of fried cod, swilling sherry, and arguing with Giles about Lewis Carroll's *Through the Looking-Glass,* obviously having a grand time.

Somehow Beth didn't think that argument was going to weigh much with her mother, either. Mrs. Finch wasn't going to care about anything except that Beth had gone *out,* without permission.

"I vote for Conan Doyle," the huge dark-haired man on Beth's right was saying. "Who doesn't like Sherlock Holmes?"

"You've already read everything Doyle ever wrote, Harry . . ."

He didn't look like a *Harry,* Beth thought, trying not to stare at the man. He wasn't just enormous—nearly a head taller even than Mab; broad enough he'd nearly turned sideways through the door—but he was black haired and swarthy, almost dark skinned. Beth could imagine the village ladies whispering, "*Is he a wog or an Eyetie?*" but he didn't sound like a foreigner. He had exactly the same university drawl as the rest.

"Maltese, Arab, and Egyptian," he said, catching Beth's eye.

She flinched. "What?"

"My father's family is originally from Malta, my mother was born to an Egyptian diplomat and the daughter of a banker from Baghdad." He grinned. "Don't be embarrassed; everyone wants to know. I'm Harry Zarb, by the way."

"You speak English very well," she managed to reply.

"Well, my branch of the family's been London based for three generations, I was baptized Church of England, then went through Kings College in Cambridge like my father and grandfather before me, so . . . be rather embarrassing if I *didn't* speak English well."

"I—I'm so sorry," Beth whispered, mortified.

"Look like me and everyone thinks you were born in a tent on a sand dune." He shrugged, but Beth was too embarrassed to answer. She let the talk pass over her head, reaching for the newspaper abandoned at the next table and turning for the crossword. It was half obliterated by grease stains but she fell into it gratefully, doing it up with a pencil stub.

"You went through that like a Derby winner," Osla laughed, but Beth just stared down at her feet. Would this night never be over?

ONE LOOK AT her mother, sitting at the kitchen table with her Bible, two bright spots of color flaring in her cheeks, and Beth shriveled down to her bones. "Now, you mustn't put yourself in a pucker, Mrs. F," Osla attempted with her winning smile as they filed into the kitchen. "It's not Beth's fault—"

"We dragged her out," Mab added. "Really—"

"Hadn't you better get to bed, girls?" Mrs. Finch looked at the kitchen clock. "Lights out in twenty."

There wasn't anything the other two could do but go upstairs. Mrs. Finch's nose twitched at the smells of cigarette smoke, beer, sherry. "I'm sorry, Mother—" Beth began, but that was all she managed to say as her mother seized her arm.

"The whole village will be talking. Did you think about that?" Mrs. Finch didn't shout, she spoke *sorrowfully*. That made it so much worse. "The ingratitude, Bethan. The disgrace." She held out her Bible, open to Deuteronomy. "'*If any man has a stubborn and rebellious son who will not obey his father or his mother, and when they chastise him, he will not even listen to them*—'"

"Mother—"

"Did you think that didn't apply to daughters? '*They shall say to the elders of the city, "This daughter of ours is stubborn and rebellious, she will not obey us, she is a glutton and a drunkard*—"'"

"I didn't drink a drop—"

Mrs. Finch shook her head sadly, holding out the Bible. Beth took the heavy book and held it straight out, tear-blurred eyes fixed on the page of Deuteronomy. The longest she'd ever had to hold it up was thirty agonizing minutes. Surely it being so late, Mother wouldn't—

"You've disappointed me, Bethan." A hard pinch to the inside of Beth's arm as the Bible began to droop, then the gentle disapproval flowed on. Beth had behaved shamefully. She had disgraced her mother, who took care of her when she was too slow-witted and head-in-the-sky to look after herself. Beth was lucky she'd never marry and have children, so she'd never know how they broke your heart . . . Fifteen minutes later, Beth was hiccupping with sobs, tears dripping off her hot cheeks, arms shaking and burning with the effort to keep the book level with her eyes.

"Of course I forgive you, Bethan. You may lower the Bible." A pat instead of a pinch to Beth's arm as she dropped the book. "This is bringing on one of my headaches . . ."

Beth flew teary eyed for a cold cloth, a footstool. It was half an hour before she was allowed to go to bed. Her arms hung loose as noodles, muscles aflame. Finally daring to massage the tender flesh inside her elbow—Mrs. Finch had strong fingers; they pinched so *hard*—Beth reached the first landing and heard voices through Osla and Mab's door.

"—poor Beth," Osla was saying.

"She could grow a spine," Mab responded tartly. "If my mother went at me like that at my age, I'd dish it right back."

"She's not you, Queen Mab. I've never seen anybody so perfectly, hopelessly Fanny Price in my life." Mab made an inquiring noise. "You know, the dishrag heroine in *Mansfield Park,* who goes about looking like a dog's dinner and raining on everyone's fun? Don't tell me you haven't read Austen—"

Beth didn't wait to hear any more. Tears sliding from her eyes all over again, cheeks burning with dull humiliation, she stumbled into her bedroom. How idiotic, how *pathetic,* thinking that because the Bletchley Park girls threw her a few nice words like a bone to a dog, they actually liked her in the slightest. Even more idiotic and pathetic to think that just because the redbrick mansion down the road had become a hive of wartime activity, life would change.

Nothing for Beth was going to change, ever.

CHAPTER 9

June rolled into July, and Osla was dying for a project. Work in German naval section might have carried on at a frenetic pace, but it was about as intellectually taxing as noughts and crosses. *I need a challenge,* Osla thought, yawning as she helped Miss Senyard notate unknown German codes to be passed up the ladder for identification. *Or at least I will when I'm back on days* . . . The nine-to-four shift wasn't bad, but when the shift change rolled around to the four-to-midnight, Osla had to fight to keep herself from falling in the dismals. It was one thing to trip home after midnight because you'd splashed out at the Café de Paris. It was quite another to fall into bed at one in the morning after a night spent making preparations for when the enemy invaded.

"There are plans to organize a mobile section of GC & CS," Miss Senyard told her girls, quite matter-of-factly. "Those members of German naval section chosen will be supplied with special passports in preparation for hasty departure."

So they can bunk off into the hills and keep up the fight once the Germans have taken over here, Osla thought with a sick twist of her stomach. Until now she'd been able to contemplate her country's takeover in the abstract, a black cloud on the horizon—but to see practical preparations being made for the day German tanks came rolling through Bletchley village . . .

If Miss Senyard's announcement had come during day shift, Osla might have been able to toss her head in defiance: *We will never need a mobile GC & CS to flee into the hills, because you'll never pull this invasion off, Herr Hitler. You'll have to run your tanks over my dead body and the dead bodies of everyone else in Britain first.*

But in the eerie, stuffy blackness of night, Miss Senyard's announcement and its implications seeped into Osla's bones like poison. If documents were being issued and orders passed down, it was fairly obvious Germany would be invading very soon.

Dear Philip: If you stop getting my letters . . .

"At least we're not on night shifts yet," one of her fellow indexers yawned, noting Osla's long silence. "The brainy boys work a midnight-to-nine shift too, because the Jerries change all the cipher settings at midnight."

"I wonder how they do it—break the ciphers." Osla wondered if she could learn to do it herself, get a transfer from filing and binding to something more taxing. Something to keep her mind from the invasion. "Not that one would ever ask; you just know Commander Denniston would have you dragged out behind the mansion and shot. But one can't help wondering. They must be fearfully clever fellows."

"Not only fellows." The answer surprised Osla. "There's a whole clutch of girls in Knox's section, that little outbuilding by the stable block? *The harem,* they call it, because Knox only recruits women."

"Let me guess—they're all slap-up lookers, and none over twenty." Osla wasn't eager for *that* kind of transfer, much as she wanted more useful work.

"No, it's not like that. Hinsley was raving a month ago how Knox poached a German-speaking girl he wanted for our section, a girl named Jane—well, I've *seen* Jane and she's got a bill like a duck. No one trying to stack his office with lookers would pick her. She's brainy, though. The brainy girls go to Dilly Knox. No idea what they do."

That was the thing about the Park; gossip ran fluid as a river, but no one knew anything for certain.

Midnight had descended black and cloudless as Osla yawned her way out of Hut 4. Codebreakers and linguists were fleeing for home and bed, as another stream of rumpled academics and girls in crepe frocks trudged in on the dreaded night shift already looking absolutely knackered. "If Mrs. F knocks on our door at six in the morning again, I'll pitch a fit," Mab grumbled, sauntering to join Osla. "I need my beauty sleep tonight. I'm going for lunch with Andrew Kempton before tomorrow's shift."

"Is that the third man asking for a date, Queen Mab?"

"Fourth." Mab didn't sound smug, just matter-of-fact. "He was born in Whitstable, read German philosophy at Cambridge, no parents—"

"Feel his withers and examine his teeth while you're at it. Are you taking a dead set at the delicious Harry Zarb, too?"

"He's married," Mab said, regretful. "At least he dropped that in right away. Most men only tell you they're married *after* trying to get a bit of the old you-know."

"Married, what a shame. You two would have had the world's tallest children." All the marriage talk made Osla think of the perennial spinster in the Finch household, and the lurking desire for a project reappeared after the night's horrified preoccupation with the German invasion. "We need to do something about Beth. The Dread Mrs. Finch has her thoroughly nobbled."

"You can't help people if they won't help themselves. She won't even look us in the eye since the literary society meeting."

Osla was quite certain, after that night two weeks ago, that she'd seen *bruises* all over the inside of Beth's arm. The kind made by strong, pinching fingers targeting the sensitive skin inside the elbow, like a bird pecking at the tenderest part of a plum. Introducing a little fizz and fun into Beth's life without putting her mother in a pucker—now, *that* was a project worth tackling.

Osla and Mab were rounding the corner through Bletchley village, walking down the center of the road to avoid the muddy ruts on the verge, when a set of headlights reared behind them. Osla shrieked and leaped into a bush, and Mab staggered and fell into a deep rut. The car ground to a halt, the driver's door flying open. "Are you all right?" A man came round the bonnet, his shadowed shape hatless and stocky. By the flare of the car's headlights, he lifted Osla easily out of the bush. "I didn't see you till I rounded the bend."

"Partly our fault," Osla said, getting her breath back. "Mab—"

Stiffly, her friend picked herself up. Osla winced. Even in the indirect glare of the masked headlights, she could see that Mab's crisp cotton print was mud from collar to hem. Reaching down, Mab slipped her left shoe off and examined the snapped heel, and Osla saw her face crumple in the shadows. Every night she watched Mab polish those cheap shoes before bed, no matter how tired she was, to give them a Bond Street shine.

"I'm sure we can fix it," Osla began, but Mab's crumpled expression vanished. She drew back and hurled the broken shoe straight into the chest of the man who'd nearly run them off the road.

"*What are you doing taking a turn at that speed, you bloody bastard!*" she bellowed. "*Are you blind, you stupid bugger?*"

"Clearly," the man said, barely catching the shoe. He stood half a head shorter than Mab, a shock of russet hair falling over his forehead as he shaded his eyes to look at her. "My apologies."

"We *were* walking in the middle of the road," Osla pointed out, but Mab stood on her one shod foot in the mud and let the stranger have it. He let it rain down, expression more admiring than horrified.

"Blew your tire," Mab finished with a withering look. "Guess you'll have to get down in the mud and change it out."

"Would if I could," he replied. "I'll just leave the car and head for the station. Are there any trains this late?"

Mab folded her arms, cheeks still scarlet with indignation. "Easier to put the spare on, if you've got a kit."

"Haven't a clue how."

Mab slipped out of her other shoe, whizzed it into his hands, marched in her stocking feet through the mud to the car's boot, and hurled it open. "Have my shoes properly mended, and I'll change your ruddy tire."

"Deal." He looked on, grinning, as Mab began yanking out tools.

"How do you know how to change a blinking tire?" Osla wondered. "I haven't the foggiest."

"A brother who works in a garage." Mab rolled up her skirt at the waist to keep it out of the mud. Her flat stare promised the stranger slow, painful death if he ogled her legs. "Have you got a torch? Shine it over so I can see what I'm doing."

He deposited Mab's ruined shoes on the bonnet and switched on his torch, still grinning. "You two are BP workers?"

Osla smiled politely, not answering that question on an open road. "Are you, Mr. . . . ?"

"Gray. And no. I'm in one of the London offices." *Intelligence,* Osla thought, approving of his vagueness. *Or Foreign Office.* "I was running some information to Commander Denniston personally, from my own boss. He was late getting me a reply, hence the midnight drive."

Osla offered a hand; he shook it over the beam of the torch. "Osla Kendall. That's Mab Churt, cursing at your tire."

"I'll need help winching up the car." Mab's irate voice floated up. "Not you, Os—no sense both of us ruining our stockings." Osla watched as Mr. Gray lent a hand. He stayed to lug the spare through the dark and pass a few more tools, until Mab snapped, "You're in my way, now; just hold the torch."

"Pity you don't work at BP instead of London, Mr. Gray," Osla said as he straightened. Hard to tell in the dark, but he looked thirty-six or thirty-seven, his face broad and calm and creased with smile lines. "We need more fellows in our literary society."

"Literary society?" He had a country voice, soft midland vowels. He spoke to Osla, but he was watching Mab do something incredibly capable to the spare tire. "I thought you BP girls were all maths-and-crosswords types."

Something niggled at the back of Osla's mind. Something about crosswords . . .

"There." Mab straightened, pushing her hair off her muddy cheek. "That should get you to London, Mr. Gray, then you can get the other patched." Her eyebrows lifted. "I'll expect my shoes back good as new."

"You have my word, Miss Churt." He shouldered his blown tire so he could sling it into the boot. "I don't want to be found dead in a gutter."

Mab nodded grudgingly, turning to look at Osla. "Coming, Os?"

"You go," Osla said as Mr. Gray nodded farewell in the dark and slipped back into his car. The bit about crosswords had dropped in her head with a *click*. "I've had an absolutely topping idea."

She hadn't been back inside the mansion since her first day; even at midnight, it hummed like a beehive with exhausted men in their shirtsleeves. Osla couldn't get in to see Commander Denniston, but red-haired Giles was in the conservatory flirting with a typist, and Osla nipped her hand through his arm. "Giles, d'you know if Denniston's still recruiting?"

"Crikey, yes. The rate traffic's mounting, they can't vet people fast enough."

"I remember hearing something about crosswords . . ."

"There's a theory that crossword types, maths types, and chess-playing types are good at our sort of work. Personally I think it's bollocks. I certainly can't tell a rook from a bishop—"

Osla cut him off. "My landlady's daughter is an absolute whiz at crosswords."

"That mousy little thing you brought to the Shoulder of Mutton? Are you mad, you dim-witted deb?"

"Her name is Beth Finch. And *don't* call me that." Osla remembered how fast Beth had finished the newspaper crossword at the pub. *Osla Kendall, not only are you not a dim-witted deb, you are a* genius. Because maybe what Beth needed was a peroxide rinse, a new dress in the latest go, and a date with an airman or two, but she wasn't going to get any of those things if she never got out of the *house*. Even sitting behind a typewriter or binding signals on night shift had to be better than toiling for the Dread Mrs. Finch until the Nazis came goose-stepping into Bletchley. "Take a puck, Giles, and put in a word with Denniston. Beth's going to fit right in at Bletchley Park."

CHAPTER 10

August 1940

"You'll do."

Beth stared in utter horror.

"Were you worried, Miss Finch?" The tired-looking man—Paymaster Commander Bradshaw, as he'd introduced himself at the start of Beth's interview—stamped something on the file in front of her. "It's not all Oxford graduates here, you know. Your background came in clean as a Sunday wash, and being a local girl, we won't have to billet you. Start tomorrow; you'll be on the day shift. You'll need to sign this . . ."

Beth didn't even hear the dire imprecations of the Official Secrets Act as they were rattled off. *They weren't supposed to take me,* she thought in a blur of panic. It had never occurred to her that Bletchley Park would hire her, even when the summons came a week ago. "It only says to present myself for an interview," Beth had reassured her mother, who had slit Beth's letter open when it arrived and demanded explanations. She'd present herself as called, but the Park wouldn't have any use for her. *Far too stupid,* she thought, wondering how they'd got her name at all. And the interview, conducted in a muggy back room behind the redbrick mansion's staircase, had seemed utterly routine: questions about typing and filing, which Beth couldn't do; education, which Beth didn't have; and foreign languages, which Beth didn't speak. She whispered one-word answers, mind half on the strange things she'd seen while trudging up to the mansion: a man cycling through the gates wearing a gas mask as though he expected an attack any moment; four men and two women playing rounders on the lawn . . . Even as she walked up the drive, Beth had already been relieved at the thought of going home and telling her mother it was all over.

Then, suddenly: *You'll do.*

"S-surely there's a mistake," she managed to stammer.

But Mr. Bradshaw was shoving a pen at her. "Sign the Act, please."

Dazed, Beth signed.

"Excellent, Miss Finch. Now for your permanent pass—" Mr. Bradshaw broke off as a commotion resonated outside. "Good Lord, these codebreakers are worse than quarreling cats."

Out the door he went. Beth blinked. "*Codebreakers?!*"

Following him out toward the entrance, she saw a weary-looking gentleman in shirtsleeves addressing a grizzled professorial type who was limping up and down the oak-paneled hall—"Dilly, old thing, do stop roaring."

"No, I will *not,*" roared the man with the limp. To Beth he looked like the White Knight in *Through the Looking-Glass,* which Osla and Mab were reading for the first literary society book pick: long, gangling, faintly comical, eyes snapping behind horn-rimmed spectacles. "Denniston, I won't have my work passed off half-done—"

"Dilly, you haven't got the personnel, and you keep turning down the new ones I send you."

"I don't want a yard of Wrens all looking the same—"

"We haven't even got any Wrens—"

"—and I don't want any debutantes in pearls whose daddies got them into BP because they knew someone at the Admiralty—"

"This one might do, Dilly," Mr. Bradshaw interrupted, and Beth shrank as every eye in the hall turned to her. "I was going to put her into administration, but you might give her a trial first if you're shorthanded."

"Eh?" The White Knight turned with a glare. His eyes behind the glasses raked Beth, and she stood frozen. "You're good with languages?"

"No." Beth had never felt so shy, slow, stilted, and stuck in her life. From Commander Denniston's grateful glance at Bradshaw, she knew perfectly well this was a diversion—chucking her into the line of fire to avert further shouting. Her face burned.

"What about linguistics? Literature?" the White Knight fired off. "Even maths?"

"No." Then for some reason, Beth whispered, "I—I'm good at crosswords."

"Crosswords, eh? Peculiar." He pushed his glasses further up his nose. "Come along."

"Miss Finch hasn't got her official pass yet—"

"Has she signed the Act? Let her start. As long as you can shoot her if she blabs, who cares about the pass?" Beth nearly fainted. "I'm Dilly Knox. Come with me," the White Knight said over his shoulder, and led her through the looking glass.

What is *this place?* Trailing after Mr. Knox as he limped out of the mansion toward what appeared to be a converted stable block, Beth couldn't stop Lewis Carroll from chaining together in her whirling head. Her brain did that sometimes, went flashing down an association and kept linking others to it to make a pattern. Glancing up at the bronze-faced clock mounted on the half-timbered upper tower, she wouldn't have been surprised to see the hands running backward. Why hadn't Osla and Mab warned her? But they couldn't say anything; they'd signed an oath . . . and now, so had Beth. Whatever happened here now, she wasn't going to be able to tell her mother a thing.

Her stomach swooped. *Mother is going to be* furious.

Beyond the old stable yard was a compact single-storied block: three brick cottages joined together in a single whitewashed unit, with two doors. Mr. Knox struck open the rightmost. "We work here," he said, beckoning Beth through a corridor. "It's like a great factory, the rest of BP. Here's where we do proper cryptography."

Cryptography, Beth thought. *I now do* cryptography.

There was no Wonderland inside the desk-crammed, chalk-dusty room where he led her, just five or six women hard at work—short and tall, pretty and plain, looking as young as eighteen or as old as thirty-five in their jumpers and skirts. None looked up. "Were you shouting at Denniston again, Dilly?" an older woman with straw-fair hair asked.

"I was sweet as a lamb. I told him just last week that he couldn't—"

"Dilly darling, no." The woman was manipulating a set of cardboard strips in a pattern Beth couldn't follow. "You didn't tell Denniston anything last week."

"Didn't I?" He scratched his head, all his earlier rage seemingly dissipated. "I rather thought last week one had said the right thing . . ."

"*One* hasn't said anything before today. *One* hasn't spoken to Denniston at all for two weeks." The straw-haired woman exchanged smiles with the younger girls.

"That would explain why he looked so puzzled." Mr. Knox shrugged, turning back to Beth. "Meet my ladies." He gestured to the room. "Dilly's Fillies, they call 'em at the mansion. Utter rot, but around here, if it rhymes, it sticks. Ladies, meet—" He looked at Beth. "Did you tell me your name?"

"Beth Finch—"

"Ladies, Beth Finch. She's . . ." He trailed off, patting his pockets. "Where are my glasses?"

"On your head," at least three of the women said, without looking up.

He located his spectacles and draped them over his nose. "Take a desk," he said, waving at Beth. "Have you got a pencil? We're breaking codes."

He flung himself down at a desk by a window, fumbling for a tin of tobacco and seemingly forgetting Beth's existence. Most of the girls went right on working as though this were a perfectly normal state of affairs, but the small woman with the straw-fair hair rose, extending a hand.

"Peggy Rock." One of the older women, thirty-five or thirty-six, a plain face that sparkled with intelligence. "I'll show you the ropes. That's Dillwyn Alfred Knox," she said, pointing to the White Knight, "and he was breaking German codes back in the Fourteen–Eighteen War. Dilly's team here researches the stuff that has to be lockpicked rather than brute-force assembly-lined through the other huts. Right now we're working the Italian naval Enigma—"

"What's *Enigma*?" Beth said, utterly bewildered.

"The machine the enemy uses to encrypt most of their military traffic," Peggy said. "Italians and Germans, naval traffic and air traffic and army traffic, and every cipher has a different setting. The machine has, well, let's just say a dizzying number of setting combinations, and the settings change every day, so that should make whatever they encrypt with Enigma unbreakable." She gave a small smile. "Not as unbreakable as they think."

Did Osla know all this? Beth wondered. Did Mab?

"We tend to get a bit more of the big picture here than the others at BP," Peggy added as if reading her mind. "They're such fiends for compartmentalization here—most people just see the bit in front of them, and maybe they put a bit together from what they see going in and out of the other huts, but that's all—"

"Utter rot." Dilly's voice floated from his desk. "I want my girls to have a large, unhampered range. You benefit from seeing the whole picture, not bits and pieces of it."

"Why?" Beth asked.

"Because we do the tricky part." Peggy Rock spread her hands. "The traffic gets registered and logged elsewhere, and once it's broken it gets translated and analyzed—but we do the important bit in the middle. The prying-it-all-open bit, every message individually. We use a technique called rodding to identify the start position of the message as seen through the window indicator setting. Let me show you—"

"I won't understand it," Beth blurted out. "I'm not clever, you understand? I can't do—" Rodding. Cryptography. *This.* Her chest was tight; her breath heaved; the walls pulsed around her. It paralyzed her to stray even a few steps outside her usual routine, and here was a whole new *world*. Any moment now she was going to panic. "I'll hold you back," she insisted, close to tears. "I'm too stupid."

"Really?" Peggy Rock looked at her calmly, fanning out a handful of those curious cardboard strips like a winning hand of cards. "Who told you that?"

CHAPTER 11

I miss you, Os. I miss you a shocking lot, to be honest.

Philip's handwriting was clear, no flourishes. Seeing it always made Osla's heart thump. *Shut up, heart,* she scolded.

"Mrs. F's really having a go." Mab was eavesdropping unashamedly downstairs, head poked into the dark landing. Beth's first shift at Bletchley Park had been today, right after her interview, and Mrs. Finch had been *twitching.* Now Beth was back, not that they could hear her. Just her mother' s insistent voice, quoting something from the Bible about *For son treats father contemptuously, daughter rises up against her mother—*

"Should we pop down?" Osla looked up from the bed where she was curled rereading Philip's old letters. "Interject various patriotic things like 'Let your daughter work, you meddling cow, there's a war on'?"

"We'll only make things worse," Mab said. "Mrs. F's on Ezekiel now."

Gnawing her lip, Osla turned back to Philip's salt-stained letter from May. *Being transferred to the* Kent *when I was just getting used to the* Ramillies; *that was a bit of a letdown. None of the ratings here are all that keen on having royalty aboard, even third-rate royalty like me. You should have seen the eyes rolling when I first came on. Whisper is we're off to hunt for some action soon. Don't worry, darling girl—*

He hadn't seen any action with the *Kent*, but now he was being transferred again, to her sister ship—who knew where it would take him? Osla shivered. U-boat wolf packs roaming the sea, and of course he'd want to charge right into the thick . . .

"Here she comes," Mab whispered as Beth's footsteps came up the stairs. Osla slid off the bed, tucking Philip's letter into her copy of *Through the Looking-Glass*. When Beth appeared on the landing, Osla and Mab whisked her into their room and shut the door.

"Well?" Osla checked Beth's arms—no bruises, thank goodness. "Your mother can't refuse, surely! You know, I thought it might take longer when I put your name in. Sometimes the vetting takes weeks—"

"So you did recommend me." Beth's voice was flat.

"Yes." Osla smiled. "I thought you might need an excuse to get out of the house—"

"*You* thought." Osla had never heard Beth interrupt anyone, but she cut Osla off now. Her cheeks flared scarlet. "You know what I think? I think I wanted to be left alone. I think I want my mother not to be angry with me, or make me hold the Bible up for twenty minutes. What I don't want is a job with strange people doing work I don't understand."

"We were just as lost the first few weeks," Mab reassured. "You'll get the hang of it. We were just trying to—"

"You want me to *grow a spine*." Beth's imitation of Mab's voice was savage. "But maybe you two should have thought that somebody like me—someone *perfectly, hopelessly Fanny Price*—would have been happy to stay home where she belongs."

She whirled out of the room. Her bedroom door banged a moment later. Mab and Osla looked at each other, stunned.

"I should have asked before I put her name up." Osla sank down on the bed. "I shouldn't have stuck my nose in."

"You didn't mean to—"

"—boss her about like her mother does?"

Mab sighed.

Dear Philip, Osla thought. *I have, if you will pardon the phrase, made a* royal *muff of things.*

CHAPTER 12

September 1940

"Hallo, can we sit here?"

Two weeks ago, Beth would have jumped out of her skin. Now she felt so weary and low, all she did was nod at the two young men who joined her table in the mansion dining hall.

"I know you." The massively built fellow with the black hair paused as he set down his tray. "You were at the first meeting of the Mad Hatters."

". . . What?"

"The literary society. We did *Through the Looking-Glass,* and at the second meet-up, Giles brought bread and margarine, moaning how Alice at least got butter when she had tea with the Mad Hatter. We've been the Mad Hatters Tea Party ever since. Less pompous than the BP Literary Society." The black-haired fellow snapped his fingers. "You were only at the first meet-up, weren't you? Don't tell me . . . Beth Finch." A grin. "I'm good with names."

Beth managed some kind of smile, pushing her food around her plate. It was two thirty in the morning, middle of night shift, and the converted dining room smelled of Brylcreem, stale fat, and kidneys on toast. All around, night-shift workers were grabbing seats, some half-asleep, some bright eyed and joking as if this were midday break at any ordinary job. Beth's stomach still wasn't used to cafeteria-style cooking, and after nearly a month her skin should have stopped prickling when she was surrounded by strangers, but it just wouldn't. "Mr.—Zarb?" she managed to say as he and his friend slung in opposite.

"Call me Harry. This is Alan," he added, indicating the young man beside him, who stared at the ceiling as he munched. "Alan Turing. We all call him the Prof, because he's such a clever bugger . . ."

Everyone here seemed to go by nicknames or first names. Everyone here seemed eccentric, too—look at Mr. Turing (Beth couldn't bring herself to think of a man she'd just met as either *Alan* or *the Prof*), with an ancient tie holding up his flannel trousers instead of a belt.

"These kidneys are abysmal," Harry Zarb went on cheerfully. "Not fit for a dog. If my son were here, he'd say we need to *get* a dog, so the kidneys wouldn't go to waste. All conversational roads lead to requests for a puppy, at least in my house—"

Beth had always wanted a dog, but Mother wouldn't hear of it. Fleas . . .

"I saw you headed into the Cottage yesterday," Harry went on, addressing Beth. "Knox's section? You must be a clever one. Dilly only takes the brainy girls for his harem—"

Beth burst into tears.

"Steady on—" Harry fumbled for a handkerchief. "I'm sorry, I shouldn't have said *harem*. No one means anything off-color by it. Dilly's a good chap—"

"Excuse me," Beth sobbed, and ran out of the room.

Bletchley Park at night might have been the dark side of the moon: every hut window blacked out to block the smallest chink of light. Beth fumbled her way across the lawn, tripped over a wooden bat left over from someone's afternoon rounders game, and finally just stopped, worn out to the bone.

It was exhausting, spending your day being stupid. Over three weeks she'd been working at the Cottage: staring at blocks of Enigma code, trying to manipulate her cardboard rods the way she'd been shown, trying to make sense of the nonsense. Hour after hour, day after day. Beth knew she was a dolt, but you'd think with three weeks of solid concentration she might achieve *something.* There was something on the other side of the curtain of code, she could feel it, but she couldn't *get* there. She was stymied. *Thoroughly dished, darling,* as Osla would have drawled. *Utterly nobbled. Completely graveled.*

"You're obsessing too much," Peggy Rock had said. "Think of it as a word game."

"I don't understand it—"

"You don't really have to. Doing this work is a bit like driving a car without having a clue what's under the bonnet. Just have at it."

Peggy had been very encouraging; so were all the other girls. But they had their own mountain of work; none of them could stand looking over Beth's shoulder all day. They sat with their crib charts and Italian dictionaries, flipping lettered rods about, and periodically someone would say something inexplicable like "Got a beetle here . . . ," and someone else would say, "I've got a starfish," and send Beth even deeper into despair.

"It's all Greek to me," she burst out her first week, and Dilly Knox had chortled, "M'dear, I wish it were!"

"He's a distinguished scholar of ancient Greek," Peggy whispered, also laughing, and Beth shriveled in her chair. Dilly was very kind, but he got so wrapped up in his own work that he barely seemed to know where *he* was, much less anyone else. The only reason Beth could think why she hadn't been sacked by now was because everyone was too busy to realize what a dismal flop she was.

And then to go home every single day and face her mother, so hurt she wouldn't even *speak* to Beth, even when Beth turned over her entire Bletchley Park salary as Mother insisted . . . "You have no idea what you're doing to her," Dad had said yesterday, shaking his head. Osla and Mab were giving Beth a wide berth; Beth flinched when she remembered how she'd hissed at them, but she wasn't sorry. Osla shouldn't have meddled. Beth Finch didn't belong here, and that was a fact.

I'm packing it in, she thought. *Tomorrow.* Three weeks ago she wouldn't have dreamed of marching up to the imposing Christmas-cake façade of the mansion and resigning, but now she knew she could screw up the courage.

Only a few girls were inside the Cottage when Beth slipped back inside—most worked days alongside Dilly. Sliding out of her cardigan, Beth sank behind her desk looking at the mess of paper slips.

"The thing about the Enigma machine," Peggy had said (though Beth hadn't even *seen* an Enigma machine), "is that it's got a great big gap we can exploit. You press the A key on the keyboard, an electrical current passes through the three wheels and a reflector, which sends the current back through the wheels and lights up the bulb of a different alphabet letter on the lampboard—A scrambles out as, say, F. Press the A key again, and another current goes through, and this time it scrambles out as Y. There's no direct equivalent, A won't always equal F—A always comes out different; that's why Enigma's so hard to crack. Except for one thing, thank goodness. The machine won't let A ever come out as A. No letter can ever be encrypted as itself."

"That's a gap?" Beth had said, utterly adrift.

"About as wide as the English Channel, duckie. Look at any block of encrypted letters: ADIPQ. Well, you know A is any letter but A, D is any letter but D . . ." Peggy had paused to light a cigarette. "Most messages that are encrypted have common phrases or words—cribs, we call them. For Italian Enigma, most messages start out with the officer the message is intended for: *Per Comandante.* So, slide through each block of letters looking for a string where not one letter matches up with P-E-R-X-C-O-M-A-N-D-A-N-T-E—the X for the space between the words—and there you are; it's a match. I'm not saying it's easy," she added. "We've been banging our heads on Italian Enigma for months, trying to figure out if it's the same machine they used in Spain in the thirties when Dilly broke their codes before. But this is how it's done—this is how you find your way in." Peggy saw Beth's despairing look. "Look, it's a bit like playing Hangman in a foreign language. You have a phrase that's all blank spaces, you guess a letter that's common in most words, and maybe it fills one or two slots in the phrase. Then you guess another letter, and the more you get, the more of the phrase you can see." She smiled. "What I'm saying is, stop focusing and let your mind play."

WIQKO QOPBG JEXLO began the code in front of Beth, five-letter block after five-letter block. She looked at the clock. Three in the morning.

Without any hope at all, she put in PERXCOMANDANTE for the machine's right-hand wheel and began trying different positions—rodding, Peggy called it, because of the slim cardboard rods with letters printed along them in the order they appeared in the wiring of each Enigma wheel. Peggy had shown Beth how to slide the rods under the encoded text to try to find a point where the text of those all-important common phrases began to appear. *Cribs,* Beth reminded herself, *not phrases. Everything has a special name here.* It sounded easy, looking for places where there was no letter overlap, but there were seventy-eight different trials to make in order to cover all twenty-six positions of each of the machine's three wheels . . .

Her eyes were aching by the time she found something. The first three letters paired up with the rod, P-E-R . . . but it gave the fourth letter as S, not X. She nearly switched over to the next, but paused.

Is there another crib starting PERS?

Beth wavered, then swiped Dilly's Italian dictionary and flipped to P. *Persona . . . personale . . .*

"Jean," she asked the nearest girl, "could *personale* be a crib?" It was the first time she'd addressed anyone in the Cottage unprompted.

"Maybe?" came the distracted answer. Beth swiveled in her chair, flipping her plait over one shoulder. "*Personale,*" she muttered. Meaning "Personal for." Surely the Italian navy had occasion to mark things *Personal for* ____. It gave her five more letter couplings to check: she had P-E-R-S; now to try for O-N-A-L-E—

Clicks. She'd heard the other girls tossing that word around for weeks, and now she saw why, because things were going *click* right on the rods in front of her. Direct clicks when both letters of a crib phrase came up side by side on the same rod; Dilly called them *beetles* for some reason. Then cross-clicks when one crib letter came up on one rod, and the other on a second rod; Dilly called those *starfish,* and Beth's breath stopped when she realized she had one. She hadn't been able to *see* it before, it hadn't made sense, but suddenly this bit right in front of her came swimming out of the rows of letters.

Well, if it was "personal for," then it stood to reason that next there would be a name, a rank, an honorific . . . She pulled out two letters, N-O. Beth dropped her rods and went pawing through the cribs again. *Signor?* Painstakingly she pulled S-I-G-out of the mess, then the R, then gobbledygook that was probably a man's name. But she had enough, she could go after some of the missing rod couplings now . . . Her braid fell over her shoulder again, getting in the way, and she twisted it up behind her neck and pushed a pencil through it. Another *click* . . .

"Beth," one of the other girls said. "Go home, your shift's over." Beth didn't hear. Her nose was almost touching the paper in front of her, the letters marching along in a straight line over her rods, but somewhere behind her eyes she could see them spiraling like rose petals, unspooling, floating from nonsense into order. She was working fast now, sliding the rods with her left hand, elbow holding the Italian dictionary open. She lost an hour on a crib that didn't work, then tried another and that was better, the clicks started coming right away . . .

Dilly Knox came in, already looking exhausted. "Anyone seen my 'baccy?" The new shift of girls went on the usual hunt for his tobacco tin. "What are you still doing here, Miss—what's your name again? I thought you were on the night shift."

Beth just handed him her worked-out message and waited, pulse racing. She'd never felt like this in her life, very light and remote, not entirely back in the present. She'd been going at it six straight hours. The message was a mess of scribbles, still gobbledygook in patches, but she'd broken it open into lines of Italian.

Her boss's smile made her heart turn over. "Oh, well done!" he all but caroled. "Well done, you! Bess?"

"Beth," she said, feeling a smile break over her face. "What—what does it say?"

He passed it off to one of the other girls, who spoke Italian. "Probably a routine weather report or something."

"Oh." Her cautious, dawning pleasure sank.

"It doesn't matter what it *says,* dear girl. Just that you broke it. We've had such trouble cracking Italian Enigma since they entered the war. This might be the best break we've had in ages."

". . . It is?" Beth looked around at the others, wondering if they'd think she was showing off. But they were grinning; Peggy clapped. "It was an accident—"

"Makes no difference. That's how it happens. Now we have this, we'll get the rest quicker. Until the Eyeties change things up, at any rate." He gave her a swift assessing look. "You need breakfast, a proper one. Come with me."

DILLY DROVE HIS Baby Austin out through the gates of Bletchley Park like the Four Horsemen of the Apocalypse were after them and was soon tearing up Watling Street with absolutely no regard for either tank traps or passing traffic. At any other time, Beth would have been sure she was about to die in a ditch, but rather than clutching the door and whimpering, she sat statue-passive in the passenger seat. She was still coming down from another world, electric and distant, spirals of letters turning lazily behind her eyelids.

Dilly didn't seem to expect conversation. Hands only now and then connecting with the wheel, he careened them down Clappins Lane and then a long woodland drive, pulling up at last before a gracious, gabled manor house. "Courns Wood," he announced, swinging out of the car. "I call it home, though with the war on, I'm hardly here. Olive!" he called, moving into a dim paneled hall. A plump graying woman appeared, dusting flour off her hands. "My wife," Dilly said, somewhat unnecessarily. "Olive, meet Beth—a budding cryptanalyst in need of sustenance."

"Hello, dear," Mrs. Knox greeted Beth tranquilly, as if utterly unsurprised to find a disheveled young woman trailing behind her husband after what had very clearly been a long night. If you were married to Dilly Knox, perhaps you got used to living in a perpetual Wonderland. "Could you eat an omelet?" she said, then answered her own question, clearly seeing Beth was beyond speech. "I'll bring two. Library, dears . . ."

Somehow Beth found herself in a disorganized study lined with books and warmed by a roaring wood fire, gin and tonic in her hand. "Drink up," Dilly said, mixing one for himself and settling into a leather chair opposite. "Nothing like a stiff gin after a hard night with the rods and cribs."

Beth didn't stop and think, *What would Mother say?* She just lifted her glass and drank half. The gin fizzed like sunshine and lemons.

"Cheers." Her boss raised his own glass, eyes sparkling. "I think you'll be a good addition to the Cottage, m'dear."

"I thought I was going to be sacked."

"Nonsense." He chuckled. "Now, what did you do before coming to BP?"

Nothing. "I was just—the daughter at home."

"University?" Beth shook her head. "Pity. What are your plans?"

"What plans?"

"After the war, of course!"

There were tank traps the length of Watling Street, and every headline was full of German Messerschmitts poking their snouts over the coast. "Are the Germans going to give us an *after the war*?" Beth heard herself wonder.

It was the kind of thing no one said aloud, but Dilly didn't chide her for letting down morale. "There's always an after. Just depends what it looks like. Finish that drink; you'll feel worlds better."

Beth lifted the glass again, then stopped. She realized in a sudden rush of returning caution how this looked: a girl of twenty-four drinking gin at ten in the morning with a man in his fifties, alone in his private library. What other people might think.

He seemed to know what was flashing through her mind. "You know why I only want gels for my team?" he asked, eyes no longer vague behind the glasses. "Not because I want pretty faces around me, though heaven knows you're all nicer to look at than a lot of university swots with horse teeth and dandruff. No, I take gels as my new recruits because they are far better, in my experience, at this kind of work."

Beth blinked. No one had ever told her young ladies were better at any kind of work than men, unless it was cooking or sewing.

"These young mathematicians and chess players in the other huts—they do similar work to what we do, rodding and cribs, but men bring *egos* into it. They compete, they show off, they don't even try to do it my way before they're telling me how to do it better. We don't have time for that, there's a war on. And I've been doing this work since the last one—I helped crack the Zimmermann telegram, for God's sake."

"What's that?"

"Never mind. What I'm saying is, I don't need a lot of young cockerels chesting about, competing with each other. Women"—Dilly leveled a finger at Beth—"are more flexible, less competitive, and more inclined to get on with the job in hand. They pay more attention to detail, probably because they've been squinting at their knitting and measuring things in kitchens all their lives. They *listen*. That's why I like fillies instead of colts, m'dear, not because I'm building a harem. Now, drink your gin."

Beth drank it. Mrs. Knox brought their breakfast, retreating with another tranquil smile, and a wave of hunger nearly flattened Beth. "I don't know if I can do it again," she found herself admitting even as she balanced the plate on her lap. No food had ever tasted so good.

“Yes, you can. Practice makes perfect. I’ve turned more schoolgirls into first-rate rodders than I can count.”

“I didn’t exactly get much training when I started.”

Dilly chewed a forkful of his own omelet. “That’s because I want you coming to it fresh and inventive, not with every instinct and impulse trained out of you. Imagination, that’s the name of the game.”

“It’s not a game.” Beth had never contradicted a superior in her life, but in this cozy library overlooking a tangled garden, none of the ordinary rules seemed to apply. “It’s war.”

“It’s still a game. The most important one. You haven’t seen an Enigma machine yet, have you? Monstrous little things. The air force and naval machines have five possible wheels, which means sixty possible orders depending on which three are picked for the day. Every wheel has twenty-six possible starting positions, and the plugboard behind it has twenty-six jacks. That makes *one hundred and fifty million million million* starting positions . . . and then the Jerries change the settings every twenty-four hours, so every midnight we have to start over. That’s what we’re up against. The Italian Enigma machine isn’t quite such a beast—no plugboard—but it’s quite bad enough.” Dilly toasted her with a tilted smile. “It’s odds to make you weep, which is why we must think of it as a game. To do otherwise is sheer madness.”

Beth was trying to figure out how many zeroes there were in one hundred and fifty million million million, and couldn’t do it. They kept spiraling behind her eyelids in five-block chunks, 00000 00000 00000, down into the rose’s heart. “If the odds are that bad, we won’t ever do it.”

“But we are. The Polish cryptanalysts were reading German Enigma traffic since the early thirties, and breaking back in after every change until ’38—we’d be nowhere without them, and now we've picked up the torch." Another silent toast for the Poles. "Bit by terrible bit, we're doing it."

"Do the Germans really have no idea?"

"None. Our fellows are very careful at the top level, how they use the decrypted information we give them. I understand there are rooms of intelligence chaps here who do nothing but mock up plausible ways our information could have been found by some other source than breaking Enigma." Dilly waved a hand. "Not our business, that part. But they must be doing it right, because the Jerries don't seem to have realized we're reading their post. German arrogance—they've got their perfect machine, their unbreakable system, so how could anyone possibly be getting around it? Especially a lot of scrubby English lads and lasses in the middle of the countryside, going at it with nothing more than pencil stubs and a little lateral thinking?"

"What's *lateral thinking*?"

"Thinking about things from different angles. Sideways, upside down, inside out." Dilly set his empty plate aside. "If I was to ask what direction a clock's hands go, what would you say?"

"Um." Beth twisted her napkin. "Clockwise?"

"Not if you're inside the clock." Pause. "See?" He smiled.

". . . Yes," said Beth Finch.

THERE WERE NO smiles the following day when she reported for her next shift. Dilly looked preoccupied, shoving Beth some new crib charts. "No Italian Enigma today. The Hut 6 lads need help getting through this lot; it's piling up and it's critical. German Enigma, mostly the Red traffic . . ."

Beth automatically coiled her plait up on the back of her head, jamming another pencil through to keep it off her neck, waiting for the nerves to swamp her as they had every day for weeks. The terrible fear that she'd fail, that she was stupid and useless and wasting everyone's time.

The fear came, the worry, the nerves—but much diminished. What Beth primarily felt was hunger: *Please, God, let me do it again.*

CHAPTER 13

September 1940

Your shoes, Miss Churt, proved broken beyond repair. I hope you will allow me to replace them, with my apologies for ruining their predecessors. —F. Gray

Mab let out a surprised *hmph,* footsteps slowing as she came into Bletchley village. A package had come in her batch of post, which like everyone else's was delivered to Bletchley Park from a PO Box in London, then sorted and sent to each hut section to be picked up after shift. Mab had torn open the envelope from Lucy first (another crayon drawing of a horse, this one with a purple mane), then turned to the package with its brief cover note. She caught her breath as she lifted out a pair of shoes: no staid replacement for her now-deceased sensible pumps, but patent-leather slings with a French heel, not too fancy for day, but perfectly gorgeous.

"Apology accepted, Mr. Gray." Mab grinned at the shoes. "Pity I didn't have you lovely things last night." She'd had a dinner date with Andrew Kempton—Hut 3, sweet fellow, bit of a bore, getting quite starry-eyed. Mab thought he'd make a very decent husband, the sort who wore starched pajamas and made the same jokes over every Sunday roast. She'd allowed a good-night kiss after dinner, and if things kept progressing, she might allow him a button on her blouse . . . No more than one, unless things proved serious. A girl couldn't let herself be carried away in the heat of the moment—that was for men, who had nothing to lose.

Mab was humming Bing Crosby's "Only Forever" as she came into the house. The sound of the radio drifted from the parlor—everyone was gathered round, Mr. Finch fiddling with the dial. The voice of Tom Chalmers over the BBC filled the room. "*. . . can see practically the whole of London spread around me. And if this weren't so appalling . . .*"

Osla was standing with enormous eyes, arms wrapped around her own waist. Beth leaned against her mother, who clutched her hand rather than pushing her aside as she'd been doing lately to punish Beth for getting a job. Mab took another step, staring at the radio.

"*The whole of the skyline to the south is lit up with a ruddy glow, almost like a sunrise or a sunset—*"

Osla spoke in a monotone. "The Germans are bombing London."

THE PRIME MINISTER'S bulldog voice, coming through the radio: "*No one should blind himself to the fact that a heavy, full-scale invasion of this island is being prepared with all the usual German thoroughness and method . . .*"

Churchill sounded so calm, Mab thought. How could he? The iron hammer of the Luftwaffe had turned away from the RAF airfields to pound London into glass. Over the radio Mab had listened frozen to descriptions of flame billowing, buildings collapsing, wave after wave of German bombers pulsing overhead dropping incendiaries on the East End docks from London

Bridge to Woolwich. There was nothing there of military value, nothing.

Only Londoners.

Those monsters, Mab thought. *Those* monsters.

Churchill's voice bulled on: "*Every man and woman will therefore prepare himself to do his duty . . .*"

Duty? Mab thought. Over four hundred dead had been reported after the morning of the first raid alone. Her knees had given out when she was finally able to put a call through to her family and hear Lucy's bright chattering voice. "It was *loud*! Mum and I ran underground—"

"Did you?" Mab had slid down to the hall floor, back against the wall. *Oh, Lucy, why didn't I bring you with me? Why didn't I* make *Mum leave?*

And now here they were, days later, and Churchill was intoning, "*This is a time for everyone to stand together, and hold firm . . .*"

Bugger that, thought Mab.

"No," said Hut 6's head of section, the moment Mab accosted him the next day. "Leave will not be granted for you to go to London to see if your boyfriend is safe."

"It's my mother and sister, not my boyfriend, and I don't need a full day. Just half—"

"You think everyone else isn't asking for the same thing? Go back to work, young lady."

"If you're hoping the chief staff officer will overrule your hut and grant you leave," Harry Zarb greeted Mab as she stamped toward the mansion, "he won't."

"Mind-reader, are you?" Mab snapped.

"Lucky guess." Harry was standing just outside the mansion, gazing over the lawn, cigarette smoldering between his big fingers. "I've been here a while smoking most of a pack, and people keep going in looking hopeful and coming out swearing."

Mab's temper subsided. She liked Harry, after all—a wry, funny regular at the Mad Hatters Tea Party. "Can I have one?" Nodding at his cigarettes.

He passed her a fag. Mab remembered being sixteen, going to films to study how the American stars smoked—how to let your hand linger around a man's as he struck a match for you. Another bit of methodical self-improvement like her reading list, like polishing her vowels. How ridiculous it all seemed. Mab didn't bother cupping Harry's hand as he lit her cigarette, just sucked down the smoke as fast as she could, like any man recently off a hard shift of war work.

"You're lucky," Harry said at last.

Her anger flared again. "I've a sister and mother in the East End, which is getting flattened by Heinkels. You have a wife, you said—is *she* in London? Have you got family in any of the zones being pounded?"

"No, I got a billet close by when I came to BP. Sheila's in Stony Stratford with Christopher." A flash of quiet pride in his voice. "That's our little boy."

"They're safe in the country, and I'm glad. But my family's not. So no, I don't think I'm *lucky*."

A tense pause. "I was trying to see if I could get released from here to enlist," Harry said at last. "I got the brush-off from Denniston; it was Giles who told me why. None of us fellows will ever be allowed to enlist. Not one, no matter how great the need. Because what if we get captured, knowing about all this?" A gesture at the lake, so peaceful with its paddling ducks; the ugly huts buzzing with secrets. "So I'm here for the duration." Harry looked at her over a vast shoulder. "You know what people think when they see a young strapping fellow like me *not* in uniform? At least no one thinks worse of you for being here."

Mab was used to the size of him by now, but reassessing the long limbs and broad chest, the massive frame that could fill a doorway, she could well imagine the glares: Harry Zarb was exactly the physical specimen made for a uniform. "It's not like this work's less important," she said, lightening her tone. "And your little Christopher would rather have his dad at home, not at the front."

"I'll tell him that, next time some grandmother spits on me at the park when I take him to spot planes." Harry dropped the butt of his cigarette, trying for a smile. "Listen to me whinge—I'd better get back to my hut. See you at the next Tea Party, Mab. Hold firm, eh?"

"Hold firm," Mab quoted back. Bloody Churchill. She finished her cigarette in the dusk, fingering Lucy's latest drawing in her pocket. The horse with the purple mane. *Hold firm.*

She managed almost an entire week.

It was near ten o'clock; Osla stood before the mirror yanking a comb through her hair, and Mab lay paging through Osla's copy of *Through the Looking-Glass.* The Mad Hatters were reading *The Hound of the Baskervilles* now, but Mab hadn't managed to finish the Carroll. "I hate this book," she heard herself saying, suddenly and viciously. "Everything upside down and nightmarish, who writes a book like that? The whole bloody *world* is already like that!" Her voice cracked. She'd had such a terrible fight with her mother over the telephone yesterday, first begging, then shouting at Mum to put Lucy on the next evacuee train out of London, *anywhere* out of London. Mrs. Churt wouldn't hear of it; she maintained that the Jerries weren't making her move one foot out of her home, nor Lucy neither. All very well and good for morale, that kind of attitude, but Lucy was a *child.* People were saying over a hundred London children had been killed in that terrible first raid alone—

She fired *Through the Looking-Glass* across the room into the hall. "Bugger you, Mr. Carroll. Bugger you and your Jabberwocky—"

Her voice broke. Mab hadn't wept since that one terrible night when she was seventeen, the night very thoroughly buried in her memory, but now she curled up on her counterpane, shuddering with sobs.

Osla sank down beside her, arms folding around Mab's shoulders. Through tear-choked eyes Mab saw Beth in a hideous flannel nightdress, standing awkwardly in the open doorway. "Your book," she said, holding out *Through the Looking-Glass*. She didn't seem to know whether to leave or to come embrace Mab too, so she shut the door and stood by Mab's bed.

Mab couldn't stop sobbing. All the tension and dread that had wound her tighter than a clock since war had been announced unspooled in one violent fit of weeping. She looked up, tears falling, as Osla squeezed her shoulders and Beth shifted from foot to foot. "How long?" She said it brutally, not caring if it was defeatist. "How long before we have Panzers rolling down Piccadilly?" Because even if the bombs missed Mum and Lucy in Shoreditch, the imminent invasion wouldn't.

"It might not happen," Osla said hopelessly. "The invasion can't go if the tides aren't—"

"The invasion was postponed."

The words flew out of Beth as if fired from a rifle. Mab and Osla both stared at her, plain prim Beth in her nightdress buttoned to the throat, flushing so crimson she nearly glowed.

"Beth—" Mab's mind flashed with all the things she was and wasn't allowed to ask, knowing they'd already transgressed those bounds. "How do you know . . ." She couldn't make herself finish, but she couldn't make herself take the question back either. Her heart pounded, and the room was so quiet she almost thought she could hear Beth and Osla's hearts thudding too.

The lights went out all at once—Mrs. Finch turning everything off at the main below, determined no one would keep a light on past her curfew. Mab nearly jumped out of her skin at the sudden blackness. An instant later, Beth's small cold hand found her wrist, presumably Osla's too, because in the pitch darkness she pulled the three of them together, so close their foreheads touched.

"The invasion has been postponed," Beth repeated in a nearly soundless whisper. "At least, I think it has. Some of my section were sent to help Hut 6 work on overflow German air force traffic. The message was broken at the desk next to mine—it was about airlifting equipment on Dutch airfields being dismantled. There was more, I don't know what, but the way the hut head reacted . . ."

"If the loading equipment was dismantled, the invasion is being pushed back." The words burst out of Osla as though Beth's confession had shattered a dam. "That could explain the messages I saw in German naval section, going out to all naval networks—"

"But in my section we're still getting messages on the buildup of forces," Mab contributed, feeling her own dam break. "So surely it's just a deferment, not a cancellation—"

"But it probably means next spring at the earliest," Osla finished. "No one would want to launch invasion barges in winter tides."

They all took that in, still frozen together with their foreheads touching in the blackness. "Who else knows about this?" Mab whispered at last.

"A few hut heads. Mr. Churchill, surely—he can't make it public; he probably won't rule out invasion this year until he's utterly certain. But he and the people at the very top—they know." Osla gulped. "And us."

This is why they don't want us talking to each other, Mab thought, remembering Commander Denniston's strictures. *We all just see one piece of the puzzle, but when we start talking and put them together . . .*

"You can't tell." Beth's words rushed. "You can't tell anyone we're safe until spring, no matter how scared they are. I shouldn't have told you. I—" Her breath hitched. "Denniston could sack us, put us in prison—"

"He won't find out. And we can't be the first to compare notes, no matter what they threaten—"

"You know how many girls ask me to look for whatever ship their boyfriend or brother's on, because I'm in German naval section?" Osla said softly. "They aren't supposed to, but they do."

The invasion postponed. It didn't mean safety from bombing; it didn't mean safety next spring . . . but it had been so long since they had heard any good news at all, it felt like a much bigger weight lifted than it really was. Yes, there would still be air raids. Yes, the Germans might cross the channel next year. But who knew where they'd all be next year? All you could think about in wartime was today, this week. There wouldn't be any German barges rolling into Dover this week, and knowing that, Mab thought she could go back to work and hold firm. "I swear right now," Mab whispered, "I won't say a word to my mum or anyone outside this bedroom. No one here will get in trouble with Denniston because of me."

"I still shouldn't have told." There was an agony of shame in Beth's voice.

Mab surprised herself by pulling Beth into a ferocious hug. "Thank you," she muttered. "I know you won't do it again, but—thank you." When a girl has broken national security to ease your mind about your family's lying in the path of an invasion route, she has officially become a friend.

ELEVEN DAYS UNTIL THE ROYAL WEDDING

November 9, 1947

CHAPTER 14

London

Marry for friendship, not love," Osla had heard her mother quip. "Friends listen better than lovers!" So what did it say when you got engaged to a friend and he didn't listen a whit?

"Darling," Osla said, trying to keep her voice even. "I've asked you repeatedly not to call me *kitten*. I've told you nicely that I dislike it; I've told you firmly that I despise it; I'm telling you now that I loathe it with every fiber of my being." Even more than she loathed being called a silly deb.

"Claws in, kitten!" He chuckled down the telephone line, still in bed by the sound of him. "Why the early call?"

Osla gave a measured exhale. "I'll be out of town for a few days. Old friend in a bit of a flap."

"I thought you were coming over tonight." His voice lowered. "Staying over."

I'm sure you can find someone else to fizz your sheets while I'm gone, Osla thought. He certainly hadn't given up other women since their engagement, and Osla supposed it didn't matter. They had an understanding, not a great love. *Let's give it a go, Os,* had been his marriage proposal. *Romance is for bad novels, but marriage is for pals—pals like us.*

Why did I say yes? she sometimes wondered when she looked at the emerald on her finger, but a scolding reply always followed fast on that thought's heels. *You know perfectly well why.* Because it had been July, the whole world positively kippered over Princess Elizabeth's recently announced engagement to Philip, and Philip's wartime girlfriend had turned overnight to an object of pity. Suddenly it didn't matter that Osla wrote for the *Tatler,* loved her work, and splashed out at the Savoy every Saturday night with a different beau—all that mattered after the royal engagement was that she was a pathetic ex-debutante, jilted by the princess's future husband and still unmarried. A week of pitying glances and sheet-sniffing journalists, and Osla had quite simply crocked up. She'd walked into the next party wearing a black satin frock slashed practically to the waist, ready to say yes to the next halfway suitable man who took a dead set at her, and an old friend had sidled up and said *Let's give it a go.*

And really, it was all going to be fine. They wouldn't be like those deadly old-fashioned couples who lived in each other's pockets. They weren't in love, and who needed to be? It was 1947, darling, not 1900. Better to marry a friend, even one who called her *kitten,* than expect some grand romance. A friend whose presence at the royal wedding would assure all onlookers that Osla Kendall was a radiant fiancée, *not* a bitter old maid.

"Sorry to snaffle your plans, darling, but I'll be back before you miss me." Osla rang off, then whisked downstairs with her traveling case. A taxi screeched to a halt, and soon Knightsbridge fell behind her. The thought of her fiancé's eyes was replaced by the memory of a woman's serious blue gaze—the eyes of the woman who had disappeared three and a half years ago into Clockwell. The last time Osla had seen those eyes, they'd been wide and bloodshot as she simultaneously wept and laughed, rocking back and forth on the floor. She'd looked utterly on her beam ends, like she *belonged* in an asylum.

The cipher message crackled in Osla's pocket. *You owe me.*

Maybe I do, Osla thought. *But that doesn't mean I* believe *you.* Believed the other half of that desperately scribbled message, the very first line, which Osla had read and reread in shock.

But she remembered those blue eyes, so painfully earnest. Eyes that had never lied.

What happened to you? Osla wondered for the thousandth time. *What happened to you, Beth Finch?*

Inside the Clock

"Into the garden, Miss Liddell! We want our exercise, don't we?"

Beth caught herself rocking again, back and forth on her bench, as she wondered what was going on in the world outside. At BP she'd been better informed than anyone outside Churchill's cabinet. Living here in this wool-padded ignorance—

With an effort, Beth stilled herself. Only madwomen rocked back and forth. She wasn't mad.

Not yet.

"Miss Liddell—" The matron hauled her up, voice dropping from sugary to sharp as the doctors bustled out of earshot. "Outside, you lazy bitch."

The thing Beth hated most here: anyone could touch her whenever they wanted. She had never liked to be touched unless it was on her own terms, and now every day there were *hands:* at her arms to steer, at her jaw to pry her mouth open, touching, touching, *touching.* Her body was no longer her own. But she moved out into the garden, because if she didn't she'd be dragged.

"That Liddell gives me the shivers," Beth heard the matron mutter an hour later, sharing a cigarette in the rose garden with another nurse. "Underneath that empty stare it's like she's thinking how to take you apart."

Correct, Beth thought, maintaining her vacant look as she wandered the roses.

"Who cares what they're thinking, as long as they're quiet?" The nurse shrugged. "At least we don't have the dangerous ones like at Broadwell or Rampton. They're docile here."

"They're docile, all right." The matron reached over to the vacant-eyed old woman who had been wheeled out to the garden in her bath chair and tapped hot cigarette ash onto her wrist. No response, and both matrons giggled.

Endure. Beth picked up the discarded, half-smoked cigarette after they wandered away, taking a welcome drag. *Just endure.*

She left the rose garden and wandered the high outer wall, which had been cleared of trees or shrubs or anything that might provide help climbing upward. A trio of burly orderlies walked the perimeter every hour, looking for knotted sheets or makeshift ropes flung over the walls. Not looking too seriously; it had been years since anyone tried to make a break for it. *I intend to be the next,* Beth thought. *And then I will come for the person who put me here.*

Three and a half years, and she still wasn't entirely sure who that was. She'd told her former friends as much in her cipher message:

Osla & Mab—

There was a traitor at Bletchley Park, selling information during the war.

I don't know who, but I know what they did. I found proof it was someone who worked in my section—but whoever they are, they had me locked up before I could make my report.

You may hate me, but you took the same oath I did: to protect BP and Britain. That oath is bigger than any of us. Get me out of this asylum, and help me catch the traitor.

Get me out of here.

You owe me.

"Everyone in, now! Exercise over." The same hard-faced matron called across the garden, sounding impatient. "Pick up your feet when I talk to you, Liddell." Giving Beth's arm a hard, careless twist as she passed.

Beth lifted the still-smoldering cigarette she'd managed to conceal between two fingers and planted the burning end on the matron's hand. "Not. My. Name."

Two orderlies dragged her to her cell, face stinging with slaps. Beth fought every step of the way, clawing and spitting as they buckled her into the straitjacket. She tried to lie low, oh, she did, but sometimes she couldn't stop herself. She snarled as she felt the needle's prick, felt her veins filling with smoke, felt herself heaved like a hay bale onto her cot. The furious matron lingered as everyone else left, waiting until she could spit down Beth's cheek. It would dry and be mistaken for drool, Beth knew. "You can lie in those sheets till you've pissed them, you little cow. Then you can lie in them a while longer."

Go to hell, you starched bully, Beth tried to say, but a fit of lung-rattling coughs erupted, and by the time she was done hacking, she was alone. Alone, straitjacketed, drugged to the gills, with nothing to think about but the traitor of Bletchley Park.

Mab and Osla would surely have the letters by now, Beth

thought dizzily. The question was, would they dismiss her claim as a madwoman's paranoid fantasy?

Or would they believe the unbelievable: that a traitor had been working at Bletchley Park and passing information to their enemy?

SIX YEARS AGO

March 1941

BLETCHLEY BLETHERINGS

BP'S NEW WEEKLY: EVERYTHING WE DINNAE NEED TO KNOW!

March 1941

Bletchley Bletherings has it on good authority that some unknown prankster smeared Commander Denniston's office chair with strawberry jam during night shift. Waste of good jam, says *BB*!

This month's Mad Hatters Tea Party is discussing *The Great Gatsby*. It is officially Giles Talbot's turn to bring the topper—for all you gigglemugs who have not clapped eyes on this monstrosity, picture a Dickensian stovepipe festooned with false flowers, ancient Boer War medals, Ascot plumes, etc. The topper is worn in dunce cap fashion by any Mad Hatter to propose the *Principia Mathematica* for the monthly read (that's you, Harry Zarb), preface every statement with "I'm sorry" (ahem, Beth Finch), or otherwise wet-blanket the proceedings. *BB* doesn't see stovepipe toppers catching on any time soon in *Vogue* . . .

Speaking of fashion trends, London continues to sport 1941's enduring, classic combination of shattered buildings and bomb craters, topped with *eau de Messerschmitt* and a dashing plume of smoke. Bomb away, Krauts—the boffins and debs of BP will still flood into London every night off and dance defiant in the rubble. There's a war on, after all, and tomorrow we might be dead!

—Anonymous

CHAPTER 15

Osla crawled along the floor, blinded by blood.

"Daisy Buchanan is one of those girls who goes about pretending they're ever so fragile," Mab proclaimed, "and really they're as tough as old boots."

"I thought she was a bit sad," Beth ventured. "I'm sorry, I didn't mean to—"

"Beth said I'm sorry *again!" A chorus of laughter from the Mad Hatters, and the ancient festooned hat was lobbed toward Beth . . .*

That wasn't right, Osla thought dimly, feeling blood run into her hair. She wasn't at the Mad Hatters Tea Party anymore. That had been this afternoon, everyone wrapped in their coats against the March chill but determined to discuss *The Great Gatsby* in the spring sunshine on the lake's shore. Mab with her legs elegantly crossed, Harry stretched full-length leaning on an elbow in the grass, Beth primly upright with her tea mug.

"You're very smart today, Os." That had been Harry, packing away the hat and the books post–Tea Party. "Night off?"

"I'm catching the evening train to London." Osla patted her bag, which she'd crammed that morning with her favorite Hartnell evening dress: emerald green satin that sluiced over her skin like water. "I've got an old friend on leave from his ship; we're going to splash out at the Café de Paris."

The Café de Paris . . . Osla looked around, blinking blood out of her lashes, but couldn't see anything through the splintered darkness but rubble and overturned tables. Humped forms lay along the floor. Her eye refused to recognize them, what they were. There—the famous nightclub staircase, taking you from the street to the intimate underground splendor of cocktail tables and champagne dreams. Osla tried to seize the bannister and haul herself upright, but she tripped over something. Looking down, she saw a girl's arm, its dainty wrist still looped with a diamond bracelet.

The girl's corpse sat slumped and armless in a blue chiffon gown at the nearest table.

"Oh," Osla whispered, and threw up into the rubble. Her mind was full of broken glass, her ears rang with sirens, and it was all coming back. She looked around at the carnage that had, minutes ago, been London's most glamorous nightclub—the safest in the city, its manager boasted. The Blitz couldn't touch you here, twenty feet belowground, so dance the night away.

"Philip," she heard herself whispering, "Philip . . ."

Ken "Snakehips" Johnson and his band had packed the floor, the Café de Paris jammed with dancers as the trumpets blared. Even when the area between Piccadilly Circus and Leicester Square was being strafed by German bombers aboveground, here you could forget the air raids. Here you were safe. Perhaps it seemed heartless or foolhardy to dance when the world above was pounded by fire, but there were times you had to either dance or weep—and Osla chose to dance, her hand in her partner's strong tanned one, his arm in its naval uniform snug about her waist.

"Marry me, Os," he said into her ear, spinning her through the tango. "Before my leave's up."

"Don't talk drip, Charlie." She executed a flashy turn, smiling. "You only propose to me when you're half-sauced." Osla couldn't help but wish she were doing the tango with Philip tonight, but he was still out to sea. Charlie was an old chum from her deb days, a young officer heading out into the teeth of the Atlantic. "No more marriage proposals, I mean it!"

"That Canadian heart of yours is frozen solid—"

Snakehips and the band swung into "Oh, Johnny, Oh, Johnny, Oh!" and Osla threw her head back to sing along. Winter was over and warmth starting to creep back over Britain; the government might still have been on alert for a German invasion, but Osla hadn't heard a peep in BP about any such operation moving forward. Maybe the headlines were still bleak, and maybe Osla was still bored to tears filing and binding in Hut 4—all right, not just bored but smarting from some drawling comment she'd overheard about *Miss Senyard's flock of dim-witted debs in pearls*—but there was, overall, a great deal more to sing about in this dawning spring of 1941 then there had been in the autumn of '40.

Snakehips sang away, dark skinned and slender in his white jacket, dancing with all the fluid grace that had won him his nickname. "He warbles it better than the Andrews Sisters," Osla half shouted over the music, jitterbugging away in her green satin pleats, and she never heard the two bombs that hit the building aboveground, then rattled down the ventilation. She only saw the blue flash exploding before the bandstand, and in the instant before everything went away, saw Snakehips Johnson's head blown from his shoulders.

And now here she was, rocking back and forth on the floor, evening dress covered in blood.

There was more light now, torches blinking on as survivors picked themselves up. A man in RAF uniform, trying to stand when one leg had been blown off at the knee . . . a boy who barely looked old enough to shave, trying to lift his moaning dance partner off the floor . . . a woman in a sequined gown crawling through the rubble . . . *Charlie,* Osla thought—there he was, faceup on the dance floor. The blast had exploded his lungs out onto the front of his naval uniform. Why had the bombs killed him and flung her clear? It made no sense. She tried to stand, but her legs wouldn't move.

Someone buffeted down the stairs, shouting, and suddenly there seemed to be a rush of feet and bouncing torch beams. "Please," she tried to ask the man who had run past, who was now moving from body to body. "Can you help—" But the man wasn't here to help; he was yanking bracelets off a woman's bloodied arm, then moving to a disembodied torso by the stage and rummaging for a wallet.

It took her a long moment to see it for what it was. *Looting,* he was looting the bodies—a man had come into a room full of dead and wounded, and he was *looting their jewelry*—

"You—" Osla struggled upright, fury like glass shards in her mouth. "You—stop—"

"Gimme that—" A young man with sandy hair reached out, and pain bolted down Osla's spine as she felt her earring torn away. "Gimme that too," he said, fingers fastening around Philip's jeweled insignia.

"You can't—have it," Osla heard herself scream, but her limbs were moving with jerky uncertainty, and she heard the strap of her dress tear.

Then a voice snarled, "Get the hell off her—" and a champagne bottle swung in a short arc through the flickering dark. There was a sound like a china plate hitting a brick floor, and Osla's attacker dropped where he stood. She felt a gentle hand on her arm. "You all right, miss?"

"Philip," she whispered. She still had the naval insignia, clenched so tight in her palm she could feel its edges cut.

"I'm not Philip, sweetheart. What's your name?"

"Os—" she began, and her teeth chattered so violently she couldn't finish her own name.

"Like Ozma of Oz?" The man's voice was light, soothing. "Sit down, Ozma, and let me see if you're hurt. Then we'll get you back to the Emerald City, right as rain." He had a torch; he guided her to the nearest chair. Her eyes were blurring so badly she couldn't see what he looked like. She had a vague impression of lean height, dark hair, an army uniform under a greatcoat. *Who's Ozma of Oz?*

The man who had attacked her lay limp among the rubble. "Is—he dead?" Osla jerked.

"I don't care if he is. Christ, the blood in your hair . . . I can't see if you've got a wound under there." He picked up the champagne bottle he'd swung against the looter's skull, popped the cork, and poured gently over Osla's hair. Pinkened bubbles streamed down her neck, still cold from the ice bucket.

She shivered, starting to weep. "Philip . . ."

"Is that your boyfriend, Ozma?" The man was examining the back of her head now, sorting through her champagne-soaked curls. "It doesn't look like this is your blood. Keep still, there's aid workers on the way—"

"Philip," Osla wept. She meant poor Charlie, but her tongue wouldn't produce the right name. She tried to stand—she should be helping, finding bandages for the others, *doing something*—but her legs still would not move.

"Keep still, sweetheart. You're in shock." The dark-haired man shrugged out of his coat and draped it around her shoulders. "I'll try to find Philip."

He's not here, Osla thought. *He's in the Mediterranean, being shot at by Italians.* But her Good Samaritan disappeared before she could tell him, moving to bend over an RAF captain who lay against the wall. The dark-haired man yanked a tablecloth off the nearest table to wad against the other man's wounds, then a line of chorus girls in feathers and sequins hid him from sight as they stumbled past weeping—they must have been shielded in the wings when the bombs went off . . .

Time slipped sideways for Osla. She was on a stretcher suddenly, still huddled in the greatcoat, and aid workers were lifting her up the stairs to the street above, where someone made another examination.

"We can take you to the doctor, miss, but you'll wait hours while they see the bad cases first. My advice is go home, clean up, see your doctor in the morning. Is there someone at home waiting for you?"

What do you mean, "home"? Philip had said that at the Café de Paris on New Year's Eve. *Home is where there's an invitation or a cousin.* Osla, standing in her bloodied dancing slippers on the rubble-strewn street, had no idea where her own home was. She was a Canadian living in Britain; she had a father under a gravestone and a mother at a house party in Kent; she had a billet in Bletchley and a thousand friends who would offer her a spare bed, but home? No. None.

"Claridge's," she managed to say, because at least she could have a hot bath in her mother's empty suite. She'd have to catch the dawn milk train to get back to Bletchley in time for her shift.

Once at the hotel, it was a long time before she could get undressed. She couldn't bear to touch the bloodied fastenings of her favorite, utterly ruined gown, couldn't bear to shed the overcoat, which was soft and worn and held her in its warm arms. She didn't even know her Good Samaritan's name, and he didn't know hers either. *Sit down, Ozma . . . we'll get you back to the Emerald City, right as rain . . .*

"Who does this belong to, Miss Kendall?" Mrs. Finch asked

the following day. Beth was usually the one she pounced on post-shift, saying reproachfully that if she was *finally done* with her *very important work,* there were spoons to be polished—but today it was Osla she was waiting for, holding out the greatcoat Osla had worn home and hung on the peg. Mrs. Finch squinted at the name tape inside the collar. "J. P. E. C. Cornwell—who is he?"

"I have no idea," said Osla, taking the coat and hobbling upstairs like an eighty-year-old woman. Every joint in her body hurt; she had not slept at all and gone straight from London into her day shift. The scent of blood and champagne lingered in her nostrils.

"What's wrong?" Mab said, following her in and slipping out of her shoes. "The way you're moving—"

Osla couldn't bear to explain. She muttered an excuse and crawled into her narrow bed, trembling somewhere deep inside, hugging the coat, which smelled like heather and smoke. *I want home,* she thought nonsensically. It wasn't enough anymore just to fight, to do her part for this country she loved and take her fun where she could. Osla Kendall was exhausted and scared, aching for a door to walk through—a door with welcoming arms inside.

She wanted to go home, and she had no idea where to find it.

CHAPTER 16

FROM *BLETCHLEY BLETHERINGS*, MARCH 1941

BP fellows, if you've got two girls on a string and are trying to keep them from finding out about each other, exercise caution. In other words, don't take your secretarial-pool blonde to the Bletchley Odeon, where you also take that brunette amazon you met by the lake on your tea break, or the amazon in question will rumble your game . . .

Lousy—little—*toad*," Mab muttered, striking each key on her Typex with special venom. Months she'd been going to films and dinners with Andrew Kempton, nailing a fascinated expression on her face as he went on about the lining of his stomach and his chilblains. Maybe he was a little dull, but she'd thought he was kind, sensible, honest. Someone to offer contentment as well as stability. He'd said he wasn't seeing anyone else; he'd hinted about introducing her to his parents. And all the time, a mansion typist on the side!

Well, so much for honesty. He'd clearly seen Mab as nothing but a girl to play with.

Men all think that about you, a poisonous whisper said at the back of her mind. *Cheap stupid slut.*

For a moment she could feel his breath in her ear, the man who'd said that. Then she shoved him back in the dark corner where he belonged and bent over her Typex again, setting her wheels in today's configuration for Red. Mab still had plenty of candidates in the marriage pool, men who *would* be kind and sensible and honest, not just making a show of it.

She finished her message and taped it up, pausing to blow on her hands. The in-hut temperature was arctic; every woman in the Decoding Room was huddled over her Typex in coat and muffler—and there were several more machines now, from the days it had just been two. Thank goodness they no longer had to run outside to get their decrypted messages out for translation and analysis; *that* work had moved to the hut right next door, and the boffins had been quick to rig a shortcut for passing information between the two. Mab took up the broom leaning against the desk, banged it briskly against the wooden hatch now seated in the wall, then slid the hatch open and called, "Wake up over there!" into the tunnel. Someone at the other end in Hut 3 shouted, "Bugger off," and then with a series of clanks, a wooden tray was yanked into the room. Mab dumped her stack of papers in, tugged the wire to send it back, then returned to her Typex.

The next report came out with a gap of gibberish in the middle, but Mab was long past the days of having to give the dud reports over to someone more experienced. "Machine error, or radio signal fading out during interception . . ." She put a request through to the Registration Room, asking them to check the traffic registers—if the message had been intercepted and recorded twice, you could often get the missing code groups from the second version . . .

A harried-looking man in a Fair Isle sweater blew into the Decoding Room. "I need the tallest girl you've got," he said without preamble. "The new operation in Hut 11—we've been sent seven

Wrens for operators, but we need an eighth, and she's got to be five eight at least. Who's the tallest here?"

Eyes went to Mab, who straightened to her full five eleven.

"Splendid. Grab your kit."

"Is this a temporary reassignment, or—"

"Who knows in this madhouse? Quick, now."

Mab gathered her things, frowning. She wasn't sure she wanted to leave the Hut 6 Decoding Room. The pace was killing, but after nearly nine months she was *good* at her job. They were more than just typing-pool girls here, she'd come to realize—it took imagination and skill to take a corrupted message and juggle wheel settings until it came clear, or to work through potential Morse errors and find the one that had thrown a message off course. She'd come to feel a certain thrum of satisfaction watching a block of five-letter gibberish sort itself under her fingers into tidy blocks of German.

Well, it didn't matter what she found satisfying; she'd work wherever she was told. Mab hurried across the gravel path toward Hut 11, squinting in the pale spring sunshine. It was Lucy's birthday soon; she'd arranged for the day off and was planning to take a cake to Sheffield, where Lucy was now thankfully living with their aunt, at least while London continued to be pounded by the Luftwaffe. Poor Luce didn't like Sheffield *or* their aunt, who had four children and hadn't wanted to take on a fifth (at least until Mab promised to send a weekly chunk of her BP wage). But even if Lucy was lonely, she was safe. Mum refused to move from Shoreditch, and Mab woke every day with the knowledge that this might be the morning she learned a bomb had flattened her mother's building.

"Good, the replacement." Mab found herself yanked into Hut 11 by a fellow she recognized from standing in line for tea at the kiosk set up by the Naval Army and Air Force Institutes—Harold

Something. Hut 11 was airless and cold, smaller than Hut 6, and not subdivided, one big room that managed to be both cavernous and claustrophobic. Along one wall stood a row of Wrens, all staring at the monstrosities in the middle of the room.

"Ladies," said Harold Whoever, "meet the bombe machines."

They were bronze-colored cabinets, massive things at least six feet high. The front held rows of circular drums, five inches in diameter, letters of the alphabet painted round each one. In this dark hut they loomed like trolls under bridges, like giants turned to boulders by sunlight. Mab stared, mesmerized, as Harold continued to speak.

"You're here to help break German codes, ladies, and the bombe machines have been designed by some of our cleverer chaps to help speed that process up. It'll be tedious work keeping these beasts going, and precision is essential, so I've been authorized to share a bit more than usual about what they do." He patted one of the massive cabinets like a dog. "Every cipher has a great many possible machine settings, and we can't get any further on the decoding till we have the settings, and it's slow going getting those by hand. These beasts will speed everything up, and that's where you ladies come in. The brainy fellows will send over something like this." Harold held up a complicated diagram of numbers and letters like nothing Mab had ever seen in Hut 6. "Called *menus*—"

"Why, sir?" one of the Wrens ventured.

"Probably because *menu* sounds better than *worked-out guess*." Harold pushed his spectacles up. "You take the menu, plug up your machine accordingly—the plugs in the back correspond to the positions on the menu. Then start the machine up, and let her rip. Each wheel on the bombe"—he indicated the rows on the nearest machine—"goes through thousands of possible settings, faster than anyone could do by hand. It finds a possible match for the wheel wiring and ring setting, as well as one possible match for a plugboard letter. That leaves, oh, a few million million possible settings to check the other plugboard possibilities. When the machine finally stops, you'll use the checking machine to match the stop position of the bombe, make sure you haven't got a false positive, and so forth. Assuming you haven't, you alert the boffins back in their huts that you've broken their setting for that key, then plug your machine up for the next menu and the next key. Questions?"

About a thousand, Mab thought. But that wasn't how it was done here; at BP it was just button up the questions and have a go.

"Miss Churt and Wren Stevens, I'm putting you on this machine here. Someone named her Agnus Dei, or maybe just Agnus—"

Aggie, Mab thought, already disliking her. The machine's back looked like a knitting basket crossed with a telephone switchboard—a mass of dangling plugs and great crimson pigtails of plaited wires like snarled yarn, snaking down through rows of letters and numbers. Wren Stevens looked similarly nonplussed. "I thought I'd ship out somewhere glamorous if I joined the navy," she whispered to Mab as Harold began showing them how to keep the wires apart with tweezers. "Out to Malta or Ceylon, getting my drinks poured by lieutenants. Not buried in wiring in the middle of Buckinghamshire!"

"Good luck getting out now you're in," Mab said, still staring up at Aggie. "Nobody transfers out of BP unless you fall pregnant or go crazy, so take your pick."

Servicing Aggie was like ministering to some cranky mechanical deity. Mab's arms ached after an hour of hoisting heavy drums into their slots; her fingers were pinched red from the heavy clips that snapped each drum in place. Plugging up the back was a horror: wrestling with a mess of wires and coupling jacks, trying not to set sparks off, squinting at a menu that looked like an arcane diagramming exercise or maybe a spell for raising the dead. Mab jumped, fingertips buzzing, as a prickle of electricity shocked her for the fourth time, and set the machine going with a muttered curse. With all the bombes at full roar, the din of Hut 11 was incredible, pounding her ears like hammers.

"Work at the other drums while you wait for the machine to stop," Harold shouted over the noise.

Mab pried open the drums to reveal circles of wire inside, going at the nest with tweezers to make sure not even a single one brushed against another and shorted the electrical circuit. Within the hour her eyes were smarting from the concentration and her reddened fingers pricked by copper wire. "What happens if the wires touch?" she called over the din.

"Don't let the wires touch," Harold replied simply.

Mab worked, sweat collecting between her aching shoulder blades, cuffs and wrists growing greasy from the bombe's fine spray of oil droplets. Pushing limp, sweaty hair off her forehead, she straightened as Aggie stopped dead, every drum frozen. "Did we break it?" Mab asked as the other machines whirred.

"No, she's telling you it's time to check her results." Harold showed Wren Stevens how to take the reading from the other side of the bombe, run it through the checking machine. "Agnus found the setting. Job's up, strip her down, load the new drums, get the next menu going. Well done."

He pushed another diagram into Mab's hand. She knew it was for an army key because she'd seen the name on reports coming through her Hut 6 Typex, but everything else on the menu was a mystery. This was an earlier part of the BP information loop than she was used to seeing—the part that helped spit out those blocks of five-letter-grouped reports that landed on the desks of the Decoding Room women.

Mab couldn't help a shiver. Working in the Decoding Room had a sheen of normality to it; a roomful of women hammering at Typex machines wasn't so different from a roomful of secretaries in an office, chattering about wasn't *Gone with the Wind* a swooner and have you seen the film yet? No one could chat in this din; no one would be admiring each other's frocks when they were all dripping sweat in the windowless fug of machine oil. Mab had worked since she was fourteen, and she already knew there wasn't a job in the world that could make this one seem normal. She finished plugging up Aggie and stood back. "Start her up."

"BREAK TIME," HAROLD called sometime later, tagging half the girls. "Relieve your partner in an hour."

Mab didn't want food, she wanted *air*. The Wrens headed for the NAAFI kiosk for tea, but Mab flopped on the lake's grassy bank. Her ears rang dully from four hours of Aggie's din; her fingers were pricked and stinging. She sucked down a cigarette and pulled her newest book out but gave up after five minutes. The Mad Hatters had picked a poetry collection for this month's read—*Mired,* it was tersely and ominously called, a volume of Great War battlefield verses—and the rhythmic iambic pentameter beat in the same *clackety-clack* pattern as the bombe machine's drums. "No, thank you," she said aloud, tossing the book onto the grass.

"I don't much like that book either," a male voice remarked behind her.

Mab tilted her head back, looking up the rumpled suit to the broad face with its laugh lines. He looked vaguely familiar . . .

"It was very dark when we first met," he said, smiling. "You changed my tire on a midnight road. Did the shoes fit?"

"Beautifully, thank you." Mab smiled back, placing his face if not his name. "You really didn't have to send them."

"My pleasure."

"Don't suppose you could spare a cigarette?" Mab was down to her last one and had a feeling she'd need it badly at the end of shift. He produced a cigarette case. "I thought you didn't work at BP."

"No, London. Got sent over on a bit of business."

Foreign Office? MI-5? Unnamed London fellows were always coming and going with their document cases and specially issued petrol coupons. Mab cast an appraising eye up at the chestnut-haired fellow, who gazed over the lake in silence. Good shoes, silver case for his cigarettes, rather lovely smile. What was his name? She didn't want to admit she'd forgot altogether. "Don't care for poetry?" she said, nodding at her discarded volume.

A shrug.

"Francis Gray isn't terrible." Educated London men liked girls who could talk about the use of metaphor and simile—you just had to be slightly less knowledgeable than they were. "'*The skyline, scarred with stars of rusted wire*'—good lines, really, it's just that the overall theme's a bit obvious. I mean, equating a wartime trench to a sacrificial altar isn't exactly original, is it?"

"Hackneyed," he agreed. More silence.

"It's this month's pick for the Mad Hatters," Mab tried again. "The BP literary society." She got another of the lovely smiles, but no reply. Didn't this one talk at all? She cut her losses, stubbing out her cigarette. "That's the end of my tea break, I'm afraid."

"Do you really dislike Gray's poetry?" the chestnut-haired man asked. "Or are you pulling my leg?"

"I don't *dis*like him. He's just no Wilfred Owen. Not his fault—wasn't he an absolute child when he wrote this?" One of those fellows who had lied about his age and enlisted far too young, Mab recalled vaguely, shoving her book into her handbag as she rose. "I didn't know anything about poetry at seventeen."

"Sixteen."

"Pardon?"

"He was sixteen. Look, I don't suppose you'd fancy going for a curry your next day off? I know a very decent Indian restaurant in London."

"I like curry as much as the next girl." She'd never tasted it.

He stood looking up at her with that faint smile, apparently unfazed by the fact she was half a head taller. Wasn't *that* unusual for short fellows. "When's your next day off, Miss Churt?"

"Monday next. And I'm ashamed to admit I don't remember your name." Mab really did feel embarrassed about that.

"Francis Gray." He tipped his hat. "Foreign Office official and mediocre poet, at your service."

CHAPTER 17

FROM *BLETCHLEY BLETHERINGS*, MARCH 1941

BB doesn't dare say a *word* about recent rumblings of upcoming action in the Mediterranean, therefore the biggest news of the week is the roach found in the night-shift pudding served at the dining hall . . .

Mother, I'm going to be late—"

"If you could wring out another cloth for my forehead . . . It feels like a spike is going through my temples." Mrs. Finch's eyes were shut tight in the darkened bedroom.

Beth flew for a cloth. "I really do have to go now—"

"You do your best, Bethan." Feebly. "I understand you don't have time for your mother—it's just so hard being left all alone . . ."

Beth was nearly crying in frustration by the time she managed to get free. Her father shook his head as she struggled into her cardigan. "Who is going to make your mother a nice cuppa, with you off at work?"

You could put a teakettle on yourself, Dad, Beth couldn't help thinking, even as she slipped out. But by the time she burst into the Cottage with a "Sorry I'm late, sorry—" the frustration and anger were gone, her brain wiped clean as a slate. It happened so fast now: in the time it took to run out her own front door and through the Cottage door, Beth's mind shut an entirely different door on everything at home and simply locked it away for later.

"We're shorthanded till midnight," Peggy said from the next desk. "Jean's home with 'flu, Dilly's having another row with Denniston, so have at it."

Beth pulled out her crib chart and her pocket Italian dictionary, fiddling with the end of her plait. Something going on in the Mediterranean, maybe something big. If only the Italian naval stuff weren't so quirky—and there was so little of it; hardly enough to work with . . . Lining up her rods, Beth got a set of easy breaks, then groaned when the next message came out of the basket. A short one—the short ones were always nasty. Ten in the evening before it clicked into place. Normally the messages meant nothing, just Italian she couldn't read, but she could make this one out. "Peggy," Beth whispered, suddenly cold.

Peggy came over. She froze when she read the words in Beth's pencil scrawl, translating the Italian.

"'*Today 25 March 1941 is the day minus three.*'" The words stung Beth's lips. She looked up at Peggy. "What's happening in three days?"

"WE'RE SWAMPED WITH urgent traffic." Beth forced herself to look the head of Hut 8 in the eye. "We need anyone you can spare." Peggy was on the Cottage telephone ringing Dilly, calling in Jean 'flu or no 'flu, summoning the whole team, and she'd sent Beth across to Hut 8 to beg reinforcements. *They borrow our people; now it's time to return the favor.* Normally Beth would have stood hunched in an agony of shyness getting the words out, but the code still had her in its spiral grip, the one that took her outside her own awkward self. "Please?"

"Oh, for—" The hut head strangled some impolite words. "You can have Harry Zarb. I can't spare more."

Beth nodded, arms wrapped around herself in the chilly spring night, waiting until Harry came shouldering out in his shirtsleeves. "Hallo," he said cheerfully. "Need a hand with the dago traffic? I can say dago," he said, noticing Beth's wince. "I get *called* a dago often enough, if not a wog. It's your inevitable fate if you're any darker than paste in Merry Olde England. Here—" He'd been about to shrug into his disreputable jacket but dropped it over Beth's shoulders instead. She started to demur, but he brushed that aside. "What's the rush in Dilly's section?"

Beth filled him in as they crossed the dark grounds. She was used to seeing Harry among the Mad Hatters, where he was wry and relaxed, leaning on his elbows in damp grass by the lake or scattering toast crumbs on his book, but he was a different man on the BP shift clock, alert and focused, brows mobile as he listened. He let out a low whistle at *Today is the day minus three,* stride lengthening until Beth had to trot to keep up. As Harry ducked into the Cottage, Peggy was on the telephone snapping, "—don't care if your nose is running like the Thames, get *back* here . . ."

"So this is the famous harem?" Harry glanced around, looking enormous and disheveled in the cramped clutter of desks. "Hugh Alexander owes me tuppence; he made a bet you'd have mirrors and powder rooms. Where can I work? It sounds like it'll be a full house."

"Share my desk." Thank goodness Hut 8 had given her someone familiar, Beth thought, not a stranger who would take over her space and freeze her solid with nerves.

He pulled up a stool on the other side of Beth's desk, black hair flopping, reaching for pencils that looked like twigs in his huge hands. "Cribs?"

Beth pushed a crib chart over. "Italian for *English, cruiser, submarine*. Here are the rods—"

"*Inglese, incrociatore, sommergibili,*" he read off the slip. "Christ, listen to us butcher the poor Italian . . ."

They reached simultaneously for the stack of messages and fell headlong into the spiral.

"TODAY IS THE day minus three." Every time someone got up from their desk, they chanted it aloud. And then it became "Today is the day minus two" because none of Dilly's team left the Cottage, not for so much as a cup of Ovaltine.

"I brought you some clothes." Osla passed Beth a package at the door, peering over at Peggy, who was coming downstairs from the attic yawning. "Are you all sleeping *here*?"

We take turns on the attic cot, when we sleep at all. Beth had done ten hours straight in her chair, fifteen hours, eighteen—she could barely even see Osla, pretty and worried looking. Beth muttered her thanks, going to the loo to tug on a new blouse and underclothes, then staggered right back to her desk, where Harry passed her a cup of chicory coffee and her rods.

Something big. They all knew it, and nine of the Cottage's eighteen women had been seconded to it, working like madwomen. Dilly had disappeared so far down into his rods he was barely even present—Beth saw him try to stuff half a cheese sandwich into his pipe instead of his tobacco as he muttered his way through a new message. She merely removed the pipe from his hand, pulled the mangled sandwich out, placed the tobacco in his palm instead, and returned to her desk. Jean was running a fever by now, honking through pile after pile of handkerchiefs as she rodded and rodded and rodded. Sometimes someone would doze off at her desk, and then someone else would chuck a blanket over her shoulders and let her doze ten minutes, before giving a nudge and a reminder of "Today's the day minus one."

"Who's our CIC in the Mediterranean?" one of the girls asked.

"Admiral Sir Andrew Cunningham," Peggy said. "Dilly said he's been notified something will be coming down."

If we can find out what. Beth reached for her next stack, only to touch the bottom of the wire basket. Dilly's Fillies paced like racehorses in their stalls then, waiting for the sound of wheels in the stable yard, which meant the dispatch riders had arrived with saddlebags full of new Morse code messages to decrypt.

"Beth?" Harry touched her arm, and she blinked—she'd got so used to his taking up the other side of her desk, she barely noticed he was there. "I'm sorry, but I've got to go—my son's peaky and I've got to help my wife. Just a few hours—"

Beth nodded, chewing a thumbnail, her mind still tumbling among the blocks of Enigma. Was there ever anything more aptly named . . .

"You're good at this." Harry shrugged into his jacket. "Very good. I'm working at a gallop, keeping up with you."

She blinked again. Ever since realizing she wasn't so terrible she was going to be sacked, she hadn't stopped to wonder if she was *good.* She'd never been good at anything in her life. "I like it," she heard herself saying, voice hoarse from going hours without saying a word. "I—I *understand* it."

"Me too." Harry had circles under his eyes and a distant, absorbed expression. Beth guessed he wasn't seeing her much more clearly than she was seeing him. "I could do this all day and be fresh at the end. It's just the old mortal frame that gets in the way. Pity we aren't machines like the ones they say are in Hut 11."

Beth nodded. The physical needs that got in the way of work had annoyed her these last two days—the need to bolt a cup of tea, the need to stretch her aching back. Irritably, she realized she was starving. "I could do this all day, too," she found herself confessing. "All day and all night."

"And it's a good thing we can. It's the most important commodity of all, isn't it?"

"What, codes?"

"What the codes protect: information. Because it doesn't matter if you're fighting a war with swords, with bombers, or with sticks and stones—weapons are no good unless you know when and where to aim them."

Hence, us. Beth smiled.

Harry glanced at his watch, looking torn. "I'll be back in a few hours, but my hut head wants me back at my usual work, not here. I hate not seeing this through . . ."

Beth pulled herself out of the mental teleprint with an effort. "We'll send word if we need to borrow you again. For now, go home."

"Just long enough to take Christopher's temperature, give him a bath, and explain again why he can't have a puppy." Harry grimaced. "Poor sprat, I hate disappointing him. What father doesn't want to give his son a puppy? But with me on night shifts and his mum at the WVS canteen, it's just not on."

"I always wished for—"

The sound of motors came rumbling from the stable yard car park then, and Beth broke off. She and the other girls were on their feet in a flash, logjamming in the doorway, exhaustion-lidded eyes suddenly sprung wide. They nearly clawed at the saddlebags to get at the new messages, even as the dispatch riders laughed, "It's got to be registered, ladies . . ." By the time they trooped back to their desks, Harry had gone and the wire baskets were filling up again.

A very long message came among the new arrivals, so long they all stood staring as it unrolled over Dilly's desk. "Battle orders," he said quietly. "Stake my pipe on it."

They looked at each other, nine worn-out women with ink-stained fingers and no nails left to gnaw. Everyone took a section back to her desk, and then, Beth thought, they all went a little bit mad. She didn't remember the following day and night, none of it. Only the rods sliding back and forth and her mind clicking away, looking up and realizing the sun had moved halfway down the sky or gone down altogether, then back to the rods and the clicks. It was nearly eleven at night before Dilly called a halt. "Show me what you've got, ladies. We're out of time."

Beth looked at Peggy, haunted. Peggy looked back, equally stricken. Out of time?

In dreadful silence, they collected around Dilly's desk again, putting their bits of message together. A frizzy-haired girl named Phyllida was sobbing. "There was a whole block I couldn't get into, not a *single* click—" Peggy put an arm round her.

Dilly's hand moved at speed as he translated the decrypted lines from Italian to English—Beth could see the linguist and professor he'd once been, in the days before when he'd translated ancient Greek texts rather than military secrets. At long last, he looked up. "Not that you're usually told details," he said matter-of-factly, "but given the work you gels put in . . . the Italian fleet is planning a major hit on the British troop convoys in the Mediterranean."

The stillness was absolute. Beth looked at her pencil-smudged fingers. They were trembling.

"Cruisers, submarines, planned locations, times of attack . . ." Dilly flung down his pen, shaking his head. "It's nearly the whole battle plan. You've done it, ladies. You've done it."

Peggy pressed a hand over her eyes. Phyllida kept crying, but in a kind of exhausted relief. Beth blinked, her mouth dry, not certain at all how to react. *You've done it.* She couldn't take that in.

Our Beth's not too bright . . . Pity that Finch girl is so slow . . .

"I'll take this over." Dilly staggered as he rose, and they all reached out to steady him. He looked exhausted, Beth realized, unshaven and unsteady after so many hours at work. More than exhausted—ill.

"I'll take it," Beth said.

"This needs to be transmitted on the Admiralty teleprinter straightaway," Dilly called. "Dear God, let Cunningham not muck it up . . ."

Beth went out into the dark, not realizing until she felt water on her face that it was pouring rain. She didn't feel the cold or the raindrops; her feet flew as she ran under the clock tower along the path, battle plans in hand. She didn't know where the Admiralty teleprinter was, so she sprinted to the mansion and with both hands heaved the double doors open. The night shift looked up as Beth Finch blew into the hall on a black gust of rain, hair plastered to her face, grim as death, holding the Cottage's precious work. *Her* work.

"Get the watchkeeper," said Beth, giving the first direct order of her life. "Get the watchkeeper *now*."

SHE DIDN'T GO back to the Cottage for her coat and handbag. She had her BP pass in her pocket, and she stumbled straight from the mansion to the Park gate and out, down the pitch-dark road through the rain. Exhaustion crashed through her in waves, battering ocean swells like those long Mediterranean rollers pushing all those Italian subs and cruisers through the night as they aimed for those precious British ships . . . but it was someone else's job to think about them. Admiral Whoever. She couldn't remember his name. She couldn't remember anything that didn't come in five-letter blocks.

The sound of a whimper came quietly through the dark. Beth barely heard it, but her feet paused. She felt her way forward in the rain, toward the chemist's shop—long shut up of course; it had to be near midnight. The whimper sounded again from the shop steps. She crouched down, peering through her soaked hair, and realized the small huddled bundle was a dog.

Beth stared at it, exhausted. It glared back, shivering, showing its teeth feebly.

It tried to bite when she lurched forward and picked it up. Beth ignored that, feeling the animal's shuddering bony ribs against her arm. The rain was coming down harder, and she turned to trudge the last dark quarter mile to her house.

A light burned in the Finch kitchen. Beth's mother was sitting at the table in her dressing gown, hands folded round a cup of Ovaltine, Bible at her side. When Beth squelched through the kitchen door, Mrs. Finch burst into tears. "There you are—three days with no word! I—" She brought herself up short, seeing the bundle in Beth's arms. "What's that?"

Beth, still numb, tugged a pristine stack of towels from the drawer and began rubbing the dog down. A schnauzer, she saw as the gray fur began to stand out in drying tufts.

"My good towels—that thing is sure to have *fleas*—" Mrs. Finch floundered. "Get it out of here!"

Beth opened the icebox. Inside was a plate with a slice of Woolton pie, probably her supper. She put it on the floor and, in a remote stupor, watched the half-starved schnauzer attack it. He had a little square head and a wiry beard like a tiny kaiser, and he kept glaring around him even as he wolfed down the pie.

"That animal is not eating off the second-best china!" Mrs. Finch looked more shocked than Beth had ever seen her in her life. She reached for her Bible as if it were a lifeline. "This lack of respect, Bethan—'*The eye that mocks a father and scorns a mother . . .*'"

Proverbs, Beth thought. Mrs. Finch held the book out, but for the first time in her life Beth didn't take it. She was too tired to hold the Bible in front of her until her arms trembled and her mother's rage was mollified. She just could not do it. With one indifferent hand she pushed the book away and stood watching the dog clean the plate. Mrs. Finch's mouth opened and closed, saying something, but Beth couldn't listen. Her mother's dutiful little helpmeet wasn't here, wasn't back yet from three days sunk in Enigma. Tomorrow, she'd apologize.

Or maybe she wouldn't.

"—and that dog is *not staying*!" her mother concluded in a stifled shriek. "You put it out right now!"

"No," said Beth.

She picked up the not-noticeably-grateful schnauzer and lugged him up the stairs past Osla and Mab, who were eavesdropping wide-eyed on the landing, and into her bedroom. She made a nest of blankets for him, observing without much interest that he did, in fact, have fleas. Then Beth and her new dog slept like the dead.

ELEVEN DAYS UNTIL THE ROYAL WEDDING

November 9, 1947

CHAPTER 18

Inside the Clock

Clockwell was a place of the living dead, Beth thought. The doctors might fiddle about with recreation therapy and hypnosis treatments, but the patients of the women's ward rarely seemed to recover and go home. They stayed here: docile, drugged, fading, and gone. Bletchley Park had broken German codes, but the asylum broke human souls.

Some of the patients were mad as hatters; some suffered such violent swings of emotion they couldn't cope with the outside world . . . but there were others, Beth had discovered over the years. The woman who had been left money her brother wanted, and he'd got her certified and locked up before she came of age to inherit it . . . The woman who had been diagnosed with nymphomania when she confessed to her new husband that she'd had a few lovers before they married . . . And the silent woman who did nothing all day, every day, but play board games. Backgammon, Go, chess with chipped queens and rooks—Beth had never played any of them before Clockwell, but she'd learned fast opposite the sharp-eyed woman who played like a grand master.

"Does the name BP mean anything to you?" Beth had asked once over a chessboard. Bletchley Park had recruited many chess players. But the woman checkmated her without responding.

This afternoon they were playing Go in the common room, a game Beth found trickier and more interesting than chess, advancing fast and vicious against each other as Beth thought about who the Bletchley Park traitor might be. The years she'd spent brooding on the question should have sanded its anguish away, but hadn't. It was someone who worked in Dilly's section, after all—which meant one of her friends had betrayed her.

Which? Beth looked at the Go board full of black and white stones. Three and a half years pondering the question, and she still wasn't sure who on the Knox team had been the black stone among the white. It wasn't her, and it wasn't Dilly—everyone else was suspect.

"Examination time, Miss Liddell. Come along."

Puzzled, Beth left the common room with the nurse. She hadn't been scheduled to see the doctor that day. "What's this for?" she asked the doctor as he examined her skull, but he only chuckled.

"Something that will make you feel much better! That mind of yours is overactive, my dear. You need a calm, untasked brain if you're to recover."

Untasked? Beth nearly spat. She had lived with an untasked brain the first twenty-four years of her life, a black-and-white film of an existence. She didn't want a calmed, soothed mind; she wanted impossible work that her brain converted to the possible by the simple process of wringing itself inside out until the job was done. Every day for four years her brain had been tasked to the breaking point, and she had lived in glorious Technicolor.

"What do you mean, '*untasked*'?" she asked the doctor. He just smiled, but a certain mutter caught Beth's ears later as she was released back into the common room.

"—glad when that one has the procedure." A sniff from the matron whose arm Beth had burned with a cigarette. "They usually stop being troublesome after a lobotomy . . ."

The rest was lost as the woman whisked away. For the first time in weeks, the thought of Bletchley Park's traitor was utterly wiped from Beth's mind. Slowly, she sat down at the Go board again; her partner slid a black piece forward as though she'd never left.

"Do you know what a *lobotomy* is?" Beth asked, stumbling over the unfamiliar word, flesh crawling with unease.

She wasn't expecting an answer, but the woman on the other side of the Go board raised sharp little eyes and drew one finger like a scalpel across her temple.

York

Mab massaged her forehead as a familiar voice drilled through the telephone, finishing-school vowels hitting her ear like crystal spikes. "What do you mean, you're *here*?"

"Just biffed in from London," Osla said. "Only arrived in York an hour ago."

Mab's hand dropped, making a fist in the burgundy folds of her skirt. "I told you when you rang yesterday, I don't want to meet." Osla's voice out of the blue, the Vigenère square—it had all unsettled Mab badly. She'd burned the message from the madhouse, told herself to forget about it, and busied herself settling two sandy, clamoring children back home after a weekend running up and down the beach under Bamburgh Castle.

"I'm here," Osla repeated implacably. "I know you're hacked off about that, but we may as well meet."

"I'm too busy," Mab lied. "I'm putting supper on."

She'd been in the dining room, in fact, determinedly *not* thinking about Beth Finch's cipher message, planning the party she was hosting in honor of the royal wedding. A dozen friends would come in their best frocks, and they'd pooled their butter and sugar rations so they could have scones and a Bakewell tart while listening to the BBC broadcast. Mab knew her husband would laugh at the royal wedding fever, but he and the rest of the men would secretly hang on the broadcast, too. Planning the party hadn't entirely distracted Mab from the worry of hearing Beth's name for the first time in years, but it made for the kind of morning Mab didn't think she'd ever stop cherishing, after having lived through a war when parties had such a desperate edge.

And now the afternoon's peace had shattered.

"Look, I haven't dragged myself all the way north to get snubbed like a Utility frock in a New Look *Vogue* spread," Osla said. "I've got a room at the Grand—"

"Of course you're at the poshest hotel in York."

"Well, I didn't see you volunteering your spare room with spontaneous cries of welcome so we could braid each other's hair at night and trade secrets."

Prickly silence fell. Mab realized she was gripping the hall table to stay upright. She knew she was overreacting, but she couldn't help the panic bubbling in her throat. She had so thoroughly buried everything that happened at the Park, damn it—once the war was done, she'd bricked those experiences up behind a wall in her mind.

But now Osla was on the other end of the telephone, and Beth had returned through the lines of a cryptogram.

You never backed down from a fight in your life, Mab told herself. *Don't start now.* So she met her own eyes in the gilt-framed mirror over the telephone, imagining she was meeting Osla's gaze. "I don't know what you thought coming here would accomplish."

"That's a bit steep, darling. You *know* we have to talk face-to-face about Beth." Pause. "If she really was put in that place unfairly—"

"If she's sane, the doctors would have released her."

"Doctors already think normal women are potty because we have monthlies. When was the last time your doctor gave you more than an aspirin unless you had a note from your husband?"

Mab remembered giving birth to her son, how her doctor had said in the middle of her contractions that she was making too much fuss and it had been scientifically proven that labor pains could be entirely controlled by appropriate breathing. Mab had been in too much agony to rip his ears off and tell him to control *that* pain with appropriate breathing.

"What I'm saying," Osla continued, "is if she's asking *us* for help, after everything that happened, it means she's absolutely dished and has no one else."

Mab's mouth was dry. "I have a family now. I'm not putting them at risk for a woman who betrayed me."

"She says we betrayed her, too. And she's not entirely wrong."

You owe me.

"What do you think of the rest of her letter?" Mab blurted out. "Do you believe it?"

It hung unsaid: *Do you believe there was a traitor at BP?*

A long silence. "Bettys tea shop," said Osla. "Tomorrow, two o'clock. We'll talk."

SIX YEARS AGO

April 1941

CHAPTER 19

FROM *BLETCHLEY BLETHERINGS*, APRIL 1941

What is there to talk about but our smashing victory in the Mediterranean? Ever since our boys broke the back of the Italian navy off Cape Matapan, someone here must have reason to grin like a cat with the cream! Since we'll never know who, let's speculate instead if whale meat is back on the evening-shift menu at the dining hall, and which fetching BP amazon has a dinner date in London with a war poet . . .

Mab stuffed the latest installment of *Bletchley Bletherings* into the bin before heading off shift. *Who's writing this stuff?* Even the establishment officer didn't know who submitted the weekly anonymous gossip sheet to be pinned up on the mansion noticeboard every Friday, but Osla's money was on Giles, and Mab was inclined to agree. "Write me up again in your illicit gossip column and I'll *skin* you," she warned him, breezing through the gates.

"Who, me?" Giles grinned. "Knock 'em dead, Queen Mab."

Mab smiled. She'd pressed every crease out of her berry-colored crepe dress, slipped on the French slings Francis Gray had given her, and Osla had lent a stunning cashmere wrap—as Mab dashed to catch the train, she knew she was looking her best. Mabel Churt from Shoreditch, taking supper with a rather famous war poet—that would be something to tell Mum.

He didn't look like a war poet—waiting for her on the platform in London, Francis Gray could have been any small-town countryman on his yearly trip to the capital, stocky and silent in a gray civilian suit, battered homburg in one wide hand, certainly no languid literary lion. Yet—"You're very lovely, aren't you," he said quietly in greeting, taking her in head to toe.

"Thank you." A man who could deliver a compliment without slavering or fumbling—that, after months of dating awkward university boys, felt refreshing. Mab's heart glowed just a little as she took his arm. All around swirled a river of uniforms hastening about their business: ack-ack girls headed for their shifts on the antiaircraft guns, fire wardens tramping toward the nightly watch on St. Paul's, everyone seemingly engaged in war business . . . but not Mab, not tonight. She was climbing into a taxi with a man who thought she looked lovely, and he was giving directions to Veeraswamy on Regent Street—an *Indian* restaurant, imagine that, with waiters in white turbans and shades of red and gold all around. Mab for the first time in days was able to put the bombes and their rackety *clack-clack-clack* behind her. She was going to take this evening and enjoy it.

Or rather, she'd try to enjoy it. Difficult when Francis Gray wouldn't bloody well *talk*.

"Tell me about your writing," she began after the waiter had taken their order. "I'm a great reader, but I don't know a thing about what it takes to put words on paper." She rested chin on hand with a fascinated expression, ready to listen at length.

"I don't, either," he replied with a smile.

She waited, but he didn't seem inclined to say more. "I know you published *Mired* after the Fourteen–Eighteen War." The facts about him at the back of the slim volume of poetry had been sparse, but she had gleaned what she could. "You wrote them during your time in France?"

He rotated his glass. "After."

"Goodness, you were still very young." He'd enlisted at sixteen in the last six months of the war, which made him thirty-nine now. "Of course, I saw a good many boys in my neighborhood lying about their age to join up in this war. I suppose it's natural to want to serve before the world thinks you're ready."

He shook his head. "They'll learn."

"I wonder if they'll become poets, too."

"Hopefully not. The world has too many bad poets."

"Not you."

"I hear my themes were a bit obvious."

Mab repressed a blush, thinking of their last meeting. It was like something out of a bad farce, criticizing a writer's work to his face, oblivious. Still, she wasn't going to reverse herself and get obsequious now; if he'd asked her for a date after she'd already shredded his iambic pentameter, he clearly wasn't looking for slavish praise. "Thematically they aren't the most original I've ever read," she said, adding a bit of sparkle to the eye, "but your use of language is lovely." That wasn't just flattery, either.

"I'll take your word for it," the poet said. "Haven't read them in years."

The waiter brought the first course. Mulligatawny soup, whatever that was—bright yellow, practically glowing. Mab picked up her spoon warily. "I heard you were invited to meet the king, at the ten-year anniversary of the peace."

"Yes."

"What was he like?"

Another smile. "Kingly."

Mab suppressed a flash of irritation. Why wouldn't he *talk*? Normally her dates never shut up: you asked a leading question or two and they were off to the races.

"Having served in one war," she tried, "it must be very surprising to find yourself neck-deep in another." The soup was hot and pungent on her tongue. What was her breath going to smell like if he tried to kiss her good night?

A faintly bitter slant to his mouth. "Wars are cyclical. It shouldn't surprise anyone when they come round again."

"What do you find different, this time?"

"I'm older."

All right, he didn't want to discuss this war *or* the last—fair enough. "So tell me about your work in London—whatever can be told, anyway."

"It's dull. Very."

For God's sake, Mab thought. It really wasn't fair to make your conversational partner do *all* the work on a date. *Why don't* you *ask a question or two, Mr. Gray?*

But he clearly wasn't going to, so she tried again.

"Where do you live, when not in London?"

"Coventry."

"So when you go home, you can say you're being sent to Coventry," she joked.

He smiled.

"I suppose you've heard all the jokes about being sent to Coventry."

Another smile, but no reply.

The soup disappeared, replaced by something called chicken madras. Mab stared at it. It was bright orange. *I am eating orange food with a mute,* she thought.

Matapan. Surely he could talk about the recent battle off Cape Matapan. Anyone could make conversational hay out of the greatest naval victory since Trafalgar. "Isn't the news about Matapan wonderful?"

"I don't know, is it?"

"Three heavy cruisers and two destroyers sunk on their side, none on ours." Mab quoted the newspaper she'd devoured with a bar of ration chocolate at the NAAFI kiosk on break. "A few thousand of Mussolini's boys killed, none of ours. I'd say that's wonderful."

He shrugged. "Unless you're among Mussolini's few thousand."

Another conversational topic as dead in the water as those Italian cruisers. Mab took a slightly defeated bite of chicken. It filled her mouth with flame. She set her fork down, trying not to choke.

"Too spicy?" he asked.

"Not at all," she managed to say. She'd be boiled in oil before she reached for her glass.

He forked up a mouthful of his without the slightest discomfort. *All right, then,* Mab thought.

She sat back, crossed one leg over the other, and composed her burning lips in a smile. He smiled back, eating. The sound of a sitar plinked. The waiter took Mab's explosive orange chicken away. Pudding arrived, something called halva that had absolutely no resemblance to pudding, but at least it didn't ignite in her mouth like petrol. She finished it, put her fork down, and smiled again.

"You don't seem particularly shy," she said at last. "So what is it?"

His fork paused. "I beg your pardon?"

"Most quiet men are quiet because they're shy. But I don't think that's you, Mr. Gray, so is there any particular reason you're not contributing to the conversation beyond monosyllables?"

"I don't particularly enjoy talking about myself, Miss Churt."

"All right. I understand that, especially when one has a job one isn't allowed to discuss. But you could ask me about myself, you know, or comment on the weather, or the food. Because it's frankly rather rude, sitting there expecting me to carry *all* the conversational weight. Why do I have to entertain you for the entire evening, and you somehow don't feel the need to reciprocate?"

"I never asked you to entertain me," he replied mildly.

"It's the usual expectation, Mr. Gray. A gentleman invites a lady to dinner, she accepts, and they make an effort to amuse one another. I promise you, I'm quite entertaining if given a smidgen of encouragement. I can imitate Churchill better than the man himself, I have an arsenal of jokes from the arcane to the profane, I've read numbers one through eighty-three of 'One Hundred Classic Literary Works for the Well-Read Lady' and have opinions on all of them." Mab pushed back her chair and stood up. "If you will excuse me, I'm going to the powder room. When I get back, I wouldn't mind having an actual conversation. Pick a topic—I promise I will hold up my end."

She half expected another shrug but got an unexpected grin.

"You should wear six-inch heels," Francis Gray said. "You'd be halfway to seven feet tall, and that speech would come out even more like a queen issuing a proclamation."

"Short men don't like very tall heels," she parried.

"I happen to like amazons." He ran a hand over his chestnut hair, hesitating. "I hate talking about myself, Miss Churt, so I assume others do too. I like silence, so I forget it makes others uncomfortable. I do apologize. When you get back from the powder room, I won't be such a pillar of salt."

She smiled, went off to freshen up her lipstick, then slid back into her seat with a slight resurgence of that glow from the beginning of the night. "Why do you dislike talking about yourself?"

He made a wry face. "Because people hear the word *poet* and get silly ideas."

"What, you aren't a poet?"

"I was an idiot of sixteen who ran off to war because I thought it would be some glorious adventure. When I realized it was not I wrote a few insipid, childish verses about my time in the trenches rather than eat my service revolver. I haven't penned so much as a limerick since." He took out his cigarette case. "I'm not a bloody poet, if you'll excuse my language. Just a chap with an office job who likes quiet."

She rested her chin in her hand. "All right, then."

They talked about his childhood home in Coventry, a small lovely city now half leveled by German bombs. Mab spun a few anecdotes about her billet-mates: "A human mouse who doesn't have two words for anybody but works with the brainiest people we have, and a Canadian deb who will short-sheet your bed and freeze your knickers outside the window in winter . . ." They talked about whether America would join the war and if the Italians were finished in the Mediterranean. Mab still found herself doing most of the talking, but at least he did his part asking questions and listening to the answers. When silence fell again, Mab was content to let it stretch, watching cigarette smoke wind between his blunt fingers. "Would you mind if I asked why you invited me to dinner, Mr. Gray? It's been a lovely time, but . . . well, you clearly aren't wooing, and if you were looking for a bit of something else, you'd have had your hand on my knee before the soup was ordered."

"I have no expectations, if that's what you're fearing." He gave a half smile. "You're a bit young and vibrant for a crumbling stone on a heath like me."

"You aren't old, if that's what you mean. Men my age are callow and boring." Older men liked to hear that, and quite often it was true. Of course, plenty of older men were also callow and boring, not that they liked to hear *that* quite so much. "Why invite me out, if you didn't expect either entertainment or romance?" She was genuinely curious.

"A reminder of civilization . . ." He trailed off. "Miss Churt, I've seen two wars. If I can sit in a lovely restaurant, eat a good curry, look at a lovely woman—that's a respite. A nice little illusion."

"Civilization isn't an illusion."

"Oh, it is. The horrors are real. This"—waving a hand—"is all gossamer."

Mab was taken aback. "What a horrible thought."

"Why? Illusion makes for a nice show, while it lasts." He offered her a cigarette. "Why don't we order coffee, and you can tell me more about your day-to-day?"

He was diverting her, but Mab decided to take the diversion. "My landlady is carrying on like something out of Dickens, or maybe Bram Stoker, because her mousy daughter took in a stray dog. *Oh,* the tears. I can't say it's a nice dog; it has fleas and it bites. But I'm on the dog's side if just to see the pinched old cow pitch a screamer every time it trundles into the room threatening to shed on her horrible Methodist furniture." Mab pressed a trembling hand to her temples in her best parody of Mrs. Finch.

The smile lines about his eyes deepened.

"I told you I can imitate Churchill, too, didn't I?" Mab flashed a V sign, deepened her voice. "'*Every man and woman will therefore prepare himself to do his duty . . .*'"

"Uncanny," Francis Gray said.

"And *this* is my little sister, Lucy, begging for a pony . . ."

CHAPTER 20

To Mr. J. P. E. C. Cornwell,

Forgive me for not knowing how to address you—you washed my hair in champagne when the Café de Paris was bombed, after knocking out the man who tried to rob me, and then you lent me your coat. My wits were sufficiently rattled that I never asked your name. Your coat has a label of J. P. E. C. Cornwell, and I managed to find an address attached to a J. Cornwell in London—but when I attempted to post it, the package was returned to me with a covering note. Apparently you shipped overseas shortly after our brief meeting. If this follow-up note finds you—I'm forwarding it to who I presume is your landlady—I wish you the very best of luck in the fight to come.

If you would like to call on Osla Kendall when you are next in England—

Osla hesitated then, not entirely sure how to finish. She didn't want to give her Good Samaritan the idea she was angling for a date—she could hardly remember anything about him except for his greatcoat, his uniform, his calm voice—but she really did want to shake his hand for the service he'd rendered her.

—I would be delighted to deliver your coat, and my thanks, in person.

"I'D LIKE A transfer, Miss Senyard." Osla met the older woman's eyes square. "My language skills are going to pot, binding reports and sticking cards in boxes."

Miss Senyard clicked her tongue. "The work we do might seem unrewarding, but it's very important."

"I have excellent command of plain and technical German. There *must* be other jobs here in German naval section that could use me." Osla gave her most winning smile. Since practically her first day here she'd found the work dull, but since surviving the bombing she'd become abruptly, violently fed up. She'd nearly died at the Café de Paris; she was not going to stagger back to BP and waste her hard-won skills on a job any schoolgirl with a little filing experience could handle. She was still alive, and she was going to do more with that life—for one, fight harder against the utter monsters dropping those bombs. "Do you know some of the chaps call our section *the Debutantes' Den*?" she asked Miss Senyard. "Let me prove I'm more than a silly socialite, Miss S."

"I'll hate to lose you, Osla." Miss Senyard sighed. "But with technical German, I suppose you could join the German translating section. I'll speak to Mr. Birch."

"Thank you, ma'am! You should put Sally Norton on translating too; her German's as good as mine." Sally had been recruited to Bletchley Park just this spring and landed under Miss Senyard too, to Osla's delight.

"Any other personnel changes you'd like to make?" Amused.

"No, ma'am." Osla was transferred in no time, still part of

Hut 4 but to a different section where a gaggle of tweedy men who'd read German at university and a cluster of twinset-wearing women who'd been "finished" in Munich and Vienna sat at a long table translating cipher messages. They made room with cheery waves, shoving over a stack of decrypts. "Decoded fresh out of the Typex machines; turn it into plain English."

Osla pulled her pink wool jacket more tightly around herself in the hut's chill—these green clapboard walls were slow to warm in the watery spring sunshine—and started translating the first cipher message. Details on a U-boat wolf pack, picked up by Morse code listeners in a Y-station in Scarborough, according to the labels. "What do we do if there are bits missing?" Whole chunks of the paragraph in front of her trailed off into blanks.

"Fill it in, given context. We don't always get all of it, and that's all there is to it."

What if that's the part that's crucial? Osla thought, staring at the blank in the message. *What if that's the part that will save lives?* Well, she'd wanted harder work, more important work—here it was. She picked up her pencil, flipping her German dictionary open. *Die Klappenschrank,* what did that mean . . .

"You should have hopped jobs at the end of March," a girl across the table said as she finished her first message. "Thrilling reading, let me tell you—all the traffic from Matapan coming through!"

My boyfriend was at Matapan, Osla wanted to say. *Because he got transferred to the* Valiant. *It wasn't till I saw the information coming through my hands in Miss Senyard's section that I realized the* Valiant *was at the battle . . .and I haven't heard from him since.*

She cut that fear off before it could grow out of proportion. Philip hadn't written because he was *busy,* for God's sake. Or maybe he'd forgot all about her, given her the old heave-ho. Fine—at this point she just wanted to know he was safe. Then she'd care about whether she'd been ditched or not.

And surely he *was* safe. She'd heard the newsreel in the little Bletchley Odeon, turned to stone in her seat, listening to the announcer over the tinny, triumphant music: "*These are some of the ships that destroyed at least three Italian cruisers and three destroyers, and crippled and possibly sank a battleship, without casualties or damage to themselves!*" "Without casualties" . . . yet, Osla knew how idiotically optimistic newsreels could be. Even in an overwhelming victory, men died. Victory came at a cost. Osla had filed the cost of victory away every day in shoeboxes.

"*These are the fifteen-inch shells that shattered a brand-new cruiser with one salvo . . . ,*" the newsreel had blithered on, and she had fought down a surge of nausea, imagining what a shell like that could do to a man's taut strength and golden skin, his clever brain inside its fragile skull. This wasn't a fairy tale; princes died as easily as any other men.

But if he was dead, surely it would have been reported. A prince's death on the front lines would be news. Unless the report wasn't in yet . . .

That gnawing fear for Philip had been the final straw that tipped Osla into begging for more vital work than copying, binding, and filing. If she was going to hurt this much, be this afraid, she was damned well going to be doing something more important.

"Wasn't it terrible seeing those Italian prisoners in the newsreel?" she heard herself asking. "The ones our ships fished out of the sea. I keep wondering how many drowned."

The others looked at her, surprised. "They're Eyeties," said a girl with a Veronica Lake wave. "If they didn't want to get sunk by British destroyers, they shouldn't have been cheering Mussolini."

"Maybe not, but . . ." Osla trailed off, frustrated. The Café de Paris explosion seemed to have blasted a layer off her polished surface, left her easy prey not only to fear but to sympathy. Looking at the bleak-faced Italians in the newsreel had nearly brought her to weeping, knowing that for every one plucked from the sea, another two or three had surely burned or drowned. So many across the world dying every day. Osla couldn't stop thinking of them: English, French, her own fellow Canadians, Australians, Poles . . . yes, even Germans and Italians. They were enemies, but they bled, too. They died. When was it bally well going to *stop*?

She'd probably know before the newsreels did, when it ran across the table in front of her for translating. There was small, cold comfort in that—that she'd clawed her way to a more vital place in BP's ladder, and here she might know first that the war was over. Even if only by minutes.

"COME IN." A worried-looking woman in an old green cardigan answered Osla's knock. "Sheila Zarb, delighted to meet you . . ." Harry's wife rushed off again before anyone could thank her for hosting tonight's Tea Party. Osla smelled stewed tea as she moved into the shabby little house. A child was roaring in the next room.

"Ah, domestic life," mused Giles, ducking in after Osla. "Why wait for death?"

"Don't be beastly," Osla retorted, slightly disgusted with herself for noticing that Harry's wife didn't have nearly the educated vowels he did. *You don't be horrid either,* Osla scolded herself as she and Giles crowded down the narrow passage. And then Osla really felt like a worm, because Sheila Zarb reappeared carrying her howling son, his sticklike legs hanging against his mother's side encased in metal braces like torture contraptions. Polio, surely—Osla had gone to boarding school with a girl who had braces like that.

"Welcome to the madhouse." Harry emerged into the hall behind his wife, scooping the child out of her arms. "Come in, parlor's that way. Christopher, chap, I know you hate your braces, but you've got to wear them."

Harry's son narrowed his eyes mutinously, still bawling. "What a darling," Osla managed to say over the din. "How old?"

"Turned three in January."

The boy looked far too small for three, thin and wasted when he should have been sturdy and bouncing. He had Harry's jet-black hair and eyes but was sallow from ill health.

"I know what this sprat needs." Mab squeezed out of the parlor behind Harry, balancing a glass of sherry and the festooned top hat. She addressed Christopher, completely at ease. "Want to wear the Mad Hatter's topper? It's magic, you know."

Little Christopher stopped yelling to consider. Mab plunked the hat on his head, Harry gave her a grateful look, and they all maneuvered into the parlor, where more Mad Hatters were passing toast and discussing *Mired: Battlefield Verses by Francis Gray.* "I prefer Siegfried Sassoon," someone was complaining.

"'Altar' is my favorite sonnet of Gray's, too eerie for words—"

"Who cares about his poetry? I want dirt on the poet." Giles turned his angelic smile on Mab. "Dish, faerie queene. You had dinner with the chap, and *Bletchley Bletherings* says he's taking you out again next week—"

"To a concert, nosy—"

"Sorry!" Beth slipped in, flushed and late. "I had to let the dog out. If he has an accident inside, Mum swears she'll get rid of him."

"Beth!" Harry maneuvered his huge frame onto the nearest chair, keeping Christopher and his braces deftly balanced on one knee. "Haven't seen you since, well, you know." He grinned, and Beth flushed, looking into her teacup Harry was filling one-handed.

"Well, well," Giles murmured in Osla's ear, alight with mischief. "Has our wallflower got a crush?"

"Don't talk slush," said Osla, who had been wondering exactly the same thing.

"Maybe he's got one, too." Giles's voice dropped even further, inaudible under the buzz of conversation to anyone but Osla. "Our Beth's a clever girl, and something tells me Harry doesn't get much brainy conversation from the missus."

"You infernal snob—"

Sheila reappeared, carrying an apron under one arm. "Sorry to leave you with bath *and* bedtime," she said low voiced to her husband as the Mad Hatters passed the teapot. "The canteen manager is insisting I cover—"

"Go on." Harry passed a hand over his son's black hair. "I've got him."

Sheila leaned down and pressed her lips to Christopher's cheek, and Osla found herself pushing back tears, looking at all the tenderness being poured on the scrawny child curled into his father's arms with complete trust. She'd have given up both legs altogether for a childhood home where there were warm laps to be counted on and kisses on the cheek at night—for any kind of home *now*. Something else she'd learned, the night after Café de Paris's destruction—how little of a home she really had.

Well, so what? Osla told herself fiercely. *You have so much else. You even finally have a job that matters.* In a world at war, surely it was greedy to want both—a job that mattered, and a home to welcome you afterward.

So Osla pinned a smile in place as the discussion got under way, and dug out a scrap of paper to jot ideas for the next *Bletchley Bletherings,* which she typed up every Wednesday. *A lively discussion on Francis Gray's battlefield verses, though* BB *wonders if war poetry is quite The Thing for morale. If you finished your shift translating, say, a U-boat casualty list, do you really want to discuss the crushed idealism of a lost generation drowned in Flanders mud as depicted in harrowing iambic pentameter? Or would you rather read some* Jeeves & Wooster*?*

Copies of *BB* were invariably zinging through every hut in Bletchley Park by Friday, followed by snorts of laughter. Osla couldn't make herself laugh these days, but by God she could dash off a weekly gossip sheet that had the whole Park fizzing.

CHAPTER 21

FROM *BLETCHLEY BLETHERINGS*, MAY 1941

Sound of singing heard from Knox's section recently—intoxicated singing, if *BB* is any judge . . .

"Not a one of you fillies can carry a tune in a bucket," Dilly remarked. "Thank God you can break codes." He conducted them with his pipe as they roared on with the next verse of his poem, specially written for the occasion:

When Cunningham won at Matapan
By the grace of God and MARGARET—
It was thanks to that girl, the admiral said,
That our aeroplanes straddled their target!

Peggy Rock shook her head smiling as Beth and the others shouted her name. Every woman in the Cottage had a verse of her own.

When Cunningham won at Matapan
By the grace of God and BETH—
She's the girl who found the planes
Our ships did then evadeth!

"I didn't really find the planes," Beth objected, "I found the coordinates—"

"Try making *coordinates* rhyme with anything!" Peggy replied.

"*Estimates,*" Beth said instantly. "*Bifurcates. Expectorates*—"

Peggy threw a wine cork at her. It was the first real opportunity they'd all had to celebrate their triumph: during those heady days after the victory, there had been new work to do. But today, Dilly had sent Beth and Peggy down to the Eight Bells pub to bring back as much wine as they could carry: Admiral Sir Andrew Cunningham himself, hero of Matapan, was coming to Bletchley Park to personally thank Dilly and his team.

When they finished singing, they raised their glasses to their boss. "To Dilly Knox," said Peggy. "The reason we're all here."

Dilly took his glasses off, blinking rather hard. "Well, now," he said. "Well, now—"

They crowded around him in a rush. Beth pushed down her dislike of being touched so she could hug everyone within reach. Her throat was so choked with feeling she could hardly breathe.

"Oh, lord," someone called in sudden panic, "is that the admiral? I swear I heard a staff car—"

They were all lined up outside the Cottage, very serious and well combed (and slightly squiffy on bad Chablis), by the time Admiral Cunningham in his gold-braided uniform came stalking along with a smiling Commander Denniston. Beth could hardly look the great man in the face as he shook hands down the line. "We have had a great victory in the Mediterranean," he said at the end, holding the glass someone had managed to find for the nasty wine. "And it is entirely due to Dilly Knox and his girls."

A very solemn moment, broken when the admiral turned and Beth saw the back of his immaculate dark uniform was blotched with white. "The Cottage was just whitewashed," giggled two of the younger women. "We maneuvered him to brush against the wall."

"That's no way to treat an admiral!" But Beth found laughter rising in her like golden bubbles, the triumph and the unaccustomed drink going to her head, and when the hero of the Mediterranean realized what had happened and shook his head in rueful amusement, Dilly's entire team burst into howls of laughter.

Beth was still smiling as she let herself in the door at home. "Not much to smile about from where I'm standing," her mother sighed. "It'll be tripe and liver hot pot for supper if I can't find an onion at the shop. And an entire basket of socks to darn!"

"I'll do it." Beth kissed her mother's cheek. *I met an admiral today, Mother. He said his victory was entirely due to me and the people I work with.* She wanted to say it, so badly. She wanted her mother to be proud.

All she could do was offer to darn socks.

"Take That Dog outside," Mrs. Finch warned, collecting her shopping basket. "I swear it's waiting for me to turn my back so it can make a mess . . ."

Beth still couldn't believe she'd won in the matter of the dog. If it hadn't been for that strange, exhilarated exhaustion that gripped her after breaking the Italian battle plan . . . her mother hadn't even quoted Deuteronomy at her the following day. Even Deuteronomy apparently had nothing to say about daughters who stayed out for three nights on shift work. The dog was seemingly just one more straw on the heap.

"You know, a dog keeps burglars away," Mab had told Mrs. Finch with a dark look implying hordes of would-be intruders, and Osla had launched a long, drawling anecdote about how "Princess Margaret has a topping little dog like that, did you see in the *Tatler* . . ." So the dog stayed, and Beth took him outside with the basket of socks, so she could do her darning on the sunny front stoop.

"Funny-looking dog," the next-door neighbor said as the schnauzer trundled crossly around Mrs. Finch's immaculate victory garden. "What's his name?"

"Boots." The name had been an accident—Mab had asked, "What'll you call him?" and Beth, still exhausted from codebreaking and expecting the question *Where did you find him?,* had mumbled *Boots,* since she'd picked him up outside the chemist's.

Osla and Mab came swinging through the front gate in their blush-pink and smoke-blue coats, passing Mrs. Finch as she departed for the grocer. "Isn't this sun bliss?" Mab sat down on the front step beside Beth. "Did you hear there's a dance in Bedford? An American band, they've got all the latest Glenn Miller tunes."

"Who?" Beth asked, rummaging for yarn.

"Told you she wouldn't know who that was." Osla grinned, sitting on Beth's other side. "Brains like hers are too busy keeping up with brilliant things to get chuffed about the latest tunes!"

"It doesn't take brilliance, the sort of thing I do. Just sideways thinking. Here—" Beth hesitated, looking around. No one in earshot. Pushing the darning basket aside, she pulled out a scrap of paper and sketched quickly. "This is a Vigenère cipher. Dilly has me doing them for practice in my spare time—it's a historic codebreaking exercise, miles different from what we do now, so it's nothing you aren't allowed to know. I'll have you solving one in twenty minutes." Still buoyed up by the Cottage celebration, the wine, and the admiral's handshake, Beth had an unaccustomed urge to share what she could do. "Here's how to crack it using a key. Though it can be done without . . ." She demonstrated. Mab and Osla both had a go, half laughing and half fascinated. It took longer than twenty minutes, but eventually they both cracked it. "See? Not so hard."

"I'd like to show this to all those fellows making jabs about 'the Debutantes' Den.'" Osla looked at her Vigenère cipher. "Hitler really would pitch an absolute screamer if he knew a lot of girls scratching pencils in Bletchley are turning his war inside out."

"'*These have knelled your fall and ruin, but your ears were far away,*'" Beth quoted one of Dilly's irreverent verses. "'*English lassies rustling papers through the sodden Bletchley day . . .*'"

"Well, these lassies are going to the dance in Bedford," Mab declared. "We deserve some fun—and so do you, Beth."

"You know she won't go." Osla smiled. "That shot is not on the board, darling!"

To Beth's surprise, she heard herself speak. "I'll go."

WITHIN THE HOUR, she was regretting the decision.

"You have no idea how long I've been wanting to get my hands on these," Osla said, going at Beth's eyebrows with tweezers.

"Ow—"

"Stop kicking up a shindy, Beth, you have to suffer to be beautiful . . ."

Mab, having shooed Boots off the bed and flung every dress Beth owned across it, held up a navy blue crepe. "This one. It's the only thing you own that isn't brown, beige, or puce. All colors you should never wear, Beth, because they make you look like a couch. What I wouldn't give to put you in something *bright* . . ."

"We'll loan her my purple satin," Osla suggested, plucking ruthlessly.

"Too small—"

"Your raspberry crepe?"

"Too big." Mab shook out the navy blue professionally. "I'll lend my red scarf, that'll add punch—"

Beth yelped as another hair was yanked out. All her life she'd hated being looked at, squirmed from being touched, and now here she was being scrutinized and poked like a heifer in a stall. Even so, there was an odd fascination to the whole process. She glanced over Osla's shoulder at her own reflection in the mirror dubiously. Could even Osla and Mab make a difference in what she saw there?

"Topping complexion, but you need color," Osla decreed. "Max Factor pancake base, a swipe of my Elizabeth Arden Victory Red—"

"Mother says women who wear lipstick are tarts."

"And she's so right about that! You're going to make a *spiffing* tart—"

"Right, about this hair." Mab had already unwoven Beth's long plait; she ran her fingers through the thin dishwater-blond waves. "If we lop off the bottom six inches—don't give me that face, I cut my sister's hair all the time—"

"My mother will kill me!"

"Beth," Osla said severely, "if you say the words *my mother* again I will knock you into next week. Poker up here! Grow a spine! Put on lipstick!"

"I've changed my mind." Beth tried to rise. "I don't want to go." But it was far, far too late. Her friends had identical slightly mad gleams in their eyes and the bit in their teeth. Her moment of rebellion collapsed back into unwilling fascination as she was stripped and whirled, plucked and pinned; six inches of her hair disappeared in a few snips, and then Osla wrestled Beth's limp locks into kirby grips as Mab basted a new hem on Beth's navy blue dress. "Too short," Beth yelped.

"Nonsense," Mab scolded, stitching away. "You have *legs,* Beth! You're a bit flat up front and you haven't got much hip, but you have legs, and they are good legs, and tonight they are going to be *seen.*"

"No!"

"Yes," her friends said ruthlessly. By the time they were done, the navy blue dress was unrecognizable: hem hitting Beth's knees, neckline framed by Mab's red scarf, skirt flared out by Osla's red silk petticoat ("it'll swish and flash around those shapely legs when you walk!") Beth stared at herself cautiously. Not exactly duckling to swan—no amount of plucking and tailoring and silk flounces was going to give her Mab's figure or Osla's sparkle—but she didn't look as ghastly as she'd feared.

"We'll give you Veronica Lake hair," Mab decreed, taking out the kirby grips. "You always duck your chin when you meet strangers—with a wave of hair over one eye to hide behind, you'll look mysterious rather than shy." She combed and parted and fluffed. "What do you think?"

My mother will hate it, Beth thought. But, well, maybe it wasn't so bad . . .

The other two were shimmying into their own dresses now, Mab's a violent blue-purple that nipped around her long figure like a lightning bolt. "It's an old curtain liner I found in Mum's rag bag last time I was in London. It'll last about three washings."

"Darling, only you and Scarlett O'Hara could dress in a curtain and still look scrummy." Osla hooked her stockings to her suspender belt. "I can't be bothered what I wear, just hand me that rose print. Now, Beth—when Mab and I distract your mother, you run out the back while we tell her you're tucked up in bed with a headache."

I am going to hell, Beth thought as they all spun through a spritz of Osla's Soir de Paris. But that didn't stop her from kissing Boots goodbye and grabbing her coat.

"Right-ho, on our way," Giles said as they all piled into his car in the pitch-black street. "I say, is that our Beth? Save me a dance, gorgeous!"

"I don't know how to dance," Beth said. "Even if I did, I'd probably hate it." And the dance was every bit as noisy and crowded as she'd feared, a big room packed to the ceiling with servicemen and local girls. Beth could barely see the stage where the band was playing "Tuxedo Junction." Giles and Mab whizzed off to the floor, and when Beth saw how Osla's feet tapped in their little diamanté-studded pumps, she urged her, "Go dance." The thought of sitting alone was alarming, but not as cringe-making as forcing her friends to nanny her all night.

As soon as Osla was whisked away, Beth found herself a chair on the side. A towheaded boy leaned over, breathing gin fumes. "Fancy a spin, Veronica Lake?"

"No, thank you." Beth couldn't say she enjoyed being in the middle of a crowd, but she found she could sit with the froth of silk petticoat rustling deliciously around her knees and let her eyes follow the dancers as the music swirled. The skirts of the women opening like flowers, the men with buttons and bars on their uniforms flashing . . . she could almost see patterns in it, like the rose-petal spirals, or the patterns of brick in a wall . . .

"Hullo there." Harry flopped into the chair beside hers, big and cheerful, black hair disheveled. He didn't look surprised at her change of appearance or seem to notice it at all. Beth smiled, realizing she rather liked that. Giles's swoony double take had felt a bit insulting—did she ordinarily look such a fright? *Obviously I do.* But if so, Harry hadn't noticed that either, and she was glad. "Didn't think I'd see you here," he continued, linking an elbow over the back of his chair.

"Why not? Am I such a wet blanket?"

"No, but you hate crowds."

"Osla and Mab dragged me out." Beth peered up at Harry through her new wave of hair and wished she could ask how the Italian naval Enigma compared to the German naval Enigma his hut worked on. But you couldn't talk codebreaking in a crowd full of outsiders, so Beth rummaged for small talk. "Did your wife come along tonight?"

"Sheila's at home with Christopher. Last night she was off at a concert with a friend, so tonight she shoved me out the door and told me to enjoy myself."

He spoke with a complete lack of self-pity, but Beth's tongue still froze with unexpressed sympathy. Having a child so frail he always needed one of you hovering . . . "Um. Do you think America will join the war?" Beth ventured, for something less personal.

"They'd better." His expression darkened. "The wolf packs are making mincemeat of us."

Another conversational dead end. Beth could have talked clicks and lobsters all day, but ordinary small talk felt like swimming upstream. *I suppose it's better than the days when* all *conversation felt like swimming upstream.*

The band swung into "In the Mood," and a bass riff growled out across the floor. "They're good," Beth said for lack of anything else to say.

"It's not bad, but I like music a bit more orderly. Patterns, you know." Harry grinned as she gave him a startled look. "You too? I had a feeling. I don't know if it's the way our brains were already wired or if it's pure habit after what we do all day. Give me Bach, anytime. There are patterns for days in *The Well-Tempered Clavier.*"

"I've never heard it."

"In Cambridge I had a job at a music shop—between customers I listened with headphones on. Made me very cross if someone came browsing when I was in the middle of a symphony."

"I've never been to Cambridge." *I've never been anywhere.*

"In the Mood" ended, and the dancers broke up. Some flooded to the side, some grabbed new partners as "Moonlight Serenade" rippled over the floor. Harry cocked his head. "Care to take a whirl?"

"I don't really want to dance," Beth confessed. "I want to be back at work."

"Me too. People like you and me, we're more hooked than opium fiends." They traded rueful, frustrated smiles. She could tell they were both itching to talk about things they shouldn't. "Come on," Harry said in a sudden burst.

Tugging Beth out to the dance floor, Harry snugged her in briskly with an arm about her waist, took her hand in his big one, and began to revolve to the slow, dreamy tune. "No one will hear if we talk like this." He lowered his head to hers, voice mischievous and friendly in her ear. "I've got some new tricks for working cribs, nothing too specific to naval section. Want to hear?"

Beth hesitated, but every other couple around them swayed with eyes closed, and he was murmuring right into her ear—even the most dedicated eavesdropper wasn't going to hear a thing over the music. "Yes, please," she whispered back with a smile of her own, relaxing into the arm around her waist.

"So, I've been working a four-wheel machine . . ."

Beth listened, the music a bright brassy pattern over the pattern Harry's words were weaving. She could almost *see* it if she closed her eyes. "Dilly has me working Vigenère squares."

"I've done those. Can you break them without a key?"

"Easy as pie."

"Christ, you're good. What about—"

"Look at you two, whispering away." Giles tapped Harry on the arm. "May I cut in?"

"No, thank you," Beth said firmly. She leaned back into Harry's shoulder, wanting to dissect Vigenère squares and four-wheel Enigmas, barely hearing Giles retreat with a laughing, "All right, keep your secrets . . ."

ELEVEN DAYS UNTIL THE ROYAL WEDDING

November 9, 1947

CHAPTER 22

Inside the Clock

One of the orderlies had red hair like Giles. Beth watched him go about his evening rounds, restocking closets, collecting dirty linen, laughing with a friend. Beth remembered Giles's voice: *Keep your secrets . . .*

Were you the one with secrets? she wondered for the thousandth time. Giles the ever friendly, the eternal gossip. Giles, who had eventually been transferred from Hut 6 to Knox's section. Giles, drollest of the Mad Hatters.

She didn't want it to be him. But she didn't want it to be any of her friends.

The red-haired orderly left the common room, and Beth slipped after him. "What do you want, Liddell?" he said, low voiced. "Cigarettes? Scent? It'll cost you."

Something else Beth had learned in her years here: which of the orderlies and nurses would trade covertly with the patients. Hoarded medicines could buy you drink, cosmetics . . . or knowledge.

"I need information." Beth swallowed hard, damp palms rubbing down her smock. "What is a *lobotomy*?"

His brows rose. "Why?"

I'm scheduled for one, and I don't know what it is. The unease had lingered all evening, since she'd heard that whispered fragment from the matrons. None of the women in the ward had any facts, only speculation. "Tell me."

"That's big information." He leaned in; Beth smelled sweat and Lysol. "What have you got for me?"

She swallowed again, bile this time, as she tugged him toward the nearest linen closet. "Come in here and I'll show you."

That was something else she'd learned. Which of the orderlies would grope under your smock if no one was looking; how to avoid them and their grabbing hands; how to bite and kick if they maneuvered you alone . . . and which of the orderlies wouldn't force you, but wouldn't say no if you offered. Sometimes, if it got you something you needed, you offered. It wasn't the first time Beth had gone to her knees in a linen closet, but her stomach roiled with just as much helpless, viscous rage as it had the first time. "What is a *lobotomy*?" she asked before she got started, voice rasping like a rusty knife.

"A head surgery," the orderly said, closing his eyes and slipping his hand into her hair. "Just a little tap to the skull, I've heard. It's done all the time in America . . . yes, keep going . . ."

Beth stopped, withdrawing. "What is this surgery *for*?"

"Just finish me off—"

"No. Not until you tell me what this surgery does."

"What does anything do here? It'll make you better, fix you. I wouldn't worry, Liddell," he added, sounding sincere. "It's not too invasive, they say. Nowhere near as bad as them electric treatments you hear about."

Beth pressed, asking more questions, but he clearly didn't know anything more. She closed her eyes and finished things, thinking of her Go-playing companion drawing a finger like a scalpel over her skull.

"Good girl." He fastened up his trousers, ruffling her hair. "Get back to your cell, now."

Beth sat back on her heels as he slipped out of the closet, red hair a winking gleam in the brief light flash from the door. She tried not to gag, smelling bleach from the folded sheets all around, lungs full of sudden fear. A surgery and a traitor to contend with, and she had no idea what or who they were, or if she would have any help in dealing with either.

Osla, Mab, where are you?

York

Bettys tea shop, Osla had said over the telephone. *Tomorrow, two o'clock. We'll talk.*

Bugger that, Mab had told her, ringing off with a bang, and gone to check on the children.

Eddie was a warm, soft weight against Mab's breast as she lifted him from his bed. He was fretful, fussing from his nap, but he settled quickly against her. She inhaled the smell of talcum and little boy, wondering if he was heavier than he'd been just last night—he was growing so fast, eighteen months and already bigger than most two-year-olds. He'd be a six-footer for sure. Mab tiptoed out of the nursery, passing a hand over Lucy's dark head. Luce was a restless sleeper, kicking her sheets off and muttering, but she stilled at Mab's hand on her hair.

Mab fed Eddie downstairs, avoiding the peas he tried to spit out onto her cream linen blouse, but afterward as she set him down to play with the toy train his father had made for him, she couldn't settle. She stood turning an unlit cigarette between her fingers—she was trying to quit—stomach churning as Beth's cipher message echoed through her mind.

There couldn't have been a traitor at Bletchley Park. Candidates were vetted before they were even invited to interview; when she transferred from the bombe machines to the mansion, Mab had heard about the boxes and boxes of MI-5 files in Hut 9. And if there was a traitor, who were they selling *to*? BP had remained safe, secret, and successful throughout the war, which argued against the Germans' ever having found out.

No. The cipher message's accusation was either a madwoman's paranoid fantasies or the lies of a desperate woman willing to say anything to get free. *Either way, what happens to me if I help her?* Mab thought. Beth was locked up on the government's orders; communicating with her could be a violation of Mab's oath. "Receiving and encouraging insecure communications of privileged information" or however they might phrase it—but it could mean prison.

Mab looked around her quiet sitting room. This home, this family, this life, was everything young Mabel Churt from Shoreditch had ever dreamed of. Her house with its three stories of mellowed Yorkshire stone and its surrounding garden of bramble roses. Her marble-tiled bathroom crowded with perfume vials and cosmetics, rather than a shared toilet down the hall. Her own bank account, with a balance she no longer compulsively checked to make absolutely certain there was enough for the electric bill, for Eddie's new shoes, for Lucy's future education. Her husband.

Risk all of this, risk her family, risk a cell—for Beth, who had betrayed her during the war?

What did she *risk to ask for your help?* the thought whispered. *What is she risking now?*

SIX YEARS AGO

May 1941

CHAPTER 23

"Out with it, Beth," said Mab.

Beth blinked, holding the red silk petticoat she'd tiptoed into the room to return, and so did Osla, who sat buffing her nails by the light of a candle stub. The three of them had only just sneaked back in from the dance, absolutely knackered, long past Mrs. Finch's lights-out, and mentally Osla was already totting up the next *Bletchley Bletherings: What shy filly splashed out at the Bedford dance this weekend? Even the most brilliant brain needs a little Glenn Miller to invigorate the old gray matter, and BP's boffins certainly sat up and took notice . . .*

"You danced five times with Harry, Beth." Mab turned away from the glass where she'd been brushing her hair and fixed Beth with a stern eye. "All slow swoony tunes, too."

Beth closed the bedroom door as Boots trundled in on her heels. "We were talking shop. You know . . ." Codebreaking, Osla knew she meant but wouldn't say, even here in private.

"Cheek to cheek?" Osla couldn't help saying.

Beth looked puzzled. "Yes. So no one could overhear." Back in her high-necked nightdress with her hair combed out of its waves, she looked very much the colorless wallflower who had never been on a date in her life.

Osla sighed. "Don't tell me you've gone moony over Harry Zarb."

Beth looked horrified. "We've worked together, that's all. He's good at what he does, I'm good at what I do, it's easy to talk . . ."

Osla and Mab exchanged glances.

"That's called getting moony." Mab tossed her brush down. "High time you started looking about for a fellow, Beth, but don't settle for a married man giving you a line."

"There was no *line*." Beth reached for the end of her plait to fidget with, but it was no longer there. "He didn't—try anything. He only asked me to dance so we could talk safely, no one hearing."

"Only at BP." Mab settled on her own bed in her nylon slip. "Not 'Let me whisper sweet nothings in your ear' but 'Let me whisper ciphers in your ear.' It doesn't mean it still wasn't a line, Beth."

Osla wasn't sure. Was Harry really the sort to step out when he had nice, tired-looking Sheila at home looking after their frail son in his leg braces? She wasn't so worried he would try things on with Beth—more like, Beth would get all starry for the first man who flirted through "Moonlight Serenade" without meaning anything serious by it.

"You can never predict what kind of man steps out on his wife," Mab said as though reading Osla's mind. "That's why you steer clear of *all* married men. Because it starts as a harmless friendship, and then you're hearing how their wife doesn't understand them and they're going to leave her soon, and then you're sneaking off behind the wife's back until *things get sorted,* which they never do. It's all rubbish. I've never got into that situation," she added, seeing the look on their faces. "But I've known girls who did, and their stories all turned out the same—*not* at the altar. Because the men were just looking for a bit of you-know."

"Bit of what?" Beth asked, perched on the edge of Osla's bed.

"*You* know." Mab looked at her. "Don't you?"

"No . . ."

Osla stared down at her hands. "Actually," she heard herself saying, "I don't, either. About . . . It." She could barely get the words out, but she couldn't lie either. Not in this blackout-curtained bedroom with two girls she'd worked with and wept with and shared untold fears with for the last year.

"Come off it!" Mab scoffed. "I'll believe that Beth here never learned the facts of life from Mrs. Finch—though didn't your sisters tell you, after they married?" she demanded, sidetracked.

Beth looked blank. "They said never to let a boy kiss me until we were engaged, so I thought maybe kissing made you pregnant."

"Methodists," Mab muttered, and looked at Osla. "All right, I believe Beth, but I don't see how you can possibly be in the same boat considering that racy mother of yours, you dizzy deb."

"*Don't call me that.*" Osla flared, knowing she was being oversensitive, not particularly caring. She was tired, tired, tired of climbing an endless ladder where she thought she'd finally reached a rung where she'd never be called *dizzy deb* or *silly socialite* again, only to find it still ringing in her ears, classifying her as dim-witted, inconsequential, ignorant. Only when it came to this, she *was* ignorant, no getting around it. You could spend your days translating Hitler's personal telegrams and still be an utter ignoramus in other spheres. "You think my racy mother ever told me anything, Mab? I grew up surrounded by hirelings. Nannies taught me to wash behind my ears; boarding school taught me German grammar; finishing school taught me to make a court curtsy. My mother was too chuffed getting married, getting divorced, and getting remarried to notice I was there, much less teach me the facts of life. So I know *nothing,* and none of the girls I went to school with did either, because everyone's mothers were too terribly *proper* to get into the whole nasty subject."

Mab still looked skeptical. "The day we met, you embarrassed a pervert on the train by asking if he needed to hide the tent in his trousers—"

"You think I had any idea what I was talking about? I fake being terribly worldly, darling, but it's all flimflam." Osla looked down at her hands again. "At the Savoy last year, I was telling a friend that I wished my boyfriend wouldn't carry his torch in his front pocket when we danced, and this old dowager at the next table rears back and hisses at me, 'You silly fool, don't you know what an erection is?' And I laughed like I knew what she meant, but I had not the foggiest. And now I'm twenty years old and in love, and I *still* have no idea how It happens." Osla ran out of breath, finally looking up. "I hate being such a—a silly deb. Can you just enlighten me?"

"Why do you think I know all about it?" Mab looked peculiarly still in the light of the candle stub. "Because Shoreditch girls are tarts?"

"No, because you didn't grow up wrapped in cotton wool like a china doll." Osla realized she had utterly derailed the conversation from Beth and Harry and the conundrum of married men, but who knew when a chance like this would come again? "*What happens?*"

There was a short, embarrassed silence. Boots broke it with a yelp, because the scarlet-faced Beth was twisting her fingers through his collar. Mab looked between Osla and Beth and shook her head. "We need a drink for this."

"Where'd you get that?" Beth blurted as Mab rummaged in her handbag and brought out a silver flask.

"Nicked it off Giles. He'll never miss it." Mab swigged; Osla swigged. Beth hesitated, but as soon as Mab said, "All right, when a man's trousers come off . . . ," she reached for the flask and gulped till she choked. Osla pounded Beth on the back, and the two of them listened, cringing, to Mab's brief, blunt lecture.

"There are things you'll hear," she finished. "Anyone who says you can't get knocked up if it's your first time—wrong. Anyone who says you can't get knocked up if a man pulls away at the end—also wrong. The only thing that stops you getting knocked up is if a man wears a French letter"—a brief explanation of what that was; Osla and Beth made faces—"or if you get a doctor to fit you for a little rubber device you push up inside." She mimed. "But no doctor will give you that until you're married or at least engaged, because doctors are men. And if a man promises he'll marry you if you do it with him, that's the lie that's been told since Adam and Eve."

"Well," Osla said at last. "I can't say I'm tempted to do it at all." It sounded perfectly horrid.

"Is it . . . nice?" Beth was nearly inaudible with embarrassment.

"I thought so." Mab's voice was carefully toneless. "Very nice. But I was only seventeen, so what did I know?"

". . . Who was he?" Osla asked.

"A fellow I shouldn't have listened to." Mab took another swallow of Giles's gin. "So is your Philip prompting this desire for information? Or is someone new putting the make on you?"

"Oh, the men I know don't try to put the make on. Maybe a kiss after a date, but that's all, or they're on the NSIT list."

"NSIT?" Beth said.

"Not Safe In Taxis."

"But you want this information for a reason." Mab refused to be deflected. "Come on, Os. You've told us all about your Philip being on the *Valiant,* and how his eyes are blue-gray and give you spasms—now give us the goods!"

Somehow that cracked the tension—Osla laughed, Mab grinned,

and an almost invisible smile escaped Beth. “I adore Philip,” Osla confessed, “and I haven’t heard anything from him since Matapan, so—what?” Beth had frozen at the word *Matapan*.

“Nothing.” Beth took another sip from the flask, looking poker-faced.

“And when he comes back from Matapan, do you think you’re getting an offer to become Mrs. Philip—” Mab paused. “You know, I don’t think you’ve told us his last name.”

“Because he doesn’t really have one.” Osla cleared her throat. “He’s, well, he’s Prince Philip of Greece.”

She looked up. Mab’s eyebrows had lofted clear to her hairline, and the flask in Beth’s hand hovered half-lowered.

“A bloody prince,” Mab told Beth. “Of course. And a *foreign* prince!”

“Not really. He’s Danish and German, but he went to school in Scotland and his uncle is Lord Mountbatten . . . it’s complicated. The family left Greece when he was a baby. He’s not heir to the throne.”

“Good,” drawled Mab, “because it would be funny if I’d just given the facts of life to the future Queen Osla.”

“Shut up!” Osla smacked her with a pillow. “This is exactly why I didn’t mention it, because you’d start talking drip, and he’s not like that. He’s just my Philip.”

Mab took the flask from Beth, turning it upside down. “Not nearly enough gin for this discussion.”

Beth actually laughed aloud. Her cheeks had faded from humiliated red to a rosy pink; she looked positively pretty. Osla wondered if Harry thought so, too. “Look, Beth, about Harry. I like him, so I want to think he wasn’t laying a line on you. But be careful.”

Beth wrinkled her nose. “Someone married—I couldn’t.” She

glanced at the candle stub; it was down to the last half inch of wax. "I'd better get to bed."

She tucked Boots under her arm and padded out. Mab looked at Osla, waiting until they heard the other bedroom door click. "I worry about Beth," she said bluntly. "Shy girls like her are just the sort to fall into the wrong man's arms and get in trouble."

"I think the appeal of someone like Harry is that he's unattainable," Osla mused, sliding between her sheets. "He's a topping good crush for a girl who doesn't actually want to step out of the shadows. I can see Beth as a ninety-year-old virgin, breaking codes and living alone with her dog, happy as a clam. A lover or a husband would break that up."

"The end of war will break that up. Who's going to be asking Beth Finch to break codes then? She'll be a spinster at home again." Mab blew out the candle. "God help her."

"Things will be different after the war." Osla stared up into the darkness over her bed. "They have to be. Or else what's it all for?"

"Some things never change." Mab's voice came through the dark, suddenly serious. "Listen, Os . . . you might know a bit more biology now, but that doesn't mean you know other things."

Osla stiffened. "What do you mean by that?"

"You don't know how men sometimes *use* women." A long exhalation. "How they use and then leave women they never intended to marry. Nice boys do that. Gentlemen do that. Even princes."

CHAPTER 24

FROM *BLETCHLEY BLETHERINGS*, MAY 1941

Goodness, who knew that the head of naval section once trod the boards in London pantomimes? Apparently his "Widow Twankey" was a smasher. The things men keep from us; how can we ever truly know them . . .

Miss Churt." Francis Gray's warm, courteous voice crackled over the line. "I thought you might enjoy dinner at the Savoy your next evening off."

Mab smiled, waving Osla on ahead—they were both leaving for the evening shift. "Will the food be electric yellow?"

"Dover sole is guaranteed. Nice white food, completely without flavor. Very English."

"I'm off Tuesday next—I'm going to Sheffield to see my sister, but I'll take the evening train to London after."

"I look forward to it, Miss Churt. Wear sky-scraping shoes."

He rang off, and Mab's smile slid to a thoughtful frown. This would make her third date with her poet—after the Indian supper at Veeraswamy, he'd invited her to a lunchtime concert at the National Gallery, where she'd heard some deeply inexplicable music—and he still puzzled her exceedingly. He barely spoke but listened attentively; he smiled a good deal but never laughed. He didn't press to use her first name—he didn't press for anything, as a matter of fact. Mab found Francis Gray something of a mystery.

"Is he on your short list?" Giles had asked after the Mad Hatters discussed Francis's unsettling war poetry.

"I don't think so." Mab knew when a man was keen, and Francis Gray didn't seem to be. He regarded everything—an air-raid alarm, a bowl of Mulligatawny soup, Mab in her berry-colored frock—with the same pleasant remoteness, like he sat friendly and removed behind an invisible curtain. She found herself rereading *Mired* from cover to cover, looking for clues to how his mind worked, but all the poetry told her was that he'd been a scared boy who tried to get rid of his trench nightmares by putting them in verse. He wasn't that boy anymore, so who was he?

"Bump him up your list," Giles had advised. "He's a catch. Parents dead, so no interfering mother-in-law. Owns a good-sized house in Coventry. No millionaire—nobody ever made a packet off poetry—but his father patented some cough medicine that's done rather well. More than enough to keep you in silk stockings and your little sister in ponies."

"I know all that." Mab always vetted her dates thoroughly. "But I'm not just after silk stockings and ponies, Giles."

"Aren't you?"

"I want someone to be contented with." She didn't ask for grand romance, but she did want contentment . . . and Mab didn't think anyone as disinterested in life as Francis Gray had it in him to be content. He was a puzzle, all right; her very own enigma in a park full of them.

"I really do not approve of *men* telephoning." Mrs. Finch appeared in the hallway the minute Mab replaced the handset. "Unless they are family."

"He's my cousin."

"You seem to have a great many cousins."

"Big family! If you'll excuse me, I've got a long evening shift ahead—"

"Doing what? Because you've started coming home with oil droplets on your cuffs . . ." Mrs. Finch smiled, but there was a glint in her eye. "And then I keep finding *these,* of course. What on earth—"

Mab examined the square of numbers scribbled in her own handwriting. "I have no idea." Ever since Beth had taught her and Osla how to crack a Vigenère square, they'd started using the cipher whenever leaving each other notes. A bit overelaborate, but none of them could resist: finally a way to cut out a snooping landlady *and* drive her mad in the process! The key was always LASSIES.

"That is *your* handwriting," Mrs. Finch accused, waving the square.

"Must dash, Mrs. F!"

The late afternoon was fragrant and beautiful. By the time Mab got off shift it would be black midnight under a half-moon. They had been so lucky out here in the countryside, no bombing raids to speak of . . . last week London had endured the worst attack since the beginning of the war. Even the perpetually optimistic newspapers couldn't make cheerful hay out of the fact that the House of Commons had been destroyed.

Coming through BP's gates and making her way to her hut, Mab had to stand a moment outside the door before she could steel herself to face those hissing, enigmatic machines. *Why haven't I asked for a transfer?* More Wrens had shipped in to service the bombes; Mab was still the only civilian assigned here. Probably because they'd forgot she was here at all. If she reminded them, she'd be back on a Typex by next week.

But she hated begging out of a job that needed doing. Even a job she hated—and bloody hell, she hated the bombe machines.

Day shifts weren't so bad; you could step outside for a welcome jolt of sunshine and suck your soul back into your lungs. But on the evening shifts the hut seemed like an airless capsule in some dark ocean, draining air and cheer away like a leech.

"Were you at the Bedford dance?" Wren Stevens asked as she and Mab received their first menu and began plugging Aggie up.

"Yes." Mab stretched to reach a plug at the top. Her turn to be on her feet tonight, as Stevens sat at the checking machine going over Aggie's settings. Oh, but her toes were going to ache by morning.

"I went with a fellow from Hut 7," Stevens went on. "Ugh, he was all hands the moment we got on the dance floor."

The men I know don't try to put the make on. Mab could hear Osla's voice asserting that. Lovely, clueless Osla who thought gentlemen were safe.

Gentlemen don't try to put the make on girls like Osla, Mab thought, setting Aggie going with a deafening racket. *With girls like me, they aren't so gentlemanly. Or so safe.*

Aggie clacked, and Mab heard the clack of the register at Selfridges as she rang up his purchase . . . his name was Geoffrey Irving; he read French literature at Christ's College, and he'd come to Selfridges to buy a present for his mother. Mab, behind the counter in her black shopgirl's dress, all of seventeen years old, had sold him a silk scarf. He'd sold her a lot of nonsense about how pretty she was.

I wasn't pretty, she thought, looking at that gawky girl who had just hit five foot eleven and hadn't ironed Shoreditch out of her vowels yet. *I was available, and I was thrilled to get a date with a university boy.* He took her to the cinema and they were kissing before the newsreel was over, his hand inside her blouse ten minutes later. He wouldn't have tried that on Osla—what Cambridge boy wanted to be labeled NSIT among all the debutantes of London?—but he hadn't hesitated with Mab, and she hadn't stopped him. He had her knickers off within three weeks, in the leather backseat of his Bentley convertible, and it had been *marvelous;* so much for any of those stories about pain and blood the first time.

"You're wonderful," he'd panted afterward. "Wonderful, Mabel . . ." And they went again with hardly a pause, Mab blissfully certain she was in love. Blissfully sure that this was the start of something special, something lasting.

Especially when he said he wanted to take her for a night on the town with his friends.

Stop there, she thought, mechanically prying open a drum, tweezing two wires apart with exquisite care. *Just . . . stop.*

It was hard to stop, in the airless depth of the night shift. Night shift was when all Mab's demons came out to play.

She still remembered the dress she'd bought to meet Geoffrey's university chums. Sunshine-yellow rayon with a big red silk rose at the shoulder. She'd spent half her savings on it, certain it was the chicest thing she'd ever owned. "Very nice," Geoffrey had said when she came tripping out to meet the Bentley, and his two friends had echoed him in identical Cambridge drawls. "How about a little joyride before the party?" They were already passing a flask back and forth when she hopped in.

Stupid girl, Mab thought, swapping out the wheel order on the drums. *There wasn't any party. The party was* you.

Seventeen-year-old Mab would have sniffed that out—*if* they'd been Shoreditch boys like the ones who had been whistling at her legs since she was twelve. But seventeen-year-old Mab, who was already head over heels for Geoffrey, assumed that young men who read literature at Cambridge were *gentlemen.*

Stupid girl.

She and Geoffrey had been kissing in the backseat, the taste of brandy on his lips, when the Bentley canted to a crooked halt and one of his friends began fumbling under her skirt. She pulled back, smacking him off with a protest of "Hey—" and Geoffrey laughed. "Wait your turn," he told his friend lazily, pulling Mab's sleeve down and nibbling at her shoulder. "I brought her, I go first."

Stupid, maybe, Mab thought, mechanically tweezing the wires apart on another drum. *But not slow.* There had been one ice-cold moment of incomprehension, looking at the boy she'd fallen for—but only that one moment. Then she'd shoved him away with all her strength, and there were hands at her back and on her breasts, and voices laughing. "You didn't say she was such a firebrand!"

Maybe they'd thought it would be easy, that they'd each take a turn in the backseat while the other two waited their turn smoking by the bumper. But they were all drunk and Mab was taller than any of them and blazing with fear and fury. Geoffrey had a set of triple-scored scratches down each side of his face, and his friend was bent over his balls in soundless groaning; his third friend had turned around to lend a hand from the front seat, and Mab had yanked his hair so hard a handful of short strands came out in her fist. She had shrieked the whole time, cursing and snarling with rage and terror. It took all three of them to wrestle her out of the car, flailing and clawing all the way, getting another rake of her nails across Geoffrey's neck as they dropped her in the road. Mab was on her feet in a flash, knees stinging and scraped, pulling her shoe off and gripping the sharp heel in one trembling hand. "You touch me," she grated, shaking so hard she could barely stand, "and I will drive this through your *fucking eye.*"

"Walk your common little arse in your common little rayon frock back to Shoreditch, you cheap stupid slut," Geoffrey bit off in that posh voice that had always turned her knees to butter, and the Bentley swerved off in a blare of headlights.

"*Go to hell, you pathetic three-inch excuse for a man . . . ,*" Mab shrieked after it, seeing the outraged white smudge of Geoffrey's face before the car disappeared. Leaving her standing on the midnight road somewhere on the outskirts of London, no handbag or money, one shoe in her hand and the other nowhere to be seen, yellow dress torn all the way to her waist, vibrating with vast, humiliated sobs.

It had taken her four hours to walk home, limping barefoot through the streets. Three words vibrated through her with every step. *Cheap stupid slut. Cheap stupid slut.*

She'd walked into the kitchen on bloodied feet, every tear long sobbed out and dried on her cheeks, and she'd thanked her lucky stars Mum was asleep. Mab peeled off her ragged stockings, her torn slip, the dress she'd thought so beautiful, and chucked it all in the bin. She'd stood tall and naked in the kitchen, lighting a cigarette and smoking it all the way down with a face like stone.

That was when she decided she was done being *Mabel.* Mabel was young and dim and easily fooled. She was going to be *Mab* instead. Cool, imperious, untouchable Queen Mab.

CHAPTER 25

FROM *BLETCHLEY BLETHERINGS*, JUNE 1941

BB spotted Dilly Knox coming to work in his pajamas again. The ladies of his section are all too brilliant to be minding their boss's wardrobe, but surely there are any number of fashion designers twiddling their thumbs—if Mr. Hartnell and Mr. Molyneux can dress royalty and Wrens, can't they be seconded to dress Dilly Knox? There's a war on, after all!

"Ladies, you've been reassigned."

Beth was down the rabbit hole on a new message and didn't look up at Dilly until Peggy reached over and took the pencil out of her hand. "Italian naval traffic is being rerouted to another section," Dilly went on, tugging the bathrobe sash holding up his trousers, "since there's now so little of it—"

"Not much naval traffic when you don't have a navy anymore," Peggy smirked. Beth smirked back, though the thought of their Matapan triumph gave her an odd feeling now that she knew Osla's princely beau had been involved in that battle. Beth usually forgot that the puzzle work she loved meant something concrete for the troops—meant life or death for men far away on a dazzling blue sea. She'd been very glad she couldn't say as much to Osla. *It was my work that flung your boyfriend's ship into the thick of the biggest naval battle since Trafalgar. Does that make it my fault, at least a little bit, that you have no idea if he's alive or dead?*

"We've been given a new puzzle," Dilly continued, passing out messages and rods. "It's a proper jabberwock, I warn you."

Beth flipped through the stack, frowning. Something looked different . . .

"The Abwehr Enigma." Dilly saw the blank looks between the girls like Beth who could work German cribs but not speak the language. "The Enigma used by German military intelligence. Just call it the Spy Enigma. Our intelligence chaps can find the German agents on our soil and feed them false information, but we haven't a clue if it's being believed by the Abwehr officers running the show in Berlin."

"What's different about their Enigma?" Peggy frowned.

"They use a four-wheel machine, not a three-wheel. Four wheel settings to find instead of three, and they turn over a deal more frequently. It's a beast," Dilly concluded, running a hand over his hair, which was already thinner than it had been when Beth first laid eyes on him. "Welchman thinks if the boys in his hut can't break it, it can't be done. Let's prove him wrong."

Beth had a go for six hours, and all she got was a headache. It felt like her first weeks in the Cottage, flailing in the dark, and she could see matching discouragement from all the others. But Dilly was sanguine. "Come back fresh tomorrow and go at it again. We'll get there—blast it, where's my *pipe*?" Beth found the pipe under a German dictionary, handed it to him, and trailed dejectedly home.

She was still wandering mentally among four-letter indicators as she leashed up Boots and set out on her mother's list of errands—fetching the post, a stop by the chemist. Mother's little helper . . . only Mother's little helper wasn't quite so content anymore. Mother's little helper now spent her time counting the hours until she could go back on shift.

Beth sighed, tugging Boots toward the chemist, where she had to step around a pair of huge booted feet. "Harry?" She blinked.

His head jerked up. Clearly he'd dozed off sitting on the shop bench, leaning against the wall. "Sorry. I'm waiting for the chemist to mix something up, and a week on the night shift got the better of me." He had circles like tar under his eyes and his collar was a wrinkled mess. Beth knew Hut 8 was working round the clock on the U-boat traffic—it wasn't any secret that the wolf packs had been bringing down close to a hundred Allied ships a month between March and June. Harry gave a hard blink, squinting up at Beth. "I haven't seen you since the dance, have I?"

Where we danced and talked codebreaking techniques, and people apparently thought we were . . . Beth felt her cheeks color. She'd been appalled when Osla and Mab thought something romantic might have been going on. Embarrassed, wondering if she'd given Harry the wrong idea. And ashamed—because yes, maybe Beth *had* developed a harmless crush on her favorite BP colleague and only just realized it.

Either way, she'd resolved to steer clear of Harry in future. "Picking up a toothbrush for my dad," she murmured, edging past, but Boots had stopped to sniff at Harry's outstretched hand.

"I'm getting a tincture for Christopher." Scratching Boots's jaw. "I don't know if it does any good, but the doctor has faith in it."

Beth hesitated despite herself. "How long—I mean, when did he contract polio?"

"He was eighteen months old." Harry's voice went flat. "Careening around the lawn one moment, the next moment screaming. By morning he couldn't stand . . . by evening he was in hospital, in an iron lung." Harry looked up. "Have you ever seen one of those damned torture chambers? Just an enormous metal cylinder, with his tiny head sticking out . . . even when he was moved to the next ward, he'd lie there in a sterile crib, crying and crying, and we'd stand at the door on the other side of the chicken wire, not able to come close because of quarantine. Five more months before we got him back for good." Harry's big hand lay still across Boots's head. "We're lucky he has use of his arms. We're *lucky*. I keep telling myself that. But he's in and out of hospital all the time. He'll need to have his ankle fused at some point, to stabilize the foot. And he's such an *active* little sprat, he cries out of pure rage whenever he's put into a cast . . ."

The chemist poked his head outside. "Your tincture's made up, Mr. Zarb."

Harry gave Boots a final scratch, rising. Beth followed him inside and took a toothbrush from the rack, arriving at the counter as Harry was putting down coins. The chemist's wife was eyeing him with distaste, gaze traveling over his vast height, his shabby tweed jacket with the button missing.

"I don't know if I should be serving you." She pushed his change across the counter with a fingertip. "A strong young fellow not in uniform, shame on you. There's a war on, you know!"

Harry paused, looking at her. "I know," he said evenly. "I *know*." He leaned forward until his nose nearly touched the woman's, even as she pressed backward with eyes growing round. "*I KNOW*."

He shoved the coins back across the counter so hard they flew up, some hitting her, some falling to the floor. He grabbed his tincture bottle and banged out, shop door rebounding against the wall. Beth pushed her own exact change for the toothbrush at the wide-eyed chemist's wife and went after him.

"Harry," she called, then hesitated. She had no idea what to say when people were angry or upset. He stood struggling with his old bicycle leaned up against the lamppost, hands moving too roughly to disengage the chain, not looking up.

"I could use some help with a problem," Beth said at last. Not much in the way of comfort, but work *was* a comfort in its way. Or maybe not a comfort, but a drug. It certainly felt that way to her. A drug that could make you forget anything—even, for a tiny space of time, the horror of seeing a child in pain.

"What problem?" He looked up, blinking as if his eyes were prickling, and Beth's embarrassed determination to steer clear of him dissolved. He hadn't been feeding her lines at the dance, for all Mab's cynicism about married men looking for fun. He wasn't going to try anything, and Beth didn't want him to, crush or not. First and foremost, Harry had always been a friend.

"What can you tell me about working a system with four-letter indicators?" Beth asked, making sure there was no one in earshot.

His gaze went from angry to speculative in a blink. "Four wheels?" She nodded. He unchained his bicycle and began to walk it along rather than mounting up, and Beth fell into step on the other side. "K Enigma uses a four-wheel machine," Harry said when they were clear of the village. The country road was empty, elms arching overhead, robins twittering. "I did a bit with that. A four-letter indicator means there's a settable *Umkehrwalze* . . ."

"It's difficult." Beth could feel both their minds ranging ahead in unison, like a pair of greyhounds bounding down this path into a gallop. "We haven't got much in the way of textual cribs."

"I might be able to help there. Have you got a bit of paper?"

CHAPTER 26

Hullo, princess—I'm back in England. Did my letter after Matapan go astray? Everything's been chaos. I've come to take my sublieutenant's courses and exams; for the moment I'm bunking with the Mountbattens. Tell me you can get to London Saturday next. —Philip

"You'll miss the next Tea Party." Beth looked up from the rug, where she was brushing Boots. "We're discussing *Carry On, Jeeves.*"

"Bugger Jeeves. Philip's not dead!" Now that Osla had the proof in his handwriting, she could laugh at her own fears. But like a child terrified of a monster in the closet, you could only laugh at the fear when the light was switched on.

"This one?" Osla pulled out a dress. "It's the very latest go—how do I look?"

"Jumpy," said Mab from the bed. "Like a Borgia who has suddenly remembered that he has forgotten to shove cyanide in the consommé, and the dinner gong due any minute." Osla gave her a look. Mab held up *Carry On, Jeeves.* "Unlike you, I did the reading."

"Oh, go boil your head, Queen Mab. Wait, do my hair? You set the most topping waves . . ."

Euston station on Saturday night was thronged with harried women and jostling servicemen, but the whole crowd might as well have been shadows to Osla as she ran for the Great Hall.

As a little girl forever shuttling back and forth between London and her latest boarding school, Osla had hurried countless times under this hall's coffered ceiling, always outstripping her luggage in her haste to get aboveground for sunshine and the start of summer hols—but today she stopped dead in the middle of the throng, not caring if she ever saw sunshine again. Because there he stood at the foot of the sweeping double flight of stairs, a man in naval uniform and greatcoat, hat over blond hair, shoulders wide and feet braced, profile bent over a letter. The sight of him nearly stopped Osla's heart.

Philip looked up as if he'd felt her gaze. He looked more like a Viking than ever: golden, hard, tanned dark by the Mediterranean sun. His gaze hunted over her a little uncertainly, as if trying to merge the irreverent Osla he'd met at Claridge's in a boiler suit with this Osla: her serious face, her blush-pink crepe dress, her little fuchsia hat tilted over one eye. An Osla who, unbeknownst to him, had spent her day translating German naval secrets.

"Os . . . ," he began, and trailed off.

"Philip." She too was suddenly floundering. "I'm on shift tomorrow morning—I only have this evening, then I have to catch the train back." Desperate for distraction, she gestured at the Great Hall around them. "Euston's a bit of an eyesore, isn't it? I always preferred coming into Paddington when I was little, because it had the statue of the Unknown Soldier—you know the one, standing there in his bronze greatcoat, reading a letter from home? I always wanted to ask him who wrote the letter. Was she beautiful, did he come back to her, did she love him . . ."

"Did he ever answer you?" Philip's eyes drifted over her face as if he hadn't quite remembered her right. They hadn't seen each other for more than a year, Osla thought. She hadn't remembered him quite right either—his eyes weren't blue-gray, they were just blue. So very blue.

She took a step closer. "No, he never answered. Being bronze, and all."

"I suppose I could answer for him." Philip held up the letter in his hand, and she saw her own writing. "The girl who wrote this letter is definitely beautiful. And he definitely survived and came back to her . . ."

Philip trailed off before the third question. *Did she love him?* Did he even want an answer?

Osla knew it would be very easy to guide this train onto safer tracks. They hadn't spent very much time together, after all, and it had been more than a year. She could play the flirtatious chum, trill, "Darling Phil, how long it's been!" and then they'd splash out at the Savoy and part with no more heartache than any other set of friends who met for a fizzing night on the town. That would probably be the wiser course, Osla thought, remembering Mab's nighttime warning about princes and the girls they wouldn't consider marrying.

But: the third question.

Did she love him?

Osla took two steps forward, flung her arms around Philip's neck, and pressed her lips to his. He pulled her against him with a yank, lifting her up onto her toes. She was too busy drowning in his kisses to notice when the lights of Euston station went out.

"I THINK WE'RE stuck here, princess."

"Such a tragedy, sailor."

The air-raid siren still sounded somewhere in the distance, but Osla could not hear the drone of planes—if bombs were falling, they were on the other side of London. The station lights had come on again, but only partly; their side was enveloped in shadow. Philip sat with his back against the station wall with Osla curled on his lap, his greatcoat draped about her shoulders so he could wrap his arms round her inside it. His hat lay on the ground with Osla's fuchsia toque on top of it beside her handbag. None of the others caught in the station paid any attention to the midshipman and his code girl hidden in the shadow of the hall, clinging so tight they nearly fused.

A sound clattered outside, and Philip's face lifted from Osla's neck, his every muscle tensing beneath her. "Just the ack-ack guns," she murmured, tugging his head back to hers. "Our side. You get used to the sound." She was drunk on him, every nerve in her body singing. They'd kissed before, but with care, standing on doorsteps where they couldn't be tempted too far. Not like this, openmouthed and yearning, hands sliding under sleeves and inside collars, the whole surface of her skin aching.

"You're so calm about the air raids," Philip muttered against her lips.

"Londoners have become terribly blasé about the Blitz." The travelers caught in the station had settled down to wait it out, unwrapping sandwiches and chatting to their neighbors. "Euston took some hits last year, but she's still standing."

"Thank God you're buried in Bucks away from the worst of it." He kissed her jaw, fingertips sliding along her skin inside her neckline—she could feel his grin against her cheek as he touched the hard little lump of his naval insignia, pinned to her brassiere between her breasts. "You kept it."

"I nearly had it stolen once." Osla pushed her face into the hollow of his neck and rested there, tasting the salt of his skin. "I came to the Café de Paris on my night off. The boy I was dancing with, he . . ." She shut her eyes, seeing poor Charlie's lungs exploded out onto the front of his uniform. "The club was bombed, and a looter tried to get my jewelry. A stranger ran him off, took care of me." *J. P. E. C. Cornwell,* whoever he was . . . Osla hadn't received any response to her letter. "I kept calling him Philip."

I'm not Philip, sweetheart. What's your name?

Philip was here now, arms tightening around her, one hand rubbing her bare shoulder where her sleeve had slipped down, the other stroking her silk-stockinged calf. Osla couldn't remember the last time she'd felt the world could be borne simply because someone was holding her. It dizzied her, this mixture of simple comfort and raw desire. "I'm sorry I wasn't there," Philip said quietly.

"You were headed to fight at Cape Matapan." *And I think one of my billet-mates knows something about what orders sent you there.*

"I wasn't in any danger, Os. We were on them that night like foxes in a henhouse." His lips touched her hair, his body suddenly still against hers. "I was on the *Valiant*'s searchlights. I'd flip the midship light and pick out the enemy cruiser until our guns set it ablaze. Then the gunnery officer would shout *train left* or *train right,* and as soon as I lit the next one up, she'd be blotted out stem to stern. Two eight-inch-gun Italian cruisers sunk in five minutes. It was as near murder as anything could be in wartime. The cruisers just—burst into tremendous sheets of flame." He exhaled into her hair. "I dream about them."

"I dream about the Café de Paris. I wake up smelling the fire, and for a moment I think I've gone mad."

"Don't say that, Os." He was already tense; now he went rigid. "Not ever."

She pulled back, looked at him through the shadows.

"Bit of a sore point with me." He made himself shrug. "My—my mother went mad."

Alice of Battenberg, from one of the German noble houses. "You've hardly ever mentioned her."

"She had a breakdown when I was eight or nine. So many doctors—they couldn't decide if she was neurotic or paranoid schizophrenic or . . ." A long pause; his eyes fixed past Osla's shoulder. "I wasn't there when they took her away. They sent the children out for the day. But I heard later how she tried to run. They had to put her in restraints and inject her before they could bundle her into a car and take her to Bellevue in Switzerland."

Osla felt him breathing against her, unevenly. "You were so young."

"It was the last time our family lived together. She was released eventually but by then my father was in France, my sisters were married, I was in England . . ."

Osla's arms tightened around his neck.

"It's just what happened," he said roughly. "She went mad. The family broke up. I just had to get on with it. You do. One does. Besides, she got better. She came out of the asylum, returned to Athens . . . she's still there. Living quietly."

And you've still had no real home since she was taken away, Osla thought. "How did she do it? Recover from that?"

"Iron will? I don't know." Philip pulled her closer into his chest. "So—don't even joke about going mad, Os."

"I won't." She took his secret like the gift it was, painful and precious. "And before you ask, I won't tell anyone. Not ever."

"I know that. I don't trust many people, but I know the ones I can." He buried his nose in her hair, inhaling. "You smell so good. I live on a tin can with a hundred chaps, you have no idea. You smell like—peonies. Earl Grey. Honey . . ."

They kissed and talked and kissed some more inside the shelter of his greatcoat, long past the all-clear siren. The lights stayed out at their end of the station, even as trains began to rumble through again and passersby resumed their bustle. Osla was dozing in the curve of Philip's arm when he stirred, pressing his lips to her temple. "Your train's coming in fifteen minutes, princess. We never even got out of the station, and it's already time to get you home."

"How long before you ship out?" She tried to say it lightly, but fear clutched her stomach. *I only just got you back.*

"Months. I need to study for my lieutenant's exams." Under the shelter of the greatcoat he helped her hook buttons that had come unbuttoned. Osla smiled as she did up his uniform collar, which had come open under her hands so she could slide her fingers over his chest. What you could do under a greatcoat in dim light during an air raid! If they hadn't been in a public place, who knew what might have happened . . .

Philip set her on her feet, looking much less flushed and rumpled as he donned his cap. Some alchemy of royal blood, maybe—the ability to compose oneself for the public eye in a blink. *But he's not just a prince,* Osla thought. *He's my Philip.* And she grinned as he buttoned his greatcoat rather hastily, because she had a much better idea (bless you, Mab!) about the biological state a man might be in after hours and hours of canoodling against a wall. "Welcome back, sailor," she said softly.

"I'm not just back." He pulled her against him, rested his chin on top of her head. "I'm home."

Home, Osla thought. The second of those twin, burning polestars toward which she tried to steer her life: a job worth doing, and a home to come back to.

Did she finally, *finally,* have both?

And for the rest of June all the way to golden autumn, Osla vibrated bright-eyed and joyous between the two—running straight from her grueling hours of translation in Hut 4 to throw herself into Philip's arms in London, riding between Bletchley and Euston station barely able to see for stars.

CHAPTER 27

FROM *BLETCHLEY BLETHERINGS*, SEPTEMBER 1941

Nothing here surprises us anymore. A gaggle of Wrens singing madrigals by the lake, attacked by the meanest swans in Bucks? Old hat. A group of naval section boys sunbathing nude on the side lawn, shrieking women fleeing the sight of all that pasty skin? Yawn. General Montgomery spotted in the dining room at three in the morning, poking at a plate of corned beef and prunes? Pass the salt, General.

But frankly, *BB* fell over in a dead faint at the sight of our latest visitor . . .

Mab was on break from the bombe machines, and a group of codebreakers were playing a makeshift game of rounders on the lawn and arguing. "Cantwell's not out. He got past the conifer—"

"No, it was the deciduous—"

Giles gave Mab a wave. "Come join, my queen. We need long legs on this team of waddlers."

The idea of stretching her legs sounded glorious. Hanging her new hat on the nearest tree branch, Mab rolled up her skirt and took a stick, which was all they had for bats. Ten minutes later she bashed the ball a great whack and sprinted for the tree. "Rounding one—rounding two—!" But then she came to a halt, jaw nearly hitting the grass, because a cluster of dark-suited figures was advancing from the mansion like a small fleet, led by Commander Denniston, who was explaining something to a short bulldog figure . . . a figure Mab recognized.

Winston Churchill stumped past close enough to reach out and touch, giving the rounders players a nod.

Giles gaped. "Was that . . ."

The PM wasn't at all as Mab had imagined him. Shorter, limping badly, hair wispy above his black pin-striped suit. No sign of his famous hat, his cigar. Mab had always imagined he would be full of noisy bravado and bluster, but he walked along quietly, looking about him with a measured gaze.

"Is he touring the place?" she whispered. "My God—" She bolted for her hut, sliding past the ministerial party when they detoured for Hut 7. She was in place at her machine's side, skirt unrolled and hair combed, when the door opened and Churchill was ushered inside. The Wrens came to attention and saluted. Mab saluted with them. She was a civilian but it was the *prime minister* standing there on the oily floor, looking at the machines she hated so much.

"Wren Stevens," Commander Denniston said. "A demonstration, if you please."

Stevens stood frozen to the spot.

"This machine is called Agnus Dei, Prime Minister." Mab spoke up when it was clear her partner couldn't summon a word. Crisply, she demonstrated: plugging up the back according to the menu, loading the drums, tweezing apart the fine wires. He fired questions, wanting to know everything—she answered as best she could. Wren Stevens eventually came forward and began responding, too. The PM whistled, impressed by the sheer din when

Aggie and her sister machines were set into motion. Waiting for a full stop might have taken hours, so Mab called a halt, explaining what it meant when a bombe machine went quiet.

As Churchill thanked them, she felt an almost violent urge to *nurture*. He looked so tired, rings under his eyes, shoulders bowed—wasn't anyone looking after him while he looked after the whole nation? She wanted to cook the prime minister a good soft-boiled egg and stand over him while he ate every bite; she wanted to tell him to have a long sleep and not worry about how bombe machines worked; she wanted to tell him they would do their jobs, never fear, so he should go home and get some *rest* before he dropped dead. She had to clasp her hands to stop from doing up his overcoat as he turned to leave.

Maybe her concern showed in her eyes, because Churchill—the most powerful man in the western world, Adolf Hitler's chief antagonist—dropped one heavy eyelid in a wink. Mab clapped a hand over her mouth but the splutter of laughter got through. Wren Stevens looked appalled, but the PM gave a nod and said cheerily, "I must head along to congratulate the chaps behind these splendid machines . . ."

They all looked at each other breathlessly as the door thumped shut. "The machines are already stopped," someone said. "No one else will be working while he's here . . ."

They all raced outside, following discreetly in the wake of the ministerial party. Churchill and his followers disappeared into Hut 8, and Mab saw to her surprise that one of the men left outside was Francis Gray.

"What are you doing here?" she said low voiced as he came to join her by the tennis court. "I didn't think you worked at Downing Street."

"No, the Foreign Office." He smiled, coat stirring about his knees. "The call came from Downing Street this morning—they were short a driver, and looking for someone who had already been to BP so they wouldn't have to use one of the ordinary drivers who hadn't been vetted at this level. Nobody needed me, so here I am."

"I haven't seen you since dinner at the Savoy," Mab replied. "When was that, May?"

"Russia joining the Allies made things rather busy after that."

"Hopefully the Yanks will get off their arses and follow Uncle Joe's example." She said *arses* deliberately, hoping for a laugh. Francis Gray had never once laughed that she could remember. But he just gave his usual smile of remote warmth.

The prime minister toured Huts 8 and 6 in turn, and there was quite a crowd by the time he came out. Mab saw Osla on the other side and was pleased to see even her cosmopolitan friend goggling at the sight of Churchill. Mab expected the PM to head back to his car, but he hesitated, looking around, before climbing up on some building rubble. Mab's throat caught, and she found herself pressing closer along with everyone else.

He stood a moment, one hand thrust in his vest pocket. "To look at you, one would not think you held so many secrets," he said conversationally. "But I know better, and I am proud of you. Here you are, working every day, working so very hard . . . I must thank you all for that." He stopped, looking down. Mab had heard him speak many times over the radio, had felt his confidence and his sheer force of will, but now he was just a rather short man standing on a heap of debris, clearly speaking around a lump in his throat, and she found tears in her eyes. "You should know how very important your skills are to the war effort," he went on. "Nothing could be more important, even if so few in Britain know what you are doing." He gave his sudden ebullient smile, and Mab tingled all the way to her fingertips. "You're my golden geese, you know. The geese who lay precious golden eggs, but never cackle!"

A roar went up from the crowd, and Mab realized she was roaring too, banging her hands together in applause. If a flight of German bombers had streaked across the sky to strafe Bletchley Park, every person there would have flung their body over the prime minister. Mab would have been at the front of the rush.

He gave a final wave, then stumped off in the direction of the mansion, phalanx of officials closing round him. The crowd lingered a moment, everyone talking excitedly before heads of huts began waving their people back to work. Mab realized she'd left her hat hanging on a tree branch in the middle of the rounders game—dashing to get it, she saw Francis waiting in front of the mansion, smoking a Woodbine. "Waiting on the PM?" she called, reaching for her hat.

"You know what I heard him say to Denniston as they went in?" A smile. "'I know I told you not to leave a stone unturned recruiting for this place, but I did not mean you to take me *quite* so seriously.'"

Mab laughed. "We're a lot of odd ducks here, no question. Oh, no . . ."

Francis raised his eyebrows.

"The brim got crumpled." Mab held up her new hat—a jet-black, dramatically brimmed take on a man's fedora, garnet-red silk band round the crown. Mab knew it made her look like a cross between Snow White and the Wicked Queen, and it was probably the last pretty thing she'd be able to buy herself for months. "You have no idea how important hats are to women."

"Enlighten me."

"Hats aren't rationed, at least not yet. I've sent most of my clothing coupons for the year to my aunt in Sheffield—she's looking after my sister, and she doesn't particularly want to, so I keep her sweet with a few coupons in the post. She'll get a new coat and I'll make do till next year, but at least I can still get a new hat." Mab sauntered toward the nearest ground-floor window, settling the hat over her head. She knew she was babbling—what was it about this man that made her feel the need to fill all the silences? "We ladies pinch and make do when it comes to darning stockings and using bootblack for eyeliner, but at least we can top a worn-out ensemble with a really smashing hat. That's very good for morale, in wartime."

His voice sounded odd. "Is it?"

"Of course." Mab surveyed her dim reflection in the window, brim slashing across her forehead. "We can't do anything about the hours or the shift changes or the airless huts, but we *can* look smart as we head off to war every day. The Bletchley Park theatrical society is cooking up a song about that for this year's Christmas revue—I've already heard them practicing." She turned, hands on hips, and sang:

Sophisticated black is de rigueur,
And a smart hat a woman's cri de coeur!

She finished with a flourish, knowing she couldn't sing. He was silent, cigarette burning between two still fingers, and her smile faded.

Mr. Gray, I officially give up trying to figure you out. You obviously find my conversation torturous. She checked her watch. "Well, I've got to get back—"

"Marry me."

She blinked. "What?"

He didn't repeat it. He stood there in the cold breeze, chestnut hair stirring, just looking at her, and there was no shield of distant amusement anymore. The veils had dropped away behind his eyes, Mab thought, revealing something that blazed like a torch.

She tried a smile. "Are you joking with me?" That seemed quite a bit more likely than getting a marriage proposal from a man she hardly knew.

"No," he said, flicking the cigarette away. There was an odd note in his voice, as if he were as confused by the offer as she. "Marry me." Bemusement in his tone or not, his gaze was steady.

"I—" How she'd dreamed of this moment, when some gentleman whose boots Geoff Irving and his filthy friends weren't fit to lick would make her an offer. She'd thought she'd be in command of things, having nurtured her suitor along a steady procession of milestones until he was brought to the precipice and thought it was all his own idea. Francis Gray hadn't hit any of the milestones. They had gone on three dates, and Mab had done 90 percent of the talking on all three occasions. "Mr. Gray—you've caught me by surprise."

"It's ridiculous, really," he said. "I'm sure there are far younger and more pleasant fellows making you offers. Still, I'm throwing my hat in the ring."

". . . Why?" Mab heard herself ask. "You don't know me." But he did, she thought. All the talking she'd done, he'd listened. She was the one who didn't know him, much as she'd tried.

He was silent nearly an entire minute, gazing at her as if he could see through her. He started to speak, then fell silent again. He reached out, touched the wing of her eyebrow, touched her cheekbone, touched her lips. "I know you." He wound a strand of her hair around his fingers and tugged her closer. She could have pulled away, but she let herself sink against him instead. Such a light kiss, to leave her so pinned in place.

"Marry me," he said, lips still brushing hers.

"Yes," she heard herself whispering back into his. Her heart wasn't fluttering in her chest as she'd thought it would; it thumped slow and hard, as if too astonished to speed up. Francis Gray, war poet and Foreign Office official, had proposed marriage. She had said yes.

She tried to catch her breath, collect her thoughts. Who knew what had swept those curtains of polite distance away from his eyes and made him blurt out a proposal, but who cared? Three-day wartime marriages blossomed all over Britain. She'd have been an absolute fool to turn him down; he was everything she'd dared to hope for in a husband, and more. Kindness, courtesy, education, career . . . maybe he was a little older, but that meant he was steady, established, not some callow boy. Perhaps she didn't know him very well, but she had the rest of her life to figure him out.

It was all so much more than she had hoped for.

His fingers untangled from her hair, picked up her hand instead. Turned it, looking at her long fingers lying across his broad palm. "This isn't very good timing," he said, and gave a short laugh. "Next week I'm being sent to America."

Mab blinked. *"America?"*

"Washington, DC. I'm afraid I can't say anything more, but I'll be overseas for months."

He hesitated, and Mab could tell it wouldn't take much to be married within the week, before he left. To say *Let's run up to London and get it done!* Servicemen and their girlfriends did it all the time, squeezing a wedding into a two-day leave. Mab nearly suggested it but bit her tongue. She was not going to race down the aisle without a few cautionary checks first; she'd known too many girls in Shoreditch who'd married in haste and repented at leisure. "We'll do it when you get back," she said, giving his hand a squeeze. "Just promise you'll meet my mother and sister before you go."

If she was hoping to bring Lucy into her home as a married woman, she had to see how Francis responded to that idea and how he got on with Lucy. If he put his foot down on it, well, that was that. But she didn't think he would. He was going to love Lucy, and she'd have every advantage in the world: snow-white socks and a day school blazer and a *pony* . . .

"Damn it." Francis glanced over his shoulder. There was motion at the door of the mansion as the ministerial party began to move outside. "Ten more minutes, that's all I ask." He looked up at her. "It will be a bit of a wait for you. Overseas post being what it is, I don't know how often I'll be able to write."

"As long as you let me know when you arrive safe," she said softly. Worry was already clutching hard in her stomach. Surely diplomats went back and forth across the Atlantic all the time; it wasn't like the convoys, getting targeted by German wolf packs. *He'll be perfectly safe,* she told herself. As soon as he came back, they'd be married. This man was going to be her husband. She'd make him the best bloody wife in Britain.

"Tea next week with your family, then, before I leave." Francis passed his thumb over her knuckles. "D'you want a ring?"

"Yes," she heard herself laugh. "I want a ring."

"Bound to be a ruby somewhere in London that matches your lips." He let go of her hand, backed up toward the little fleet of cars. The prime minister had already climbed inside and his chauffeur was starting up; the aides hovered by the next vehicle, waiting for their driver. Francis looked at Mab another long moment, the curtains still swept aside from his naked gaze. No one had ever looked at Mab like that in her life.

Her fiancé climbed into the car. It moved off, and Mab walked, still in a daze, back toward her hut. *Mab Gray,* she thought. *Mrs. Gray.*

Mab saw Winston Churchill's face turned out the window of the lead car as it swept around the drive toward the gates. She put up her hand and flashed a V with two fingers, his famous sign. *V for victory.* Because today she'd won, damn it. She'd *won.*

The prime minister put a hand out the window and flashed a V back.

CHAPTER 28

FROM *BLETCHLEY BLETHERINGS*, OCTOBER 1941

"Preoccupied"—adjective, "engrossed in thought." Taken to an entirely new level by BP personnel, who are frequently too preoccupied to notice if they have put their knickers on backward, if the prime minister has dropped in for tea, or if everything except the pencil actually in their hand is on fire.

Beth missed everything that autumn. Churchill's visit, Mab's engagement—it all passed Beth in a blur. "Honestly, where do you Cottage girls go?" Osla demanded. "The blinking *moon*?"

Beth just stared, exhausted. She was sleeping very badly—at night her brain roiled so much with five-letter groups and quartets of wheels, she was lucky if she got more than a few hours of tossing and turning. Boots had given up sleeping on her feet and retired in disgust to the basket on the floor.

"MI-5 manages the controlled German agents," Dilly had mused aloud at the beginning, with his usual complete disregard for Bletchley Park's paranoia about keeping its workers in the dark. "MI-5 makes them send out false information on their own wireless transmitters, as directed by our case officers, using their own hand cipher given to them by the Germans. Their controllers are usually in Lisbon, Madrid, or Paris; they analyze everything before transmitting to Berlin. We just need to crack the one *they* use to make sure Berlin is swallowing it . . ."

But "just" hadn't happened yet, even though Dilly's entire section had been banging their brains against it for three months so far. This wasn't like the three-day sprint they'd flung themselves into to break the Matapan battle orders—excruciating but finite. This was a desperate, endless slog of dead ends, going down one promising path until it petered out, then trying another. With no time for recovery or rest.

"If I analyze the hand-cipher traffic from the individual network, we should get some good cribs," Dilly muttered, but he'd been analyzing the traffic all this time and nothing consistent came up. With Italian naval Enigma, cribs gave you something to rod for. Here they had nothing. It was those damned four wheels used in the Abwehr Enigma, turning over much more frequently with no predictable pattern.

Have to crack it, have to crack it. Her entire body was tense as wire, and she was so far down the rabbit hole she felt like screaming. If she screamed, she'd probably scream in five-letter clumps. *Have to crack it.*

Beth wasn't going anywhere except the Cottage, where she overstayed her shifts and barely came home in time to walk Boots before being hauled into the kitchen. Then she'd stand stirring rice pudding over the heat, watching boxing chains unspool in her head until her mother had her by the elbow, shaking her. "Bethan, you've burned it—"

Five minutes later Beth would realize she'd gone sideways in her thoughts all over again, not listening to a word of the lecture.

Sometimes she managed to mumble, "I'm sorry, Mother, what were you saying?"

And Mrs. Finch would walk away quivering with anger, saying, "I think you're going mad, I really do!"

I think so too, Beth sometimes thought.

Dilly burst into the Cottage one interminable night shift, waving his glasses. "Lobsters!"

Beth traded looks with Phyllida at the next desk. "Lobsters?" When Dilly was in one of his Catherine wheel moods and started firing ideas off like sparks, it was best to patiently ask questions until he started making sense. Peggy was better at it than Beth, who knew she wasn't making much sense these days herself. Only yesterday she'd noticed the big ruby glinting on Mab's hand, and said, "How long have you had that?" Mab had looked at her a little strangely and said, "A month, Beth. Francis gave it to me before he went overseas. After I took him to meet Mum and Lucy."

"After there was that tempest in a teapot the high-ups made about the new Agatha Christie book?" Osla had prompted when Beth looked blank. "Don't tell me you forgot that, too!"

Beth had, apparently. And now she was being asked to think about *lobsters.*

"The moment all four wheels in the machine turn over between the first two letters of the indicator and again in its repeat position—think of that as a crab." Dilly waved four fingers like crab legs all moving together.

"It's not a way into the cipher." Beth poured cold coffee into a cup and pushed it into his hand.

"But if there are four-wheel turnovers on both sides of the throw-on indicator key-block, there could be more turnovers on *one* side of the key-block alone. Think of that as a lobster . . ."

He made lobster claw gestures, spilling coffee, jabbering as Beth listened. Nothing made sense, but she was used to Dilly's Lewis Carroll logic by now and found her brain diving down the right angle he'd just proposed.

"If we could find your lobster," she said slowly, "and a long block of text after it, maybe we'd have better luck breaking key-blocks of indicators on the same setting . . ." She didn't really know where she was going with that yet, but the best way to find out was to *have a go,* as Dilly always said. Beth pulled out the pencil stub holding her knotted-up hair. "Let's go lobster hunting."

It took four days to find a message with the right turnover, but as soon as Beth had it, numbers started spiraling and chaining madly. "Yes," she yelped in the middle of the day shift. "Give me a cipher letter pairing in position one, I can chain together some deductions about the other pairings . . ." Her words tumbled madly. "Don't you see?" she finished in a rush, blood fizzing.

Phyllida rubbed the bridge of her nose. "Sort of."

Peggy peered closer. "Show me."

"Where's Dilly?" Beth looked around. "Did he go home?"

"Yes, he did." Peggy's face was drawn. "And we aren't bothering him. Show me . . ."

It had gone October, trees flaming yellow and orange around the lake, by the time Beth could crack one wheel setting. November frosts had hardened the ground before the Cottage girls could theorize how often the German technicians, when they picked four-letter wheel settings for the day's traffic, fell back on particular words: NEIN, WEIN, NEUN . . . "Four-letter names, too," Peggy mused.

Then Beth broke a wheel setting on some Balkan-based traffic after she broke S-A for the two right-hand wheels, and made a grainy-eyed, dawn-hour guess that the Balkan operator had a girlfriend named ROSA. With R and O fixed in position, everything fell into place; generated alphabets of text and cipher could then be swiftly buttoned up, and lists of four-letter German names and words were soon pinned up on every Cottage wall.

"We're getting there," Dilly encouraged, sprinkling tobacco all over Beth's work. "It's coming, ladies."

In early December, the moment came. Everyone clustered around Beth's desk, barely breathing as she pulled blocks of German out of the chaos. There it was, a decrypted message—the German-speaking women confirmed it was legible. Beth didn't ask or care what it said. She put her knuckles to her mouth and bit down savagely, little dying fragments of code spasming across her vision. She was suddenly hungry and didn't know when she'd last eaten, didn't know when she'd last been home or what day it was. She didn't know anything except that she'd done it. They'd all done it. They'd broken the Spy Enigma.

Peggy swayed where she stood at Beth's shoulder. She put her head in her hands, and suddenly the silence snapped. Phyllida threw herself into the arms of the puzzled tea lady, who had just trundled in with fresh chicory coffee. Several girls laughed as if they were drunk, several cried, all so finely balanced between elation and exhaustion they couldn't speak a single coherent word.

At last Peggy lifted her head from her hands, looking like she was swimming up through deep water, and said, "I'll telephone Dilly, then inform Commander Denniston." She reached for the message on Beth's desk, giving Beth's shoulder a fierce squeeze.

Someone else was looking at the schedule, calling out the girls who were on until midnight. "Beth, it's your day off tomorrow. Go home before you drop."

Beth struggled into her coat and stumbled outside, winter chill striking her in the face. It was full dark, but whether it was six o'clock or midnight, she had no idea. Beth's ears were roaring as she came out of the stable yard, and it took her a fuddled moment to realize the roar wasn't in her head—it was coming from the mansion. Men and women were spilling out the front door, shouting, laughing, calling out to each other. "You heard—" "I heard!" "About bloody time—"

"What?" Beth called, buffeted by the stream of ecstatic codebreakers. "What happened?" She caught sight of a familiar red-banded, slant-brimmed hat and caught Mab's elbow. "What is it?"

Mab threw her arms around Beth, all her usual cool poise gone. "They're in, Beth! The Americans are in the war! The Japanese attacked one of their bases—"

"They *did*?"

"Don't tell me you missed that, too. Pearl Harbor?" Mab took a gulping breath. "The announcement was coming, we all knew it. Everybody's been cramming into the mansion round the radio. Not an hour ago President Roosevelt came on, and the Yanks are in it!"

America in the war, and the Spy Enigma broken—after so many months of hoping and waiting for both, they'd come all at once. Beth took a shaky breath and began sobbing. She stood there with tears pouring down her face, utterly spent and utterly, utterly happy.

Mab put an arm around her shoulder and squeezed, a flash of light from the mansion sparking red fire off her ruby ring. "Cry all you want, I won't tell. Have you got a day off tomorrow, like Os and me? We all need to sleep late . . ."

By the time Beth had cried herself into hiccupping silence against Mab's shoulder, she was limp as a dishrag and Osla had found them. "Darlings, isn't it *topping*!" She and Mab steered Beth between them as they headed for home, chattering excitedly. The world was coming back to Beth's eyes in its usual shapes by the time they came through the Finch door, and as she unbuttoned her coat, she called eagerly, "Did you hear, Dad? Have you got the radio on?"

"We heard." Beth's father came into the corridor smiling. "Lovely news, lovely—the war will be over in no time! Mabel, your fiancé telephoned. He's back from America earlier than expected."

Mab paled. "My God, did he sail in the middle of—"

"No, he was back day before yesterday. Said he was quite as surprised by Pearl Harbor as we were. He's at his London digs if you want to ring." Beth's father smiled indulgently as Mab flew for the telephone, but that smile shuttered as he looked back at Beth. "Your mother's in the kitchen. She's had a very difficult day—"

Beth kissed her father's cheek, blew into the kitchen, and flung her arms around her mother's waist where she stood at the stove. "Isn't it wonderful news? Let me take over, I know I've been gone forever, you wouldn't believe the workload." The exhaustion and frustration of the past months were fading like a dream. The first message had been broken; they'd break more. *I can break anything,* Beth thought, smiling. *Give me a pencil and a crib, and I'll crack the world.*

She reached for an apron, looking around. "Where's Boots?" She was hours overdue to take him out.

"Do set the table." Her mother kept stirring. "Yes, it's lovely news. Though when I think of those poor people in Pearl Harbor—"

"Let me take Boots out, then I'll set the table." Beth whistled, but no woolly gray shape trundled crossly into the room.

"I told you, Bethan." Her mother looked up from the pot she

was stirring, her smile serene. "I told you that dog was out if it ever made a mess in the house. You said you'd always be home to take it out. I told you—"

Beth took a step, suddenly numb. "What did you do?"

"BOOTS!"

Beth caught her foot on a stone, stumbling. Bletchley after sundown was a black pit, every chink of light battened down. She had a torch but it was pasted over with regulation paper so only a shadowy beam emerged. A village she'd walked her entire life suddenly became an alien landscape.

"Boots!"

Her dog had made a puddle in the parlor when Beth was late coming home. And her mother had taken him by the collar, put him outside into the dark street, and shut the door.

"Now, Beth," her father had said, placating. "See it from your mother's side—" But Beth had grabbed the torch and run straight out into the street, forgetting everything except that her dog was blundering through the winter night alone.

She stumbled again, filling her lungs in a hitching sob. "*Boots!*"

A chink of light showed down the street as a door opened. The indistinct ripple of Osla's voice: "Pardon me, have you seen . . ." Mab had the other torch, looking in the opposite direction. They'd followed Beth without a moment's hesitation, as Beth's mother stood with arms folded, shaking her head more in sorrow than in anger. "I told you what would happen, Bethan. You can't blame me."

Yes, I can, Beth thought. But she couldn't focus on the flickering rage; despair welled up over it. How was she going to find one small dog in the middle of the night? He was gone, the longed-for dog she'd claimed in the most monumental act of will of her life. He was gone and she was never going to find him. Or if she did it would only be his body, half-eaten by foxes or crushed by a car careening through on the way to London . . .

She screamed into the dark, ripping the paper off the torch. "*Boots!*"

"Beth!" Mab's voice. Beth reversed, stumbled toward the bouncing beam of Mab's torch, heart suddenly cannoning inside her ribs. Mab's tall shape formed up in the black, clutching a small, shivering bundle.

"Found him under a bush four houses down," Mab said. "He didn't go far—stop snapping at me, you little bugger, I'm on *your* side."

Beth pulled her dog into her arms and for the second time that day sobbed all over Mab's shoulder. The schnauzer was damp and smelly and quivering with cold, harrumphing like a cross old man when she hugged him too hard. Beth didn't know if she'd ever be able to put him down.

"There'd better be a good reason you girls are making a ruckus," a disapproving voice sounded. One of the civilian ARP wardens, busybodies all. "Uncovered lights despite blackout regulations . . ."

Mab switched her torch off and Osla caught up and began pouring verbal honey. They got rid of him and turned for home, steering Beth between them. With Boots safe, a hot spark of something diamond-hard had lodged itself in Beth's throat, and with every step toward her house, it grew bigger.

"Is your mother going to let you—" Osla began, and then stopped.

Beth came through the door, tugged her mother's jumper off the coatrack, and rubbed Boots dry right there in the entryway. She could see Mrs. Finch's shoes on the hooked rug but refused to look up. Osla and Mab crowded in behind, making bright noises about how cold it was outside, but the silence under their exclamations stretched like a sheet of ice. Beth didn't raise her eyes until Boots was dry and had stopped shivering. Then she straightened, meeting her mother's gaze expressionlessly.

Mrs. Finch heaved a gentle, put-upon sigh. "It can stay *one* more night, Bethan. If tomorrow you find it somewhere else to—"

Beth didn't plan it, didn't think about it, didn't even know it was happening until she saw her hand flash up and hit her mother across the face.

She'd never hit anyone before in her life. She'd probably hurt her hand more than she'd hurt its target. But Mrs. Finch fell back, fingertips flying to her own cheek in shock, and Beth fell back a step too in horror. *I didn't mean to,* she almost said—but she had meant to. *I'm sorry,* she almost said—but she wasn't sorry. The diamond spark of rage in her throat was still burning, larger and larger.

She couldn't think what to say, so all she said was, "How dare you?"

Red-faced, Mrs. Finch reached for her Bible. "'*He that smiteth his father or his mother shall surely—*'"

Beth didn't wait for her to finish Exodus 21:15 or extend the book and tell her to hold it up until her arms burned. "No."

"What did you say to me?"

Out of sheer habit, Beth almost dropped her eyes and fiddled with the end of her plait. But when her fingers reached for the wispy end of the long braid, which she'd spent her whole life hanging on to like a lifeline rather than meet anyone's eyes, it wasn't there. She had a smart shoulder-skimming wave now, and she had a dog and a circle of friends and a job breaking German ciphers.

So Beth said very quietly, "I'm not holding the Bible up for the next half hour while you harangue me. And you are not throwing my dog out."

"We'll discuss it tomorrow." Beth's father spoke loud enough to make everyone jump. "We're all overwrought, this news about the Americans—"

But Mrs. Finch rode over him, eyes filled with tears. "Why are you behaving like this, Bethan? Why? You haven't been the same since that job."

"Why is this about my job?" Beth had to raise her own voice to be heard. "You threw my *dog* out! What kind of person would—"

"—you didn't have to take that job. They don't need *you*!"

"Yes, they do." Beth threw her head back. "There isn't anyone there who can do what I do."

"And what is it you do?" Mrs. Finch's voice rose. "If it's so important, tell me. Tell me *right now*."

Beth refused to get sidetracked down that path. "I won't apologize for taking the job at BP." Ever since she'd started working, all she'd done at home was apologize for it. No more.

"Your job is here! You're my little helper. What am I supposed to do without extra hands at home?"

"I help you every minute I'm home. I'm *happy* to help. And you still *threw my dog out in the damned street*—"

"You care more for a dog and a job than your own mother." Mrs. Finch pressed a hand against her temple. "Your own mother, who isn't well—"

Mab's voice sounded behind Beth, amused and contemptuous. "Here comes the headache."

"Right on schedule," Osla agreed.

"Don't you talk back to me, you two tarts," Mrs. Finch snapped. "Encouraging my Bethan to behave like a common—"

"A common *what*?" Suddenly Beth's words were pouring out. "Mother, I work for the war effort. I meet with friends to talk about books. I have the occasional glass of sherry. Why does any of that make me a tart?"

Mrs. Finch poked her Bible at Beth. "'*Do not profane your daughter by making her a harlot—*'"

Beth swatted the book out of her hands to the floor. "I'm not doing anything wrong, and you bloody well know it. So why does it *bother* you?"

"I didn't give you permission to—"

"I am twenty-five years old!"

"It's my house, you'll obey my rules—"

"BP pays me a salary of one hundred and fifty pounds a year, and I give it all to you! I've earned the right to—"

Mrs. Finch seized Beth's arm. For the first time, Beth put her hands to her mother's shoulders and shoved her back. The skin inside her elbow stung, and she realized how unerringly her mother's strong fingers always found that spot where the flesh was the most tender. She couldn't remember the last time her arms hadn't been bruised blue.

"Please." Beth's father stood wringing his hands. "Can we all have a cup of tea and—"

"Where were *you* when she put my dog out?" Beth rounded on him. The spark of rage had grown to a cloud, billowing up inside her throat, choking her. "Why didn't you stop her? Or why didn't you get out of your armchair and take him out yourself when I was working late, so he didn't make a mess in the first place?"

"Well—" Mr. Finch shifted, uncomfortable. "She said I shouldn't—"

"It's your house, too!" Beth cried. "But you never tell her no. *Do* it, Dad. Tell her I can keep my dog. Tell her to stop badgering me. Tell her to *stop*."

Mrs. Finch folded her arms tight, a spot of color burning high in each cheek. "I want that dog gone, and that is final."

Silence. Boots whined beside Beth's feet. She could feel Osla and Mab behind her like sentinels. Mr. Finch cleared his throat, opened his mouth. Shut it again.

Mrs. Finch gave a sharp nod, eyes boring into Beth. "What do you have to say now, miss?"

"If the dog goes, so do I," Beth said, drawing a long breath. "And the next time you get a headache you can wring out your own washcloth, you Sunday school bully."

This time it was Mrs. Finch's hand that whipped out. Beth stepped back, and the blow missed. Mr. Finch seized his wife's arm before she could swing again. "Muriel—Beth—let's sit down—"

"No." Beth turned away and fumbled her coat on, numb and shaking. "I'm going."

"So are we." Mab brushed past Mrs. Finch, Osla marching straight after her. A moment later Beth heard their footsteps up the creaky stairs, heard the bedroom door open, heard the sound of traveling cases sliding out from under beds. Mrs. Finch turned a mottled red, lips pressing together in a tight line. Beth looked at her another long, dreadful moment, then turned away to fetch her handbag and a lead for Boots. She knew she should go upstairs and gather some things, but she couldn't make herself retreat even one step further into the house. The dreadful stillness spread and spread.

In no time at all, Mab and Osla clattered back downstairs, carrying not just their own traveling cases but Beth's, exploding with hastily stuffed slips and blouses. "The road you are walking leads to *hell,*" Mrs. Finch said, white with fury.

"At least you won't be there," said Beth.

The three of them walked out of the house where Beth had lived all her life, Boots trotting at their heels, and shut the door behind them.

CHAPTER 29

As far as Mab knew, princes married princesses, not Canadian commoners—therefore, Philip of Greece had no business making Osla fall head over heels, and Mab wasn't prepared to warm to him. Still, she had to admit he was a looker as he picked the three of them up from Euston station in his rakish little Vauxhall, fair hair rumpled. "Hullo, princess," he greeted Osla, and his grin made even Mab's impervious pulse flutter. "I hear you and your damsels are in need of rescuing."

"No daffing about, Philip, we barely escaped with our lives." Osla leaned over the Vauxhall's door to kiss him, and though it was a brief kiss, the heat of it made Mab wonder if that midnight talk about the facts of life had come just in time. "Philip, meet Mab Churt and Beth Finch," Osla continued. "The three of us are temporarily homeless and absolutely knackered."

Philip hopped out and shook hands. Mab did her best to look like she met princes every day, and Beth spoke for the first time since leaving Bletchley on the train they'd caught by the tips of their fingers. "Do you have anything to drink?"

"Fizz, coming right up." Philip's eyes gleamed as he threw their bags in the boot. "So, why the SOS so late at night? I sense a story."

Osla shrugged. "Beth's mother flipped her wicket—"

"Bitch," Mab couldn't help muttering. "I'm sorry, Beth, but she is."

"She is," Beth agreed. She looked pale and wrung out, climbing in the backseat with Boots, but Mab thought something inside Beth had *unwound* somehow. It had left her shaky but defiant, shoulders squared as never before. *Hurrah, Beth,* Mab thought with a rush of pride as the Vauxhall shot off into the night. Wherever the BP billeting officer bunked them next, it simply couldn't be worse than Mrs. Finch. No more nosy questions, no more leathery Woolton pie . . .

"Claridge's, darling," Osla was saying to Philip. "My mother's at Kelburn Castle on a house party, so her suite's empty . . ."

The hall porter at Claridge's greeted Osla like a long-lost niece, and Mab and Beth like royalty. "A gentleman waiting inside for you, Miss Churt. A Mr. Gray—"

Mab flew inside. The art deco hotel court with its glittering chandelier and black and white tiles was thronged with women in satin and men in uniform, champagne corks popping as everyone celebrated the Americans' entering the war. To Mab, that already felt like it had happened a year ago. She craned her head, and there was Francis, standing hands in his pockets, watching the party with that air of distant enjoyment she knew so well. He looked less tanned—evidently he hadn't seen much sun, these last two months in America—but the smile was the same.

"Francis," she called, and there was a moment's awkwardness as they both hovered, visibly wondering whether to embrace or shake hands. They hadn't worked any of that out yet—they hadn't worked *anything* out, really, though they'd been engaged since September. Finally Mab stepped forward and kissed his cheek. He smelled like sandalwood and his hair looked so soft she wanted to run her hands through it, but she didn't quite dare. "I didn't think you'd be able to meet me on such short notice." Mab had managed to ring him from Bletchley station, but what a way to reunite after nearly three months.

"You look well." His eyes went over her, that look that made her feel naked. "Your family, they're well too?"

"Yes, Lucy's back in London with Mum now that the bombings have tailed off." Francis had met them both, two days before he left for America—Mab's mother had been flustered by the posh tearoom and Lucy had been wary, not at all convinced that this stranger wasn't going to take Mab even more *away* than she already was . . . but Francis had been friendly, unflappable, and he hadn't raised even the hint of an eyebrow at Mab's post-tearoom suggestion that Lucy might live with them. With that, Mab had exhaled her last bit of caution. It was all going to be just fine.

Another silence fell.

"I wish we'd been able to write more." Mab tried not to sound accusatory. Overseas post was spotty, and telephone calls cost a fortune—Francis had sent a telegram when he'd arrived in Washington, but there had only been postcards afterward. It had been difficult not to wonder if he was regretting his offer. If he'd come back wondering what he'd been thinking when he folded that big ruby into her hand . . . "I can't believe it's been nearly three months!" she said brightly.

"Two months, one week, and four days," he said, and the knot of anxiety in Mab's stomach eased. If a man was counting the days, it wasn't because he was looking to take his ring back.

"How was Washington?"

"Not much I can tell you, I'm afraid. Busy. Cold. Too many Americans. Your work?"

"Not much I can tell you, I'm afraid. Busy. Hot. Too many machines."

Another exchange of smiles, a visible sense of wondering if they should join hands or kiss again, or . . . *Surely we'll learn to talk to each other,* Mab thought, *once we're married.* Once they could do their *not talking* in a bed. Mab wished they could get on with that side of things now—his tie was rumpled, and something in her was rising, wanting to yank it *off* . . .

Give away nothing for free, the steely voice in the back of her mind said. The voice that had held her upright when Geoffrey Irving and his friends left her on the side of the street. *Give away* nothing *for free. Even at the eleventh hour.*

By this time the others had squirmed through the celebratory crowd. Introductions were made, Osla embellished the story of their departure—"Beth was an absolute *brick*!"—and Philip went off to order Bollinger and came back with brimming coupes. Beth slugged hers with surprising speed.

"Steady on—" he said as she swallowed the second glass before he'd half refilled it.

"I just told my mother she was a Sunday school bully," Beth said.

"Drink up." He refilled her glass before turning to Francis. "You're a lucky man, Mr. Gray. When's the happy day?"

Francis looked at Mab, one of those quiet glances with something burning behind it. "I'm leaving London again day after tomorrow," he said. "No time to arrange a proper wedding and honeymoon until I get back. Three more weeks—"

"Or there's the registry office," Mab heard herself saying. "What about tomorrow?"

"MR. GIBBS," OSLA SAID, descending on the hall porter with a ravishing smile. "My friend is getting married tomorrow, and she is going to need a slap-up wedding party. Can you help me?"

"Yes, Miss Kendall," he replied, not batting an eyelash.

"Good. Bollinger, enough to get all London kippered, and the best wedding breakfast rationing will allow. How many eggs can you get your hands on? Foie gras? What about beluga? Put it on my mother's bill. I'm also going to need the room number of every guest currently staying in this hotel with a daughter aged . . ." Osla looked back at Mab. "How old is Lucy?"

"Nearly six." Mab choked, helpless with laughter.

"Between the ages of five and seven," Osla finished to Gibbs. "Please send notes to all their parents, and beg emergency morning loan of their daughter's best frock. I will be by at nine sharp tomorrow morning to inspect the selection."

"I'm not sure I—"

"Don't let me down, Mr. Gibbs." Osla pressed a wad of bills into his hand and turned, hands on hips, a general surveying the troops. "Francis, I'm sending you home so your bride can get her beauty sleep. Come back at eleven tomorrow, in your best suit, with rings and whatever bits of paper one needs for a marriage license. Philip, if you can collect Mab's mother and sister tomorrow morning at nine, and deliver them to Cyclax round the corner, where we'll get our faces done. Your mother's address, Mab?"

Mab, giggling, gave it. *Mum is going to faint, being chauffeured to my wedding by a prince!*

"Right," Philip grinned, clearly thinking it the best lark in the world to use up his precious petrol coupons in a mad dash across London for a Shoreditch mother of the bride. Mab's urge to distrust him melted. "Come on, old man." The prince clapped Francis on the shoulder. "I'll drop you home tonight. I might know a chap who can grease the wheels at the registry office . . ."

"Excellent. We convene here at eleven tomorrow, and you slackards will *not* be late! Say goodbye to your fiancé, Mab, you and I have a closet to raid." Grabbing the bottle of Bollinger and three glasses, Osla headed for the stairs. Beth followed with Boots, and after a hasty kiss to Francis, Mab floated along behind, still laughing. "My mother's suite," Osla said, waving them into the opulent set of rooms, with its massive bed, the bathroom with its huge tub and shining mirrors. "You can borrow it for your wedding, you and Francis—Mr. Gibbs can find Beth and me another bunk."

"All right," Mab said immediately. She'd been prepared for a wedding night in Francis's bachelor digs before he left London and she departed for Bletchley, but my God, did she want a night of luxury if it was on offer. Not just because she'd never stayed in a sumptuous hotel, but because surely it would be easier to get to know a brand-new, all-but-silent husband when you were surrounded by satin sheets and champagne in ice buckets . . . Mab swigged from her coupe, feeling the first surge of wedding nerves. She was a bride. She was getting married *tomorrow.* To a man she'd only met six times . . .

"Beth, keep the fizz topped." Osla yanked open her mother's wardrobe and began flinging dresses around. "Now: a scrummy frock that will pass as a wedding gown . . ."

"Your mother's going to know if I raid her rack of Hartnells!" Mab yelped.

"She'll never miss one, and you are *not* getting married in your blue curtain liner, Scarlett O'Hara." Osla held up a dress: long sleeved, tight waisted, cream satin pleats cascading from the waist in devastating knife-edge folds. "This one."

Mab coveted that dress more than air. "I can't . . ."

Osla paid absolutely no attention, bless her. "It won't hit the ground on you, since Mamma's much shorter, so we'll hem it to the knee. Knee-length is better for a day wedding, anyway. Now, for Beth . . . we'll be your bridesmaids, of course. This smoke-blue chiffon would look scrumptious with some sashing . . ."

"This has been a very strange night," Beth said, sitting on the bed drinking straight from the champagne bottle. She looked tipsy and tired, but a smile hovered at the corners of her lips. "A *very* strange night," she repeated, looking at Boots ensconced on the nearest down pillow, snoring.

Osla raised her glass, beautiful alabaster face flushed pink. "To Mrs. Gray."

"And to you, Os." Mab lifted her own glass. "And Beth—" She wanted to say something about what they meant, the two of them. How she'd never in her life had such friends. But she didn't have the words to explain how much she felt, so she just raised her champagne, throat choked. "To Bletchley Park."

TEN DAYS UNTIL THE ROYAL WEDDING

November 10, 1947

CHAPTER 30

York

Osla could feel the waiter of Bettys tearoom hovering, irritated that the woman in the scarlet New Look coat and smart black toque hadn't ordered yet. Osla kept watch through the floor-to-ceiling windows for Mab's tall figure hurrying across the square but couldn't stop looking at the shop sign. *Bettys.* The lack of apostrophe was driving her potty. Why couldn't people punctuate properly, for God's sake?

And suddenly Mab was standing in the doorway, dressed in the latest go: huge-skirted midnight-blue coat, tiny sapphire-blue hat tilted over one eye at an insolent angle, black pearls at her ears and throat. Her gaze crossed the room to Osla with the force of a rifle shot. *Take the high road if she pulls out her claws,* Osla told herself, gazing back without smiling. *Stick to the matter at hand.*

"Tea?" The waiter sprang forward as Mab rustled through the nest of little tables and elegantly dressed women, and sank down at the table Osla had chosen—a secluded nook against a window, where no one would be able to hear their conversation if they whispered.

"A pot of Earl Grey," Mab said, as Osla said, "Scones, please." The waiter whisked off, and Mab arched those scimitar eyebrows.

"Scones? I thought you'd be watching your figure for the royal wedding."

So much for the high road or *the matter at hand.*

"Such a thumping bore," Osla said airily. "Can't believe I have to dig out Mamma's diamonds just to park myself in that old stone heap with a stunning view of a column and absolutely nothing else."

Mab tugged off her ink-blue gloves. "You're in the papers even this far north. The scandal rags, anyway. So much speculation about whether *a certain dark-haired Canadian beauty* would attend Prince Philip's stag party."

"You know the scandal rags." Osla stripped off her own gloves so Mab could see the emerald. "Thank goodness my fiancé doesn't give any credence to gossip columns."

Mab admired the ring. "Pity green doesn't suit you . . . Does your fiancé know the reason for this little jaunt?"

"Naturally not, darling. I'll wager your husband doesn't either. Just like he doesn't know you chose him less for his smile and more for his *assets*."

"I'm a practical woman, Os. You're the one writing *Tatler* fluff. Fairy stories . . . only in those, doesn't the girl usually get the prince in the end?"

The waiter chose that moment to return with tea and scones. Flowered Minton cups and saucers clattered in the charged silence. They sipped, staring daggers.

"Look, let's stop talking slush," Osla said finally. "Much as I would like to sit here trading unpleasantries, we have a decision to make."

Beth hovered almost visibly at the table. Mab's mocking expression shuttered, and her voice automatically dropped to a murmur inaudible to anyone but Osla. "I have trouble believing this guff about a traitor. If someone had been selling information to the Germans, the Luftwaffe would have bombed us flat. The fact that we went through the war without being targeted proves they never found out we were reading their bloody post."

Osla had thought of that, too. "They could have been running counterintelligence, feeding false information to misdirect us."

"Then they wouldn't have *lost*."

"Well, maybe it wasn't the Jerries this traitor was selling to."

"But the war's over. Why is this still so urgent?"

"Don't be dense; treason has no expiration date. And her note said this traitor is still very much a threat—"

"That sounds like a madwoman's paranoia to me," Mab stated.

"Paranoia, or just someone who worked at BP? Look at *us*." Osla gestured around the tearoom with its dazzle of crystal and silver, its brocade drapes. "We picked the table furthest from the others, and even so we're whispering and breaking off every time someone walks near. When I had a tooth worked on last year, I was so worried I'd mutter something classified while sauced on chloroform, I made them do the whole procedure while I was awake. It was *agony*."

Long pause. "I wouldn't take anything for pain when I gave birth." Mab stirred her tea, looking like it killed her to agree with anything Osla said. "The same reason."

"See? We're *all* paranoid. It's second nature by now. Beth's being cautious, not necessarily lying."

"Or she believes her own story. People who are insane tend to do that."

Osla picked a scone off the untouched plate. "If she's insane."

"Remember how hysterical she was at the end? We both thought—"

"I know," Osla admitted. "But looking back now . . . did she go mad or just get pushed to the brink? We were all strained to the limit by that point. I was on my beam ends, you were getting bottled every night—"

"I was not."

"You were a blinking mess, and everyone knew it."

Mab glowered, recrossing her legs under a swath of midnight-blue crinoline. "You think Beth's sane, then?"

Osla looked at her scone, which she'd reduced to a pile of crumbs. "Until the day she was carted away, I'd have laid money that Beth Finch was the least likely person at BP to crock up. She was a perfectly functioning machine. And even if she *did* crock up, she might have got better. People can." Osla remembered Philip's telling her how his mother had recovered from her breakdown and been released from Bellevue. *Iron will,* he'd guessed. Who had a more iron will than Beth?

Mab looked at her. They took simultaneous gulps of Earl Grey, and Osla had the feeling they were both wishing it were gin. Maybe they should have met in a pub, not a tearoom.

"Even if she's not mad," Mab said finally, "I can't swallow this idea that one of Beth's friends in Knox's section was a rat. They were supposed to be the best of the best. Who on earth could it *be*?"

"That's why we have to ask Beth." Osla looked her in the eye. "That's why we're going to Clockwell."

Inside the Clock

The asylum nurses talked of nothing but the royal wedding.

"Eight bridesmaids, all dressed by Hartnell. Princess Margaret, of course—"

Shut up about the wedding, Beth would have liked to shout through the door of her cell. *Talk about this surgery the new doctor here is so keen on, this* lobotomy.

"—Princess Alexandra of Kent; Lady Caroline Montagu-Douglas-Scott—"

Beth turned over on her cot, trying to listen, pushing down the wet cough that had lingered since her springtime bout of pneumonia. She was trying to get an afternoon doze—last night had stretched empty and sleepless, with the relentless seeping cold and her bitter flashing back to the minutes she'd spent on her knees before the red-haired orderly.

"—you know the princess had to use clothing ration coupons for her wedding dress, just like any other bride. I remember my sister's wedding during the war, she made a veil out of parlor doilies—"

Beth remembered Mab's wedding in London. The dash to the registry office, Mab in her ivory satin pleats; the wedding breakfast at Claridge's of ham salad and champagne followed by eggless cake; little Lucy twirling in a borrowed frock of pale pink lace as Mab and Francis were practically carried upstairs to the bridal suite . . .

That was a beautiful day, Beth thought, swallowing more coughs. No pompous Westminster ceremony could match it. Though ironically, Osla's escort to Mab's nuptials was the bridegroom of the upcoming royal wedding.

"Have you seen Prince Philip's picture?" A sigh from one of the nurses outside. "*So* handsome."

"He's German, though. You'd think our princess could do better than a Hun."

"I thought he was Greek . . ."

"He fought on our side. Besides, the Germans aren't enemies now. I'd be a lot more worried if he was a Russky . . ."

Russia—the new enemy. When Beth wasn't sifting through mental evidence on who Bletchley Park's traitor might be, she pondered who they might have been working for. She was fairly certain it couldn't have been Germany—the evidence she'd decrypted had been Soviet in origin, not German. Besides, if the Nazis had had access to the kind of information that passed through Dilly's section, they would surely have targeted Bletchley.

Silence outside. The nurses had moved on. Beth gave way to a fit of coughing, the sound from her lungs wet and ugly. *The pneumonia will come back this winter,* she thought, hacking into her pillow. *And this time it might kill me.*

If this lobotomy surgery didn't, whatever it was . . . but Beth pushed that thought away. She coughed up what felt like half a lung and finally turned over, mind limping in old, spent circles. Osla and Mab, cryptograms and traitors, Germany and Russia . . . the traitor had to have been working for the Soviets. The USSR and Britain had been allies back then, but that didn't mean Churchill trusted them—Beth could well imagine Uncle Joe snooping for more information than his colleagues were willing to share. And BP had always had its share of Marxist sympathizers, political dabblers from Cambridge and Oxford who quoted Lenin and talked about the proletariat.

Which of my friends sympathized with Russia? she wondered now. And wished for the thousandth time that she hadn't been so far inside the spirals of her work that she missed the discussions flying around her in Knox's section.

Because the war against Germany might have been over, but the struggle against the Soviet Union was only beginning. And Beth, doubling over in another fit of hacking, couldn't help but wonder if the traitor who had put her here was still sending information to the USSR.

FIVE YEARS AGO

February 1942

CHAPTER 31

FROM *BLETCHLEY BLETHERINGS*, FEBRUARY 1942

The madhouse has a new warden! Commander Travis has taken over from Denniston, at least on the Service side. Good luck to him controlling the inmates . . .

Not you again," Commander Travis said ominously.

"Is that any way to greet your favorite naval section translator, sir?" Osla grinned.

The other men in Travis's office—suited types, probably London intelligence men—gave censorious frowns, but Travis just sighed. "What is it this time? Sneaking an electric cooker ring into the signals cupboard so you could make toast on the night watch?"

"That was last week," Osla said.

"Sneaking into the new block the minute the walls were half-constructed, riding the wheeled laundry bin down the hall into the gentlemen's loo?"

"Two weeks ago."

Travis sighed again, looking out the window where, distantly, off-duty codebreakers were ice-skating on the frozen lake. "Then enlighten me."

"No pranks this time, sir." Though Osla didn't see what was wrong with a few hijinks. BP *needed* a little laughter to keep up morale—after the jubilation of December, everyone rejoicing in the joy of the Americans' entering the war, the New Year hadn't really started with a bang. The Yanks might have been in the fight but weren't here yet, and the fall of Singapore last week with more than sixty thousand British, Indian, and Australian soldiers heading into Japanese POW camps had plunged the entire Park into gloom. And something dire was happening in Hut 8 with the German naval codes—Osla had no clue what, but Harry and the rest of his section were going around looking like absolute death. "I'm actually here to make a point, Commander Travis," she said, bringing herself back to business.

Travis and the men behind him watched with bemusement, then embarrassment, then alarm as Osla fished discreetly among her clothes, removing a folded square of paper from her skirt waistband, another tucked inside her stocking top, and a third that had been wedged into a T-strap pump. She laid all three on Travis's desk. "Nobody saw me smuggling these out of Hut 4, sir."

His voice went from weary to cold. "What do you mean by sneaking decrypted intelligence out of your workplace?"

"Just blank scrap paper." Osla unfolded each square, demonstrating. She wasn't dim enough to try to illustrate her point here with real cryptograms. "I am proving to you that it is too blinking easy to get bits of paper out of one's hut. Ever since I went to work as a translator, I've been noticing how simple it would be to smuggle messages out of BP. I thought if I brought it to your attention—"

"There is no one here who would think to misappropriate intelligence, Miss Kendall. Our people are thoroughly vetted."

"I'm not saying it's likely we've got a spy at BP, sir. But if the wrong person here was blackmailed or threatened into obtaining information, they could do it rather easily, depending on where they worked—it's the simplest thing in the world to tuck a slip of paper in your brassiere when everyone's yawning on night shift." The men shifted at the word *brassiere,* and Osla nearly rolled her eyes. Point out a security leak and they shrugged; mention a woman's underclothes and everyone got in a wax. "Obviously I only know about naval section, but areas like mine would seem the obvious places to tighten up. Where the information goes through the translators and is legible—"

"I don't think we need security advice from a silly deb," one of the intelligence men behind Travis said rather nastily.

"You clearly need it from *someone,*" Osla shot back.

"Miss Kendall, I'm sure you meant well, but the matter has been considered. Stick to doing your job," Travis said sternly, "and writing your gossip-page fluff."

Osla refused to ask how he knew she wrote *Bletchley Bletherings.* This was an intelligence facility, after all. "Just because I write gossip-page fluff"—*And what on earth is wrong with fluff if it makes people laugh during a war, for God's sake*—"it does not mean I have fluff between the ears."

"Your concern about our security is noted. But it was very foolish to smuggle anything out of your hut, even blank paper. Go back to your section, and do not pull a trick like this again."

Osla stamped out, fuming. "In hot water?" Giles greeted her, leaning against one of the stone griffons flanking the mansion's front doors.

"Yes, and this time I didn't deserve it." What would it take to ever, ever be taken seriously? Osla knew she was the best translator in her section; she maintained a cracking pace of work and still found time to dash off a weekly chin-wag that had the entire Park in stitches; she had brought a legitimate potential security problem to the attention of her superiors—yet she was still just a bit of Mayfair crumpet. "Why aren't you ever in trouble, Giles? You take so many cigarette breaks, I'm amazed you get anything done at all."

"I'm not on break this time." Giles exhaled a stream of fragrant smoke. He refused to smoke anything but Gitanes; who knew what he paid for them on the black market. "My hut head told me to take twenty before he knocked my block off."

Osla blinked. "What about?"

"I was at the NAAFI kiosk getting some tea and listening to Harry express the rather mild opinion that the Russkies might be doing a touch better against Operation Barbarossa if we actually shared information with them. Uncle Joe being an ally, after all."

"How do you or Harry know we *aren't* sharing it?"

"If the Russians saw half the stuff that passes through my hut, they wouldn't be getting stomped quite so thoroughly on the eastern front." Giles offered Osla a Gitane. "Harry got quite hot under the collar about it."

"Maybe they aren't properly using the information we give."

"No, I suspect the PM is keeping his cards close. Doesn't trust Uncle Joe."

"Nothing we can do about that, surely."

"That's what I told Harry, but he was on a bit of a rant, and then my hut head said that was commie talk. Harry said you didn't have to be a commie to want to help an ally, I said he had a point, and my hut head told me to take twenty or he'd pound me." Giles rolled his eyes. "It was Harry's rant, not mine!"

"Yes, but Harry's enormous. No one's going to threaten to pound him." *If I were Harry's size and a man, they'd have taken me seriously in that office . . .* Osla took a long drag, still hacked off at that contemptuous *silly deb* from the intelligence fellow. "I really cannot stand those MI-5 types." She was going to absolutely roast them in the next *BB*.

"It's mutual, I assure you," Giles said airily. "Intelligence chaps hate that the information they rely on comes from the kind of people they used to bully at school. Namely women, weedy fellows who were better at maths than games, and pansies."

"Who here's a pansy?" Osla asked, intrigued.

"Angus Wilson, for one. You hear things about Turing, too."

"Goodness, who knew?"

"Me, because I'm all-knowing."

"You're not all-knowing, you're *annoying,*" Osla informed him.

"Granted, but you love me anyway."

"Oh, do I?"

"Because I don't slaver over you, and girls like you are so used to being slavered over, you'll adore any fellow who just wants to be chums."

Osla grinned. "Aren't you perceptive?"

"Perceptive enough to know no one else is going to beat Prince Charming. Don't waste any time nailing him down, that's my advice. I dithered about too much and lost the girl of my dreams."

"Giles, I never. Who is she? Maybe it's not too late to take a puck at her."

"Oh, it's too late. The ink's barely dry on Queen Mab's marriage certificate." Giles clapped a melodramatic hand to his heart. "I'm soft as a sponge about her. Daft as a basket. By the time I was ready to make my move, Mr. Sensitive Bloody War Poet swooped in."

"You don't seem *too* heartbroken, Giles. If I know you, you'll console yourself with a string of Wrens."

Giles snorted, Osla ground out her cigarette, and they parted ways. "I told you Travis would give you a set-down!" Sally Norton called over when Osla came back into Hut 4.

"I'm already missing Denniston," Osla grumped, squeezing in at the crowded table of translators. The close quarters didn't make it any warmer; they all sat shivering over their stacks of reports, wrapped in scarves and mittens against the hut's arctic chill. Osla was snuggled inside the huge wool overcoat belonging to her Café de Paris Good Samaritan, Mr. J. P. E. C. Cornwell—who cared if it was like wearing a circus tent; it was *warm*. And it still smelled like him, some combination of smoke and heather . . . She might not know the man's name, but just from wearing his coat she knew he had excellent taste in cologne and shoulders like Alps.

She blew on her hands, steeling herself to pick up the half-translated report waiting to be finished: a page of idle chatter between German radio operators who should have kept better discipline on air, but the Y-stations transcribed idle chatter as well as official traffic . . . and these men had been discussing the rumor that Jews were being murdered on the eastern front, lined up on the lips of ditches and shot as the German army advanced.

It's not verified, Osla told herself. *It's vicious gossip between bored men.* But even in a spotty transcript with missing words, she couldn't miss the lightheartedness, the fact that those radio operators thought it all a great joke. Even if it wasn't true, they thought it was a perfectly decent idea.

My God, but I wish I was Mab or Beth. Or at least, sometimes Osla did. She wasn't begging off the job she'd worked so hard to get—it was too important—but neither Mab nor Beth spoke German, so they didn't have the burden of understanding whatever information came through their hands on duty. Osla dreamed at night of the things she translated, dreams that inevitably got muddled with the explosion at the Café de Paris. Sometimes she could wake herself before she had to watch Snakehips Johnson's head be blown off, but more often she was bound inside the memory until the bitter end. Only it *didn't* end; she just shook and wept in the bloodied rubble, and no one wrapped her in a coat that smelled like smoke and heather, and called her Ozma of Oz.

Sit down, Ozma, and let me see if you're hurt . . .

"Who's Ozma of Oz?" she mused aloud when she met up with Mab and Beth at shift's end.

"What?" Mab asked, buttoning her coat.

"Never mind. Is that another letter from Francis I see poking out of your pocket, Mrs. Gray?" They climbed aboard the transport bus—the one disadvantage of their new billet was that it was eight miles away, no longer a five-minute stroll from the Park. Not that it wasn't worth a daily bus ride just to avoid the Dread Mrs. Finch. "Are you finally getting a proper honeymoon?"

"Francis is taking me to the Lake District."

"About bally time. Have you had a single night together, these last two months since you tied the knot?"

"Not the way our schedules clash. It's just been the odd café dinner or tea at a railway station between shifts." Mab's face didn't exactly soften at the mention of her husband—Queen Mab wasn't the sort to go buttery around the edges—but she gave her wedding band a pleased twirl, and Osla felt a jab she couldn't even pretend wasn't envy.

As soon as she got home, she rang London. "Hullo, sailor."

"Hullo, princess."

Philip's voice came warmly down the line. He was staying with Lord Mountbatten until the lieutenant's exams—Osla could hear the rustle of paper. "Burning the midnight oil?"

"Writing a letter, actually."

"Sending love notes to some tart?" Osla teased. "I just know you fell into the arms of a hussy or two whenever your ship nipped into port."

"Darling, that's not something a gentleman can talk about." Which meant, of course, that it had happened. Women had to be good, but not men out to sea halfway around the world. Unfair, but there it was.

"As long as those hussies are on the other side of the world, I can leave them be," Osla decided. "Who's the letter for?"

"Cousin Lilibet, and she's still in the schoolroom, so don't get a case of the green-eyed monster."

"Princess *Elizabeth*? That cousin?"

His shrug was almost audible. "She began writing me when she was thirteen. I send her a line now and then. She's a nice little thing."

Every so often, it struck Osla all over again that her Philip was, in fact, a prince. She knew he was descended from Queen Victoria; she knew he sometimes visited Windsor Castle—and apparently he was posting letters to the future queen of England, whom he was allowed to call *Lilibet*. Still, it was difficult to reconcile the prince with the irreverent, tousle-haired naval officer who drove too fast and kissed her senseless.

"What's on your mind, Os?"

So many things. The frustration of being tossed out of Travis's office without a fair listen; the worry that someone really *might* smuggle decrypted reports out of BP. Nightmares of the Café de Paris; the horror of hearing that Jews were being murdered in eastern Europe . . . if only she could say it aloud. Philip told her so much: his mother, his dreams about Cape Matapan, his sadness at being cut off from his sisters in Germany. What could she tell him? Absolutely nothing.

How could you hope to build anything with a man, when so many of the things you had to tell him were lies?

"Nothing," she answered brightly. "Just bored to tears out here!"

"Better bored than in danger. You've no idea how glad I am you're safe in boring old Bucks." A pause. "I love you, you know."

Osla caught her breath. He'd never said that before, not aloud. She hadn't, either. "I love you," she whispered back.

So let's make it official, Philip. The words trembled on her tongue. *Run off to the registry office like Mab and Francis, make a home in hotel rooms whenever you're on leave. Why not?*

"Because princes don't marry commoners," Mab would have said. Sometimes Osla thought she was right—that surely there wasn't much future for Philip and herself, even if they *had* been going together for more than two years. At other times she was inclined to set her jaw and challenge the odds. Philip didn't have a kingdom to rule; he'd made his home in England like Osla; he fought for England like Osla. There was no reason he couldn't please himself, marry whom he chose. It wasn't as if Miss Osla Kendall were a chorus girl dancing on a bar in her garters—she'd been presented to the king and queen; she had funds from her dead father that she'd inherit when she was thirty or when she married, whichever came first. She had a job that mattered, helping save lives, and she was damned good at it. *I'm good enough for Philip of Greece,* Osla thought defiantly. *I'm good enough for* anyone.

"Are you sure nothing's on your mind, princess?"

"Flimflam and feathers, darling. You know me." If there was still a world left by the end of this war, there'd be time to work out what that world held for her and Philip. Today, there was only the now, and she wasn't going to waste the now obsessing about what lay ahead. "Want to take this dizzy debutante out dancing?"

"You're far more than a dizzy deb."

"I'm glad someone thinks so."

CHAPTER 32

FROM *BLETCHLEY BLETHERINGS*, FEBRUARY 1942

Those men who slither up from London, you know the ones, with their pin-striped suits and their hints about all the secrets they know . . . why are they all such crashing bores? Ian Fleming from the Admiralty (known as the Phlegm among the many BP females he has backed into a corner) is a classic case in point: damp hands, gin fumes, slinks about like something out of a cheap spy novel. *BB* wonders if his Berlin equivalents are just the same . . .

Mab groused when their joint alarm went off, and Osla burrowed under her pillow with a moan, but Beth always sprang from bed early, blood humming in her veins.

"I hope you three don't mind sharing the top room," their new landlady had said as she welcomed them to the redbrick Queen Anne house in Aspley Guise. "I know you girls like your privacy, but I've already got a philosophy professor billeted in my other spare room."

"We'll be snug as biscuits in a tin," Osla had reassured her as Beth stood in the middle of their new digs, bursting with happiness. A big light-filled room with two beds and a wide couch for a third; a bathroom of their own to share—no more outdoor loo!—and an overgrown lawn behind the house where the landlady promised to take Boots every day if Beth was working late, because she *liked dogs*. It had seemed too much to hope for, getting a decent place the three of them could share. Beth had been terrified she'd get lobbed in with new billet-mates—strange girls who would think she was odd, laugh at her absentmindedness, tap their temples with one finger when Beth said something that didn't make sense because she was thinking about the Abwehr Enigma.

It was Giles who pulled strings and landed the three of them together. "It's a beaut of a place," he said of lovely, friendly Aspley Guise. "I will happily accept physical demonstrations of gratitude—" Mab and Osla had promptly kissed his cheeks, and Beth managed to give him a hug.

It wasn't just the house. *I do not have to see Mother. I do not have to see her or hear her or feel her nails in my arm.* And Beth had her work—work she was getting so good at. A tricky new network had popped up at the beginning of the month, the one Dilly called the GGG after the call sign of the Abwehr office in Algeciras, which used it constantly. "Put Beth on that," he said, standing up too quickly and steadying himself with a hand on his desk. "She'll turn it inside out if you give her a lever, a chisel, and enough coffee. It's all their traffic on the Strait of Gibraltar, and God knows we can't let their spies start messing with *that* . . ."

Beth didn't really care what the GGG Enigma did or what kind of information it passed. It was just a new puzzle. "Are they transmitting weekly?" Taking the stack from Dilly with one hand, she raised the other to pluck the spectacles off his nose where he'd perched them upside down and drape them back right-side up.

"Messages from Abwehr offices in Tetuán, Ceuta, and Algeciras to Madrid nearly every day. Shipping movements and aircraft spotted near the entrance to the Mediterranean, likely. It goes to Berlin on the standard Abwehr cipher, but this local one is its own beast."

Yet Beth had an eye for the beast now. *You're just another ugly little four-wheel egg waiting to be cracked,* she told the stack of messages, plucking her pencil out of her knotted hair. She had a *feel* for the way those four-wheels worked; she couldn't describe it any better than that. Not that it wasn't hard, painstaking work, of course it was, but she had a sense of what she needed, what kind of message might produce the prized crack. Of course, they were trying to find the message sent on GGG *and* its corresponding message on the main cipher . . . "I need a GGG message where the time and length of the intercept pinpoints the actual repeat message with a minimum of textual additions—" She gave a yelp of triumph when one landed on her desk. "Come here, you—!"

It took Beth two weeks. She dearly wished she could have had Harry to work on it with her—it would have been much less frustrating—but when that wheel wiring came out of the fug of letters in front of her, she let out a whoop. "I've got it," she said, looking around the room. "With the right-hand wheel locked, standard rodding and charting will pry it the rest of the way open." She massaged her neck, which she only now realized ached like it had been squeezed in a vise. "Where's Dilly?" She couldn't wait to tell him.

Phyllida and Jean were looking at her a little oddly. "Don't you mean Peter?"

"Peter who?"

"Peter Twinn. From Hut 8? He's running our section now."

"What?"

"For God's sake, Beth. He might be on a different shift rotation, but he introduced himself to the whole section weeks ago. When he took over for Dilly."

"Well, yes. But that's only temporary . . . ?" Beth felt the statement trailing upward into a question. She remembered someone giving a speech, *Hallo, I'll be heading things up now,* but she'd been eleven hours into a double shift, following the chains down the spiral, barely listening. "I thought Peter was filling in until Dilly was feeling better." He couldn't be gone for good. The entire section was now designated Illicit Services Knox—what was ISK without Dilly?

"Dilly isn't ever going to feel better. Don't you ever get your head out of the rods and lobsters?" Phyllida drew a short breath. "He is *dying*."

"HULLO, DEAR." MRS. KNOX greeted Beth at the door of Courns Wood, not looking at all surprised to see her there, white faced and twisting her hands. "Did one of the transport drivers drop you?"

"I've brought some papers for Dilly." Files were usually assigned a courier, but Beth had leaped on the chance today. "May I see him?"

"Of course, dear. He'll be delighted to see you; he talks of you so often. Peggy Rock comes when she can . . ."

Beth cringed with shame as she followed Mrs. Knox up the passage. Peggy had come to visit. Peggy knew Dilly had been cutting back his time at BP since autumn, and why. Beth hadn't even realized he was coming into work less and less, never mind guessing the reason behind it. She hadn't seen anything, really, not for months, unless it was in a cryptogram waiting to be deciphered.

Dilly looked up as the library door opened, glasses perched on top of his head. He was sitting in his leather chair facing the long view onto the terrace, and he had a lapful of messages and rods. "Oh, hullo, Beth," he said absently. "Have you seen my glasses?"

For a moment, Beth couldn't speak. She wanted to weep, because now that she was actually looking, she could see how thin he was, how his hair, which had once been largely dark, was graying. She walked across the room and took the glasses off the top of his head, her hand shaking. "Here, Dilly."

He rearranged the specs on his nose, peering up at her. "I see someone's been telling tales," he said. "We'd better have a drink."

He set his papers aside, rose stiffly, and went to the decanter. As he'd done the day Beth made her first break into Enigma, he mixed a gin and tonic. "Drink up. You've been working all night, I take it?"

"Yes," Beth managed to say. "I broke the GGG Enigma."

"Well done, you!" He beamed. "The best of my Fillies. You and Peggy, and you might be a hair tougher than Peggy."

"Is something wrong with her?" Now that Beth was looking back on the last few months, at all the things she'd completely ignored, she realized she hadn't seen Peggy at work for a while either. "I thought she'd changed shifts . . ."

No, Beth told herself brutally. *You didn't think that.* She hadn't even noticed that her favorite colleague, a woman she considered a friend, was gone in the first place.

"Peggy's a bit run down." Dilly eased back into his chair, and Beth didn't miss the pain that flashed across his face. "Pleurisy, but it's as much nervous exhaustion as illness. She's been sent home for bed rest."

Nervous exhaustion. Breakdown. There were a hundred euphemisms at BP, but everyone knew what it meant. It meant you'd cracked, snapped, broken. Peggy Rock, as impervious as her name, had cracked. Beth sat clutching her glass. What else did this day hold?

"She'll be back." Dilly seemed quite certain. "It happens, you know. Strain. It gets even the best brains in the business. Sometimes the best brains are the ones that get it worst."

They sat quietly, sipping.

"How's Peter Twinn carrying on?" Dilly asked finally. "He's a good chap, for a mathematician. Promised he'd let my girls work the way they were used to working."

"Have you really stopped working yourself? This doesn't look . . ." Beth waved at the messages and rods he'd laid aside.

"Oh, I'm not out of the game. Twinn runs my section day-to-day, but I've still got my hand in, working from home where Olive can keep an eye on me. I'll be at the rods and cribs till they carry me out in a box."

He laughed, but Beth flinched as if she'd been struck. "Don't say that. Surely it can't be as serious as—"

"Lymphatic cancer, m'dear. Had my first surgery right before going to meet the Polish cryptanalysts in '39, pooling our knowledge on Enigma." He smiled. "Don't look so long faced! Some rest and a cruise will put me right, I'm sure."

Beth wasn't. He looked *so* ill . . . How obscene that in the middle of a world-enveloping war, with so many dying in bombing raids and on battlefields, people could still suffer from mundane diseases. Perhaps it was also obscene to be so overwhelmed by one man's mortality with so many others dying every day, but she couldn't help it. A small choked noise escaped her before she could stop it.

Dilly handed her a handkerchief, then picked up his pile of messages and decrypts and walked to the library wall, clearly giving her space to compose herself. He pressed an oak panel, and it sprang open to reveal a little wall safe. "As long as I take a few precautions, Travis lets me take home whatever I want. The odd networks, the ones no one has time to work on but me." He stuffed the heap of paper inside, started to close the door, peered back in, and pulled out a pipe with a murmur of "So that's where you've been hiding." Then he locked the safe with a key hanging from his watch chain before closing up again. "Can't leave raw intelligence lying about, even in the middle of Bucks! Now tell me, how'd you break GGG?"

CHAPTER 33

FROM *BLETCHLEY BLETHERINGS*, FEBRUARY 1942

What recently wed BP amazon is dashing north as we speak, headed for a romantic weekend in the Lake District with her war-poet husband? Pack your Wordsworth, that's all *BB* can say—and does anyone else think all those Lake District poets should have got jobs rather than gassing on about daffodils . . .

Mab Gray. It sounded like a Brontë heroine, a woman who strode fearlessly across hilltops. Someday, Mab thought, she *would* stride across hilltops; Francis said his house in Coventry wasn't far from the countryside. Mab imagined walking along a sunny meadow, picnic basket swinging between them, Lucy running ahead, getting hooked up in golden brambles of gorse. *What* is *gorse, anyway?* wondered the London-bred Mab. It sounded picturesque, anyway.

The compartment was cold, jammed with soldiers who kept pestering her to get a drink with them. Outside, icy gray rain slashed down the train windows, and Mab wondered if the Lake District was always this wet. She'd proposed meeting in Coventry, but her new husband was politely firm. "I'd rather not take you to our house until we can live there for good," he'd said over the telephone last week, when they realized they'd have a whole thirty-six hours together at the end of the month. "What about Keswick? It's a postage stamp of a place in the Lake District."

Mab rotated the gold band around her ring finger, still wishing it was Coventry she was traveling to. If she could walk through the house that was going to be their home someday, maybe she'd feel more . . . married.

It was so *strange,* this limbo they were living in. That madcap London wedding, and the following day a hasty goodbye at Euston station as Mab caught the train back to Bletchley with Osla and Beth, and Francis headed out on another journey for the Foreign Office. They'd agreed it would be best for her not to relocate to his single boardinghouse room in London—after all, he was at his office or traveling nearly round the clock, and Mab too had important work to do. "I'd rather have you safe in Bucks than in London anyway," Francis said. "The bombings have tailed off, but there's no guarantee the Luftwaffe won't come crashing in again."

Since the wedding night at Claridge's, they hadn't had a single night together—only the occasional meet-up for tea or an early supper in a London suburb or railway café. Mab had never anticipated life after marriage proceeding more or less exactly as it had before.

It's hardly a unique situation, she reminded herself. Husbands and wives all over Britain were in the same pickle: the men off fighting, the women up to their necks in war work; weekends snatched whenever someone had leave. At least Francis wasn't on the front lines as a younger man would have been; he spent his days in an office and Mab didn't have to worry like Osla had when her prince was out to sea being targeted by U-boats. *We just have to wait out the war, then married life can start.* When they would live under the same roof, when Mab would butter her husband's toast in the morning, make his house welcoming, and ensure she was a wife to be proud of.

How did you do that at long distance?

Write letters, Mab had told herself. Cheerful letters, not too long—men didn't want to be inundated, just know that they were missed. And she *did* miss him, so she put the first letter together like a dress pattern, meticulous, affectionate, wifely, not expecting any kind of lengthy answer. Everyone knew men hated writing letters, and Francis barely had two words to say in person. So Mab was startled by the thick packets that started arriving from London.

> *Darling girl—a quick line on my tea break. The tea here is disgusting: viscid, gelatinous, mouse-colored dishwater through which a tea leaf has perhaps in the last generation or so briefly passed. You would arch your regal eyebrows at it and it would slink wetly out of the cup, never to return. I lack your courage to challenge this gelid mess in my saucer, and drink it down with little more than a mutinous whimper. I miss your regal eyebrows . . .*

> Or: *My dear Faerie Queene—what a day. Can you keep me from dreaming of it? I'm sure you can. Queen Mab is the mistress of dreams if we can believe Shakespeare (and whom else in this world can we believe, if not him?). Come galloping through my sleeping brain tonight in your squirrel-made chariot, and make me dream of love. Though Shakespeare does call his Mab a hag, which doesn't seem gallant for a husbandly metaphor. Maybe you are Y Mab Darogan of Welsh legend rather than*

a faerie Mab—the Destined One who will drive the English from the island. I can certainly see you leading armies, sword lifted high, face streaked blue and fierce . . .

Mab didn't know what to make of such letters. How could a man who talked like his vocabulary was as rationed as his meat be so verbose in print? Not just verbose, but funny, wry, moody, tender . . . yet she wasn't sure she understood him any better. Nothing he wrote ever touched on himself, but an envelope still winged from London nearly every other day. What was she supposed to write back? That the new billet was very nice, that the new landlady was very nice, that the weather was very nice? She couldn't say anything about her work and didn't have her husband's knack for spinning pages about daily trifles. Trying to carry on a conversation with Francis seemed destined to be one-sided—but whereas he was the silent one in person, by letter, *she* felt like the mute.

It will be different, she told herself, *after the war.* When they weren't trying to conduct a marriage almost entirely by post.

He was waiting on the platform when Mab stepped down, hatless under an umbrella streaming rain off its edge. "Not the weather I hoped for," he said, kissing her gloved knuckles.

"No walks around the lake, no picnics by the water? Whatever shall we do?" He smiled, eyes going over her with slow care. Mab laughed, touching her hair. "Do I look a fright?"

"No." He picked up her overnight case. "I forget you a little, every time, and then the sight of you shocks me all over again."

"It's—lovely to see you too," Mab said inadequately. "I, um. I got your letters."

"I blather. It's a bad habit."

"No, I like them . . . mine are very dull."

The hotel was narrow, Edwardian, looking out over the rain-lashed expanse of Derwentwater. Their room would have been cheerful in sunlight but it looked gray and rippled, as though it were all underwater. "We can take tea downstairs if you're hungry," Francis began as the door shut, but the words disappeared half-spoken as the overnight case clattered to the floor and they gripped at each other, pulling together like magnets.

On the night of their wedding in the borrowed suite in Claridge's, Mab's oh-so-new husband had been opening a half bottle of champagne when she came out in her negligee, and he'd gone so still he could have been a waxwork. Something flickered across his features, an expression too fast to catch, but something about it made his broad, calm, unremarkable face almost handsome. "Come here . . . ," he'd whispered as the champagne crashed over unopened. Mab had fallen into him wholeheartedly, focused on being warm and welcoming under the rumpled sheets. *Let me make you happy.*

"I take it you realize—I've done that before?" she ventured hesitantly afterward. She'd devoted many sleepless nights planning exactly how to broach the fact that she wasn't any schoolgirl innocent. She felt guilty for not saying it before the wedding, but she'd been too afraid it would ruin everything. Maybe it still would—if he rounded on her now and said anything about *spoiled goods,* she was going to shrivel up and die. "I'm no tart, Francis. It was only one—"

"Oh, darling girl. Not important," he said drowsily, and Mab fell asleep nearly limp with relief. The last hurdle cleared . . . only later that same night, Mab had wakened to see Francis sitting at the window in his half-buttoned shirt, sash hauled open to the icy winter night, cigarette drifting smoke between his still fingers. His face as he gazed out over the dark London streets had looked so shuttered Mab sat up in bed, half asleep and half alarmed.

"Francis?"

Slowly his eyes turned to her; he half smiled in that opaque, polite way. "Go back to sleep, lovely Mab."

Her drowsy ears listened for air-raid sirens, even as she slid back toward dreamland. "Nothing's wrong?"

"Only the world," she thought she heard him say.

Did you say that? Mab wondered now, even as her arms twined about his neck. *Do I know you at all?*

Well, this was surely a way to know him better. She began drawing him toward the bed, as she had in Claridge's, but Francis stopped her this time, taking her hands and turning them over in his as if he'd never seen anything so lovely before. He lifted them upward, lowering his head to press his lips against each palm, and then he took her face in his hands and gave her one of those long looks that nearly scarred her bones. Mab couldn't hold that gaze; she shied away from it, pressing her mouth to his so he'd have to close his eyes. He kissed her with his hands in her hair and at her shoulders, fingers sliding to feather her spine in unhurried strokes, not just using her mouth as a place to rest his while they pushed clothes out of the way. Not self-conscious at all that she was the one to bend her head to kiss him.

"You're the perfect height," he murmured against her breasts, and the room's underwater light filtered over his stocky shoulders as his shirt dropped atop her dress on the floor, followed by her slip and stockings, his braces and trousers.

"If you'll give me a moment—" Mab remembered with a jolt, stepping back and reaching for her handbag. "I have to do something first." She wordlessly showed him the little bag with her rubber device to prevent conception, feeling herself flush. On their wedding night she had taken care of matters when she changed out of her wedding dress; later, as he searched his wallet for a packet of French letters, she'd simply murmured, *No need, I saw a doctor and was fitted for, you know . . .* He'd grinned, put his wallet aside, and that had been that. But now she had to disentangle from him, take her bag awkwardly into the loo, fumble about in there while the clock outside ticked. Oh, this was awkward! She came out again, naked and self-conscious, aware she was blushing.

"Lovely Mab." Her husband didn't seem embarrassed at all, taking her back into his arms without any haste. He was solid, brown, stocky—he looked like he should have been walking a farm, not the corridors of the Foreign Office. He smiled, running a hand down Mab's long, pale-skinned leg. "How did a hill-bred cob like me land such a long-boned thoroughbred?" he said, kissing each of her shoulders.

Mab had always thought husbands would want things proper—done in the dark, under the covers; she could remember the rhythmic nighttime grunts coming through the thin wall when her father had still been at home. The wedding-night suite at Claridge's had been all shadows in the candlelight, and Francis had made no objection when Mab slid under the sheets; he'd come under them as well, and pulled her silently against him. Now he reached over and flicked the light on, and when Mab climbed under the covers, he turned them back. "Let me see you," he said quietly.

No, Mab almost said. She didn't know why it made her uneasy to be looked at; she wanted to prickle and hide; she wanted to pull him over her and get on with it. She didn't really like being naked, being seen. She didn't know if any of that flashed through her gaze, but he came on his side instead of moving over her, pulling her back snugly into the curve of his chest. ". . . Like this?" Mab blurted, startled. It occurred to her that for someone who had instructed both her billet-mates in the facts of life, there were a good many things she didn't know.

Francis kissed the space between her shoulder blades. "Like

this." He rubbed the length of her back, up and down, probably feeling the tension Mab couldn't stop from coiling through her, having someone at her back where she couldn't see them. "Trust me," he said against her spine.

I don't really trust anyone, Mab couldn't stop herself from thinking. Such a cold, hateful thought to have in bed with your own husband who had never given you any reason for wariness, but she couldn't help it. She could feel herself going rigid in his arms, and she couldn't stop it, but he just slowed, lips resting in the hollow behind her ear, one broad arm cradling her against his chest, one hand stroking unhurriedly up and down the length of her body. He stroked until her wary muscles loosened, and then he stroked even more slowly until they began to wind taut again for another reason entirely. Mab bit her lip as his hand traced over her belly. "Trust me," he said again against her ear, and Mab saw the outline of the rain sliding down the windowpane outside, making rippling shadows over his arm as his hand slid lower, agonizingly. Lower. "Relax . . ." He stroked her so slowly, unfolding her a touch at a time. Her back arched hard against him as she squeezed her eyes shut, and he only held her tighter against his chest, tethering her to the bed, tethering her to the world.

"I have you," he whispered as the shudders racked through her, and she felt his lips at the nape of her neck. Mab opened her eyes, limp and dizzy, trying to turn and pull him over her, but he only wrapped her more firmly in his arms, his knees behind hers, his shoulders behind hers, every inch of her already cradled inside his body before he moved into hers. Dimly Mab could hear the rain beating as they rocked together, nested like a pair of spoons. She gripped at his hands where he held her, hanging on for dear life, feeling the answering squeeze of his fingers as they fell into each other.

Francis didn't pull away afterward, only unwound one arm enough to pull up the covers over them, tucking the warm edge around her shoulders. Mab opened her mouth to say something, she wasn't sure what—*Do you think we've missed tea downstairs? Goodness, it's raining hard!*—but to her horror, she burst into tears. She didn't know why.

Francis moved a hand through her hair, tipping her head back against his shoulder. He kissed each of her wet eyelids. "You can trust me, Mab," he said very quietly.

She lay silent, her body limp and boneless, her eyelids still leaking, and she thought, *Maybe I can.*

But when she woke in the soundless blackness of three in the morning, his half of the bed was empty and she saw him sitting at the open window again in his half-buttoned shirt, staring into the night.

THERE WAS A note on her pillow when she woke in the morning.

Darling Mab, Francis had written. *I went for a walk at dawn. Yes, in the rain—I can see your eyebrows shooting up.* They were. *I always need a walk after night is done, weather regardless, and you were sleeping so soundly I didn't have the heart to wake you. You snore, by the way. It's delightful. Have a leisurely bath and I'll bring you up some toast. —F*

There was a postscript: *I shan't ask you his name, if you don't wish to share it, but I am rather assuming he hurt you in some way.*

Mab hesitated, fighting her immediate, spiky prickle of reaction, the urge to slam the door on that entire subject. She had never spoken about Geoff Irving or his horrible friends or that horrible night to anyone, ever. Had it been so obvious that someone . . .

Yes, maybe it was. If a man cared to look.

She still didn't think she could force the words through her lips.

Maybe I don't have to, she thought, eyeing the pile of hotel stationery.

Dear Francis—she couldn't quite bring herself to say *darling;* it didn't feel natural. She hesitated a long time, then wrote the words:

Yes, he did.

And I do not snore. —M

She was scrubbing her hair in the bath when she heard him come in on the other side of the door. She heard the crackle of paper unfolding, and she sat there in the tub, hugging her knees, water sliding down her naked back.

A moment later, a folded sheet of paper pushed under the bathroom door. She maneuvered an arm across the chipped black and white tiles and retrieved it.

I thought so. I shan't mention it again if you don't wish.

You do snore. But a very ladylike snore. Jane Eyre would snore like you. —F

Mab smiled, climbing out and wrapping herself in a towel. Wiping her hands dry, she fetched about and found a stub of eyebrow pencil from her cosmetics case. Cosmetics were too precious to waste, but she couldn't resist scrawling an answer and pushing it back under the door, heart jumping absurdly.

Now you're trying to impress me with books you haven't read. I have never met a man in my life who read a Brontë novel.

You wouldn't believe how the fellows in the Mad Hatters griped about Jane Eyre. *—M*

She heard an answering snort from the other side, and took her time toweling her hair and fixing her little contraceptive device again. Her heart leaped when the sheet of paper came back.

I have too read Jane Eyre. *Do you want a dog named Pilot someday, like Mr. Rochester? —F*

Yes. —M

Mab came out, wrapped in a towel. Francis was bent over the desk, scribbling something next to a cooling rack of toast. His collar stood open; drops of rain sparkled on his hair. He looked up, smiled, dropped the pen at the same time Mab dropped the towel, and they collided in another rush. They were still kissing as he lifted her to the edge of the table—Mab made a noise, feeling high and insecure away from the bed. She had to cling hard against him, her arms about his neck, her legs about his waist.

"I've got you." He put his lips to her ear, murmuring, "Thrash all you like, I won't let you fall." Mab clung, limbs coiling through his like a vine, his hands under her hips holding her steady, and by the end she trembled so she could hardly stand. Francis looked wry, touching a red mark on her breast and then rubbing his day's worth of stubble. "I didn't shave this morning," he said. "Bachelor habit—I'll have to do better."

He was lathering up over the washbasin in the bathroom, all bare feet and trousers and braces, as Mab closed the door just for the purpose of sliding the note under it. She heard him unfold it.

Lunch?

For the first time since meeting Francis Gray, she heard him laugh.

SHE WAS ON the train the next day. It had rained the entire weekend, and Mab hadn't set foot out of the room. She ate meals Francis brought up on trays from the coy landlady, plowed through half of *For Whom the Bell Tolls* (next week's Tea Party pick, since all men save her husband appeared unwilling to read *Jane Eyre*) when Francis left on his morning walks, made love to him when he came back, passed notes back and forth in a strange competition to see who could say the fewest words and write the most, made love again. He said nothing on the train platform, only picked up her hands, turned them over, dropped a kiss into each palm.

"You're not returning to London?" Mab asked finally.

"Some business in Leeds first." A half smile. "I'll see you when the stars align for another weekend, lovely girl." Who knew when that would be. Mab kissed him fiercely, not at all sure if she was relieved or upset. She had never felt so turned upside down and inside out—part of her welcomed the thought of BP's frenetic routine and midnight cups of Ovaltine; nothing unexpected to leave her unsettled. But part of her wanted to stay with her silent husband, and see where he led her next.

It wasn't until Mab settled into the compartment that she found the letter Francis had slipped into her coat pocket.

Darling girl—you're asleep as I'm writing this. You wonder why I sit up every night smoking and looking out the window, don't you? The truth is, I haven't slept more than four hours at a time since coming home from the trenches in '19. There used to be thrashing and shouting, hallucinations, dreams—but I found over the years that a cigarette and an open window does the most good, and then a walk at dawn to clear the cobwebs away. It doesn't leave me entirely settled, I'm too much a patched-together pot for that, but at least the pot is fit to hold water through the day to come.

There—now you know. It was troubling you, wasn't it?—F

Mab put her head back on the seat and blinked rapidly, wondering if she knew another man anywhere who would simply *admit* something like that in black and white. In her experience men either denied such things altogether or, if forced to acknowledge them, did so with crude jokes and rough shrugs.

She looked at the sheeting rain, buffeting down on the curve of the railroad track ahead. She still had the sensation that she was naked, even armored in her coat and gloves. Even though he was no longer here. Before the feeling faded and the armor was back, she took a pen from her handbag.

His name isn't important, she wrote on a scrap of notepaper, her mouth utterly dry, *but I thought I loved him.* She wrote out the whole story of Geoffrey Irving and his friends, factual and ugly; stuffed the page into an envelope; addressed it to Francis's London boardinghouse; and sealed it before she could change her mind.

You can trust me, Mab.

I hope so. She dropped it in the nearest postbox when she changed trains, heart thudding. *Don't ask for any more of my secrets, Francis.*

Because I can't give you the last one.

CHAPTER 34

FROM *BLETCHLEY BLETHERINGS*, MARCH 1942

It's not every day we see a vice admiral at BP, but the chief of combined operations himself turned up for a tour out of the blue. Isn't the whole point of an installation like this one that the top brass can't drop in whenever they feel like it? Commander Travis looked like he'd swallowed a moth . . .

Uncle Dickie, what are you doing here?" Osla blurted, jumping up from the translators' table. Not just Uncle Dickie but an entourage of naval types and some harassed-looking BP staff cramming into the room behind him.

"I knew my favorite goddaughters were here." The vice admiral beamed at Osla and Sally Norton, who stood equally frozen, though not so frozen they weren't hastily turning over the work in front of them. "I thought I'd see how you're getting on, eh? Show me this cross-reference index I've heard about . . ."

Osla saw tight, angry glances from the BP officials behind her godfather. Oh, *topping;* Commander Travis was absolutely going to flip his wicket. She tried to fade back as Sally led Lord Mountbatten to Miss Senyard's section, but her godfather pulled Osla's arm through his as the party trailed through Hut 4.

"You keep looking after my scamp of a nephew! Philip gets into trouble when you're not around. Smashed up my Vauxhall last weekend, racing with David Milford Haven. The lad sails all over the Mediterranean getting shot at and earns his first wound in a London blackout . . ."

Osla laughed dutifully as the naval party had their look-round, then trailed outside. This morning's rain had tailed off; the air was bright, and a good many curious codebreakers had nipped outside for a gander at the visitor in his gold braid. "Though after Churchill, how chuffed can one get over an admiral?" she could hear Giles saying, ambling over from Hut 6.

"We're sunk," Sally said, low voiced, at Osla's side. "Travis is going to have us hanged, drawn, and quartered."

"Don't talk slush. Not our fault Uncle Dickie showed up out of the blue."

"They can't shout at a vice admiral, so they'll shout at us, just you wait."

"I've no intention of waiting. I've got work to do." Osla saw her godfather off to the mansion, then fought her way back through the milling crowd toward Hut 4. Goodness, but the Park was getting crowded, every week bringing new recruits: Oxford boys and secretarial-pool women, shopgirls and invalided-out soldiers . . .

Hut 4 was almost empty, the workers yet to straggle back after the naval interruption. Osla's eyes were dazzled, coming into the dark hut after the flare of sun outside, and as she shaded her eyes she saw the flick of motion—a jacket, or a skirt—quickly sidling out of the room.

"Hello?" she called, puzzled. There were people coming and going in-hut all the time, but generally muttering and juggling mugs of tea, making no secret of their exit. Not furtively slinking out as if trying to remain unseen.

Osla followed the whisk of motion, coming into what was

laughingly called the Debutantes' Den. Miss Senyard's neat shelves of box files had become a proper index room, boxes stacked on boxes, everything filed and cross-correlated within an inch of its life . . . and two lids sat crooked on boxes of indexed reports, as if someone had been rummaging in a hurry. *Probably someone who made a request for information,* she told herself. But she went and poked her head into each of the other rooms. Nothing out of place at her own section; Mr. Birch's office was still locked . . . she thought she heard another footstep, a quiet creak of shoe leather on lino, and reversed back across the hut.

The door to the outside was still swinging. Osla pushed through, coming to a halt. The path between Hut 4 and the mansion was still thronged with people, not just codebreakers but aides from Uncle Dickie's entourage. Whoever had slipped out just ahead of Osla could be anywhere in this crush. And she had no idea what she was looking for, if that furtive whisk of a hem had been a skirted woman or a man in a jacket.

It likely wasn't anything sinister, Osla thought with a little mental shake. Just a filing girl hurrying for a look at the top brass, leaving a few boxes open in her haste. Slowly Osla went back inside, going through the two boxes with the lids askew. Hundreds of notecards; impossible to tell if anything was missing. Surely nothing was.

But she heard her own voice just a matter of weeks ago, arguing to Travis: *How simple it would be to smuggle messages out of BP . . . it's the simplest thing in the world to tuck a slip of paper in your brassiere when everyone's yawning on night shift.*

Or distracted by an admiralty's worth of distinguished visitors.

Someone had been in here. Osla drew a deep breath to steady herself, and the back of her neck prickled. She smelled something that teased her memory, something tantalizingly familiar. A cologne or perfume, hanging on the air? She inhaled again, but the room was heavy with the fug of coke stoves, overlaid by the morning's rain and the Odo-Ro-No some woman had dabbed under her arms this morning. Whatever that smell was that had prickled Osla's skin, it was gone.

You're imagining things, she told herself. But she went to see Commander Travis anyway as soon as Uncle Dickie's staff car had purred away, only to find Sally in tears before his desk, swearing that she had never peeped a word to her godfather about the naval section. Before Osla could say a thing about rifled file boxes, she was coming in for a rating, too. "Lord Mountbatten may be privy to a certain amount of information about Bletchley Park, but if you or Miss Norton have given him specific details about your work—"

"We have *not.*" For a long moment, Osla could feel her job hanging in the balance. The job she had worked so hard for. Sally was sobbing; Osla managed just barely to keep the tears out of her own eyes.

"All right." Travis sounded gruff, but he offered Sally a handkerchief. "I believe you, young ladies. Mop up, now."

"Sir, if I could report one more thing . . . ," Osla began, and trailed off. What had she seen, really? A whisk of skirt hem or jacket, a box left open, a familiar scent . . . and Travis was already in a flap. *Do you want to look like a champagne Shirley having the vapors?*

"Miss Kendall?"

"Never mind, sir. Nothing important."

CHAPTER 35

FROM *BLETCHLEY BLETHERINGS*, APRIL 1942

Hut 8, what on *earth* is wrong? You all look like you haven't slept since the Yanks were "those bloody colonials" rather than allies. *BB* has no idea what's going on in there, obviously, but get some sunshine and some gin before you all keel over.

The Mad Hatters had been holding their monthly Tea Party for nearly two years, but it was the first time Beth could remember anyone coming to blows.

"*Gone with the Wind* is a lousy book," Harry snapped.

"How dare you," Osla laughed. "It is an absolutely topping book."

"It's too long," Giles complained, lounging under the overadorned top hat. "Eight hundred pages . . ."

April had come in silky and fresh, and they'd taken the meeting to the lawn outside the mansion, the women sitting on their coats, the men leaning on their elbows in the grass. Beth arrived late, coming from a visit to Dilly, and now she wished she hadn't come—Harry was snappish, and his irritation was spreading.

"It's rubbish." He tossed *Gone with the Wind* to the center of the circle. "All that guff about the slaves being happy and grateful—does anyone believe that?"

"Scarlett does because it's what she's been taught," Mab pointed out. "It's mostly her point of view; we can't see things she doesn't."

Harry yanked a slice of bread off the plate. He was thinner, Beth thought, and his big hands had a fine tremor. She was trying to be more observant of her friends since realizing how colossally she'd failed to notice Dilly's deterioration. "Scarlett doesn't deserve to be the heroine," Harry went on. "She's a selfish cow."

"Agreed," Giles yawned. "She's hard as a fistful of nails."

Mab rolled her eyes. "God forbid women in books be any harder than a powder puff—"

"God forbid women in *life* be harder than a powder puff." Osla's dark curls ruffled in the breeze. "Living in a war zone isn't all fizz and bobbery. All of us have harder edges than we did a few years ago, and we don't have Germans actually setting fire to our homes like the Yankees with Tara. Why shouldn't Scarlett be hard?"

"She supposedly adores Mammy but never once calls her by name, or even seems to know if she has one," Harry began.

"Taking it a bit personally, aren't you?" Giles drawled.

"Maybe if your father-in-law asked you to your face if you had Negro blood, you'd take it a bit personally too," Harry said shortly.

"It's a flawed book." Beth tried to steer a middle course. "But I like Scarlett. I can't remember the last time the heroine of a book was good at maths or numbers—"

But Harry and Giles were still going at each other, ignoring the discussion. ". . . bit touchy, aren't you?" Giles said. "Learn to laugh, Harry. No need to be *thin* skinned as well as dark skinned."

In an eyeblink, Harry grabbed Giles by the collar and levered him halfway off the grass. Beth froze, seeing his fingers ball into a fist, but Mab grabbed his elbow before the blow could fly. "Not where Commander Travis can see you," she said sharply. "He's cracking down on everything since those Hut 3 decrypts got misplaced. He sacked two Decoding Room women just for trading BP gossip at the station, and you're going to start brawling within view of his office?"

Harry's arm dropped. His face was set and furious.

Giles looked contrite. "Sorry, old boy. Didn't mean anything by it." He proffered his pack of Gitanes. "Peace?"

"Go fuck yourself," Harry said very clearly. He rose in a fluid, angry motion and stalked off down the bank.

"Clearly we need a less controversial book next month," Osla said, trying to lighten the mood. "How do we all feel about *A Little Princess*?"

Mab spun on Giles and started giving him hell. A few of the others joined in, some defending, some arguing. Beth rose and followed Harry.

He'd gone down to the lake, sitting with his elbows resting on his drawn-up knees. He looked at Beth briefly as she sat beside him, then looked away.

"I wish I'd hit him," Harry said.

"I know this isn't only about what Giles said," Beth answered. She wasn't any good at comforting people, but she understood Harry a bit better than the others did, so she felt obligated to try. Share a desk for forty-eight hours decrypting battle plans, and you get to know someone. "Is it work? Or something at home?"

"Sixty-four days," Harry said.

"What?"

"Sixty-four fucking days we've been locked out of the U-boat traffic." Harry looked at her, eyes sunken. "Admiral Dönitz set the submarine codes to a different key than the surface naval vessels, and"—he snapped his fingers—"we're out."

"You can't tell me that . . . ," She couldn't help flinching.

"You don't know the name of the key, you don't know the details. Besides, half of BP has probably guessed. One look at the bloody papers, and anyone could see the number of sunk ships in the last sixty-four days." Harry was ripping up grass by savage handfuls. "We're locked out. And I have no idea how we'll get back in."

"You'll do it." She remembered banging her head on the Spy Enigma all those months. "It took me six months to get my most recent break."

"But we haven't got any cribs. The key's been changed on us, and we've got nothing. We all sit there, day after day, night after night, trying to wedge a foot in and getting nowhere. Sixty-four days of goddamned *failing*—I'm going mad with it, Beth. It's driving me bloody mad. I see the traffic coming, those bloody five-letter clusters, night day night day night day. It never stops. Even when I'm asleep it just keeps spooling—"

His voice cracked. *Breakdown,* Beth thought sickly. She'd missed it happening to Peggy, but there wasn't any missing it here. Harry was on the edge, and Beth had no idea how to make it better. *Let me help,* she wanted to say—maybe ISK could lend her out to Hut 8, as 8 had lent Harry to them during the Matapan crisis. But ISK couldn't spare her, not with Dilly gone and Peggy still not back from her attack of pleurisy. No one else broke the Abwehr traffic as fast as Beth. "Keep it up," Dilly had told her this afternoon. "I've been informed that the information from our Spy Enigma decrypts has built up such a good picture of Abwehr operations, MI-5 is in control of every German agent operating in Britain." They wouldn't keep up that level of success if Dilly's section couldn't turn over the Abwehr traffic at speed.

"I wish I could help," Beth told Harry at last. "I'm sorry."

"I'd give my liver to have you at my desk, but it wouldn't make any difference. It's not more brains we need, it's information to get us in the door. One good look at a U-boat weather book to see how they've changed their methods . . ." He gulped in a breath, and Beth realized his enormous shoulders were heaving. "We need a bloody miracle, Beth. Because convoys are going to be coming from America, bringing that aid we were so damned happy about getting when they joined the fight in December. As things stand, those ships are sitting ducks. Thousands and thousands of—"

His shoulders shook again. He turned away from her, roughly, and lay back in the grass, folding one elbow over his eyes, chest rising and falling like a bellows. Beth sat there, desperately looking for something to say.

"Did I ever tell you," she began at last, "about the funniest Enigma break I ever had?"

"No." His voice was hoarse. "Please tell me."

"Italian naval Enigma . . . old news, so it's nothing you can't hear." Beth lay back in the grass, too, her shoulder firm against Harry's. She looked up into the endless sky, not at him. "I picked up a message, and I knew right away there was something off. A second later, I had it—there wasn't a single L in the entire page. All twenty-five other letters of the alphabet, no L. And the machine can't encrypt any letter as itself, so . . ."

She waited. He moved his elbow, dropped his arm back into the grass.

"Right," she said as if he'd answered. "The operator must have been told to send out a dummy message, the way they do after they change the wirings. Just gibberish. But he didn't bother to make something up. He just pressed the letter L for an entire page, and the machine pushed out every other letter *but* L. So I had the longest, nicest crib anyone could ask for. A whole page of Ls."

"Christ." Harry's voice was ragged, but that strangled heaving of his shoulders had stopped. "What an arse. Probably having a fag late at night, deciding 'Hell with protocol.'"

"Just hitting L over and over, thinking about his girlfriend," Beth agreed. "I get wheel settings off girlfriend names, too. There was a Balkan operator who kept setting a four-wheel machine to R-O-S-A. Another operator in the same district was also using R-O-S-A. We kept debating among ourselves if it was the same Rosa."

"Not very nice of her, keeping them in the dark."

"A woman whose only romantic options are fascist Balkan wireless operators has bigger problems than not being nice."

"True." Harry turned his head on the grass to look at Beth.

Beth looked back at him. "You'll get your L," she said. "At some point."

"If we don't, we're sunk." He said it very quietly. "That traffic is everything. It's not just that we can't keep the Americans safe without it. We don't get the convoys full of supplies without it. We don't eat without it. We don't win without it. And I can't get in. I cannot get in."

"You'll get in."

He raised himself on one elbow, dropped his head to Beth's, and gave her one fast, ferocious kiss. He tasted like strong tea and utter desperation. He pulled back before she could react, rising and brushing the grass from his sleeves. Beth sat bolt upright, feeling her face heat like a forge. Her mouth burned.

"Don't worry." He stood big and expressionless against the sun, hair disheveled, hands sunk in his pockets as though to stop them from reaching toward her. "Won't do that again. I just—one time, that's all."

Beth looked wildly up and down the bank. No one in view. She still found herself whispering as she blurted out, "You are *married*."

"I'm not—that is, my wife and I, we aren't married in the way you think—" He shook his head, cutting himself off. "Never mind. I won't make excuses. The heart of it is this: I want you, I can't have you, and for a moment I forgot. I'm sorry."

"Are you just looking for a bit of fun?" Beth flared. Maybe he'd sensed she had a bit of a crush, noticed the involuntary smile that came over her whenever she saw him. *Beth, darling!* The thought came in Osla's slangy Mayfair drawl, except Osla was never cruel. *You're too, too utterly pathetic!* Beth wanted to crawl into the lake.

"No, I—Christ." Harry looked at her squarely. "You're so bloody brilliant you take my breath away. Ever since I watched you crack Italian Enigma, I can barely breathe around you."

Beth couldn't think of a thing to say. She was twenty-six years old and she'd never come remotely close to being kissed before. No one thought of shy, backward Beth Finch that way in BP or the village. *They would,* Mab had said when she last gave Beth's hair a trim to keep its Veronica Lake wave, *if you didn't try to melt into the background.*

I like melting into the background, Beth had replied. The promise of a film or a few kisses wasn't tempting enough to make it worth the agony of trying to converse with a stranger on a date. She already had everything she needed: a home away from her mother; work she loved more than life; Dilly Knox and wonderful friends and a dog who curled on her feet at night. It hadn't occurred to Beth to want more.

It certainly hadn't crossed her mind that someone wanted her.

Her mouth still burned. The kiss had been glorious, and that filled her with fury. A crush had been safe, a little private glow to enjoy. Now that was spoiled. "You shouldn't tease," she said tightly, aware she was still blushing, mortified by it. "It's hateful, teasing someone with something they can't have."

"I'm not teasing you. I'm yours if you want me." Harry sounded deathly tired. "I just don't know why you would. There's not much of me left over, Beth. But all of it belongs to you." He stared across the lake at the huts, and she could see the five-letter blocks start to spiral into him, working through his shoulders until they looked like stone walls. "And all of it would rather die than hurt you."

He set off for his desk like he was walking toward a gallows.

CHAPTER 36

Darling girl, Francis had scribbled hastily on Foreign Office stationery,

I can't get away from the office until this evening. Pop in on your family, then come back to my rooms and make yourself at home. I shall see when I can get out—hopefully not so late I cannot pin you to my exceedingly narrow bed and do a number of ungodly things to you which I have been daydreaming about, most inappropriately, during work hours. —F

Mab repressed a violent urge to curse. She would undoubtedly shock her husband's grandmotherly landlady, who had passed the letter over and now stood in the shabby-elegant corridor looking sympathetic. "He sent the note round an hour ago, dearie. Asked me to give his lovely wife the key to his room if she wanted to wait for him."

I don't want to wait, Mab wanted to shout. *I want him* here*!* Already gone May, and she had barely seen her husband at all since the Lake District. They simply hadn't had any luck when it came to timing. First Francis had been sent to Scotland for nearly five weeks, completely out of reach, then when he came back and they had managed to line up another weekend—Mab hoarding her days off, working twelve days straight so she'd have forty-eight hours' leave—that had been scuppered by Wren Stevens, who begged, crying, for Mab to take her shift. "Jimmy's shipping out to Ceylon, it's my last chance to see him!" What was Mab supposed to say? Well, she could have said *no,* if she was as much of a hard-boiled egg as some seemed to think, but she didn't have the heart. Francis wasn't shipping out somewhere dangerous; they'd have all the time in the world once the war was done—who knew if poor weepy Stevens's fiancé would come back alive?

So the only time together Mab and Francis had managed in the last few months had been tea in a railway café between London and Bletchley, surrounded by irritable waitresses and squalling children. They could barely hear each other over the din; conversation died utterly after a few feeble fits and starts. All they could do was hold hands over the rickety table, smiling in silent rueful acknowledgment of their situation, Mab unable to ask in the middle of the noisy café, *What did you think of my letter?*

Her husband had answered that spilling of her soul with a short letter of his own: *I think you are brave and beautiful, Mab. And I shan't ever bring the matter or the man—though he doesn't deserve the word—up again, unless you wish to discuss it.* Mab had grown weak-kneed with relief, reading those words, but she'd still wondered if something would change in the way Francis looked at her. She didn't *think* anything had, but how could you tell from twenty-five minutes in a crowded café?

Now they were supposed to have an entire afternoon and night and morning before Mab returned to Bletchley, and Francis was stuck at the office. Mab unloaded every East End curse she knew in a silent scream.

The landlady was still chattering. ". . . pleased as punch to see Mr. Francis marry! Such a fine man, one of my best guests. Do you wish to wait upstairs, dear?"

"I'll pop out to see my family first."

Lucy greeted Mab's arrival in Shoreditch with a shout. "I drew a picture! C'n I show you? Mum's making tea, she's too busy to look—"

"Beautiful," Mab said over the sound of clanking dishes, admiring Lucy's latest sketch on the back of an old envelope—a horse with a green mane and yellow hooves. Lucy still wanted a pony more than life. "I can't get you a pony, Luce, but I brought you mounds of paper. You'll be sketching ponies for months."

Lucy gave her a careless kiss and began sorting through the scrap paper Mab had hoarded from Bletchley Park. Lucy was six years old now, lively as a monkey, hair exploding in uncontrollable dark curls. Mab frowned, calling to the kitchen. "Mum, Lucy shouldn't be running around in skivvies." The flat was too stuffy even on a rainy May day to be chilly, but Mab wanted to see Lucy in something better than a grubby vest and knickers.

"You ran around like that till you were eight." Mab's mother came in with the tea mugs, cigarette dangling from the corner of her mouth. "And look how you turned out, Miss Fine and Fancy."

Mrs. Churt couldn't keep a slightly adversarial awe out of her voice whenever she addressed Mab now. Being chauffeured to a fancy London hotel by a Greek prince, getting kitted out in a borrowed silk dress, and watching her Hartnell-clad daughter recite her vows to a gentleman in a Savile Row suit had knocked Mrs. Churt for a loop. "Why couldn't my other girls turn out like Mabel?" Mab had heard her mother saying to one of the neighbors. "They settle for dockworkers and factory men, when she nabs herself a dyed-in-the-wool gentleman easy as taking candy from a baby!"

"Don't suppose you could spare a few quid?" she asked now as Mab handed over all her extra clothing coupons for Lucy.

"That's near a week's wages, Mum—"

"What, that husband of yours doesn't give you pin money?"

Francis had offered, but it seemed greedy when her billet and meals were covered. Mab didn't want him thinking she was the kind of woman who always had her hand out. "I don't keep house for him yet, so it's not necessary." Mab pushed a couple of pound notes across the table, then bundled Lucy into her clothes and took her to the park. "Do you want to live in Coventry after the war, Luce? It's in the very middle of England, and there's a house there that will be mine, and you could learn to ride."

"I don't want to learn to ride *later*. I want to learn *now*."

"I don't blame you." Mab took her hand as they crossed Rotten Row. "There are a lot of things I want now, too. But there's a war on."

"Why does everyone say that?" Lucy said crossly. She probably didn't remember when there hadn't been a war on.

Mab headed back to Francis's digs at twilight, hoping . . . but the landlady shook her head. "He's not back yet, dearie. Would you like to wait in his room? Normally I'd insist on seeing a marriage certificate before letting any young lady into a gentleman's quarters under my roof, but Mr. Francis is such a perfect gentleman . . ."

Not so perfect as that, Mab thought with a certain grin, mounting the carpeted stairs. Francis could, in his quiet way, pen an absolutely indecent letter. Something else she'd learned about him, since the Lake District.

I'm sitting at my desk in my shirtsleeves under a hideous gaslight, smudged in pencil, dreaming of the long map of your body unscrolled across my unmade bed. A map I've nowhere near finished charting, though I know a few landmarks well enough to dream on. Your hills and vales, your valleys and mounds, your wicked eyes. You're an endless serpentine ladder to paradise, and I wish I could coil your hair in my hands and climb you like that great mountain in Nepal where countless explorers have died in ecstasy searching for the peak. I am mixing my metaphors horribly, but longing does that to a man, and you already knew I was a terrible poet. I'd fall back on a better one and pass his work off as my own, except you read far too widely for that to work. "License my roving hands, and let them go, before, behind, between, above, below . . ." O my Mab, my newfound land! Is John Donne on your list of classic literature? He is probably considered too indecent for females. Certainly he's no help to a gentleman's peace of mind either, especially when dreaming of you, my lovely map, my unclimbed ladder . . .

Francis's room was at the top of the house. Mab let herself in, realizing she had no idea how he lived—for all his letters, he had never once described this place. She looked around the neat, anonymous bedroom, not seeing Francis at all; it was cluttered with the Victorian landlady's crocheted antimacassars and silk flowers. Nothing here smelled like him, his hair tonic or his shirts or his soap.

Make yourself at home, his note had said. She didn't want to pry, but she was desperately curious. His bedcovers were pulled taut enough to bounce a shilling—clearly he'd never lost the army habits from the last war. The desk was bare except for pen and blotter and stationery. One photograph in a much-handled frame, facedown on the desk . . . turning it over, Mab saw four young men in uniform. With a stab to her gut like a bayonet thrust, she realized the shortest was Francis, his uniform so big it puddled at his ankles. He stood clutching his weapon with a huge grin, as if he had joined the greatest adventure in the world. The three men around him looked grimmer, their smiles more cynical, or was she reading too much into those blurred, unknown faces? The scribbled date in the corner read *April 1918*.

"You poor bugger," she said softly, touching her husband's young face. She'd never once seen Francis smile that wide—she wondered if he *ever* had, since April 1918. There were no names written under any of the men around him. *They didn't live,* Mab thought, replacing the picture where she'd found it. *I'd stake my life on it.*

No other photographs, not of his parents, not of Mab. She didn't have a single picture of herself to send him—she'd have to do something about that—and they hadn't snapped any wedding photographs. Osla hadn't been able to find a camera on short notice. Mab went to the bookshelf—no poets, mostly treatises on distant history, long-ago Chinese dynasties and Roman emperors. He seemed to like his reading to take him as far from the twentieth century as possible. At the very back of the shelf, wedged almost out of sight, she found a copy of *Mired: Battlefield Verses by Francis Gray,* with a copyright page from 1919—it must have been from the first printing run. The spine cracked as if it hadn't been opened in years, but there were angry scribbles all over the pages, almost every poem marked up. From "Altar," his most well-known poem:

Where stinking mud spreads
wide as any nave
Where prayers are thickly
muttered in the lull — no one prays formally in foxholes, it's just GodGodJesusshit
Where stillness hammers,
rotted as a grave,

Is embattered even a word, you hack?

On shell-embattered ears
in parchment skulls.
The skyline, scarred with
stars of rusted wire
The spark of cigarettes in
hands that quake
The spider limb, sprawled
limp, of one expired
So many faces, young and like to break.

KitArthurJo
MichaelRobH
MarcusBernard

A yellow cloud of blindness and decay
A rank of lambs in too-
large khaki shoes
A scarlet arc in fountain-graceful spray

You are such a [unintelligible]

The stack of telegrams
and dreadful news.
As in the mud the trampled
daisies died,

daisies? daisies don't grow in trenches who fact-checked you

The wire trapped the
lambs, all crucified.

You should have damned well died there

Mab laid the book aside, feeling stripped to the core. All the letters he'd written and never a word about any of this. But why would he? No one talked about their war when it was over. If the day ever came that Hitler was defeated and Bletchley Park closed for good, Mab suddenly knew down to her bones that she and everyone else wouldn't need the Official Secrets Act to tell them to scorch it from their minds. They'd do it anyway. That was what Francis and his surviving friends had done after the last war; it was probably what the Roman and Chinese soldiers in his history books had done after their wars long ago.

In the top drawer of his desk, she found a packet of her letters. She leafed through them, every one clearly much handled, all the way back to the very first note she'd written him after they became engaged—just a few lines suggesting a date he could meet her family. Underneath her signature, he'd scribbled in pencil:

The girl with the hat!

A knock sounded, and Mab jumped out of her skin. Still holding the bunch of letters, she rose to answer.

"Mr. Gray telephoned, dearie. He won't be able to get away at all tonight—possibly by tomorrow morning. He's very sorry—some line of questioning he can't get free of."

Mab's heart sank.

"Would you like some supper? Just mock duck and turnip-top salad, but no one goes away from my table hungry, even with a war on."

Mab demurred politely, then shut the door and looked around the little room. It might not have looked like Francis, smelled like him, or carried the shape of him in its shadows, but at that moment she swore she could almost feel him breathing at her shoulder. Before she could lose the feeling, she sat down at his chair and helped herself to his pen and paper.

Dear Francis—sitting in your room without you in it fills me with questions. I know the direction you slant your hat when you cram it over your hair with one hand. I know you take your tea without sugar, even when sugar isn't rationed. I know you have a ticklish spot at your waist, and I know the song you hum while shaving ("I'm Always Chasing Rainbows"). But sometimes I don't feel I know you at all . . . and you seem to know me so well.

I wish I had known the boy I saw in the photograph on your desk, the one with a smile that nearly runs round the back of his head. I wish I knew who his friends were. I wish I knew why you called me "the girl in the hat."

I wish you were here. —M

Darling Mab—I missed you by eight bloody minutes this morning. I ran all the way home, shamelessly shoving small children into ditches and old ladies into oncoming traffic. Your scent was still lingering when I wrenched the door open. I said a good many words then of which my landlady did not approve. Damn my job, damn the Foreign Office, damn the war.

Don't regret never getting to know the boy in that photograph. He was an idiot. He'd have been utterly tongue-tied in your presence, and you'd have spent all night talking to his three friends, who would have charmed you. They were all far better men than Private F. C. Gray. (C stands for Charles. Did you know that? It's entirely possible I never told you.)

As for the girl in the hat, she's you. Or rather, she's become you.

I was sixteen, and I'd been in the trenches four months, quite long enough to lose every ideal I'd had. You've read the wretched poetry, I won't repeat anything trite about barbed wire or flying bullets. I had forty-eight hours' leave coming with my friend Kit—in the photograph, he's the towhead on the end. The other two had already died, Arthur two weeks before of peritonitis, George three weeks before that of a scrape gone septic. It was just Kit and me left, and he was hauling me to Paris on our next leave. Only he was killed six hours beforehand, gut-shot in a pointless skirmish. I listened to him scream for an hour before a sniper on our own side finally finished him. So I went to Paris on my own.

The Eiffel Tower, the Sacré Coeur . . . I wandered round in an utter daze, looking at all the things we said we'd see, and

I don't remember any of it. A sort of veil had dropped over the whole world, and I stumbled along behind it, peering through the fog. The world had simply gone gray.

There was a hat shop on the Rue de la Paix, and for some reason I stopped in front of it. I wasn't looking at the hats in the window, I wasn't looking at anything. I wasn't thinking anything. But slowly I became aware there was a girl inside, trying on hats.

I don't remember what she looked like. I know she was tall, and had a pale blue dress. For the Rue de la Paix she looked rather shabby. She'd clearly saved up to buy a hat at this very expensive shop, and by God, she wasn't going to be sniffed at by any of those coiffed vendeuses. She was scrutinizing those hats like Napoléon inspecting his artillery. Clearly the perfect hat was going to seal her fate in some way, and she was determined to find it. I stood there dumbly, staring through the window as she tried on one after the other, until she found The One. I remember it was pale straw, with a cornflower-blue ribbon round the crown and some wafty sort of netting. She stood before the mirror, smiling, and I realized I was seeing her as if in a bright light—as if she'd stepped out from behind that veil that was bleaching all the color out of the world. A pretty girl in a pretty hat in the middle of an ugly war. I nearly wept. Instead I stood transfixed. I could have watched her forever.

She bought the blue-ribboned hat and came out, swinging her hatbox happily. I didn't follow her. It wasn't about trying to find out her name or where she lived. It wasn't about falling in love with her, whoever she was. It was one bright, beautiful moment in the middle of a hideous world, and when I went back to the trenches, I pulled that moment up and slept on it every night until the war was over. The girl in the hat, in the moment of her joy.

The veil mostly dropped back over me, Mab—it hasn't ever really gone away. I haven't seen the world in full color since I was sixteen years old and buried in mud at the front. I came back from that terrible place with all my limbs and most of my sanity, but I can't say I entirely rejoined the human race. I've never been able to shake the feeling of standing in the wings of a play, separated from it by a curtain.

Only sometimes, every now and then, the curtain sweeps back and I see things in full color—I get yanked onto the stage, blinking and dazzled, and I feel.

There was a moment at Bletchley Park during the prime minister's visit, where you put on your new hat and sang a little song about how a smart hat was a woman' s cri de coeur. In that moment you became the Girl in the Hat.

I'd enjoyed your company before then, because you were lovely and entertaining. A pleasant companion on a night out, for a man who periodically tries to remind himself that the world has civilized things to offer and not just horrors. But there on the lawn, you dazzled me. You want things so fiercely—you're so determined to wrest your fate out of the world, horrors be damned, and the odds never seem to daunt you. You will simply put on a smart hat, and conquer the world. And in that moment, I loved you.

I can't say the veil over my eyes has disappeared simply because you have come into my life. Mostly it's still there, making it hard for me to reach you. I have spent decades not really trying to reach anyone. But it's beginning to part more often than it did. When you lift an eyebrow skeptically. When I sink into you and feel you arch against me. When I see you straighten your hat.

Darling Mab, you are and always will be the Girl in the Hat. The girl who makes life worth living.

—F

Mab brought the letter to her evening shift, reading it at the checking machine as she waited for Aggie to halt. She read it three times, then she put it away, hands trembling. Francis didn't even have to be in the same bed, or the same room, or the same *city* to give her that feeling of being unshelled, naked as a chick peeled from its egg. She wanted to cry and she wanted to smile, she wanted to dance and she wanted to blush.

Her well-ordered plan for life had always included being married, but had nothing at all about being loved. Because love was for novels, not real life.

And yet . . .

She smiled and read the letter again.

CHAPTER 37

FROM *BLETCHLEY BLETHERINGS*, MAY 1942

Everyone likes to think cloistered academics are such sheltered innocents, but the goings-on among BP's racy set would make a sailor blush. Partner-swapping that would put a Highland reel to shame, enough adultery for a dozen Oscar Wilde plays—you wouldn't believe what this hothouse of cloistered academics gets up to off shift! If only *BB* could name names . . .

"Excuse me . . . you wouldn't be Beth by any chance? Beth who works at Bletchley Park?"

Beth looked up as she settled Boots into the basket of her bicycle. The tired-looking woman in her green cardigan looked a few years older than Beth, holding a shopping basket. "Do you work at BP?" Beth asked warily, eyeing the sign posted just past the woman's shoulder: *Tittle Tattle Lost the Battle!* Beth was rubbery legged from the long bicycle ride back from Courns Wood, where she'd been giving Dilly the news that Peggy was returning to ISK soon; it was nearly nightfall and she'd only stopped to let her grumbling dog relieve himself against a post. She didn't really want to get stuck talking to some curious stranger.

"I'm not at BP," the woman continued, looking Beth over from the wave of hair falling over one eye to the red-sprigged cotton frock she was now able to wear without imagining her mother sniffing *Only tarts wear red!* "But my husband works there."

"I'm afraid I can't discuss the work with anyone." Beth could deliver that statement without blushing or breaking eye contact now, even when she had to say it to strangers. Though the woman looked familiar . . .

"Mum!" A little boy lurched through the shop door, seizing the woman's skirt. "Can we go home?" Lurched because he wore bulky leg braces, and that was when Beth knew exactly who his mother was.

"Sheila Zarb," she said. "Harry's wife. You came to the house once, for the literary society. I met so many new people, I couldn't remember which was Beth."

Beth felt a horrendous blush sweep up from the collar of her dress. She stood like a tomato with ears, remembering exactly how it felt when this woman's husband had kissed her.

"You're definitely Beth." Sheila nodded. "D'you fancy a drink? It'll make this easier."

THE BAR AT the Shoulder of Mutton inn was cozy and bright lit—worth the walk for a little privacy, Sheila Zarb said, carrying her son as Beth wheeled her bicycle. She asked the barmaid if they could borrow the private sitting room, then went behind the bar and deftly drew two pints. "I fill in the odd shift here," she told Beth, who stood silently gripping her dog's lead. She had no idea if she was going to be slapped or shouted at, she had no idea what Harry had told his wife, and everything inside her was cringing. *I didn't do anything,* her mind insisted. *I didn't ask him to kiss me.*

You certainly enjoyed it though, a second inner voice said unhelpfully.

Harry's wife carried the pints into the private room, motioning Beth after her and closing the door with one foot. "Oh, stop blushing. I'm not going to eat you. Can Christopher play with your dog?"

Beth released Boots, who stumped toward the enchanted little boy. Clutching her glass, Beth eased down at the table opposite Harry's wife, who sat looking at her with clear, curious eyes. Beth examined her back. Harry's wife was tall, rawboned, with sandy hair and a face that was pleasant rather than pretty.

"Mrs. Zarb—" Beth began.

"If you're the one my husband's lost his head over, you can call me Sheila."

Beth's face heated again. She glanced at Harry's son, but he was playing unconcernedly with Boots on the other side of the long room, and the sound of someone playing the piano in the bar outside gave their voices cover. "What—what did he tell you?" Beth found herself asking.

"Almost nothing. Harry's a vault. But he got plastered a few nights ago—which isn't like him—and he mumbled something about kissing Beth at the last Tea Party. Went on and on about how you'd think he was a rotter now."

Beth hadn't told anyone what happened. Osla would have issued dismayed warnings, and Mab would have hooted, "Of course he'll tell you he doesn't have a *real* marriage. They all say that!" So Beth pushed the afternoon kiss ruthlessly behind her and focused on the avalanche of work. And during shifts, that was fine. It was after work, staring in grainy-eyed exhaustion at the ceiling over her bed, gradually drifting out of the mental spirals of code, that she wondered what would have happened if she'd let Harry keep kissing her. What would have come next, how it would have felt. One kiss had wakened her curiosity with a vengeance—she wanted to *know.*

"D'you fancy him?" Sheila asked bluntly.

Beth dropped her eyes, thinking despite herself of the sheer joy she'd taken in working with Harry—pushing rods and cups of coffee and Italian dictionaries back and forth, waiting in wordless impatience for the dispatch riders to bring in new traffic, the quick grin they'd exchange when the cars rolled in . . .

Ever since I watched you crack Italian Enigma, I can barely breathe around you.

"I'll take that as a yes," Sheila said.

"It doesn't matter." Beth made herself say it, looking up. "I wouldn't do—anything. Because he's your husband."

"Is that what's holding you back?" Sheila took a long swallow of her pint. "Look. I've got someone. Harry knows; doesn't mind a bit. We stay married for that little fellow there." She nodded at her son, lying nose to nose with Boots at the other end of the room, and her face softened. "He's a ruddy miracle, and I'd die for him. We both would. Our son's the only thing we have in common. Henry Omar Darius Zarb with his university education and his fancy family full of diplomats and London bankers, and Sheila Jean McGee the former barmaid at the Eagle in Cambridge, where he used to study over a pint. It wasn't ever any grand romance. He liked me because I didn't call him a wog or a dago, I liked him because I thought he looked like a sheikh in a film. He did the right thing by me when I found out Christopher was coming, and he's a grand dad, but he drives me round the bend sometimes. Him and his equations and the fact he can't pick up his ruddy socks to save his life." Her voice was fondly irritated; she sounded like an older sister rather than a wife. "We bump along well enough, but if he wants a fling with someone like you—well, if you want it too, have at it."

Beth stared at her. She picked up her glass and swallowed about half the beer. "That would be *immoral,*" she couldn't help saying, hearing her mother's voice.

"Why is it immoral if it isn't hurting anybody?" Sheila shrugged. "We keep things quiet, so nothing comes back on Christopher, and otherwise we let each other be. I'd like to see Harry happy. He's the best friend I've got, and he lets me be happy—my fellow and me. Not a lot of men would do that. You're a brainy sort, like Harry. I don't know what you people do at BP, but it's clearly important. He'd like a woman he could talk equations to, or whatever pillow talk is for you Cambridge sorts."

"I didn't go to university."

"You're still just like him. There's a sort of staring-into-space thing you were doing when I saw you outside the grocer's—Harry does it too." Sheila shook her head. "I don't know if you're mixed up in the same thing he is at BP, but it's got him wound tighter than a clock lately . . ."

It'll be more than eighty days locked out of the U-boat traffic now, Beth thought. She knew just from passing Harry in the new-built canteen, seeing his slumped shoulders and drawn face over his supper tray, that they hadn't cracked it.

". . . When I caught sight of you today and wondered if you were the one he liked, I thought it wouldn't hurt to tell you how things stood."

"I'm not a fling," Beth burst out. "If he wants one of those, he can pick up some tart at the cinema."

"He probably does, now and then. I wouldn't know." Beth wondered how Sheila could sound that unruffled. The thought of Harry with some other woman made Beth want to spit. "Men like a bit of the old you-know," Sheila went on, "and Harry and I don't anymore, not since I met my Jack. So maybe he's had a fling or two to let off tension, or maybe he hasn't, but I can tell you this—he hasn't fallen head over heels for anyone but you. It's your name he's mumbling when he's sozzled, not anyone else's."

Beth sat tongue-tied all over again.

"Look." Sheila finished her pint, pushing the glass aside. "I'm not matchmaking. If you'd rather keep your distance from married blokes, that's fine. Probably the smarter thing, because Harry won't ever leave Christopher and me. He broke with his posh family over us, when his dad wanted to pay me off to get it taken care of. Harry wouldn't hear of it, and his father cut him off without a bean, and that's why a chap named Henry Omar Darius Zarb with a First from Cambridge lives in rented digs and has holes in his jacket elbows. There was a time we were planning to separate and get a quiet divorce, once we realized it wasn't ever going to be love between us—but then our boy got sick, and that was that. Christopher needs us both, always will, and that means Harry and I are in it to stay. I'm not ever going to have my Jack past the occasional evening he's on leave from the RAF, and Harry won't put you or any woman above Christopher." A pause. "But somewhere around the edges of that, if he can find happiness, he deserves it. And if you feel like being that woman and you're willing to keep things quiet, you've got my blessing."

She rose then, holding her arms out to Christopher. "Come here and give me a hug, lad. What do you say we take some fish and chips home for supper? Your dad'll like that." She helped him with his braces, collected her basket, and was gone before Beth could utter more than a dazed goodbye.

Beth sat looking at her half-drunk beer. *What do you want?* a thought whispered.

No answer. She sighed, collected Boots, and left the pub. Walking straight out without looking, she ran smack into a statuesque bulk of flowered housedress. Before she even heard the outraged exhalation, Beth knew who it was. "Hello, Mother."

"Bethan!" Mrs. Finch's eyes darted over Beth's red-sprigged dress, her shoulder-waved hair, the red T-strap pumps borrowed from Osla. "What are you doing in a *pub*?"

"Having a pint." *And discussing the finer points of adultery,* Beth added with a certain inner smile.

"Bethan—" Mrs. Finch composed herself visibly, gripping her handbag. "You really must give up this disgraceful gadding about. Why, just yesterday . . ." Beth let her get it out of her system, leaning down to give Boots a rub. He was eyeing Mrs. Finch coldly through his shaggy brows. ". . . do you know what people at chapel are saying about you?" Beth's mother finally finished.

"Not much," Beth said. "Everyone smiles at me just the same. I enjoy chapel so much more now that I don't have to go home and hold the Bible over my head for fifteen minutes because I got distracted during the sermon." These days, Beth sat in chapel letting the hymns wash over her and thinking about the Abwehr Enigma, and she didn't think God minded at all. Beth didn't think God was nearly as severe as her mother made Him out to be.

Mrs. Finch took a hitching breath. "If you will come home, all will be forgiven. The prodigal daughter will be welcomed, I promise. You may even keep the dog. Isn't that what you want?"

"I want quite a lot more than that, actually," Beth said. One hand drifted up to her lips, and she smiled. "Goodbye, Mother."

CHAPTER 38

FROM *BLETCHLEY BLETHERINGS*, JUNE 1942

BB has ranted before about those pin-striped sorts we're always seeing eel their way over from London on secretive business, but they really are *snakes*. Braying, bottom-feeding, bombastic, web-footed cretins in homburgs, and *BB* will brook no quibbling with this verdict.

"Oh, for heaven's sake." Osla spoke first, before Commander Travis could utter a word from behind his desk. "I don't know what's thrown a spanner in the works this time, but it wasn't me." Was she going to be raked over the coals every blinking time something went wrong at BP?

"Last Tuesday, you were seen in Hut 3." Commander Travis's voice was cold, and the expression on the man lounging against the wall behind him, fleshy and florid in a pin-striped suit, was equally icy. "Why?"

Osla had to stop and recall. "Mr. Birch had me nip over with a message. I waited for an answer."

"Did you invite yourself inside to wait?"

"Just in the corridor. It was pelting rain—"

"It was not your business to put a toe over the threshold of any hut where you do not work. We keep things compartmentalized for a reason."

"I—"

"And you didn't wait in the corridor. You were seen in one of the inner rooms."

"A girl I knew from the canteen waved at me. I stuck my head in to wave back, but I didn't go in." Osla looked from face to face. "What's this about?"

"Did you take anything from Hut 3, Miss Kendall? Files, perhaps?"

"Of course not. Has something gone missing?"

They didn't answer that. They didn't have to. Osla's mind flashed to the box files she thought might have been rifled the day of her godfather's visit—but Travis had said Hut *3,* not 4. "I didn't take anything," she repeated, pulling her flying thoughts together. She'd just about convinced herself she must have imagined that whisk of furtive motion the day Uncle Dickie came; now all her doubts came roaring back. She was about to unpack it all when Travis spoke again, even more icily.

"You have taken things from your section before."

"Oh, *really*. I smuggled out a few blank pieces of paper to prove how easily it could be done."

"Were you trying to prove something again?"

"No. I'm dished if I know what happened in Hut 3." Though Osla wouldn't have been surprised if someone else had reached the same conclusion she had, about how easily files could be snatched. Never in her life had she wanted so badly to say *I told you so*.

The florid man in the pin-striped suit—MI-5 or MI-6, Osla was suddenly, unpleasantly certain—cleared his throat and opened a file under his arm. "It's my understanding that you are, ah, *involved* with a certain Prince Philip of Greece."

Osla blinked. "What has that to do with anything?"

"Answer my question."

"That wasn't a question. It was a statement." *A statement with a nasty little implication ladled over the word* involved, *I might add.* But this was not a man with whom she could afford to get snippy. "Prince Philip is my boyfriend, yes."

"You two went out last Thursday to the cinema."

"*That Hamilton Woman.* Not a very good picture." Philip had howled with laughter at how the Battle of Trafalgar was depicted.

"Did you happen to . . . *give* your boyfriend anything that night?"

"What on earth do you mean?" Osla asked frostily.

"You are aware several of his brothers-in-law are members of the Nazi party?" There was a superior note in the man's voice. As if she was too dense to connect the dots. "He's related by blood and by marriage to a pack of Nazis."

"So is King George," she shot back. "It hasn't snaffled his game any."

"Don't be flippant."

"Philip's relatives are neither a matter of choice nor a reflection on him." She could feel rage shortening her breath. "He abhors his family connections to the Third Reich. He just passed his lieutenant's exams for the Royal Navy. If he has the royal family's approval, to the point where he's allowed to correspond privately with the future queen of England, how can he be considered a risk?" The man in the pin-striped suit looked peevish. He couldn't lose face by backing down, Osla knew, but he couldn't say the king was a dupe, either. She crossed her arms. "Now you're the one who hasn't answered *my* question."

He shifted tack instead. "Are you quite certain he doesn't write to those sisters behind enemy lines? Who knows what he might be telling them. Especially when one considers his girlfriend has access to so much critical intelligence."

"Don't talk slush, sir." Osla could feel Philip's tousled hair under her hand, the exact feel of it. The roughness of the reddish beard he'd been growing on leave. "He does not write his German relatives. And even if he did, he has no idea that I have access to critical intelligence. He thinks I have a boring office job."

"Oh, come now, Miss Kendall. Not one single cozy confession over a pillow?"

Icicles dripped from Osla's voice. "There is no *pillow*."

"No need to be indelicate," Travis said at the same time, looking rather disgusted.

Pinstripes shrugged, unapologetic. "You have to admit it looks bad. She's careless with rules, knows how to smuggle information, let things slip to her godfather—"

"I did *not*—"

"—embroiled with a damned wog who has a pack of Nazis in the family tree. Specifically reported to us for turning up in Hut 3 where she shouldn't have been—"

Someone reported me? Osla thought sickly. *Who would do that?*

"—and Canadian, to boot."

"Like the Canadians who are fighting for England right now?" Osla's voice rose. "Are those the Canadians you mean?"

"Lower your voice."

"I will not. I left Montreal and came back to Britain to fight for this country. I have lied to everyone I love, including Philip, rather than violate the Official Secrets Act. I will not be labeled an outsider, and I will not be accused of being untrustworthy." Osla unfolded her arms. "I would never have helped myself to a file of reports against all rules and regulations. I am as careful and clever a worker as you have ever hired at Bletchley Park."

They looked skeptical. To them she was that silly girl who didn't have a thought in her head but hijinks and handsome princes—who would believe a word she said?

"If you want to prove your loyalty," Pinstripes said at last, "then I'm sure you'll have no objection to turning over all your correspondence with Prince Philip."

For a moment Osla couldn't speak. Could an oath demand this?

Apparently it could. She jerked out a nod, tasting bile.

Pinstripes looked satisfied, but Travis put up a hand. "It would be better for BP if you broke things off with this fellow altogether," he said bluntly. "A girl with your access to sensitive information cannot have Nazi connections, however thirdhand."

Osla's stomach rolled. *Take everything,* she thought. *Just take it all, why don't you.* The two things that had brought her happiness after the shattering darkness of the Café de Paris: Philip, whose arms had become something like a home, and her pride in her job. So much for her shining hope, once she'd moved to translation duties, that she'd finally proved herself enough to be taken seriously. Her word of honor clearly meant nothing here. A girl like her couldn't be trusted to keep her mouth shut around her boyfriend, so just *break things off, you silly socialite.* She wanted to lash out, pound the desk in rage.

"I understand, sir," she forced out.

What else was there to say?

PHILIP'S VOICE DOWN the telephone line was jubilant. "I've received my posting, Os. Sublieutenant on the *Wallace.* Just an old Shakespeare-class destroyer, but she's got teeth."

"Topping," Osla managed to say. He wouldn't tell her where the ship would patrol, but she already had a very good idea, after translating so many reports on surface navy action. Probably E-boat Alley, that treacherous passage between the Firth of Forth and Sheerness . . .

"I'm off in two days. Any chance you can get to London for a final hurrah?"

Osla closed her eyes tight. She had to swallow twice, but her voice came out light, careless. "I'm simply knackered, darling. See you on the other side?"

Then she rang off, going upstairs to gather all his letters. The idea that someone would be pawing through their correspondence made her sick, but the sooner Pinstripes saw it was all innocuous, the better. Turn the letters over, and then she'd better start discouraging Philip from writing any more. Being close to a Bletchley Park translator was clearly agitating London intelligence about his loyalties—it was absurd, but Osla knew exactly how paranoid MI-5 could be. She'd heard all about the fuss they'd kicked up last year over an Agatha Christie novel, for God's sake, just because the mystery writer had named a spy *Colonel Bletchley* . . .

Osla's vision blurred as she finished bundling up Philip's letters, but she wouldn't let the tears fall. Any Agatha Christie heroine worth her salt would poker up here and do what she had to. Even if it meant breaking her own heart.

An Agatha Christie heroine might do a little digging, too, if she were in Osla's situation. Might poke around after those missing files. Because this was the second set of files that had been either rummaged or nabbed, and Osla couldn't help but wonder, disquiet running through her bones, if someone here was stealing information.

TEN DAYS UNTIL THE ROYAL WEDDING

November 10, 1947

CHAPTER 39

Inside the Clock

Back in the straitjacket again. One of the matrons, it seemed, had reported Beth's throwing up her morning pills.

"Just until you're calm," the doctor said as she was buckled in.

"If I take those blasted tablets I am halfway to a *coma,*" Beth snarled, thrashing. "How calm do you want me, you pill-peddling hack?"

"An extra dose, doctor?" The matron spoke up, cream smooth—the same matron whose arm Beth had burned with a cigarette. "Liddell has been misbehaving lately. An orderly said she made indecent overtures to him, in a linen closet. These nymphomaniac types . . ."

Her eyes danced, spiteful. Beth reared back and spat on the front of her apron.

A needle pricked. "Just wait, you nasty little thing," the matron said as soon as the doctor left. "When they get you under the scalpel—"

"*When?*" Beth hissed, but the matron was gone, the world sliding away into smoke and mirrors. Beth's veins felt unclean, as if her blood had been greased. She found herself weeping at some point and forced the tears away. Tears would wear her mind down like water on stone, and her mind was all she had.

I break codes. I eat secrets. Enigma was no match for me—neither is this place.

Breathe in, breathe out. Ignore the numbness of her trapped hands. Think of something else, not scalpels and spiteful matrons and oblivious doctors with their unfair punishments.

Unfairly punished . . . Beth's drugged memory turned up something long forgotten: Osla hauled up by Commander Travis at BP, raked over the coals about Prince Philip's Nazi relatives, interrogated about what Osla had guessed were some missing decrypted messages from Hut 3. When had that been, June '42? If someone had snatched files, they could easily have reported beautiful, highly visible Osla, who had sauntered over from Hut 4 on routine business and diverted attention from the presence of a traitor.

Who? Beth thought. Back to that again, endlessly turning over old memories, hoping for some fresh insight—but none of her ISK colleagues had ever worked in Hut 3.

So don't focus on the where, Beth thought. *Focus on the* when. *June of '42 . . .*

Peggy Rock had returned to Bletchley Park from her breakdown that same month. Peggy, the cleverest woman Beth knew. Had there really been a breakdown? Or had she been . . . somewhere else? Meeting someone, passing information?

Beth had weighed Peggy's name before on her list of suspects and always cringed from the thought. Peggy a traitor? Fair-haired, brilliant Peggy who had shown her how to rod?

But Peggy worked in ISK. She had disappeared and been gone for months. She had returned to work, Dilly's best codebreaker aside from Beth. A woman as clever as Peggy could have found a way to walk into Hut 3 and out again with a file, surely. And with Dilly no longer keeping an eye on his section's day-to-day routine . . .

Peggy. Yes, she might be the one.

Or any of Dilly's team. Dear friends all, because Beth had made friends almost exclusively inside Knox's section. Except for Osla and Mab, who now hated her.

What a cruel twist of fate that her friends were all suspects, and her enemies were the only ones she was sure of.

Come on, you two, Beth thought throughout the endless afternoon, canvas-bound and helpless. *Come through.*

York

Mab dropped her teaspoon. "You want us to go *where*?"

"To Clockwell, to see Beth." Osla saw they were getting glances from the other patrons of Bettys tea shop, and no wonder—two well-groomed women in New Look billows of skirt, dagger eyed, going at each other over the teacups for the past half hour. "Try not to look so hacked off, will you? We're attracting attention."

Mab bared all her teeth in a smile, violently stirring her tea. "I am not going to a madhouse."

"You're willing to leave her there, because you're afraid?" Reverting to whispering, making sure no one was walking past. "When she may be perfectly sane, and there may be a traitor who betrayed Bletchley Park—who betrayed *all* of us who worked there—walking free? Now, that really takes the biscuit, darling." Osla gave Mab a withering look. "I knew you were a ruthless cow, but I didn't think you'd become a coward."

"I'm not afraid, you featherweight gossip-page hack." Mab reverted to whispers, too. "I'm pointing out that we could be breaking the law by contacting her at all."

"We would also be breaking the law if we allowed the secrecy of our work to be compromised." Osla leaned forward. "I may be a featherweight gossip-page hack now, but I take my oath seriously."

"But you can't possibly entertain the notion that someone at BP—"

"Yes, I can. Remember the time I was hauled into Travis's office and accused of lifting files from Hut 3? I ranted to you and Beth about it." The rifled Hut 4 box files, too . . .

Mab fiddled with her strand of black pearls. "So we report this to someone higher up. Someone unconnected with Beth's section."

"No one is going to take it seriously, because they think Beth's gone potty. But we lived with her for years, and we know her better than anyone. If we see her in the flesh, put the question to her ourselves"—*However we can make* that *happen,* Osla thought—"we'll know if she's crazy. We'll *know* if she's lying."

Mab spoke very low. "And what if we don't think she's lying?"

A long silence.

"We'll think of something." Osla pushed her teacup away. "Perhaps there's something my godfather could do. Pull strings—"

"Or you could ring Philip," Mab suggested. "It must be nice having the future royal consort in your address book. He's got to be worth a ring on the telephone, even if he came up short as far as rings on the finger."

"Mention Philip again," Osla snapped, "and I'll cram those pearls up your nose until you are sneezing nacre, Queen Mab."

"You aren't exactly endearing yourself to me, considering you want my help."

"I don't *want* your help, you blithering bitch. I need it. I need another pair of eyes on Beth to figure out if she's talking straw or gold." Osla began tugging on her gloves. "The eleven oh five leaves tomorrow morning, and it stops two miles from Clockwell. I plan to be on it."

"Don't count on me joining you." Mab finally broke down and took a scone, reaching for the butter dish.

"No one could ever count on you for anything, Mab. Break form for once, why don't you." Osla rose, smiling sweetly. "Not *too* much butter, darling. Watch that waist! Right now, it's all you've got going for you."

FIVE YEARS AGO

June 1942

CHAPTER 40

FROM *BLETCHLEY BLETHERINGS*, JUNE 1942

Boffins and gents, stop trying to peek into the hut with all the machine racket going on inside. It is *just a rumor* that the Wrens sometimes strip down and work in their knickers.

Job's up!"

It was always a moment, Mab reflected, when a proper stop was logged on one of the bombe machines—when all the checks came back and it wasn't a mistake that had stopped the drums' whirring, but success. Who knew what might come from the bombe's latest break? Maybe intelligence important enough to go straight to Churchill's desk. Ever since his visit, Mab had felt a bit proprietary about the prime minister. He wasn't just Britain's PM, he was *her* PM.

"Strip down," Wren Stevens sighed as she and Mab began unplugging the great wired back of the machine. "I wish *we* could strip down." They'd finally moved from windowless, claustrophobic Hut 11 to new-built 11A, which had an actual air-conditioning unit—but the unit was on the fritz, as the Yanks would say, and the summer heat inside the hut was overwhelming. Mab felt sweat running down her back, and the Wrens in their smart brass-buttoned uniforms had it even worse.

"Well, why don't we?" she replied with a grin. "Who's going to see us?" The Wrens laughed uncertainly, but Mab was fizzing along, carefree and happy. She was going to see Francis tomorrow—they'd have three days together in Keswick. "Let's have a bit of mischief!" She yanked her sweaty frock over her head and her gummy slip after it, hanging them on a nail. She stretched her arms, standing in her knickers and brassiere. "Much better."

"Right, I'm with you." Stevens began unbuttoning her uniform, and soon they were all stripping down and going back to man their machines in their unmentionables. Mab carefully tweezed the tiny drum wires apart, plugged up the back for a new menu, and gave Aggie a pat. "Ready to go, you cranky cow." She set it in motion, for once not minding the clacking drone. There were many more bombe machines now besides these—so much traffic poured through BP, the handful of bombes here couldn't possibly cope. And it would be dangerous, anyway, to keep all the machines in one place where a single Luftwaffe strike could knock out Britain's entire decoding capacity. The Wrens said that there were stations in Adstock Manor, Wavendon, and Gayhurst now—Mab wondered if any of the Wrens at those stations were on duty in their knickers.

The shift was about to turn over, and the operators shrugging back into their clothes, when a young Wren slid through the door with a miserable look. "Why the long face?" Mab asked.

"Does anyone know Wren Bishop?" the girl blurted. "Stationed at RAF Chicksands?"

"I knew her from training in Dunbartonshire," one of the other Wrens volunteered.

"She's being sent home. It's terrible." The Wren lowered her voice. "There was a *baby*. She was seeing an American officer . . .

supposedly she was six months along, trying to keep it hidden. Until last night. Last night she—she had it. Or something happened. And it was dead and she tried to hide it in a d-*drawer*—and the officers I overheard talking about it, they didn't even care. They were just saying things about l-loose morals—"

She burst into tears. Two of the others hugged her. Mab wrapped her arms around herself, suddenly chilled despite the choking heat.

"Bloody *men,*" one of the Wrens spat. "She's done in the WRNS now, and what's going to happen to the fellow who got her in trouble?"

"He'll be giving some other girl the same line in a week." Mab quoted the rhyme: "'*Same old Yank, same old tune.*'"

She hadn't known Wren Bishop, but the news cast a pall over her mood. She couldn't muster a smile on the train ride north the following morning, not until she descended in a fine mist of Lake District rain and saw Francis. He was leaning against the station wall, hat brim slanting over his brow, and when he looked up and saw her he went utterly still. Mab stood, letting him look, letting the other passengers stream around her. She'd scoured London for the hat—pale straw, with a cornflower-blue ribbon round the crown and silk netting. As close as she could find to the hat he'd described the long-ago girl choosing in a Paris shop in 1918, in the letter Mab had read about three hundred times. She'd spent a shocking amount of money on it, and she didn't care. Mab lifted her chin, straightened the hat as if before an imaginary mirror, raised her eyebrows.

By the time he was done kissing her, the hat had fallen off and blown clear across the station. "That's no way to treat a poetical inspiration," Mab scolded, retrieving it.

"How did you find the exact one?" He placed it tenderly back over her hair.

"By enduring the rolled eyes of every clerk in London when they heard me ask for 'wafty sort of netting.' You couldn't have been more specific in your details when you decided to fix this memory in your mind forever?" Mab slid her arm through his. "Remembering spotted netting or close-weave netting would have been a lot more helpful."

"I stand by *wafty*. I know nothing about female attire. Let's get to the hotel so I can peel you out of yours."

I don't deserve this, Mab thought as they tumbled into bed. *I don't deserve him.* She'd always thought of being a good wife in terms of keeping a tidy house, setting a good table, warming a welcoming bed . . . how did you return this? This quiet, devastating riptide of devotion? How did you earn it?

"Mab?" Francis said in astonishment when she dragged herself out of bed in the pink light of dawn as he was pulling on his walking boots. "You don't have to come along on my morning walks. You hate rising early, you hate getting your hair wet—"

"It's time I learned to be a country lass," Mab said determinedly. "Long walks in the woods, sensible shoes. I'll love it!"

She was cursing inside before they made it out of Keswick. "There's a lovely view up the hill quite close," Francis said—apparently *quite close* meant *five miles*. He strode along easily, hands in his pockets, shaking off whatever cobwebs of war came in the night, so Mab did her best to struggle in silence, her hair flattening in the fine drizzle.

She was too out of breath to enjoy the view when they reached the top. It was pouring anyway, too hard to see anything but gray waves of rain gusting across Derwentwater. Francis whistled through his teeth as he looked off the rocky point over the water. The bloody man wasn't even out of breath. "Well, it's *usually* a lovely view," he remarked.

"Spiffing," Mab bit off, massaging her toes.

"All right, country lass." Francis grinned. "How much did you hate this?"

"I look at a view like this," Mab said, waving a hand at the water, the trees, the sweep of clouds, "and I want to see something *paved*."

"That's my city girl." He slid an arm around her waist. "Maybe tomorrow morning we both stay in bed. Stow the hike."

"At least it's not hot." Mab gave a half smile. "You wouldn't believe the sweatshop my hut has turned into." She told him the story of the Wrens' stripping down and working in their underwear, glad she could tell him about her work, even if just a little. She'd hate to be Osla, always keeping mum with her royal suitor. Francis laughed as Mab finished, and she felt rich. He still didn't laugh very often.

"You realize every chap at Bletchley Park will turn into a Peeping Tom once the word gets round? And when the Yanks arrive—"

Mab's smile faded as she remembered the Yank who had supposedly got Wren Bishop into trouble.

"What's that you just thought of?" Francis caught the flicker of her expression.

"A Wren I heard about at BP." Leaning back against the nearest rock, her shoulder against Francis's, Mab surprised herself by telling him. She hadn't ever imagined talking to a husband about such things.

"Poor girl." He shook his head. "That's . . . ugly."

"An old story," Mab said. "Women get in trouble, and if the men won't marry them, there's only a handful of choices. Hoping for a miscarriage"—or doing something to help that along, something that might well kill you in the process—"or going off somewhere to have the baby and give it up."

"Or going somewhere with your mother, somewhere no one knows you, and giving her name at the hospital instead of your own," Francis said calmly. "Then going home and telling your friends and family she had the baby and you have a new little sister."

Mab froze. For a moment she thought her heart had stopped altogether.

"Oh." He turned, hands in his pockets, looking wry. "I wasn't trying to give you a shock . . . I thought you'd guessed by now that I knew."

Mab still didn't know if her heart was beating or not. "How—" she managed to say before her throat locked.

"The first time I saw you with Lucy. The way you looked at her, just a flash when you touched her hair."

I gave myself away, Mab thought. So much obsessive discretion over the years, and all it took was the wrong glance when someone who cared was watching.

"It didn't shock me, Mab. I've heard of such things before."

It hadn't been till weeks after that horrible night Mab had been left by the side of the road that she'd realized Lucy was coming. By then she'd have rather been torn apart by red-hot fishhooks than ever, *ever* contact Geoffrey Irving again.

"It's why the first thing you asked of me was how I felt about taking Lucy into our home," Francis said. "I could see why it meant so much."

"My mother—isn't a very good mother." Mab felt the words wrench and twist, as if they were being forged between her teeth. "She's free with the slaps, she doesn't care if her children run about with holes in their knickers, she'll take Lucy out of school and send her to work as soon as she can. That's what she did with all her children. She's not a bad woman, just worn out and impatient. But I can't really harangue her. Because she agreed to raise my—" Mab stopped for nearly an entire minute. She had never said the two words out loud before, had hardly ever said them in her head. From the day she'd given birth in an anonymous charity hospital and seen the baby carried out in a blanket, she'd told herself over and over, *That's my sister. That's my sister Lucy.*

"—she agreed to raise my daughter for me," Mab whispered, and felt the tears begin to slide. "Mum didn't have to do that. She could have tossed me out on my ear. She could have given me a few quid and told me to get rid of it. She could have told the whole neighborhood I was a slut. She called me that plenty of times, and she slapped me black and blue, but she said she wasn't going to see her youngest dying in some back alley with a coat hanger and a bottle of gin. And then she said she guessed I wasn't going to be her youngest after all, and by the end of the week there was a story about how she and my dad had had a weekend when he was last in town, before she kicked him out for good, and there were plans to go visit him up north with me and see if things worked out. No one really looked surprised when she was back six months later with a baby . . . Some people knew, of course, but it had all been properly explained." Mab scrubbed at her cheeks. "So I don't really have the right to say my mum's not doing such a good job raising Lucy. She didn't have to raise her at all."

"But you want more for Lucy." Francis was listening with every drop of concentration in him, leaning against the rock, his shoulder pressing Mab's.

"Everything I made myself into, I had to fight to do. The books, the clothes, the secretarial course, all of it. With Mum and everyone else saying I was an uppity bitch. I don't want that for Luce. I want her to go to school, a proper school where she gets to play hockey in a clean gym slip and learn maths. I want her to have the kind of vowels I had to teach myself by eavesdropping on university students. I want her to have little shiny riding boots and a *pony*."

Francis put his arms around her. Mab sagged against him, raw to the core. “Please,” she heard herself beg—tough-shelled Mabel from Shoreditch, who never begged anyone for anything, suddenly needing reassurance more than she needed air. “Please tell me what you’re thinking.” *Please tell me I won’t lose you over this.*

“I’m thinking”—he pulled back, tugged a strand of wet hair off her cheek—“that my blasted office is sending me to Scotland for a few months, but that when I get back, you should bring Lucy to Coventry so we can show her her future home. Including where the pony will live.”

Then he held Mab quietly as she clung to him. Blinking over his shoulder, she saw the rain clouds had rolled back from Derwentwater. The lake had turned a sudden, spectacular blue and the fields around it exploded like green and gold velvet under a sudden drenching of sunshine. “You’re right,” she choked. “It’s a lovely view.”

CHAPTER 41

FROM *BLETCHLEY BLETHERINGS*, JUNE 1942

This fine summer weather means romance, judging from the number of BP engagements rumored! What the huts and night shifts hath joined together, let no one put asunder . . .

Two weeks after the conversation with Sheila Zarb, Beth became a thief.

"Beth Finch." Giles's voice hovered somewhere between amused and offended. "Are you actually rummaging in my wallet?"

"No. Yes." Beth could feel the things she'd taken, nearly burning a hole in her pocket. She'd just managed to ease Giles's wallet back into his jacket where it hung over his chair—a much easier job in the large, crowded new-built canteen than it would have been in the old mansion dining room—but he'd ambled back with his tray faster than anticipated. "I needed something . . . I didn't steal! I left you two shillings in place."

"I don't really fancy anyone taking a poke in my wallet who isn't me." He dumped his tray on the table. "What did you need so badly?"

"I—" Beth couldn't say another word. It was four in the morning and the canteen was full of tired people jostling for plates of corned beef and prunes. Beth ducked her head, avoiding his eyes. "I—can't say."

Giles went through his wallet. His brows rose. "Well. I'm plus two shillings and minus two—"

"Pleasedon'tsayit." Beth squeezed her eyes shut in agony. "*Please,* Giles."

He sat back in his chair with a grin. "Wouldn't dream of it."

She fled before he could make any more jokes.

"Beth?" Harry stopped in surprise, coming out of Hut 8 five hours later. Beth had been wondering what to do if he worked a double, but here he was, rumpled and tired looking, shrugging into his jacket.

"You're off shift?" Of course he was, it was nine sharp and people were streaming into the bright summer morning toward the gates, but so much of ordinary conversation seemed to be about stating the obvious. How did anyone stand it? "Where are you off to?"

She'd been expecting him to say "home" and she had an answer for that, but he surprised her. "Hopping the train to Cambridge for the day. Sheila's already there, visiting her parents with Christopher—it's better if I don't go with them, so I'll loaf about until afternoon and then bring them home."

"Why can't you visit her parents?"

Someone jostled past Harry; he moved to one side near the brick half wall erected to shield the hut from bomb raids. "Once her dad is two pints in, he'll start making digs at me, and her mum always frets about how dark Christopher turned out and argues about me teaching him Arabic." Harry's face was taut.

"I don't see Sheila putting up with that."

"She gives them hell. But Christopher cries, and—" Harry broke off. "How do you know what Sheila would or wouldn't do?"

"We met again a few weeks back"—Beth looked down at her handbag—"and talked."

". . . About what?"

Beth couldn't manage the answer. "You're off to the train station then?"

"Yes."

She took a breath. Let the breath out. "I've never been to Cambridge."

He looked at her then, exhausted, direct. "D'you want to come?"

THEY DIDN'T SPEAK on the station platform, or on the train. Harry angled his big body in the crushing crowd so Beth had a bit of space, and then stood silent, expression abstracted. Beth knew the look, having seen it in the mirror often enough. She was still fighting off the code's mesmeric hold herself, and she'd had a *good* shift's work, hard concentration giving way to clean, decrypted script. She hadn't spent hours banging her head against an impenetrable wall. In the cramped space between them she raised her hand, flashed five fingers rapidly like a cluster of Enigma traffic, and then swirled them like a whirlpool, letting her eyes cross. Harry nodded, lids lifted briefly as he grinned. As she dropped her hand back to her side, the backs of their fingers brushed together with the swaying of the train. Beth stood quietly, focusing on the haphazard touch.

They got off at Cambridge, Harry taking her hand quite naturally, pulling her through the crush on the platform. He didn't drop it, and she didn't tug away. She saw spires and goldenstoned buildings; a city half-medieval and utterly untouched by bombing—she couldn't help turning her eyes everywhere, astounded.

"Cambridge is lovelier than Oxford," Harry said. "Don't let any of the Oxford blokes tell you different."

Beth didn't see how anything could be lovelier than this. They meandered, Harry pointing out his favorite spots: "There's the Eagle, best pub in town; I used to work proofs over a pint in the evenings . . . the tower there marks Caius College—my cousin Maurice dared me to climb the roof at night and make the Senate House leap across the lane below. Maurice got recruited to BP too, you know—I had no idea, till I saw him flashing his pass at the gate . . ." Cambridge wasn't as intimidating as London but was much bigger than Bletchley. *And not a soul here knows me.* All her life Beth had lived in a glass bowl where she couldn't cross the road without meeting five people who called out her name.

Harry bought a packet of ersatz meat-paste sandwiches, and they ate on the grass in a loop of the river. He sat with his knees up, shoulders giving an irregular hitch now and then, and a lingering fear flashed in Beth—*breakdown*. Like poor Peggy, who had returned from bed rest pale faced and elusive about her time away. "You're not going crazy, Harry." Beth said it blunt and direct.

"It feels like it." He looked at her, speaking equally bluntly. "What did Sheila tell you?"

Beth had hoped she could get through this without blushing, but she might as well have wished for the moon. "About someone she sees . . . Someone you don't mind about."

"I've never met him." Harry tossed a crust into the river. "But I hope he's head over heels for her."

"You—really don't mind?"

"She should be happy while she can." Harry shook his head. "She fell for a *flier* . . . if he lives through the war it'll be a miracle."

"So . . ." Beth couldn't finish the sentence or her sandwich.

He looked at her straight. "This is all I've got to offer you: the occasional afternoon. Because I'm not leaving Sheila or my son. Wouldn't you rather be off with some fellow who can take you to meet his parents, give you a ring someday?"

"No." Mab seemed to love being married, and clearly Osla wanted to be, but Beth didn't feel that tug. She'd just got out of a household that felt like a prison; the thought of starting things up with a man who might trap her in another household someday made her want to scratch and howl. Beth wanted the life she already had, only—

"Why are you here?" Harry asked, low voiced.

Because I don't know if you're the only friend I have who does what I do and loves what I love—or if you're something more, Beth thought. *And I want to know. Because you make me dizzy.*

She didn't know how to say that. "Why did you ask me to come along today?" she asked instead.

"Because you've got a great, big, beautiful brain all teeming with lobsters and wheels and roses," Harry said, "and I could get tangled up in it all night."

You said it better, Beth thought dizzily. She spoke before she could stop and think, before she could find an excuse to dive back into the shadows.

"Can we go somewhere?"

Harry smiled. He still looked exhausted, but the smile lightened him all over, as if he were hovering over the grass and not sunk into it like a boulder. He reached out, linking his fingers through Beth's. "D'you like music?"

THE SIGN OVER the door read *Scopelli's Music Shop*. The premises were closed and shuttered—it was Sunday morning, Beth realized; everyone was at church or at home. She could have been in chapel right now, ignoring her mother's reproachful stares—instead she was hand-in-hand with a married man, thinking . . .

Well, things that weren't suitable for chapel.

"I had a job here my last year at King's College." Harry let them into the shop and began turning on lights. "Old Mr. Scopelli let me keep a key so I can come on my afternoons off and listen to music."

Most of the shop was in shadow, but Beth saw booths with chairs and headphones. "What do you listen to?" She'd heard so little music, only what was on the radio that Mrs. Finch thought appropriate. At Aspley Guise, they didn't have a radio at all.

Harry went to the wall of records, running his fingers along the top shelf. "Since the U-boat blackout, Bach."

"You said once it was splendidly foursquare," Beth remembered. "Patterns for days."

"Maybe that's why I've been burying myself in it. Trying to find U-boat keys in *The Well-Tempered Clavier*—at least it's something we haven't tried at work." His face darkened briefly, then he gave his head a fierce shake as if to shove Hut 8 and everything about it back into the hole it came from. He pulled a record down. "There . . ." Nodding to the booth at the back. Beth took a seat and Harry dropped into the chair beside her, putting the record on and fiddling with various dials. He shrugged out of his jacket and pushed back his sleeves. "We'll both hear it this way," he said, picking up two pairs of headphones and slipping one over Beth's ears. The world sealed away with a suddenness that surprised her, and she wished she had a pair of these at ISK—then she'd really be able to focus, no distractions of Phyllida's throat-clearing or Jean's slight humming . . .

In the artificial silence she looked at Harry, then looped her fingers round his wrist and tugged. His big hand rose to the nape of her neck, then his other hand moved to her hair, tangling slowly through it, and the silence filled up as he kissed her. Not with sound, Beth thought, gripping his loosened collar and pulling him closer, with color. Honey yellow, sunshine yellow, flooded her to the bone in the utter stillness.

He pulled back, hand still warm at the side of her throat. He looked a question at her. She smiled.

He lowered his head, kissed the space between her collarbones, then drew back and pulled the record from its sleeve. Beth saw the label: *Bach's Partita Number 2 in C Minor.* He dropped the needle, and a piano began.

Patterns—Beth could *hear* them unspooling, golden horizontal lines, more melodies adding in, undergirding the first. Patterns mingling, left hand and right. Patterns she didn't have to solve, just admire. Harry kissed her again. Beth closed her eyes, following the left-hand pattern as it surged, following the pulse in Harry's neck as it surged under her fingertips. She followed the strong lines of his throat down into his collar, listening, moving her lips to his neck. She felt him swallow, felt his hand make a fist in her hair, and it hurt wonderfully. She had never liked to be touched, but now she couldn't get close enough. Normally Harry hunkered down in chairs as if to keep his vast size from intimidating anyone, but now she had the feeling of being pulled into the unyielding granite loom of a mountain. He could have broken her between his huge hands like a toothpick and it didn't frighten her at all—if anything Beth had a fierce thrum of pleasure, because he was nearly shaking with the effort to hold all that strength back, let her be the one to move first.

The world jolted as he tugged her earphones away. "—should stop," he was saying.

"Why?" Everything was too loud. Beth was curled in his lap,

her blouse and brassiere on the floor, Harry's shirt unbuttoned; they were both breathing hard. Music came tinnily from the discarded earphones.

"I'm not going to get you in trouble." Harry went through his pockets with a muttered curse. "I didn't bring anything—didn't think the day had anything like this in store."

Beth reached over to her handbag and showed him what she'd swiped from Giles. "I did."

Harry burst out laughing. "Don't tell me you marched into a shop and asked for—"

"As if anyone would sell them to me!" She felt the blush come. "Nicked from Giles."

"Christ, Beth." Harry put his forehead against hers and laughed in huge, gusting waves. He sounded like he hadn't laughed in months.

"Does this make me a . . ." Beth hesitated. "I thought I should be prepared. Just in case."

"You're a bloody genius." He swiped the two small packets from her hand. "Mr. Scopelli turned his back room into a bomb shelter—there's a camp cot and blankets . . ." Harry paused, giving her a look up and down that scoured like coal fire. "Christ, even your nipples blush."

"Shut up." Beth reached for the earphones. "I want to hear the end of the partita—"

He swung her off his lap, holding her off the ground close against him, eyes black and ravenous. "Bugger. The partita."

CHAPTER 42

Letter from Osla to her Café de Paris Good Samaritan, posted to his London landlady

I don't know why I'm writing you—my first letter after our meeting at the Café de Paris had no reply. Are you still overseas? Are you even still alive? I hope you are. You provided comfort in one of the worst moments of my life, and somehow you've become important to me. Perhaps that's silly . . . I suppose I'm also writing you because I can't write my boyfriend anymore (let's not get into why*) and sometimes I need a page to scream into. This is such a bloody awful war, and I'm so tired of making everyone laugh . . .*

"Nothing missing." Miss Senyard lowered the lid on the last box file. "Will you give it a rest now, Osla?"

Osla nibbled a nail. Months and months it had taken to go through those boxes she thought might have been rifled. She'd told Miss Senyard she was worried about possible missing files, and the older woman had been dubious, but no one could say she wasn't careful: she and her girls (and Osla, too, pitching in at least an hour after every shift) had gone through every single box and cupboard where signals, reports, and copies were stored. The stacks took up whole walls now that German naval section was consolidated. "Goddamn," a visiting American colonel had whistled last week. "If this were the Pentagon, there would be rows and rows of shiny filing cabinets with nothing in them, and you do it all in goddamn shoeboxes."

Well, Osla had seen every one checked and cross-correlated, and she was floored at all points: nothing appeared to be missing. *Maybe whoever rifled through just copied down what they wanted before scarpering,* she thought. But if there was a way to check for that, she didn't know what it was.

"Thanks awfully, ma'am," she told Miss Senyard. "I know you're glad to call this project a dead end." She'd made inquiries about the missing Hut 3 files too (the ones Travis wouldn't admit to) and met a wall of *You dinnae need to know*. There was no uproar or further investigation from the mansion, and no one had been sacked from BP for carelessness—that sort of news made itself known all over the Park—so perhaps the missing files had turned up without fuss. Perhaps they'd simply been mislaid. With thousands of reports flowing through BP, surely the odd stack of paper ended up in the wrong drawer from time to time.

So let it go, her common sense advised as she headed back to Aspley Guise, but Osla didn't entirely *want* to let it go. At least the mystery had kept her occupied, and there hadn't been much in the way of bright spots lately. No more Hut 4 now that they'd moved to the big, anonymous new block; fewer jokes and more strange faces all around. No Philip to bring a jolt of sunshine into her veins; he was out at sea. No escape from tragedy when Osla translated gleeful Nazi reports in July about tracking Convoy PQ17 and sinking twenty-four of thirty ships . . .

And certainly no cessation of nightmares when she closed her eyes at night. Osla wrote her Good Samaritan about that, mainly because she couldn't think who else to tell, wrapped up in his old overcoat, which still smelled like heather and smoke. Sometimes she slept in it. It smelled like a man, even if it wasn't Philip, and then she could pretend she had her head on his shoulder and wasn't just lying in the dark in her narrow bed, dying of loneliness.

"Come up to the roof," Mab proposed when she got back to Aspley Guise. "We won't get another warm day like this until spring, and you look peaky."

"It's the new block." Still the *new* block, even though the naval section had moved over in August. "I never thought I'd miss that creaky old hut, but these big blocks have all the boundless charm of a TB sanitarium. Conveyor belts cranking away, pneumatic tubes, Park messengers whizzing in and out . . ." Osla shook off her blue funk, shimmied into her bathing suit (midriff-baring white dotted with red cherries), and followed Mab up the attic stairs to the rooftop, which was flat, remote, and perfect for sunbathing. Osla laid out her towel as Mab stripped down to her unmentionables; no one was going to see them up here. The day was summer-warm, more like June than October—Osla watched a Hurricane drone overhead from the nearest training base and began working through a comic weather report for *Bletchley Bletherings: Warm and hazy, with a thirty percent chance of Messerschmitts!* Writing *BB* was about the only thing that gave Osla's days any fizz now.

"I got your Vigenère message." Beth's voice floated behind them. Even without the Dread Mrs. Finch snooping, the three of them had never dropped the habit of leaving notes for each other in code. *Up on the roof, bring your bathing suit!* Osla had ciphered before dashing upstairs after Mab.

"Letter came for each of you," Beth continued, wind stirring her blond hair as she came up onto the roof. Osla had marveled before at the change in her quietest billet-mate—something had shifted in Beth, beyond the hair and lipstick. She hardly seemed to be *present* now unless she was on her way to BP, straining like an eager greyhound to get to work. If she wasn't working, Beth didn't even seem to be there. Not in the *please don't look at me* way of the silent, henpecked girl Osla had first met—more in the sense that she wasn't really interested in anything that took place outside Knox's section. That, or heading to Cambridge every day off to listen to records; something else the old Beth would never have done, so Osla supposed it was progress . . . Still, there was something Osla found unsettling in her billet-mate's preoccupied stare lately.

"For you, and you—posted here, not through the London PO Box." Beth handed over the letters, sitting down on the slates and tilting her face upward. "That plane's doing another loop."

"A Hurricane. I used to make them."

"Did you?" Beth asked vaguely.

"Yes." Osla heard her voice grow tart. "And you've heard that story several times. Can't you at least pretend not to utterly ignore anything that isn't in bally code?"

Beth looked puzzled. Osla sighed and tore open her letter, getting a familiar jolt of joy as she recognized Philip's writing.

> *Darling Os—I haven't had a letter in ages. Did I do something to offend? Don't tell me you've met someone else, because if you have, I'll paste him.*

On the heels of joy: pain. Because she couldn't tell Philip why she'd stopped writing.

You might hurt for a while, Osla told Philip silently, *but I'm keeping you safe.* Her commander had been clear—if she failed to keep Philip at arm's length and there was another security breach, Osla wouldn't be the only one called to account. Philip could be too, and he had more to lose. His shining new lieutenancy, his pride in serving at sea, his acceptance from the royal family when he hardly had family of his own left . . . all that could go if there was talk of treason.

He would never recover from a blow like that. Even a brave man like Philip had his Achilles' heel.

I'm protecting yours, Osla thought, folding up the letter. *Even if you never know it.*

Her ears rang suddenly as Mab let out a whoop. "He's coming home! *Francis is coming home!*"

"From Inverness?" Osla asked as Beth said, "From where?"

"I thought they were going to keep him there till he sprouted heather." Mab shuffled a ream of pages, still reading—her husband was always writing her thick packets, and all summer long she'd been scribbling thick packets back.

Osla took her involuntary tendril of envy, squashed it flat, and stamped on it repeatedly. "How long has it been now?"

"Four months, ages longer than he originally thought . . ." Mab hugged her knees. "He'll have three days, the eighth through the tenth of November. How am I going to wait *another* month? He wants me to take the train to Coventry, and bring Lucy." A dizzy smile. "He's going to show us his house—the house we'll all live in after the war."

Osla's envy raised its head again, and she gave it another vicious stamp. "Absolutely topping!"

"Come with me," Mab said promptly. "I'll need someone to help look after Lucy."

"So you can boff your husband senseless each night?" Beth said.

Osla and Mab turned to stare at her. "Where did you learn an expression like that, Miss Finch?" Mab laughed. "Clearly you have been falling into bad company."

"Beth, are you sloping off to meet some fellow?" Osla exclaimed in mock horror. "All these Cambridge Sundays . . ."

She meant it as a joke but Beth looked upward, avoiding eye contact. "That Hurricane's back."

Osla's senses pricked. Maybe if Beth seemed distant lately there was a better explanation than overwork. "Don't get in a flap, tell me—"

"Look, Coventry—can one of you come?" Mab pleaded.

The pink in her cheeks made Osla forget about Beth. Mab was positively shining, not with the cool, hard confidence she'd radiated from the day they met, but with pure joy. *She's in love,* Osla thought. *She may have married Francis for hardheaded reasons, but now she's head over heels.*

"Well, I'd better come along so you get your idyll," Osla said lightly. Three days alongside a husband and wife fizzing with mutual adoration—this was going to require a *lot* of mental stamping. But Osla couldn't say no, not when Mab sat there visibly clutching her own happiness like it was the most fragile of vases. "If you brought Beth, she'd get the swithers, disappear down the center of a rose for an hour, and next thing you knew Lucy would turn up in Timbuktu."

The Hurricane circled round again, even lower. Mab grinned, eyes sparkling. "Let's give him something to look at, ladies."

She stripped off her brassiere and whirled it over her head as the plane droned overhead. Osla pulled off the top of her bathing suit and did the same, laughing. "No, thank you," said Beth, keeping her blouse buttoned, but she waved. The Hurricane waggled its wings in return, and Mab blew a kiss. "Guess what, flyboy!" she shouted upward. "*My husband's coming home!*"

CHAPTER 43

FROM *BLETCHLEY BLETHERINGS*, NOVEMBER 1942

What on earth is the local RAF squadron to do now that it's too cold for the BP ladies of Woburn Abbey and Aspley Guise to go rooftop sunbathing in their skivvies? Go buzz the Fräuleins in Berlin, boys, and drop a few bombs while you're at it . . .

One hour's break for every eight-hour shift. Sometimes Beth and Harry were too exhausted to do anything but bolt sandwiches side by side in the canteen before heading back to their respective blocks, but more often than not they'd trade a wordless glance, make separately for the Park's abandoned air-raid shelter, and fall on each other. It wasn't lovemaking in there, when they were inside BP's clock; it was fast, urgent relief. In Cambridge on days off, they could stretch out on the cot in Scopelli's, talk, laugh—but coming together in the middle of a shift, they were both too far inside Enigma's pathways to pull entirely free.

Beth's mind had been knotted up for weeks in the Spy Enigma; by the time she fell into Harry's arms on break, all she wanted was a few minutes to *stop thinking*. Harry was nine months into the U-boat traffic lockout; after four hours of fruitless work he'd slam into the air-raid cellar with every muscle drawn stone-hard, balanced on such a knife edge of frustration and rage that all he wanted was an outlet—an urge Beth understood perfectly. They'd take a few silent minutes to claw it all out on each other's flesh and then trade soft, wordless kisses and go back to the code.

The code and Harry—Beth didn't know what she'd do without either. *When we win the war,* people were beginning to say with increasing optimism, because the war was starting to look winnable: American troops and supplies were coming across the Atlantic despite the U-boat lockout, Hitler's eastern advance had bogged down in the Soviet Union's implacable ice, and something unspeakably secret was taking shape to tackle Rommel in the desert. Most people were cautiously jubilant—but when Beth heard the words *When we win the war,* she had to push down a surge of panic. Without a war she didn't have this work. Without a war there was no excuse to see Harry. Without a war, would she be an unemployed spinster with a dog, forced back home because she no longer had a billet and a salary?

I feel myself cracking round the edges, Harry sometimes said quietly into her hair when they were alone. But the only thing that made Beth's mind bend at the edges was the thought of losing all this. She could take the hours, she could take the secrecy, she could take the grueling pace, but she couldn't take the thought that it would all someday disappear.

"Where's Jumbo?" someone called out as she let herself back into her section after shift break—they'd moved from the Cottage into a gothic redbrick school building adjacent to BP. Beth missed the whitewashed cottage off the stable yard, but it was too small now with so many new additions to Illicit Services Knox. Not just more new women but men ("Men in my harem," Dilly sighed on one of his rare visits to the section). It didn't matter where ISK was housed or how many new people joined; the women who had broken Matapan together were still the heart of the operation. "*Where's Jumbo?*" Jean repeated, sounding agitated.

"Here." Beth plucked a stuffed plush elephant off her seat and handed it over for a ceremonial ear-rub. The elephant had come from Dilly, living in the cupboard until they were in the middle of a jumbo rush, and the rush had been overwhelming all through October and the start of November. Scads of Abwehr traffic about something called Operation Torch (whatever that was) drawing to a head.

"I'll wager it's confirmations," Giles speculated. He'd been moved over to ISK some weeks ago; Beth still found it strange to see him working at the desk next to hers. "If it's really true we've got all the German double agents under our thumbs, we'll be using them to feed false information back as cover-up for Torch. No good planning a big push without misdirection. Convince the Krauts the Allied convoys are heading one way, when they're headed another . . . all this Abwehr stuff is just checking to confirm if they're buying what we're selling."

"Maybe." Beth was rodding for the right-hand wheel position, fast and automatic.

"You aren't even the tiniest bit inquisitive?"

"No."

"I can't decide if you're monumentally incurious or the purest bloody brain I've ever met." Giles linked his hands behind his head, studying her as if she were a rare scientific specimen. "Hitler's private telegrams or the Sunday crossword—it's all the same to you."

"I crack messages. I don't interpret them." Beth swept her hair out of her face. "It doesn't matter to me what I'm breaking. Why complicate things when there aren't hardly enough hours in the day as is?"

"Especially at my pace." Giles made a face. He wasn't a bad cryptanalyst, but he'd got used to three-wheel work in his old hut, and wading through four-wheel stuff like Abwehr took him ages.

"You're getting faster," Beth said charitably.

"Won't ever be up to your speed." He said it without resentment, which Beth appreciated. Some of the Hut 6 men were disconcerted by the unconventional working methods of Dilly's team. *That's not the way this is done,* one of the new mathematicians had said his first week, and Giles had bounced a wad of paper off his forehead and said, *You crack the Spy key all by yourself, Gerald, and I'll do it your way. Until then I'm going to do it Beth's way.*

Beth cracked through her whole stack of messages before looking up and stretching her neck. "What else have we got?" Giving Jumbo's ears a rub.

Peggy brought fresh chicory coffee over. "Night shift's done, Beth. Go home."

"This is what calms me down." Osla and Mab were leaving this morning for Coventry—it would be dull in Aspley Guise without them, and Beth would far rather work the day shift. "Give me the Hut 6 duds if there's nothing else."

Peggy pushed a stack over. "More possible bombing sites—Giles has the list of city codes."

"*Loge* for London, *Paula* for Paris . . ." Giles reeled them off. Beth pulled her crib sheets and rods over and began working. Not nearly so many air raids now as earlier in the war, but you never knew when a wave of German bombers would pop up like a nasty surprise out of a jack-in-the-box.

"Giles," Beth called over absently, some hours later. "What city is *Korn* code for?"

"*Korn . . . Korn . . .*" He dropped his pencil, massaging his fingers. “Coventry. Don’t tell me poor little Coventry is due for another raid?”

“Did they get hit before?”

“Do you live in a box? They were nearly flattened two years back.”

Beth stared at the jumble of German words coming out of the message before her. She still didn’t speak German, but there were words she saw often enough to recognize. She looked at this one and she saw *Korn* and numbers that might be coordinates . . . and then her eyes caught on the raid’s attack date. *8 November.*

“Giles,” Beth said slowly, “what day is it today?”

CHAPTER 44

Mab was used to the sight of air-raid damage, but gazing at Coventry, she realized how much London's sprawl lessened the impact of the destruction. There, if you saw a house missing at least there were houses still standing on either side; if you saw bomb craters in a street, you saw automobiles swerving busily around them. Coventry, so much smaller and more compact, had been far more comprehensively wrecked. Mab barely counted one building in three that wasn't either reduced to rubble or sporting boarded windows. The ancient cathedral stood open to the elements, stone floor dusted with snow, medieval windows with their fire-scarred stone tracery stark against the gray sky. "'Bare ruined choirs,'" Mab echoed. The Mad Hatters were reading Shakespeare's sonnets this month.

"The big raid was in November of '40," Francis said, also gazing at the cathedral. "More than five hundred killed. I wasn't in town, but I knew so many who died. There've been two more raids since, but nothing like that one." He ruffled a hand through his chestnut hair. "It's all in dismal condition, but I hope you can see Coventry for what it will be again, after the war."

He said it low voiced so Lucy, running ahead through a puddle, wouldn't hear. "Come back, Luce!" Osla called, sauntering after in her blush-pink coat. She and Mab had said goodbye to Beth at the BP canteen this morning, then collected Lucy, who had been put on the train to Bletchley in care of the conductor, and they'd all headed for Coventry. Francis had greeted them at the station, a flat box under one arm that he hadn't yet explained. Lucy had hung back behind Mab, regarding him warily through the fringe of her bangs. "Hello, Lucy," he'd said easily. "What would you say to a walk around the city?"

"No," Lucy said. "I'd rather look at ponies than take a walk. Are there ponies?"

"We'll see if we can find you ponies." Off they went, the four of them bundled in coats and scarves, and Mab was glad for Osla's easy chatter, which acted like bright paint over Francis's habitual silence and Lucy's careful glances. *Wait till we see our home-to-be,* Mab promised her family silently. When the three of them all lived here together, Lucy would relax and Francis would laugh more and Coventry Cathedral would have a roof again. All it took was peacetime.

"I think it's a beautiful city," Mab said as they turned away from the cathedral.

Francis gave a half smile. He was even quieter than usual, his face paler after months under Scotland's gray skies. Mab wondered what he'd been doing there. Maybe when they were married forty years or so and none of these secrets mattered anymore, they could tell each other.

"So . . ." Francis offered his arm. "Do you want to see the house?"

It was tall, tawny stoned, surrounded by a tangled garden dusted with snow. Mab envisioned roses, no more victory garden vegetables, because when the war was over she would just buy cabbages at the greengrocer's. The front door creaked invitingly when he unlocked it.

Mab almost tiptoed inside. A flagstone entryway, a grandfather clock ticking at the end . . . Lucy, instantly fascinated, tried to climb in. Mab looked into a parlor with a towering stone hearth—she could see cozy fires dancing in the evening—a dining room for Sunday lunches in a future where roasts and butter were no longer rationed . . .

Francis began throwing blackout curtains open and Mab saw how big the windows were, how the house would look flooded in summer sunshine. "A housekeeper comes weekly to keep things aired and dusted," he said. "She's left us a cold lunch. I'll put things out, you ladies look round."

"Good for sliding," Lucy said, running her hand over the polished oak bannister.

"Very good for sliding," Mab agreed, following her upstairs. A bedroom upstairs with an enormous four-poster; three more bedrooms. She saw Lucy hesitate in the one with a cushioned window seat. "This could be yours," Mab said, and held her breath.

Lucy frowned. "Mum wouldn't mind?"

"No." Mab's mother hadn't been able to hide her relief at the idea that she wouldn't have to shepherd another child all the way through to majority. *No, I don't mind if you take her on, are you mad?* Mab had no doubt her mother loved Lucy in her brusque way, but she was past fifty and tired. She didn't really want to keep trimming bangs and scrimping for shoes. "Mum won't mind," Mab assured Lucy now. "We'll go see her every week, but you'll be living here with me."

"Now?"

"After the war."

"Would he live here too?" A glance through the door, toward where Francis clattered in the kitchen downstairs.

"Yes, he would."

Lucy frowned. She was wary of all strange men, and Mab wondered in a surge of bleakness if that was something she'd unconsciously passed to her daughter. "He's a very nice man, Luce. You'll like living here with us."

"It's not London . . ." In Lucy's short life she'd been uprooted from London and sent to Sheffield, then shuttled between the two depending on the ebb and flow of German air raids—Mab could tell the idea of yet another upheaval was making her daughter balk. But Lucy kept looking at that window seat, exactly the right size for a little girl to curl up in while drawing.

"Let's call this your room," Mab said, and led Lucy downstairs.

Francis and Osla had set the table in the kitchen for lunch—a pot of tea, cold sandwiches, an eggless sponge pudding with raspberry jam. Osla, bless her, was chattering pleasantries while Francis quietly poured tea. He gave Lucy a proper cup, not just nursery tea with hot water and milk, and on her chair Mab saw the flat box he'd been carrying earlier. "That's for you, Lucy," Francis said, sipping.

Lucy pushed back the lid, looked into the nest of tissue paper . . . and her face flushed pink. Mab had never in her entire life seen a child look so happy. "*Oh,*" Lucy breathed, and lifted out a pair of tiny, glossy, knee-high riding boots.

"For when you start riding lessons," Francis said. What he must have spent in clothing coupons and favors for such a gift! "There's a riding school not far away."

"Really?"

"Really."

Mab looked at her daughter, hugging her new boots and glowing like a small sun as she whispered a shy, ecstatic *thank you,* and felt her heart shatter. *I love you,* she thought, looking across the table at her husband. *How I love you, Francis Gray.*

CHAPTER 45

The air-raid siren went off long after midnight.

Osla jerked awake. It took her a moment to remember she was sharing one of the ground-floor bedrooms of Francis's Coventry house with Lucy. They'd all played backgammon and charades, then turned on the radio and listened breathlessly to reports of joint Allied landings in North Africa. Once Lucy was drooping, and Mab and Francis on the point of going up in smoke if they didn't get some time alone, Osla suggested heading to bed.

Now the air-raid sirens wailed outside.

"Lucy, wake up—" The little girl was still sound asleep on the other side of the bed. How many air-raid sirens had a child of the East End heard by 1942? Lucy probably didn't bother waking up for anything less than five hundred Junkers overhead. But Osla hadn't faced an air raid since the Café de Paris had been blown to pieces all around her, and fear rose thick and foul in her throat as she fumbled for her shoes and flung her coat over her nightdress. *Don't panic,* she told herself, scooping up the sleeping Lucy and stumbling out into the pitch-dark corridor.

"Mab?" Osla called. A bone-humming drone sounded above—were bombers here already? Osla groped to the front door and flung it open. Outside the darkness was thick enough to choke on, pierced by finger-beams of searchlights stabbing at a roiling, reddened sky. Osla saw something metallic flash through one of the searchlights—a plane. A German bomber, piloted by some fresh-faced Luftwaffe pilot who was right now doing his best to blow Osla and Lucy and the rest of Coventry to cinders. She felt a stab of hatred so silver-bright it nearly staggered her, and then she heard footsteps down the stairs, Francis in trousers and shirtsleeves, Mab wrapped in his coat.

"There's an air-raid shelter a quarter mile down the road," Francis said, sounding so blessedly calm Osla's pulse steadied. "Safer than the cellar . . ." And they were all piling out through the tangled garden. Francis struggled into his spare coat as Mab tried to take Lucy, but the girl clung to Osla like a limpet, still mostly asleep.

"Leave her," Osla gasped. "At least she's quiet." Mab put her arm around Osla, squeezing in fierce, wordless love, and they joined the flood of people thronging the icy street: a child dragging a panicked dog, a woman with a kerchief over rag curls, a man with pajama bottoms stuffed into wellies. It was not really loud yet; it was all labored breaths and shuffling feet, muffled cursing and droning engines. Osla's stockingless toes scraped inside her shoes; her arms ached supporting Lucy's warm, solid weight. She could see flares drifting down like fireflies from the planes, lighting the ground for strikes from the air, and she thought of Philip at Cape Matapan, lighting the enemy cruisers for strikes from the sea. *As near murder as anything could be in wartime . . .*

Lucy stirred muzzily, but Osla tugged the blanket back over her head. "We're playing a game, darling. You've got to keep quiet as a mouse, that's the game—"

"Almost there," Francis said as the crush grew thicker. He had one arm around Mab and his other hand grasped Osla's shoulder, calm and reliable, and Osla had her panic firmly gripped between her teeth. The imagined air-raid shelter gleamed like a beacon: a cozy underground place where everyone would share blankets, someone would have a flask of whiskey, and maybe they'd sing "Could You Please Oblige Us with a Bren Gun?" until the all-clear sounded. It would be nothing like the Café de Paris.

Then Francis's hand tore away from Osla's arm as a crowd of young men pushed through the throng, shoving ahead at a flat run. Jostled, Osla's foot missed the curb and slewed sideways. Pain shot clear up to her knee. She fell, managing to twist to one side so she didn't crush Lucy as the two of them hit the street with a jolt. Osla's entire body vibrated as though she'd been slammed through the windscreen of a car. Lucy yelped, fighting free of the blanket.

"*Lucy!*" Mab's voice, high and panicked. Osla couldn't see her friend. The night was black and red, people streaming in all directions.

"Lucy, here—" The world tilted and spun, but Osla levered herself up, lunging to grab hold of the little girl. Her fingers locked round that tiny wrist. "Stay with me, sweetheart—"

A vast percussive *whump* sounded, and Osla heard the shatter of exploding windows. For an instant she saw the blue flash of the explosion that had torn the Café de Paris apart, torn her dancing partner's lungs from his chest—and she flinched, fingers springing open.

In that moment, Lucy wrenched away and fled into the night.

CHAPTER 46

"*Lucy!*" Mab's throat was raw with calling. She nearly fell over a chunk of masonry in the street, staggered upright, and rebounded off a woman dragging a human chain of children toward the air-raid shelter. The din was deafening; bombs fell, smoke billowed, screams rose, but Mab could hear nothing, see nothing, that wasn't Lucy. How could a child surrounded by three adults disappear in an instant? Her daughter had slipped into this rushing torrent of panic and bombs and disappeared like a minnow into white water. "*Lucy!*"

"Mab—" Francis's hand like a steel band over her arm. "Get to the shelter, let me look for her."

She didn't even answer, just tore away and shoved further up the street, panic rising red and clawing in her chest. Osla reached out with one shaking hand, the other clapped to her face, which had been scraped raw against the street. "Mab—" Blood ran through her fingers. "We'll find her, I promise, we'll find her—"

"Why didn't you keep hold of her?" Mab snarled. She would have struck Osla if Francis hadn't seized her again.

"You two look here, I'll see if she's making for the house."

Mab dimly saw the sense of that and began to fumble down her side of the street as Osla staggered across to the other side and Francis took off the way they'd come. Mab saw the flash of his hair in a jagged spear of red light, and he was gone. She flung herself against the nearest door, a house with blackout shutters blown to splinters. "*Did you see a child—*"

No use. The din was deafening, explosions and toppling timber and the dry growing rush of fire rising every second. Everyone was sprinting openly for the cover of a shelter or a cellar. The night choked black on terror, and Lucy was nowhere to be seen. Mab sobbed, stumbling from house to house, banging on doors, fumbling behind pots and lampposts—anywhere a child could have curled up, small and cowering as a beetle. Dimly she saw Osla searching across the street. A deafening crash sounded as a house collapsed, and Mab felt a sickle-sharp splinter carve a path across her hand.

"*Lucy!*"

No answer. Overhead the roar of engines as planes throbbed through the sky. Searchlights stabbed the air, hunting them out so the antiaircraft defenses could line up a shot. *Shoot them down,* Mab wanted to scream, *shoot them all down so I can find my* child—but the bombers droned on untouched, disappearing into billows of smoke. Another house collapsed, and arms locked around Mab, dragging her down. "Get down," Osla was shouting, "get *down—*"

No, Mab wanted to scream, but Osla half threw her to the ground in the shadow of a big brick depot, wrapping her arms around Mab's head. The explosions were all around them now, cobbles and bricks cracking and leaping like drops of fat in a hot pan. She tried to stand and a wave of smoke forced her down again, choking. Mab didn't know where the sky was; this was her very first air raid, and the world had turned to black smoke and shrieking metal. She felt Osla trembling, taut with terror, and held on to her for dear life.

As soon as the deafening wave overhead passed, Mab was back on her feet and stumbling down the street, calling her daughter's name. Calling until her throat scraped.

"*Mab!*" Osla was screaming right into her face. Mab's ears rang so badly, she could barely hear. "Mab, it's stopping!"

Mab swayed, gulping in a breath that tasted like ash. She looked overhead—no waves of bombers showed in silver splinters against the searchlights. There was still the hungry crackle of fire, but she thought she heard the shouts of fire wardens, the hiss of water being trained through hoses. "It's stopping," Osla repeated. Mab had never seen her stylish, beautiful billet-mate look such a wreck, curls clinging ash-matted to her neck, face darkened with smoke.

"It's stopping," Mab repeated shakily. She could feel blood trickling from her blasted ears. "Lucy will come out from where she's hiding now." She was only hiding; it was all right.

People were coming out even before the all-clear sounded, cautiously putting noses round doors, trailing up cellar steps. Mab rushed up to every face she saw. "Have you seen a little girl, six, dark haired?" People stopped, no longer pushing past in panic; they stopped to listen.

No one had seen her.

"Mab," Osla began, voice quivering, but Mab pushed her away and lurched down the street toward Francis's house.

She got lost in the dark tangle of unfamiliar streets, straightened herself out as the all-clear sounded at last. The sky had lightened to gray, Mab realized dully—how long had the attack lasted? It felt like a century.

She let out a choked gasp. The house beside Francis's had been sheared nearly in half, the front façade collapsed into rubble, the inside open to the elements. A sink hung over the garden below, sagging in midair, and the outer wall snugged up nearly to

Francis's chimney was listing outward as though about to topple. But the tawny-stoned house where Mab had led Lucy yesterday afternoon—where they had eaten sponge with jam and Mab had fantasized about peacetime Christmas dinners; where Lucy had picked out her bedroom and Francis had made slow, sleepy love to Mab at midnight in their own—was untouched.

And the front door was opening with an ordinary, everyday creak.

Mab clung to the garden gate as Francis came out of the house and down the steps, Lucy riding comfortably in his arms. He was in his shirtsleeves, russet hair glinting in the dawn; his coat was wrapped around Lucy, who had linked an elbow around his neck. With the other arm she hugged her new riding boots against her little chest.

"She went back for her boots," Francis called, perfectly calm, and Mab's throat closed in a half sob, half laugh. Lucy was giving Mab a sunny wave, as if the city had not been stirred to ash and terror all around her.

Mab heard Osla crying with relief behind her. "It's all right, Os," she managed to say, reaching back to give her friend's hand a squeeze. "They're all right."

Francis looked up at the house beside his with its sheared-off front face. The clawfoot bathtub had been blown from the first-floor loo and landed on his own front walk. "Let's get out over the side fence instead, Lucy-girl," he remarked with one of his rare grins, skirting the mess of ceramic shards. "Since there's a bathtub in our front yard."

Lucy was gurgling with laughter, Mab smiling as Francis swung her daughter over the side fence—and it happened.

It happened so fast.

Just as a relieved Mab was reaching out her arms to Lucy, the leaning outer wall of the bombed-out house toppled outward in a sudden three-story roar of bricks and beams, collapsing directly into the fenced garden.

Francis had time to look up.

Lucy had time for a thin, terrified wail.

Then they disappeared, buried in a torrent of stone.

—I WOULDN'T DIG *if I were you, ma'am—*

—My daughter's in there, she can't breathe—

—Ma'am, your daughter is—

—MAB, COME AWAY. *Please come away—*

—Get off me, Os—

—CHRIST, LOOK AT *her hands—ma'am, stop tearing at those stones—*

—Mab, stop. Stop, they're dead*—*

—Go to hell, Osla Kendall—

—DON'T LOOK, MA'AM. *You don't want to remember them like that—*

—Will someone get the damned woman out of here—

—Mrs. Gray—

—I TOLD YOU *not to look, ma'am . . .*

—I told you not to look.

SOMEONE WAS SCREAMING—

Someone was scraping blood and wood splinters from under her nails—

Someone was wiping at a wet gray slurry on her sleeve, stone dust and flecks of brain—

Mab realized it was her.

CHAPTER 47

FROM *BLETCHLEY BLETHERINGS*, DECEMBER 1942

The final couplet of "Spark," sonnet from *Mired: Battlefield Verses by Francis Gray:*

The spark is snuffed—and then another, too—
Too fragile-fine to flame above the rue.

Two sparks have gone out, and Bletchley Park mourns alongside one of its own.

There were more people present at the funeral than Osla expected—a group of Francis's colleagues from the Foreign Office, some Coventry friends, his London publisher, a handful of literary admirers . . . and Mab. The widowed Mrs. Gray in the front pew of the Keswick church, red lipstick perfectly applied, black dress contrasting against a curiously frivolous straw hat with a blue ribbon.

"Why did Mab decide to bury him here?" Giles whispered when the service ended and the mourners filed toward the graveyard.

"Because she and Francis were happy here." Osla hadn't wept during the service, but she nearly wept now, thinking of Mab's happy face after her Lake District weekends.

"But you'd think she'd do it in Coventry where he died," said Beth.

"Why would she ever want to go back there? For God's sake . . ."

Beth flushed dully over her ugly black dress. "It's not the town's fault. They didn't know the raid was coming. Even if they had, they couldn't have evacuated in time."

Osla choked down the urge to scream. *You've said that about eight times, Beth.* What did it matter if the town couldn't have evacuated if they'd known? No one *had* known that one of the bigger raids of the year was coming to hit poor little Coventry all over again.

"Even if they'd had word, the town couldn't have emptied in time," Beth insisted, as if she had to convince someone.

"It doesn't matter. Mab doesn't want to bury Francis in Coventry, and he has no family to say otherwise, so why shouldn't she please herself?"

Mab hadn't spoken to either of her billet-mates since the Coventry raid. She'd gone straight to London and refused to come to the telephone when they rang. Mrs. Churt had been the one to tell Osla, hoarse voiced, that Lucy had been buried already. *Here, where our family could attend. Mabel's gone to Keswick now, to put her man in the ground.*

The mourners clustered around the grave as the coffin was lowered in, and Osla wished the Mad Hatters could have come. But Mab hadn't spoken to any of them, either, and only Osla, Beth, and Giles were able to get last-minute leave.

They watched Mab drop the first clod of earth into the grave. Her face was a pale mask, the same mask Osla had seen when she was wrenched away from the terrible heap in the Coventry garden. Her rending shrieks had stopped as if a switch had been flipped. *Oh, Mab, come back,* Osla pleaded silently, looking at her friend's empty face.

Would Mab come back—not just to herself, but to Buckinghamshire? What would Bletchley Park be like without Mab?

Somehow the graveside service was over. The mourners broke up, shepherded by a middle-aged woman in black crepe. "There's a bit of luncheon laid out in my parlor," she told Osla. "Do come get a bite, dear. How did you know Mr. Gray? Such a fine man . . ."

Osla watched Mab walk out of the churchyard in her pale hat. "Yes, he was."

Beth was still looking at the grave. "Coventry couldn't have been evacuated," she whispered when the middle-aged woman hurried off.

"Shut up!" Osla exploded.

Beth started as if she'd been slapped. Giles put a consoling arm around her, and Osla looked away, strangling her black-bordered handkerchief. She knew she should apologize, but she couldn't. All she could see was her own fingers letting go of Lucy's tiny wrist—the silent, terrible heap of stones and beams—Mab on her knees in the rubble, cradling a tiny riding boot and giving those terrible choked screams . . .

In the hotel parlor, Mab managed to accept a tight hug from Giles before being walled off by suits and condolences. Osla and Beth stood with untouched plates of prune pudding, waiting for a chance to speak with her, but there wasn't one. At some point the crowd cleared, and she was simply gone.

"She went walking," the hotel landlady said, clearing plates. "Around Derwentwater, up to the lookout. A lovely view up there."

Osla and Beth exchanged glances with Giles, and Osla knew they were all sharing the same thought.

Mab wouldn't throw herself off . . . would she?

No, Osla thought. *Not Mab.*

But her stomach rolled in sudden terror, and her mind flashed with a horrifically clear image of Lucy's tiny body, pulled from the rubble. *It was your fault,* the thought whispered. *You let go of Lucy. And if something happens to Mab, that will be your fault, too.*

"Go," Giles said, moving to head off some incoming gossipers. "She needs you both right now."

CHAPTER 48

Last time Mab had taken this walk, it had been with Francis. *We'll bring Lucy,* she'd thought at the time, head against his shoulder as they looked out at the lake. She let herself sink into that dream now: Francis pointing out the flowers she couldn't identify; Lucy running after butterflies; Mab following in a summer straw hat. Francis would have carried Lucy over the steep bits of the climb—Lucy would have allowed that. At the very end in Coventry, she'd let him pick her up. She'd been learning to trust him. She would have let him carry her all the way to the top of the lookout here.

Only now she never would.

Why. The word had been echoing through Mab's brain for three weeks now, about everything. Why. *Why. WHY.*

Why didn't you marry him at once, instead of waiting until you were sure he was a good prospect?

Why didn't you quit working at Bletchley Park and make a home right away for him and Lucy?

Why were you so careful not to conceive a child?

Why and *if.* The two most painful words in existence. *If* she'd married Francis Gray the week he proposed, they'd have had three more months of married life. *If* she'd resigned from BP, she would have had her family together every night when Lucy came home from school and Francis came home from work, not spread out and waiting because war work had somehow seemed more important. *If* she hadn't been so careful to avoid conception, she might have had something of Francis besides a packet of love letters.

You have more than that, she reminded herself bitterly. *You have everything you ever dreamed of, Mab Gray.* She'd wanted to ditch the name *Churt* and remake herself as a lady of means, with no whiff of scandal that she'd ever been a cheap East End slut who gave birth out of wedlock. Well, she was Mrs. Gray now, and she was certainly a lady of means: Francis's will named her sole inheritor of his modest royalties and not-so-modest accounts. She could afford all the fine hats and leather-bound books she wanted, and no one would ever know she'd given birth out of wedlock because her child was dead.

She realized that she was ripping her blue-ribboned hat to pieces and flinging them off the lookout. The ribbon went drifting down the hillside, as blue as the surface of Derwentwater, then the straw brim, then the wafty netting. In Francis's wallet, returned to her with his effects, she had found a folded sheet of paper with a few scribbled lines in his writing:

The Girl with the Hat
a sonnet by Francis Gray

The mirror shows a faery queen in red
Posing, turning, angling with a smile
She tilts a straw-made hat upon her head

Christ, this is awful stuff, Gray. Who ever said you could write poetry?

But there were more lines, reworked and crossed out and reworked again, and at the very bottom he'd squeezed in a note: *Work Lucy into the metaphor? Titania's sprite Peaseblossom? Or is Luce more of a Mustardseed . . .*

The pain clawed Mab like some hungry beast, doubling her over. It never hit when she expected it to—she'd stood entirely numb through Lucy's funeral in London, through Francis's here. Sometimes it crept up on her at night, leaving her sobbing, or it overcame her when she was pouring a brandy and wondering if she'd sleep if she drank an entire bottle. She never knew when it was coming, only that it would never stop. She was twenty-four years old; she'd been a mother for six years and a wife for less than one, and the pain was never going to stop.

Then she turned and saw Osla and Beth coming up the path onto the lookout.

Mab didn't wait for either of them to speak. She pulled her head back and spat at Osla, hitting Osla's black cashmere coat hem. "How dare you show up at his funeral, Osla Kendall. How *dare* you."

"I came for you," Osla whispered. "I'm your friend."

"You killed them," Mab rasped. "You let go of Lucy—you let her go, and Francis went tearing off after her—"

"Yes." Osla stood chalk white and shaking, but she didn't flinch from the accusation. "It's my fault."

"*All you had to do was hold on to her, and you let her go.*" Mab heard her voice scaling up and choked it off. She would kill Osla and Beth right here and now if she cried in front of them. "We—if we'd got to a damned air-raid shelter—"

"You can't blame Osla," Beth whispered.

"Yes, I can." Mab felt herself smiling mirthlessly. The smile hurt. She welcomed the pain, dug into it, ate it raw and sopping red. "I can blame everyone." The Luftwaffe, for bombing Coventry. Herself, for insisting Francis take them there. Francis, for stepping left instead of right to get out of the garden. "But all Osla had to do was hang on to Lucy's hand, and she *fucking let her go.*"

"I did." Osla's eyes overflowed, tears streaking sooty and black down her cheeks.

"She was my daughter," Mab whispered. "You killed my *daughter.*"

"She was your sis—" Beth began automatically, literal as ever, and then even Beth stopped dead, her eyes huge and horrified.

Osla trembled. "Oh, Mab—"

"Shut up." Mab was shaking, too, now. "Don't you say a goddamned word to me ever again, Osla Kendall. Don't you *dare.*"

CHAPTER 49

The tiny lake at Bletchley Park sometimes froze thick enough in wintertime for skating. Some off-duty codebreakers were playing hockey today, bashing sticks around the ice, but Beth ignored them. She stood on the bank, looking at the beaten-steel sky, thinking of Coventry. Francis and Lucy—Mab's *daughter*. Osla and Mab . . .

I can't tell them, Beth thought, breathing raggedly. *Not ever.*

Couldn't tell them how all hell had broken loose in ISK, tearing Beth away from the message she'd been decrypting about the Coventry raid . . . someone shouting about Allied forces and North Africa. Suddenly everyone had been gathering round the radio, breathless with excitement. It was the kind of turnaround that made all the double shifts worthwhile, Beth thought—the moment you finally understood what you'd been working on for so many months. "So *that's* what Operation Torch was," she'd marveled, hearing of Allied landings in Tunisia, Morocco, and Algeria, and Dilly's women had all cheered because now they could look back at the October rush and realize what they'd done. Because they'd cracked the Spy Enigma, the German agents had been turned and forced to feed false information about where Operation Torch's convoys were headed. Because of ISK, Operation Torch had hit like a bolt from the blue and Rommel in his desert headquarters was having a very, very bad time of it.

Beth hadn't come back to the message about the Coventry raid for hours, and when she did, her duty had seemed quite clear. She'd just witnessed the importance of secrecy firsthand—even the slightest leak outside Park walls could have turned Operation Torch into a slaughter. *You can't tell Osla or Mab,* she'd thought, filing the Coventry message. *You swore an oath.* So when she bid them goodbye in the canteen later that morning, knowing they were off to catch the Coventry train, she'd done it with barely a hitch. What were the odds, after all, in a city well accustomed to bolting for air-raid shelters at the first blare of a siren, that her friends would be hurt?

You were wrong, Beth thought now, breath catching painfully.

But it didn't matter. What was the point of telling now, when the damage was done?

So she gulped a breath, took the secret, and mentally filed it away as she stood beside the frozen lake. She had begun to find it quite easy, dividing life into compartments. There was the code and everything that came with it. And there was everything else—her friends, her family, Harry, everyone—who had to come second.

The code came first.

When Coventry and all its losses were neatly boxed up, Beth waved to the hockey players and picked her way across the icy lake path, pausing midway as she saw a mass of Hut 8 cryptanalysts spilling across the lawn, cheering at the top of their lungs. Brilliant Joan Clarke, whom Dilly wished he'd poached for his section; Rolf Noskwith drinking directly out of a wine bottle—and Harry, veering away from the pack and picking Beth up, swinging her over the frosty grass.

"We did it, we bloody did it! A pinch off U-559—we're back in. We're back in the bloody U-boat traffic!"

"Harry!" She kissed him jubilantly, every worry that had been consuming her falling away. "I knew you'd get in."

People were spilling out of huts and blocks, letting out cheers as the news spread. The U-boat blackout had gone on too long not to be common knowledge at BP, even if no one outside Hut 8 knew details. "Christ, Beth," Harry was whispering into her hair, still holding on to her like a lifeline. "I wish I could tell you how we got in. I wish you'd been there."

"You can't tell me anything, it's all right, I don't care—"

He kissed her again, hands pulling through her hair, and Beth heard ripples from the people around them. It would be all over Bletchley Park in hours: little Beth Finch and Harry Zarb who had a wife and child at home. She didn't care what people thought. It wasn't an important secret.

Not like the one she'd just buried.

TEN DAYS UNTIL THE ROYAL WEDDING

November 10, 1947

CHAPTER 50

Inside the Clock

Beth wasn't released from the straitjacket until after supper. Chafing her numbed hands, fighting the hangover of the injections, she wandered into the common room looking for a game of Go and her partner. But the board sat abandoned, the sharp-eyed woman nowhere in sight. "Didn't you know?" another of the women said. "She was taken off this afternoon. Surgery."

Beth fought a swell of unease. "What kind of surgery?"

Shrug. Beth sat behind the game board, fighting her disquiet. A matron came in with a list of tomorrow's visitations, but Beth ignored her. In three and a half years she'd only had one visitor.

That was why it had taken so long to smuggle her coded letters out to Osla and Mab.

So many dead ends . . . Trying to sneak the cipher messages out with the asylum post. Trying to bribe an orderly to post them off-grounds. Wheedling a fellow inmate into sealing a letter inside one of theirs. She'd been shut down or caught every time—*Miss Liddell, no post in or out for you!* When she'd been sent here, MI-5's instructions had clearly been strict: an inmate like Beth with her headful of secret information was *not* allowed to exchange news with the outside world.

Only a few weeks ago had she finally been able to send her ciphered call for help.

"Visitor, Miss Liddell!" the nurse had sung out, shocking Beth speechless. Three and a half years with not a single visitor from the outside world . . . *Harry?* she'd thought, pulse ratcheting as she approached the visiting room.

"Bethan." Her father stood in the middle of the room, which could have been her mother's parlor except that all the knick-knacks were bolted down to stop hysterical inmates from hurling them at their visiting loved ones. Seeing her father's horror as he registered her chopped hair and gaunt face, Beth wouldn't have minded slinging a vase or two. "Are you—all right?" he ventured as the orderlies left them alone.

"Do I look all right?" Beth had answered coldly.

"You look . . ." He trailed away. "Are you improving? I'd love to have you home again."

"Why? Mother wouldn't."

"Of course she would! Well, not that she said—that is, she doesn't know I'm here." An unnecessary statement if there ever was one, Beth thought. "She's visiting your aunt in Bournemouth, and I thought I'd—"

"Sneak out behind her back?" Beth's throat burned constantly from throwing up her pills twice a day; looking at her father, it felt like she was choking out hot coals along with words. "More than three years, Dad. Not *one* visit."

"Your mother didn't think . . . that is, we decided to give you time to heal." His eyes darted across her smock, her chapped lips. "They said it was a good place."

"Mother was only too happy to believe that, I'm sure. A place where I'm no longer underfoot, embarrassing her." Beth choked herself off. She could rage at her father forever, but all that would do was drive him away. *Don't waste this chance.*

"Thank you for coming," she said, making her voice gentler.

He relaxed then, telling family news, answering questions she kept innocuous. No, he didn't know what had happened to Boots . . . Beth choked down bitter disappointment but kept nodding.

"I'd get you out if I could," her father had said at last, hesitant. "The Bletchley fellows said parental rights didn't have sway here. You're committed as an employee of the government, by order of the government, for your own good and for the sake of security."

"I know." Perhaps the right person could make enough fuss to get her case reviewed, but her father didn't have it in him to kick down doors in London. He had barely summoned the nerve to visit her today behind his wife's back. Her contempt nearly choked her, but at the same time she wanted to cry, remembering how he'd let her help with his crossword when she was small. *Oh, Dad . . .*

Then she remembered how he'd stood by her entire life while her mother bullied her.

"Dad, I need you to do something for me."

"Bethan, I can't—"

Her voice cracked across the room like a whip. "*You owe me.*"

And he'd walked out with two scribbled cipher messages in his pocket, promising to post them to Mab and Osla wherever they might now be living.

He promised he'd do it, Beth thought now, two weeks later, staring at an empty game board. He'd promised.

But no one had come.

York

Mab couldn't sleep.

Go to Clockwell, or not?

It was near midnight when she slipped out of bed and tiptoed downstairs to sit in the dining room's big window. The table was stacked with damask napkins—Mab had brought them out to iron for her royal wedding listening party. There had been a certain amount of hilarity when her husband caught her practicing folding them into swans.

I used to decode Nazi battle orders, Mab thought, *and now I'm folding napkins into swans.*

The switch her life had made sometimes astounded her. She'd be going through the market squeezing pears for ripeness, or sharing a gossip with her neighbors, and it would hit her all over again: just a few short years ago she would have been surrounded by racketing machines, exhausted and oil stained and pushed to her limit, but doing something that *mattered*. Now she had peace, prosperity, all the things she'd dreamed of during the war years, and sometimes it felt . . .

Mab searched, but there wasn't a word. It wasn't that life now didn't *matter*—by God, it did. Being able to bring up your children in peace, praying the peace would last, was a gift she would never cease treasuring. Looking at the stack of napkins, she wondered if it was *purpose* she missed; hands that folded damask swans yet yearned for war machines . . . She looked upward to where her husband slept, wondering if he ever felt a similar restlessness in turning his skills from war to peace. If he did, he never said so. These were things no one seemed to say. They all just put the war behind them and got on with it.

And is that such a bad thing? Mab scolded herself. Perhaps life wasn't exactly exciting anymore; there were no great sweeps of passion or purpose to her days, but there was no grief or stress, either. Adventure, excitement, passion; those things were unreliable. The Bletchley Park years had offered all that, love and change and friendships to outlast the world, or so it seemed—but all that had come crashing down, and Mab had built this new life over the ruins, stone by painful stone.

Why on earth would she risk it all for a woman she hated?

But . . .

You may hate me, Beth had written, *but you took the same oath I did.* And whether Beth was mad or conniving, she had risked a great deal to reach out past asylum walls for help.

Mab scowled, and made a decision.

FOUR YEARS AGO

October 1943

CHAPTER 51

FROM *BLETCHLEY BLETHERINGS*, OCTOBER 1943

Bletchley Park is infested—not by mice, but by Yanks. *Pestus Americanus* can be identified by its unnaturally white teeth and Camel cigarettes . . .

Mab shattered into pieces exactly three hundred and forty-four days after Lucy and Francis died. She worked out the figure in the sickroom, as she lay in bed staring at the ceiling.

She'd been called to demonstrate the one remaining bombe machine in Hut 11A. All the others had been moved to outstations, along with the Wrens who serviced them, but demonstrations were still required from time to time, and a cluster of Americans was getting the show now. "This is how we set the bombe in motion," Mab said tonelessly over the machine's racket.

"Awfully finicky work." A lieutenant hovered, jostling. He had fair hair and an easy smile and was probably just trying to be friendly, but Mab could hardly stand looking at him. She didn't want to be friendly. The only reason she'd returned to Bletchley Park was because it was work here or do service elsewhere; because working here meant she could help stop the German bastards who had killed her family—and finally, because Francis would have been disappointed if she'd curled up in bed after the funerals and let the grief eat her alive. He'd have told her to carry on the fight.

So Mab had come back to BP a shocking two days after Francis's funeral—she knew people had whispered—and she hadn't missed a shift since. She threw herself into her work, and why not? Francis and Lucy were dead, and that wasn't a false stop. She couldn't wire her life up like a bombe and get it running again. Everything had just—stopped.

"Marvelous machines I've seen here," the Yank wittered on, oblivious. "And so many attractive ladies. As far as I can tell, the machines were made by the British Tabulating Machine Company and the ladies by God!"

He honked laughter. Mab looked at him. She didn't lower her eyebrows in her old scowl, she just gazed at him blankly until his smile dripped away. Mab didn't know what was in her gaze these days, but very few people seemed to want to meet it for long.

She finished with the drums, changed up the wheel orders, checked the wires on the new wheels. Her lips were cracked and dry from the hut's airlessness; Mab reached for her pocket mirror and set it above the bombe's cables, pulling out her lipstick. She had a scraping of Elizabeth Arden Victory Red left in the tube—a sudden memory flashed of the time Lucy had rummaged in her cosmetics and used half a tube daubing her face in war paint. *I shouted at her. Why did I do that?* Mab's hand shook as she lifted the lipstick, steadying the mirror with her other hand, and an electric shock from the cables jolted thorough the metal mirror to her fingertips. She turned numbly, and the American let out a surprised shout, pointing at her throat. Mab raised her stinging fingers and touched something sticky, saw red on her fingertips.

I'm dead, she thought calmly, looking in the mirror and seeing the red line across her windpipe. But it wasn't blood she smelled on her fingertips, just lipstick. The recoil of her electric-shocked hand had jerked the lipstick across her own neck; it must have looked like she'd cut her own throat.

I'm not *dead,* she tried to say, looking at the ash-pale Yanks. Instead, she found herself laughing at a high pitch, laughing and shaking beside the bombe machine, which kept on with its horrible, monotonous whirring. Mab tried to steady herself, but somehow slipped to her knees instead on the oily floor, still laughing, smearing and tearing at the red line on her throat.

Then there were hands pulling her away from the bombe. "Get her to the infirmary." When Mab pulled herself together, she was standing wan and swaying before a starchy-looking matron in a ward she'd never set foot in before.

"What's the matter with you, then?"

"I don't know," Mab said, dazed. "What month is it?"

The woman looked at her a moment. "October, love. 'Forty-Three."

Ten months since she'd buried Francis and Lucy. Ten months. Soon it would be a year. Where had the days gone? Mab couldn't remember getting out of bed this morning, or taking the transport bus here. She didn't know if she was on day shift, evening shift, or night shift. She clutched for the blanketing cotton wool that had battened her senses for months, but it thinned and shredded, electrified away. Mab began to cry in huge wrenching sobs.

She hadn't cried since Coventry.

"That's all right, love." The matron steered her to a narrow white bed behind a screen. "You've got a touch of nervous exhaustion, I'll wager. Four days' bed rest—"

"My husband is dead," Mab managed to say. She wanted to add *my daughter is dead,* but she couldn't have anyone thinking that Lucy had been a bastard, and she couldn't say *my sister* after a lifetime of saying nothing else. So just—"My husband is dead."

"I haven't got a cure for that, love. I wish I did." Giving Mab's shoulder a squeeze. "But plenty of sleep and water will still do you some good. Strip down and climb in—"

"*Job's up,*" Mab whispered. "*Job's up, strip down . . .*" She peeled out of her black crepe, crawled between the sheets, and slept like the dead for nearly three days.

When she woke, she saw two male blurs at her bedside, one huge and dark, one skinny and ginger. The sight of any man who wasn't Francis sometimes hurt her, but Harry and Giles were so absolutely, comfortingly different in every way that she could look at them without flinching.

"Sleeping Beauty awakes," Giles said. "The Mad Hatters have been dropping in between shifts to see if we can catch you when you aren't snoring."

*—You snore—*Francis's voice. *But a very ladylike snore . . .*

"We brought the Mad Hatter's topper," Giles was burbling, oblivious. "Thought it might be just the thing." He plunked the outrageous object into her hands, and Mab stroked the spray of silk flowers, trying to remember when she'd last gone to a Tea Party. She couldn't even remember when she'd last read a book. *I've gone a little mad,* she thought unsteadily, *mad as the Mad Hatter.* She didn't think it was over yet, either. There were broken pieces jabbing everywhere inside, now that the cotton wool was gone.

"You just missed Beth," Harry was saying, linking his big hands between his knees. "She had to go on shift. And she's not really sure what to do around sickbeds. You aren't a line of code, so she's stumped."

You and Beth? Mab wondered, looking at him. There was a thing a man's eyes did when he was in love, a softening at the very centers—she'd learned that from Francis. Abruptly, she wished Harry would go. She didn't want to look at a man in love when she'd lost her own. Mab remembered reading something rubbishy about the ennoblement of grief . . . what rot. Grief didn't make you noble. It made you selfish and hateful. She made herself smile at Harry, but she was glad when he left.

Giles lingered, looking like a bony heron perched on his too-low stool. "You want to scream," he said, "don't you?"

"Yes." Her hand left the Mad Hatter's topper and crept up to her throat where the line of lipstick had looked like a knife slash. *I wish it had been.*

"What you need," Giles said, "is a transfer."

"Where?" When the bombes were moved out and the Wrens with them, Mab had been stuck back in Hut 6, first on a Typex, more recently in the Machine Room, where she mechanically sorted and tested bombe menus. "I'm not a brain like Beth or Harry. I don't speak German; no use pushing me in with women like—"

Osla. The name stuck in her throat like a spike of ice. Perhaps she didn't loathe Osla with the visceral hatred that had gripped her after the funeral, but a tiny whisper inside remained uncompromising: *If you hadn't let go of Lucy's hand . . .*

It wasn't fair. Mab *knew* it wasn't fair. She knew if she picked her anger apart, the feelings beneath would be far more complicated than simple hatred. But she didn't have the energy, and every day the gulf grew wider, so Mab simply kept to the road of avoiding her old friend. Hating Osla was less complicated, more comforting—and avoiding her was child's play. Keeping your distance from someone at BP was easy if you didn't work the same hut or shift schedule. Mab had moved from their shared room to a parlor cot, so even billeting under the same roof, she hardly ever crossed paths with Osla.

"There are all kinds of posts here," Giles continued. "You're not tied to Hut 6—let's see if we can get you swapped into the mansion. Travis's team, maybe . . . I'll pull strings."

"Thank you," Mab managed.

He seemed to realize what an effort it took her. "Things have been damned awful for you this year. I'm sorry."

Sorry. Everyone told her they were sorry. Why didn't they tell her how to go on living, instead? How to keep going, day after day, when soon it was going to be a year since she'd buried Lucy and Francis—then two years—then three?

Why did no one tell her how to keep living?

CHAPTER 52

FROM *BLETCHLEY BLETHERINGS*, NOVEMBER 1943

To the American officers who condescended to tell the ladies in Knox's section how to do their work—all *BB* can say is: Really, gentlemen? Did you fail to notice these women have a CMG on their wall? You don't win the Companionship of the Order of Saint Michael and Saint George for Best Radishes in the Victory Garden . . .

"'*Loveliest of trees, the cherry now is hung with bloom about the bough . . .*'" Dilly's voice echoed, happy and careless.

"But it's covered in snow," Beth answered aloud, looking at the tree arching overhead. Earlier this year, a warm winter had meant it blossomed unseasonably fast; she'd come to Courns Wood with Abwehr traffic, alternating days with Peggy, and she and Dilly would spread a blanket in his garden and sit boxing and rodding as white petals drifted down. Now it was nearly winter; the cherry tree was bare.

And Dilly Knox was dead.

Beth stood alone under the tree—but not really alone. Turning her head, she could imagine Dilly beside her so vividly: smoking his pipe, no longer gaunt and graying because in her imagination he was restored to health. When she came here, she could replay entire conversations they'd had before he died, tell him what had happened since, imagine his answers . . . sometimes she pictured him sitting in the desk beside her at work, so she could ask his advice on a tricky crib.

"Gives me the creeps when you do that," Phyllida said, shivering. "It sounds proper mad, you having conversations with a dead man."

"It helps me work." *Cope, too.*

"The cherry covered in snow, that's the poem's third verse," Dilly went on in Beth's imagination. "You should read more poetry, m'dear."

"When?" Beth asked the dead man. She tossed a stick for Boots, who ignored it as he trundled over the frozen ground. Her dog looked like a grumpy tin of Scottish shortbread in a little tartan coat Mab had made out of an old blanket. Mab . . . but Beth pushed that familiar guilt away. "I've been trying to break back into the KK traffic, Dilly." A pinch during Operation Torch had produced a multi-turnover Abwehr machine, rewired and used for a link that hadn't been broken cryptographically before. "Six weeks of back traffic broken, but we haven't been able to get back in. Where's the time for poetry?"

"Verse can be handy in our line of work. I've broken more than one key that was picked out of a line of Goethe. Operators are supposed to choose random letters, but they don't. It's not in human nature to be random." He sounded affectionate at this universal failing. "So sometimes they pick fragments of poetry as keys instead."

"Or dirty words," Beth replied. "I've decrypted a lot more traffic keyed to dirty words than lines of Schiller."

"Dear me. My well-bred gels are being subjected to Germanic cursing?"

"*Scheisse,*" said Beth, and Dilly laughed until he choked. "How's that new cipher you're working on?" she asked. Dilly had told her about it on her very last visit: *Tricky, tricky stuff. Reminds me of a rose, petals overlapping downward toward the core.* His hands had made vague blooming motions over the bed—a bed he was too weak to leave by then. *Travis didn't mind if I took it home to pick at, not that I've made much headway . . .*

Beth wished he were here, to tell her more about it. "I miss you," she whispered aloud.

Nothing felt the same. Her billet-mates were still avoiding each other, leaving Beth stranded in the middle, very determinedly *not* thinking about what had caused the breach and if part of that might be her fault. Bletchley Park, with all the new blocks and new recruits, wasn't quite the haven it had once been; Beth felt waves of her old crippling shyness every time she stepped into the streaming mass of strangers at shift change. Yet things were going *better* now than they had during the old Cottage days, Beth had to admit—with U-boat operations suspended in the Atlantic, American soldiers and supplies were flowing steadily; German and Italian troops were surrendering in North Africa; the massive invasion of Sicily had kicked down the door for the move to mainland Italy and now the Allies were celebrating in Naples. An Allied return to French shores was being discussed in pubs and over tea tables as something that *would* happen, not something everyone hoped might happen. Things were better.

But . . .

"I miss my ladies," the imagined Dilly said wistfully. Wherever he was now, Beth was sure he missed them. "I wish I'd been there when you took those Yanks down a peg."

"Catching sight of your CMG set them straight." It had been January when word came down that Dilly Knox, in recognition of his wartime achievements, was to be awarded the CMG. Dilly had been far too ill to travel to London for the ceremony, but he'd received the palace emissary at Courns Wood, accepted the award . . . which he'd kept for all of ten minutes before dispatching it by car to ISK with a note:

Awards of this sort depend entirely on the support of colleagues and associates. May I, before proceeding, refer them back!

It is, I fear, incumbent upon me at the same time to bid farewell.

Everyone, Dilly's whole section, had wept.

He died not long after.

Beth realized she was crying, tears dripping off her chin. She collected Boots's lead and without another word trailed back toward the house. She didn't need to look back to see him sitting there, in his university scarf, thinking of inward-folding ciphers and A. E. Housman verse.

Mrs. Knox came out of the kitchen, drying her hands on her apron. "Beth, could you take a stack of papers back to Bletchley for me? Commander Travis gave permission for Dilly to keep them in his library when he was working, but now . . ."

Her voice trailed off. Her eyes were reddened, and Beth couldn't meet them straight on. Too much grief.

Mrs. Knox rallied to complete the thought. "They should be back under proper security. I should have thought of it months ago, but no one came asking, and I've been in such a state. I can't think it was anything terribly important if they didn't send for it before now, but one still shouldn't leave these things lying about."

"Of course I'll take them." Beth followed her into the library, waiting as Dilly's small safe behind the wall panel was unlocked and a folder of messages extracted. Beth was tempted to peek, see if this was the cipher Dilly had compared to a rose, but tucked it unopened inside her coat. She'd ask if she could work on it in her spare time, if she had any. There was going to be another jumbo rush as soon as plans firmed up for the invasion, which would *surely* be this coming year. More work for Knox's section, feeding false information through double agents, then cracking the Abwehr traffic to make sure Berlin swallowed it . . .

Beth telephoned the transport pool. She'd be early for her shift, but carrying a folder of Enigma meant getting a BP transport back to the Park, and immediately. Drawing up to the Park gates the better part of an hour later, Beth was surprised to see a familiar figure arguing with one of the guards.

"Drop me here," Beth told the driver, and swung out. "Dad?"

He turned round, red faced, frustrated. "These fellows wouldn't let me in."

"They won't let anyone in without a pass." She pulled him aside from the gate. "What is it?"

"Your mother is in a state. The things she's been hearing about you . . ."

The last time Beth had paid a dutiful call home, Mother had called her a tart and a serpent's tooth, and Beth had turned and walked right back out. She hadn't been privy to much family news after that. "What's she raging about now?"

"There is *talk,* Bethan. That you're mixed up with some *dark* fellow. The pastor's wife saw you in Cambridge walking with some chap she insisted was at least half black—"

"He's not black," Beth said.

"Well, I'm glad to hear—"

"He's Maltese, Egyptian, and Arabic. Shall I bring him round for tea?" Beth couldn't resist.

"You're joking, surely. A *heathen*?"

"He was raised Church of England like his entire family." Though Beth thought Harry's faith lay more in mathematics than God; they'd had some spirited theological discussions along those lines. "His name's Harry Zarb. He speaks Arabic as well as English; it's a lovely language. Oh, and he's married! But he's absolutely *wonderful,* Dad."

"Bethan"—plaintively—"just come home."

"No." Beth spoke mildly but firmly, bringing Boots to heel. "I'm happy to visit if Mother can manage not to pitch a fit, but I'm never moving back."

"I'm your father. I have the right—"

"No, you don't." Beth looked him in the eye. "You didn't stop her throwing me out. You never defended me. You never told me I was clever, even though I can do the Sunday crossword ten times faster than you. You never told me I was anything." She thought of Dilly Knox, frail and bright burning, telling her she was the best of his Fillies. "I have to go to work now."

"Bethan—"

"Don't call me that," she said without turning. "It's not who I am anymore."

She made sure the folder of Dilly's work was properly registered, then took it to ISK (now moved over to one of the new blocks) when no one seemed sure where it should be filed. "What's this?" said Peggy as Beth opened the file. "And what's *that*?" Looking at Boots.

"That's a schnauzer. This is something Dilly was working on."

"Why does ISK need a schnauzer? The Yanks already think we're potty because of Jumbo."

Beth arranged her coat into a nest under her desk for Boots. "He'll be quiet as a mouse. I couldn't go all the way back to my billet to drop him off, not when I was carrying those. Do you recognize the cipher? Dilly was working on it."

"It's an odd one . . ." Peggy frowned. "He told me he was working on Soviet ciphers."

"But the Russians don't use Enigma machines, and this is definitely Enigma traffic."

"That doesn't mean they haven't captured the odd machine or two from the Germans, in the back-and-forth on the eastern front." Peggy flipped through the stack. "Perhaps they're experimenting with a machine."

"Even if they are, why are we flagging it? The Russians are our allies. We aren't reading their post."

"Goodness, whatever gave you that idea?" Peggy handed the folder back. "Put it in the stack of duds, and anyone with a free hour can have a crack at it."

Beth put it aside, reached for the day's Abwehr traffic, and immediately forgot about Dilly's Russian project.

Later she looked back at that moment, screaming in the ear of her past self. *Don't forget about that file. Pick it up right now, Beth Finch.* Pick it up!

CHAPTER 53

FROM *BLETCHLEY BLETHERINGS*, NOVEMBER 1943

Addressing the lovers who left a set of frilly knickers on the lakeshore after what one presumes was a tryst—for heaven's sake, fake a marriage certificate and go to a hotel!

Again," Mab coached Beth.

"My fiancé is an airman stationed in Kent," Beth recited, standing in the icy street before the narrow front of the gynecologist's office. All around them people pushed and hurried. "He has forty-eight hours' leave to get married before Christmas. I'm not looking to have children until after the war—"

"Say it's your fiancé who wants that," Mab corrected. Most doctors would only fit married women for a contraceptive device, but given the war, some would fit affianced women. Mab had come here herself almost exactly two years ago, before her wedding. *Don't think about that.* "If you say you're the one who doesn't want babies yet, you'll get a lecture."

"Right." Beth looked determined. She'd barely even blushed when Mab collared her, shortly after leaving sick bay, and said bluntly, *I know what you and Harry are up to. I think you're an id-*

iot, but please tell me you're taking precautions. Beth had mumbled something about using French letters, and Mab had sighed, *There are safer options.* Whoever would have guessed shy Beth would end up part of BP's fast set, the ones who unabashedly worked off codebreaking stress in dark corners with any partner they could find? Though Beth didn't seem to be sneaking off to dark corners with anyone but Harry. Mab had Beth go through her story again, then pulled off her left glove. "You'd—better borrow this. The doctor won't believe you without a ring."

It hurt, taking Francis's ruby off. Beth slipped it on, seeming to know what it cost Mab. "Thank you. I know you don't approve—"

"It's not my business," Mab said shortly. "You want to get mixed up with a married man, well, you already know what I think about that."

"I'm not ashamed." Beth's chin went up. "And I'm not hurting anyone."

"Just yourself, if you think it's going to end in wedding bells."

"I don't want wedding bells."

Beth really had to be the oddest duck Mab had ever befriended. *And now she's about the only female friend I've got left.* No Osla, no Wrens . . . most of the other women at BP didn't seem to know how to talk to Mab anymore. Those like herself who had lost husbands, fiancés, boyfriends, were so raw in their own grief that Mab avoided them, and the women who hadn't suffered such a loss either were awkward in the face of the pain Mab couldn't conceal, or flinched from her mourning black because they were afraid for their own loved ones. Whether they thought Mab was bad luck or bad company, they tended to avoid her now. All except Beth, who was looking up at the doors of the doctor's office.

"Does it really work, this cap thing? Better than, you know." She blushed.

“It works.” Mab bit the words off. Lately she’d been having dreams about children—never girls, all little girls were Lucy, but boys. Baby boys with Francis’s russet hair; boys of ten with Francis’s stocky build, running about with cricket bats . . . boys so real she could almost reach out and touch them before they dissolved into the dream’s mist. She’d wake up retching with longing.

Beth disappeared into the office, and Mab went on to her own meeting in Trafalgar Square. Even on a cold winter’s day it was thronged: lovers meeting under Nelson’s Column, children throwing crumbs to the pigeons.

“Tell me about your husband, Mrs. Gray.” The journalist met her beside the great bronze lion on the south side of Nelson’s Column, as arranged. An exchange of names and pleasantries, and he was already pulling out his notepad. *He’s rather a well-known correspondent,* Francis’s publisher had said when he telephoned Mab. *Doing a piece on Francis. Perhaps you might answer a few questions when you’re next in London?* Mab would rather have chewed glass than rake over her memories for a stranger, but since she hadn’t given Francis a russet-haired son for a legacy, she’d force herself to talk about his poetry.

“What do you want to know, Mr. . . .” His name had already slipped her memory. She couldn’t seem to keep anything fixed in her mind nowadays.

“Graham. Ian Graham.” He had a beautiful baritone and public school vowels: a tall man, wire-lean in rumpled overcoat and battered fedora. “I’m writing a series on the role of art in wartime. First a piece on Dame Myra Hess and the National Gallery lunchtime concerts—what?”

“My husband took me to one of those concerts.” Mab huddled deeper into her black coat. “Our second date.” She’d spent the performance scrutinizing the clothes of the women in the audience, while Francis sat transfixed by the music. *Such a marvelous thing,* he'd said afterward. *You know how these concerts came about? The art was taken out of the gallery for safekeeping, then Dame Myra organized the most famous musicians in Britain to come play for the public among all the empty picture frames, just so blacked-out London has something beautiful to listen to.*

Marvelous, Mab had said, eyeing an ivy-print silk frock in the next row.

"It won't be a puff piece, Mrs. Gray." Ian Graham evidently took her silence for mistrust. "Francis Gray's poetry helped define trench warfare to an oblivious generation. In war, art is a balm."

"Then ask what you'd like," Mab said brusquely.

"More about you first . . . I understand you're billeted up in Buckinghamshire, doing war work."

"Yes, office work. Too boring for words." It really was, no fibbing required. Giles had got her a post filing and typing in the mansion; it was quiet and monotonous and Mab thought she could do it forever.

"Where in Buckinghamshire exactly?" The pencil jotted.

"A little town hardly more than a railway depot."

"Really . . . You're not the first person I've met who does something terribly boring and vague up in Bucks, in a little town with nothing but a railway depot."

"Is that so?"

"Yes. Most of the others were—how shall I put it? Whitehall sorts, Foreign Office sorts. They'll talk about their own work readily enough, especially with a scotch or two down the hatch, but they all clammed when it came to anything about Buckinghamshire."

Mab gave him a blank look. "I don't know what you're talking about."

Ian Graham grinned, a quick sunlight shaft of a smile. "Right," he said, and changed the subject. Routine questions: how long she and Francis had been married, where they had met. Mab's nails bit into her palms as she made herself recount their dates, the hasty wedding . . .

"Your husband enjoyed music—what about art? Paintings, sculpture?"

"I—I don't know."

"Did he ever say anything about his war, Mrs. Gray?"

"No."

"He took a rather well-known tour in 1919, collecting earth from battlefields for the families who hadn't been able to bury their boys. His letter about it was published in the *Times*. Did he—"

"I—he didn't tell me about that," Mab jerked.

Mr. Graham changed tack. "I don't mean to pry, Mrs. Gray. It's merely that you were Francis Gray's wife—his publishers and readers can tell me about the poetry, but you can tell me about the man. A personal anecdote, perhaps?"

Personal. Suddenly Mab couldn't breathe. This wasn't like the hysteria that had gripped her during her bombe demonstration. This was rage and despair, two emotions flaming up in red and black. Turning, she seized the surprised journalist by the sleeve. "I need a drink."

He bought her a gin at the nearest pub, not batting an eye as she slammed it back. The perfect place, dark and grimy, full of drinkers who didn't want to be bothered. No one glanced over as the choked words began pouring out of Mab.

"You want a personal anecdote, Mr. Graham?" She took her second drink, turning to the journalist. "The truth is, I don't have any. Francis Gray was the best man I have ever known, and I was his wife less than one year. You know how many times we saw each other? Fourteen. He was always traveling, and I had a job we agreed was important, so we did our best. We had a forty-eight-hour wedding-and-honeymoon. We had two weekends in the Lake District. We had the odd meal in a railway café. We made love a total of fifteen times." She didn't care if she was being indecent. She didn't care she was saying it to a journalist. She had to say it to someone, after thinking it for so many nights, or she would burst. Ian Graham listened without interrupting, and that was all that mattered. "We loved each other by proxy, Mr. Graham. He loved me through a girl he saw once in Paris in 1918, and I loved him through his letters, but we hardly spent any time together. I don't *have* any personal anecdotes about my husband. We didn't have time to create any."

Her voice cracked. She bolted half the gin.

"I know he liked curry and dawn walks. I know he hated his own poetry and never slept the night through, because of the things he saw in the trenches. But I didn't know *him*. You have to live with someone to know them. I've lived with my billet-mates for three and a half years; I know them inside and out. I loved Francis Gray, and to me he was perfect, and that's proof I didn't know him very well at all. I never got to realize all the ways he wasn't perfect. I didn't get to reach the point where the song he whistled while shaving drove me mad or learn how rainy days made him short tempered. He never got to realize that I'm not some great wartime love, just a shallow cow who lives for pretty shoes and library novels. We never got to quarrel over the milk bill or whether to buy strawberry jam or marmalade . . ."

It was the thing that killed Mab every night. When she grieved Lucy, she grieved for the woman her daughter would never become—the young girl taking her exams, the coltish student heading off to university—but at least she had known the six-year-old Lucy of November 1942 to her very bones. So much of Francis had still been an unmapped continent, a man she was only beginning to truly know.

And he didn't know me, she thought, *or he wouldn't have loved me the way he did. He would have realized I was a social-climbing tart who would marry a good man like him as a ticket up the ladder. He would have realized he deserved better than me.*

"I don't have one single photograph of the two of us together." Mab stared into her glass. "Not one. We couldn't get a camera on our wedding day, it was short notice, and after that we were too busy cramming in time together to pose for a flash. An entire marriage gone, without one picture to commemorate it."

She looked up at the journalist's grave face. "There's something titillating for your story," she said, mocking. "Francis Gray's drunken Shoreditch widow, slopping gin all over you in a pub. I don't care if you print it. I don't care what you say about me—"

"I'm a journalist, not a monster," said Ian Graham.

"—but I do care what you say about Francis. Do justice to him. He was a good poet and a great man." She finished her gin in a gulp.

"Is there anything I can do to help?" the journalist asked, his voice quiet.

Mab turned sharply, nearly sliding off her stool. He caught her hand, steadying her, and Mab's skin prickled. Oh, God, how she missed Francis's hands. His fingers through hers, his palm on her waist. So much of her numbness had burned away in sick bay—at night, she now lay awake holding herself in her own arms, trying to pretend they were Francis's arms, longing to be held again.

Stay with me, she started to say. The impulse went through her in a bolt of desperation: take this man she didn't know up to some rented room and let him do anything he wanted, as long as she could keep her eyes shut and pretend he was Francis.

Then she shoved that away, so sick with shame she almost vomited.

Ian Graham got a glass of water and lemon from the barman

and pushed it toward her. "Drink that down." He waited while she drank, then rose. "I have what I need. May I take you to catch your train, Mrs. Gray?"

"I'm meeting a friend—we're returning to Bucks together."

He hesitated, clearly not wanting to leave her alone, but Mab put out her hand. "Goodbye, Mr. Graham. I look forward to reading your piece."

He tipped his hat and departed. She wondered where he'd be sent next, what blood-laced beach or bombed-out town he'd report on, then she ordered another gin and thought only about Francis and Lucy.

Three drinks later, she was staggering. She nearly missed the doctor's office when she went back to find it, and Beth almost had to carry her home.

CHAPTER 54

Letter from Osla to her Café de Paris Good Samaritan

I wonder why I keep writing you in such a void. Posting all these letters (five now? Six?) into limbo, or at least to your landlady . . . it feels a bit like sealing a message in a bottle and hurling it out to sea: you never know who will read it, or if anyone will. Maybe it's better if no one ever does, the way I've talked my soul out.

Happy Christmas, Mr. Cornwell, wherever you are. —Ozma of Oz

Osla was in a good mood for once when she sauntered through the ivy-hung doors of Claridge's. The last decrypt she'd translated on shift before running to catch her train was a radio message to a German destroyer off Norway: "Please inform Oberleutnant W. Breisbach that his wife has been delivered of a son."

Congratulations, Oberleutnant, Osla thought, smiling. *I hope you survive to see your son grow up.* Surely at Christmastime it was allowable to wish an enemy well as a fellow human being. Osla wanted Lieutenant Breisbach to raise his son in a world where that son wouldn't have to join the Hitler Youth, and assuredly that wasn't too much to hope for. It was the cusp of 1944—surely now they could hope for the beginning of the end.

"I understand felicitations are in order, Miss Kendall," the porter Mr. Gibbs greeted her. "I heard your mother's happy news."

Stepfather number four, what a rum thought. "Is she home tonight?"

"I'm afraid not. The Windsor pantomime—"

Osla sighed. "I don't suppose you could rustle me up a suitable escort for her wedding next month, could you, Mr. Gibbs?" Once upon a time, Osla would have brought Mab. Mab would have been a capital friend for a chichi London wedding, analyzing every dress, making fun of every horrendous hat . . . but for an entire year now, she'd barely caught sight of Mab except across the canteen. Osla's smile slipped as the memory rose of another wedding: Mab and Francis in this very hotel, looking so happy they stopped people in their tracks.

I miss my friend.

"Prince Philip will not be escorting you, Miss Kendall?"

"I don't think so." Philip had given up writing some time ago, after all . . . Trying to recover her holiday cheer, Osla bid Mr. Gibbs good night and swanned upstairs. If Mamma wasn't here, at least Osla could stay the night in her suite and work up the next *BB*. Ever since Coventry, she'd been having trouble keeping *BB*'s tone light. The jokes still came, but they came with more bite. Still, maybe that was all right; humor could cut at the same time as it made people laugh. Maybe Osla Kendall would take a puck at becoming the next great satirist, once the war was over.

Oh, who was she fooling? If you were a man and you wrote funny pieces about daily life, they called it satire. If you were a woman and you wrote funny pieces about daily life, they called it fluff.

Scowling now, Osla came out of the elevator, rounded the corner—and crashed straight into Philip.

"Oh! Um—"

"Sorry—Os, is that—"

They stopped. *My God, it's been so long,* Osla thought, trying not to stare and also trying not to laugh. Philip loomed impossibly tall and tanned, more like a Viking than ever . . . but he was also in a bathrobe and slippers, and no Viking ever looked at ease caught out in a bathrobe and slippers. He stuck his hands in his pockets, clearly mortified. "You look well, princess."

"I didn't know the *Wallace* was back."

"Yes, well . . . I'd be at the Mountbattens', but they've a houseful of Christmas guests."

They stared at each other some more. Philip didn't look entirely welcoming; his expression was closed off in a way Osla remembered from the few times she'd seen him angry. *You're right to be angry,* she thought. *I ditched you—for very good reasons, but you don't know that.* She couldn't say it, so she started chattering.

"I've only popped in tonight, to surprise my mother. Of course she's not home—and to think I passed up an outing to the cinema with the Glassborow twins, too. I always wanted a twin sister but given all the tandem giggling from those girls, I probably wouldn't have heard a word of the film." Osla ran out of breath. "How are you?"

"Getting over a touch of 'flu." Now that she looked closer, she saw his face was flushed under his tan, and his forehead had a sheen of sweat. "I was poking my head out for some handkerchiefs the bellboy left me."

Philip scooped the packet off the threshold, and Osla saw him sway. "Steady on, sailor." She put her hands to his shoulders, righting him, and his arms came reflexively around her waist. They both paused in the act of moving toward each other, and she could all but see him thinking, *I don't want to get you sick.* Osla didn't care. She pulled his head down to hers and they were kissing, pressed against the door. His mouth was hard and angry, but his hands at her back were soft, as if he couldn't stop from melting against her. He was warm with fever. "You *are* ill," she said, breaking the kiss.

"Not too ill to notice how good you smell." It seemed to come out involuntarily, and he scowled, pulling back. Osla did too, realizing where they were. No hotel in London would allow a young woman upstairs with a young man unless they'd presented a marriage certificate . . . but here they were, with a room at his back and no eyes to see.

"I'm supposed to be attending the royal pantomime at Windsor tonight," he muttered. "*Aladdin*—the princesses are acting."

"You're not going anywhere." Osla put a hand to his forehead. "Get inside." She pushed the door open, following on his heels. A modest room by Claridge's standards; nothing like her mother's suite. Philip's kit bag lay in a corner; the bed was mussed as if he'd been tossing and turning. "In bed," Osla ordered, kicking off her shoes. "I'm going to look after you."

"YOU'RE A LOUSY nurse, princess."

"You're a terrible patient, sailor. Put that thermometer under your tongue—"

"You're enjoying this," he accused, looking ready to bite it in half.

"Too bally right." Osla hopped onto the foot of the bed, pulling his feet into her lap. He had long bony toes, and she thought she could get quite inordinately foolish about them.

"It's just a chill—"

"You're one of those fellows who say *it's just a sprain* when the bone is poking through the skin, aren't you?"

He looked offended. "You don't know that."

"Yes, I do!"

Philip stared at the ceiling, thermometer pointing skyward.

"I never had anyone look after me when I was sick before. Not really . . ."

"Other than servants, you mean, or boarding-school nurses with cold-fish hands?" Osla paused. "I never have, either."

She bounded off to get him a glass of water. *I'm enjoying this.* Maybe it was the domesticity of it all, so ordinary and yet so strange. In her experience, getting involved with any man meant *going* places: driving, dancing, the cinema. The plain, everyday ordinariness of walking around barefoot in Philip's room, making herself at home . . .

"Down," she ordered, pushing him flat again as he tried to sit up.

"Bully," he said, spitting out the thermometer.

"Too right, darling, and it's working—your temperature's down. You haven't been very good, but I suppose we can crack the fizz." She'd had him order a bottle of champagne along with chicken broth. Fizz was good for invalids; everyone knew that. "You've been in town a few days?" she asked, popping the cork.

He regarded her steadily. "Are you going to ask why I didn't ring you?"

She topped up two tea mugs. ". . . I know why you didn't ring me."

An awkward silence.

He struggled up on one elbow. "Did you meet someone, Os? Is that why you stopped writing?"

"No, I did not meet someone. Don't talk such slush."

"Then why'd you go off me?"

I was protecting you.

"I thought maybe you were backing off," he said eventually. "Letting things cool down. Can't say I liked it, but that would probably be the best thing."

"Why?" Osla looked at him, but he only shrugged. "I wasn't

backing off . . . it's been a terrible year, Philip. I saw my best friend's husband and little sister die in front of me in a bombing. She blames me, in part"—Osla still blamed herself, for letting go of Lucy's hand—"so I lost her, too. And then every day at work I'd type up war reports, and the details could be horrifying." There, not too many lies in that mix. A few things omitted, like her fruitless, months-long hunt for files that were missing and then not missing. A thief or informant who might or might not have been real . . . Osla still wasn't sure. All she could do was keep her eyes open; so far nothing else seemed to have disappeared.

"Anyway," she finished, "I've been in such a blue funk, and I didn't want to write if I couldn't think of anything cheerful to say, and the longer the silence stretched, the harder it was to reach out." Osla touched his hand. "Forgive me?"

"I've had a bad year, too." Quietly.

Osla hesitated. *Keep your distance. It's better for him that way.* But she couldn't walk away from Philip like this, not feverish and alone in an impersonal hotel room at Christmastime. Besides, since she'd made the decision to back away from Philip, she'd seen Mab lose Francis—seen her rage and grieve that they hadn't had more time, more love, more everything . . .

Osla stretched across the bed opposite Philip, twining her stockinged feet with his bony ones. "Tell me."

It came slowly, in terse fits and starts as they sipped their fizz. Across the Atlantic and back with a convoy; dive-bombed by Stukas all through the Mediterranean when the *Wallace* was posted to assist in the invasion of Sicily. "There was one night in July," Philip said. "The moon lit everything up bright as day. We were leaving a wake that glowed like the Yellow Brick Road. The ship had already been hit, everyone knew they were coming back to put us down for good. We had to come up with something quick—I don't know why the captain listened to my idea, but he did. We banged a big raft together out of crates and timber, heaped debris on it, slung a smoke float at each end, and cast it off—then steamed as fast as we could in the other direction and cut the *Wallace* dead, engines, lights, and all. All of us sitting there in the dark, hoping the Krauts would assume we'd gone down and that raft of debris and smoke was all that was left . . ."

"I'll guess that they swallowed it," Osla said when he fell silent. "Or you wouldn't be here."

"They swallowed it, all right. We heard bombers screaming overhead, hitting the wreckage to send it to the bottom. Those bastards, strafing what they thought were sailors clinging to debris . . ."

"But they weren't. It sounds to me like you saved your sailors, Lieutenant."

Another shrug. "I swear I aged five years that night, Os."

"Five years . . ." Osla turned over and he snugged her up into his chest, tugging the coverlet up over them both. "Wasn't it only five years ago we met?"

"Four."

"That's all?"

"End of '39, at the bar downstairs. You in your boiler suit. You looked like Winston Churchill, but adorable."

"My God. I was an absolute infant."

"I was, too. I thought war was going to be such a lark."

They lay quiet, feet entangled, curled up close in the dim room. To Osla, drifting off to sleep, it felt like home again.

AT SOME POINT in the night she woke. Philip's warm chest wasn't against her back; instead she felt something soft and fluffy. "Why did you wedge a pillow between us?" she yawned.

"I didn't have a sword," he mumbled, half-asleep.

"What?"

"A sword . . . it's an old story. A knight puts a sword in the bed if he has to sleep beside his lady. So she knows he won't cross over it."

"What if she wants him to?"

No answer.

Osla slid out of bed and began unhooking her gray wool dress. They hadn't drawn the blackout curtains; moonlight threw a little silvery light into the dark room. She could see Philip sit up in bed—he must have got feverish in his sleep, because he'd tossed off his shirt and blankets and had the sheet drawn up around his raised knees. It was the first time she'd seen him without a shirt, and dear God, was it a sight.

"Os," he said drowsily as she peeled off her stockings, "I'd better go sleep on the sofa."

"You'll do no such thing, sailor. You've still got a touch of fever."

"I'm not made of marble, you know." He waved a hand at her satin slip. "There's only so much a pillow can do . . ."

"Well, I'm not sleeping in a wool dress, and I'm not sleeping on that blithering sofa either." She climbed back into bed on his side, hearing her own heart hammer.

"You're a devil," he said through the dark, reaching for her. His skin was still hot with fever and Osla caught the flame, losing her breath, making him lose his as they tossed and rolled in the crisp sheets. "Hang on to me," he said at one point, hands and lips sliding along the edge of her slip, and did something Osla didn't have a name for, something she didn't know people did, only it left her wrung limp and breathless, hanging off his broad shoulders like she was about to fall off a cliff. She could feel Philip's smile against her skin. "You're finally communicating, princess."

"Communication should go both ways, it seems to me," she managed to gasp, and figured out a few ways to do so, letting his hands and his strangled curses guide her along. They came to a stop, clinging and breathing hard, pressed full-length, forehead rocking against forehead. A gentleman never pushed things past a certain point with a girl unless there was some kind of understanding that things would soon be made permanent. Before, whenever they'd reached that point, Philip had never pushed further . . . but they'd never had an opportunity to be alone like this, either. To do whatever they wanted. This time, Osla sensed, she could push past his protests. He was light-headed enough tonight to be reckless—if she was ruthless enough to push till he forgot himself.

But he wouldn't have pushed if she were the one laid low with fever and forgetting herself.

"Os," Philip said, sounding strangled. "Better put that pillow back."

Osla let her head drop, banging her forehead gently against his shoulder. "I hate doing the honorable thing."

"Oh, so do I," he growled. They managed to rearrange themselves, limbs aligned back more or less where they should be, pillow wedged virtuously between, Osla's head on his shoulder. "We could do this any time we wanted, you know," Osla said into the dark. "Nothing's stopping us from being—more."

It was the nearest she'd come to saying it, or even hinting it. *Stop calling me princess, because I'm not one—but I could be. If you wanted.*

But he'd already slid back into dreamland.

They slept late, and by noon his fever was entirely gone and he was sitting up in bed demanding toast. They ordered from the hotel kitchens, ate in bed . . . Osla looked at the clock, sighing. "An hour till I catch the train."

"And I have no more excuses to skip the Christmas pantomime at Windsor."

She brushed a crumb off his lip. "Can't see you at a children's panto."

"It's more than that. The princesses do it every year for a private audience, to raise money for the men at the front." He smiled. "Lilibet always gets stuck doing the men's parts, because Margaret has to get the princess role."

"She already is a princess. Can't she play something else for one night?"

"You don't know Margaret." Philip looked down at his plate, tearing the last piece of toast to bits. "Os . . . you never really answered my question last night." He looked up. "Why you stopped writing."

"I said—"

"—a lot of vague stuff about it being a terrible year. That's not an answer." His gaze was keen. "I know you. Terrible year or not, Osla Kendall keeps her chin up and goes right on fizzing along. So what happened?"

She couldn't look at him. "You'll have to trust me, Philip."

"Are you going to write when I ship out again? Or go out with me while I'm in town?"

I'm not sure it's wise, Osla thought. This meeting had been accidental. If they started being seen around town again, she might be called on the carpet to face more questions. *Turn over his letters. Tell us if he contacts his family. Tell us what he says over a pillow* . . . And her oath meant she'd have to do it.

Philip's face shuttered as she remained silent. "Thanks for playing nurse, princess."

"THOUGHT YOU OUGHT to hear it from a friend," the voice on the telephone said.

"David, what on earth are you blathering on about?" It was the day before New Year's; Osla had been working up this week's

BB with a razor-sharp lampoon of the Bletchley Park dramatic society's Christmas revue when her landlady had called her to the telephone. Osla had been puzzled to find Philip's chum David Milford Haven on the other end. "I know Philip went to Windsor for Christmas after the pantomime. It was in the papers."

"What's not in the papers is that he and Princess Elizabeth sparked like a bonfire. Charades with the family after Boxing Day dinner, dancing to the gramophone—"

"So? Philip and Lilibet have been pen pals forever. *Charades*—that's something you play with your little sister."

"Not so little—she'll be eighteen this April. Solemn, wants to join the ATS, blue eyes, lovely legs. Philip got an eyeful of those when she was prancing round the panto stage in tights."

"Do you have to slaver quite so audibly?" Osla wrinkled her nose.

"I'm serious, Os. All through Christmas, our princess was looking at Philip like he was God, and he wasn't exactly looking away. There'll be gossip soon; I thought you might want to hear it from me first."

"Out of the goodness of your heart? That's just topping of you."

"Fancy drinks at the Four Hundred? Just you and me—"

Osla rang off. She stood in the passage a moment, looking at her own legs, which were rather sturdy and wouldn't be much of a sight in tights.

Princess Elizabeth. The future queen of England. And *Philip*? *He calls her* Cousin Lilibet. *He thinks she's a child.*

"Osla!" Beth's voice floated in from the front gate. "The bus—"

"Coming!" Osla flashed out the door for work, where she tried all day not to think about princesses with big blue eyes.

CHAPTER 55

FROM *BLETCHLEY BLETHERINGS*, JANUARY 1944

What is the worst toll taken by BP's necessary secret-keeping? The worry of disclosing information while under anesthesia at the dentist, the pressure of lying to one's friends? No, according to an informal *BB* poll, it's having to bite one's tongue when Cousin Betty purrs yet again over the Christmas roast, "At least my husband/brother/father is in uniform, unlike yours!"

Beth sat in one of the listening booths at Scopelli's, earphones clamped over her ears, chin on her folded arms. Harry wasn't coming today; he had a pack of six-year-olds coming over for Christopher's birthday, so he'd given Beth the music shop key for herself. Bach's parallel lines of melody were pouring into her ears now, precise and rippling, and behind closed eyelids Beth saw the new cipher. The cipher Dilly had been working on before he died.

Who knew what the Soviets were sending over their captured Enigma machine, or why—Beth knew it was probably dummy messages, but the cipher itself fascinated her. It seemed to have been sent over a three-wheel German army Enigma machine, but it was somehow different from the others she'd seen. Dilly was right about its spiraling inward; it seemed downright hostile to being wedged open.

"Why waste time on that?" Peggy asked one slow night shortly after the year turned. "We've got stacks of more recent unsolvables if you're bored." As long as Beth had worked in Knox's section, there had been a basket heaped with the messages that couldn't be broken—you worked on the duds when you were at loose ends, but no one had much free time now, with the Allied invasion of France looming. "Why waste time on Dilly's old stuff?"

"Because it was his last work." On and off since bringing it from Courns Wood, she'd turned back to it whenever she had a spare moment, working her way patiently through all the exercises she knew. Nothing to show for it, but being stalled didn't give her the colossal, mind-shattering frustration Harry had experienced with the U-boat blackout. Maybe because Dilly's discarded traffic hadn't been deemed critical—no one was dying in the cold waters of the Atlantic because Beth couldn't crack this cipher; it was merely a puzzle. She was starting to have dreams where a rose bloomed into lines of Enigma that then folded up on themselves like a bud flowering in reverse.

She was turning the record to the second side when the shop door banged open. Harry came in like a thunderstorm, hands balled into fists.

She pulled her earphones all the way off. "Is it Christopher? His party—"

Harry slammed the door so hard the frame rattled. "I've been uninvited."

"What?"

"Christopher asked me not to be there. He says his friends will tease him. Because he's the only one whose father isn't in uniform."

That little brat, Beth barely managed not to say. She hoped Sheila had smacked him.

"Sheila gave him what for," Harry said, as if reading her mind.

"Good," said Beth. "You should have stayed anyway."

"It's his birthday." Harry began to pace. "He wasn't throwing a tantrum or trying to be cruel. Boys that age, the boys he goes to school with . . . They play war, they brag about whose father is off killing the most Nazis. Christopher's already a wog and a cripple"—he spat the words out with savage precision—"which puts him at the mercy of any bully who wants some fun. And on top of everything else, he doesn't even have a father he can be proud of."

"Yes, he does," Beth said.

"He has no idea what I do."

"Sheila doesn't know either, but she knows it's important."

"Christopher's *six*. All he knows is that the other boys torment him because his dad's a coward, and I can't protect him. And when he asks me why I'm not fighting, I don't have an answer." Harry dropped into the chair opposite Beth, face bleak. "The women working at BP—no one gives you dirty looks because you're not in uniform. Strangers don't stop you in the street and ask how you can hold up your head every day when other able-bodied young men are dying. Blokes don't give you a shove and say *You don't belong in this country, and you won't even fight for it.*"

"I'm only allowed this work because there's a war on," Beth said, "and I still don't get paid what you're paid, Harry. Don't tell me I've got it easy."

"I'm not," he snapped, eyes flaring. She held his gaze, not backing down, and he reached across the table, enveloping her hand in his bigger one. "I'm sorry. I shouldn't whine like this."

She studied him. "It's not just Christopher, is it?"

Harry looked at down at their hands, spreading her fingers like a fan. "If I'd known coming to Bletchley Park meant I could never fight—that none of us BP chaps would ever be allowed to enlist, because they can't risk us being captured—I'm not sure I'd have come. And I'm not the only one who feels that way."

"You wish you'd joined the RAF and died somewhere over Kent in 'Thirty-Nine?" Beth asked, incredulous. "Or been a gunner and got captured at Dunkirk? That would have been a better use of your brain?"

"Being clever shouldn't exempt me from danger. I'm not saying they aren't right to keep me from joining up now—the Park's secrecy is more important. But I wish I could have had the chance to do more than I've done."

"Are you saying you have no impact on this war? Estimate how many transports have crossed the ocean safely because you broke the U-boat traffic." She paused. "Anyone can be fodder for machine guns, but only a few can break top-level ciphers. This war needs your skull intact. Let someone else get blown up—better them than you."

"You're not saying we're better than the boys who get blown up—"

"A lot of them, yes. You are. *We* are. Our souls aren't worth more to God, but our brains are worth more to Britain."

Harry looked at her a moment. "God knows I love you, Beth," he said. "But sometimes I find it hard to like you."

"*What?*" She felt like she'd been slapped.

"Our brains work a certain way—a way that makes us useful. And yes, we save lives. But it is colossally goddamned arrogant to look down on those lives we save because their brains don't work like ours."

"It's not arrogant to know what we're worth, Harry. And it's ridiculous to think that shooting our enemies is a nobler or more effective part of the fight than decrypting their battle plans. We might fight with paper and pencil, but that doesn't make it less of a fight."

"I know that. I know the fight is worthwhile. But it's hollowed me out until I've wondered if I'll end up in a padded cell, and it's put a target on my son's back, and I'll be damned if I pretend I don't have regrets." He pulled away, rising and beginning to pace again.

"I wouldn't have you if not for this job," Beth said, feeling cold. "Is that something else you regret?"

Harry stopped. She saw the tension in his broad back. "No," he said quietly.

But . . . ? Beth thought.

"I envy you sometimes." Harry turned, leaning an elbow against the doorjamb. "How you sail through every day, oblivious to everything but work. I can't decide if you really don't care, or you care but you're so focused it all ceases to exist as soon as you fall down the rabbit hole."

"Care? About what?"

"The war, as it exists outside a stack of ciphers. Your friends, whom I know you love but you don't pay much attention to—"

"I do, too—"

"Mab's drinking herself sick in the Recreation Hut after every shift. She's hanging by a thread. Haven't you bloody well noticed?"

". . . No." Mab was *unhappy,* of course she was, but hanging by a thread? Mab who still trimmed Beth's hair in its Veronica Lake wave every month, who had taken her to London for her contraceptive device. "I didn't realize," Beth said in a small voice.

"And I just told you I love you, and you didn't even blink." He folded his arms across his chest. "Do you love me, Beth?"

"You also said you found it hard to like me," Beth rallied. "That might have hit a little harder."

"When you're clicking along like a clockwork mechanism completely oblivious to everyone around you, yes, I find that hard to like. It doesn't mean I don't love you. I do. Fairly incurably."

Beth looked down, fiddling with the earphones on the table, feeling one of her persimmon blushes sweep over her face. "I don't—know what to say to that," she said finally. "Or what to do with it. We can't change anything. I don't *want* to change anything. So why do we have to discuss it?"

Harry came over, tilted up her face, and kissed her gently. "Beth," he said, "you don't know what to do with it because it doesn't come in five-letter clusters."

CHAPTER 56

FROM BLETCHLEY BLETHERINGS, FEBRUARY 1944

"Dutch gin," as served in the Recreation Hut, bears no resemblance to either Holland or gin. It's drinkable only when you've had the worst day in the world. For example, the kind of day *BB* had, upon coming across the phrase *zur Endlösung* in the course of work. It referenced a transportation of Jews, and it means "for the final solution." *BB* has never come across that particular expression before, but it doesn't take a great deal of imagination to fill in the possibilities, does it? *[Draft destroyed unread by anyone but its author, and replaced with humorous write-up of BP chess tournament]*

"Four months? God help us."

"Preparations are well under way."

"Better hope so . . ."

The conversation in Commander Travis's office retreated as Mab picked up the tea tray and a stack of reports, closing the door behind her. It was all anyone had talked about since the year had turned: the Allied invasion of France, which Mab now knew was planned for June or thereabouts. She was also privy to the exact number of Lancaster bombers and Flying Fortresses headed to flatten Germany's airfields in long-term preparation for the invasion. Mab supposed indifferently that she was better informed about Britain's war plans than the cabinet.

Ditching the tea tray, she went to lock up the files she'd just collected. Nothing important was ever to be left lying about unlocked, even for a moment—Mab knew one of these cabinets had reports about assassination attempts against Hitler, and reports about the new and improved computing machines here at BP that would supposedly crack Enigma traffic even faster than the bombes. But she didn't think about any of it. Her brain wasn't required in this new job. She was in administration now; filing, typing, and organizing records. Pure secretarial work; something to get up for each morning, but requiring no deep thought or focus.

Mab came off shift at last, and ten minutes later had her first drink sitting in front of her at the Recreation Hut. She downed two Dutch gins in quick succession, then ordered a pint of lager and sipped slowly. Two quick, one slow; that was the ticket. Get drunk too quickly and she'd end up weeping into her glass; too slow, and she wouldn't get as numb as she needed in order to sleep. Two quick, one slow—repeat for four hours, until it came time to sway dizzily toward the transport bus. She was fine. It was all fine.

She rummaged in her handbag for a cigarette, squinting when she found the ring of keys for the cabinets where she'd finished today's filing in the mansion—she'd forgot to turn them in to the watchman in the main hall. He already had another set, thank goodness, so she'd just pop back in and hand hers over when she left here. All was well as long as the keys stayed on Park ground and were never left unattended.

"Queen Mab, you gorgeous thing. May I get you a drink?" Giles asked, his face agreeably out of focus. "Any good gossip?"

Dropping his voice to a near whisper under the cheerful noise of off-duty codebreakers drinking, playing table tennis, and dealing bridge in the background. "Has Travis hit the bottle yet from the stress of the coming invasion?"

"I'm not saying a thing about work, Giles." Even three drinks in, half-drowning in grief, and ensconced here at the heart of BP, the knee-jerk was reflexive.

"Darling girl, I want *gossip,* not work secrets. *Bletchley Bletherings* isn't very funny these days—letting down the side. So tell me whose nerves are in a lather picking the invasion date; tell me if the PM really is screaming down the line every other day about Montgomery. We can't talk secrets, but we can talk people. Nothing? Well, I've got plenty for you. The Glassborow twins have joined the Mad Hatters—you know, the brunettes in Hut 16? My God, but they're irritating. They never stop giggling. If that's what youth is coming to, we should throw in the towel and let Hitler *have* the empire. We're reading *Bleak House,* by the way, for the monthly pick. I'll save you five hundred pages: it's bleak."

Mab remembered plowing through most of Dickens on "100 Classic Literary Works for the Well-Read Lady." Had she ever finished the list? Not that it mattered now.

"—You're missed at the Tea Parties, Mab. The Mad Hatters aren't the same without you. Osla's too gloomy lately to provide much sparkle—have you heard the whispers about that prince of hers?—and sweet Beth may be brilliant but she's never been one for banter. Though I confess there's a certain amusement value in watching her and Harry sit across from each other, pretending they haven't just been at it like rabbits in the air-raid cellar. Who those two think they're fooling, I have no idea . . ."

Mab swallowed the rest of her drink, ordered another. The sides of her head felt soft. She looked past Giles, and sat bolt upright. Francis was sitting in the far corner of the Recreation Hut—his back was to her, but those were unmistakably his stocky shoulders, his hair with its tracing of gray . . . she slid off the stool so quickly she almost fell, pushing past a quartet of bridge players. "Excuse me—" It was Francis, he was alive, and he was going to turn round smiling and tell her Lucy was asleep in the nursery.

Her hand fell on his shoulder. The man turned his head and it wasn't Francis. Of course it wasn't. Just a stocky fellow with a red face, nothing like Francis. Mab nearly wept. She turned and blundered back toward her stool, missing it as she tried to slide back on.

"Careful." Giles put a hand on her shoulder. "You don't look too steady on your pins."

Mab had been cursed like this since Christmas—*seeing* Francis and Lucy everywhere. But not really seeing them at all. Every skinny-legged girl playing with a ball turned into Lucy; every man with a chestnut gleam in his hair was Francis. Mab knew her mind was playing tricks, but she couldn't stop running up to strangers, hoping against all reason. Cruel, mad mind. Crueler, madder world. *Turn it off* . . .

She swallowed the dregs of her beer and looked at Giles, stretching her lips into a smile. "You were saying . . ." She didn't listen to his answer, just kept nodding and sipping until the world transformed into fizzing and sparks. Mab woke with sunlight in her eyes.

She sat up, looked around a strange room with a sheet sliding down her naked body, pain splitting her skull, and realized Giles lay stretched out in the bed beside her.

"NO NEED TO blitz out of here like you're making for the last lifeboat off the *Titanic*."

Mab straightened, a wave of nausea rolling through her stomach, snatching up her clothes, which had apparently been dropped on the floor wherever they fell. This had to be Giles's bedroom—he'd been one of the lucky ones billeted in the Shoulder of Mutton. He was sitting up in bed, red hair standing on end, coverlet drawn to his waist. Mab's stomach rolled again. "Am I late for shift?" Perhaps it was a pathetic point of pride, but all the times she'd stumbled home to bed half-drunk, she had never once allowed it to make her late the following day. She'd failed all her promises to Lucy, she'd failed all her promises to Francis, but she hadn't failed the oath to her country. "*Giles—*"

"It's not even six." He reached for the pack of Gitanes on his night table.

She would have sagged in relief, but that was only the first of the worries making her stomach clench. "Did—" she began, still clutching the clothes against her own nakedness. Giles appeared to be wearing his drawers still, but she could hardly bear to look. "*Did we—*" She didn't remember a single thing past being helped through BP's main gates.

"We did not." He struck a match. "Try not to look quite so surprised, will you? You were keen enough last night, and I admit I was fairly keen, too, but you were out cold the moment your back hit the mattress. I don't require protestations of eternal love from the women I take to bed, but I do require consciousness. So I put the covers over you and climbed in myself for some shut-eye. I'd have taken the couch like a gentleman, but as you see"—he gestured around the tiny room—"there isn't one."

"Th—thank you. I'm sorry to impose, I—" Mab managed to pull her slip over herself. Her stomach churned again. *What else did I do? What spectacle did I make of myself?* This had never happened before, in all her hours drinking at the Recreation Hut. How had she got drunk and thrown herself at Giles, of all people?

An entirely different panic seized her as she remembered her ring of keys from the mansion. She grabbed her handbag. "Giles, my keys—"

"Relax, darling. You insisted on dropping them with the main hall watchman before we came here. You might have been plastered, but irresponsible? Never."

Mab exhaled relief. "Can I use your washstand?"

Giles exhaled a cloud of smoke. "Be my guest."

The water was freezing cold, just enough to gulp down a half glass, then splash the rest over her face and neck. Straightening, she looked at herself in the mirror and recoiled. The soot with which she meticulously blackened her lashes in place of mascara now ran down her cheeks like black tears, and her hair was a rat's nest. She didn't look like Francis Gray's elegant wife in her chic hats and perfectly shined shoes. She didn't even look like Mab Churt, the pugnacious Shoreditch girl in rayon frocks who was going to tow Lucy out of the hole they'd both been born in.

"You cry in your sleep." Giles's voice came quietly behind her.

Mab began crying now, hunched over the basin.

"You've had a rotten time, haven't you?" Giles stretched out a pale, freckled arm. "Don't be ashamed. You were drowning your sorrows last night, and frankly so was I."

Somehow Mab found herself crawling onto the bed and under his arm. She shook, racked by sobbing, as Giles passed her a handkerchief and talked lightly in a way that required no reply.

"I used to have a dreadful pash for you, you know. I got over it when you married the war poet, though I can't say my luck got any better, because I promptly lost my head for another woman I can't have. Which is why I thought last night it might be a good idea to forget about her in *your* arms, but you're the one who needs arms right now. Poor Mab . . ." Squeezing her shoulders. Mab's sobs were subsiding, even as her head continued to throb. "Part of me envies you," Giles continued. "At least your Francis loved you back. I can't even get Beth to look my bloody direction."

He wasn't really equating his unrequited crush with Francis's death, she knew. He was trying to distract her, and she was grateful. "Giles, don't tell me you've lost your head over Beth." Mab pressed the heels of her hands to her eyes.

"Ever since getting transferred to ISK. You can't really know someone at BP till you see them work. I never knew what Beth *did* until I came there." Giles whistled. "When she's really working, she practically shimmers. I used to think I was fairly bright, but here everyone has a First from Oxford or translates Egyptian papyri. Brains like mine are plain tuppence pieces to Beth's golden guinea. Harry, now, he's a solid pound sterling. No wonder she looked past me and snapped him up."

"I'm sorry," Mab managed to say.

"I'll get over it." A shrug. "Besides, if I wait a bit, Harry might bugger off home to his wife and Beth might look my way. A chap can dream, eh? Until then . . ." Giles placed his last half inch of cigarette in the saucer on the bedside table and cupped a hand to her cheek. "You've got someone you'd like to forget, and I do, too. Now that we're both sober, what d'you say we give it a try?"

Part of her wanted to, just to get out of her own miserably aching head. But he was Giles, one of her few remaining friends, and he didn't deserve a woman who was only going to shut her eyes and wish he were someone else. "I can't, Giles."

He smiled, dropping his hand. "Then what do you say to breakfast, my queen?"

CHAPTER 57

FROM *BLETCHLEY BLETHERINGS*, MARCH 1944

Trains and train stations—what a thing they become in wartime. How many heartbreaks and homecomings, ecstasies and agonies, have we experienced with a rocking floor, a platform crowd, and a sweaty ticket clutched in hand?

This time Osla was the one to wait on the platform at Euston. A gleam of ash-gold hair—there was Philip, right on time, coming through the crowd with his loose-limbed stride. He hadn't written since Christmas or invited her to meet up before today. He'd said he was up to his ears, reassigned to a new W-class destroyer in Newcastle upon Tyne . . .

Perfectly reasonable, Osla thought, watching him approach. She was up to her ears too; the clock was ticking down to June and the planned invasion, and the Hut 4 translators were swamped. But her mental insistence that things were fine couldn't entirely banish Philip's cool voice at Claridge's: *You never really answered my question last night. Why you stopped writing.*

And the voice of Philip's friend David: *He and Princess Elizabeth sparked like a bonfire . . .*

Philip stopped before her. "Hullo, princess." Eyes traveling over her blush-pink dress—the same one she'd worn the very first time they'd met at this spot—and landing on his naval insignia pinned between her breasts. He smiled despite himself, scooping up her hand and kissing it. "I'm only in town the one night. Tomorrow it's back to Newcastle—lots to do, overseeing the *Whelp*'s finishing touches."

"*Whelp*—what a name for a fighting ship."

"She's a nice, fast piece of work . . ." He waxed technical, hands flying. He wanted to be back at sea, Osla knew. A man like Philip was meant for heavy seas and dodging fire, not squiring ladies around London.

"And you?" He tucked her hand in his arm, drawing her back toward the shelter of the wall. A train had just roared in, soldiers spilling out hauling kit bags, harried-looking women scolding children. "What are you up to in that dull job of yours, Os?"

Yesterday, my fellow translators and I were all having a good snicker at Herr Hitler, Osla thought. *The Führer seems to have written off the idea that the Allied invasion is coming through France. He thinks it'll be* Norway; *isn't that an absolute screamer, Philip? You really have to wonder about Hitler—if a lot of dabbling debs can point out there's no practical way a huge amphibious force could bang through those North Sea choppers and then clamber over those rocky shores inland, you'd think the supreme leader of a Reich that's supposed to last a thousand years could figure it out. But he hasn't, and a hut full of women is laughing their heads off at his expense. That's my week in a nutshell! Isn't it a hoot?*

"Oh, you know. Nothing to tell!" Osla squeezed his arm. "According to your friend David, *you've* got something to tell. He rang me after Christmas, saying poor Lilibet has a mad crush on you. I hope you haven't broken our princess's heart."

She made her voice warm and teasing, inviting him to laugh.

But Philip glanced down at her, and an expression shifted across his face. "I wondered if you'd heard anything."

"Is there anything to hear?"

"No. There isn't."

"Then what . . ." Osla didn't know where to go with that, so she trailed off. They stood silent on the platform. How much time had they spent here, waiting for each other? "Philip, I'm not *jealous*. Though I think that was David's aim—why else call up your friend's girl and tell her he spent Christmas getting ogled by a seventeen-year-old in pantomime tights?"

Philip sounded clipped. "Elizabeth is far too young for people to be hashing out wedding plans—"

"*Wedding* plans?" Osla's heart pounded unpleasantly. "Who's hashing those?"

A pause. "I'd rather not talk about this anymore, Os."

"I'm not trying to pry into—royal matters," she managed to say. "But you gave me this to wear"—touching the naval insignia—"and you've told me you loved me more than once over the last four years. Even if things have been strained lately, I think I have a right to know if your name is being seriously bandied about in *wedding plans* to someone else."

"It isn't." He rounded. "Far too early for that."

"Well, isn't that topping." There really was something then. Something besides idle whispers. Osla let out a slow breath. "Shall I wait a year or two and bring it up then? Will that still be too early? Or too late?"

"Osla, let's drop this. Go get Dover sole and champagne at the Savoy."

"I've lost my appetite."

They stood looking at each other. The platform was almost empty; the crowd from the last train had cleared out, and passengers for the next had yet to gather. "I'm not discussing this here," Philip said at last. Osla heard the bite of royal disdain that so rarely cropped up in his voice; disdain for saying anything remotely personal in public.

"This is about as close as we'll get to private, Your Highness, given that we don't have a room at Claridge's this time. So I'd like to hear what is happening with you and dear Cousin Lilibet."

He thrust his hands into his pockets. "She's fond of me," he said finally. "She has been since she was thirteen."

"That's a silly girl's crush."

"She's not silly. She's very serious, actually. Solemn. She knows what she wants."

"And she wants you. And now that she's nearly eighteen"—*the age I was when I met you*—"people are starting to think about whom she might marry one day."

"I suppose." He looked restless. "I've never given it a thought, Os. I'm still not. I've got a ship to think about. I'm heading out to fight—that's what I'm thinking about. There's a war on."

I know there's a war on, Osla wanted to shriek. *I know! I know!* But something else went on at the same time war did, and that was life. It kept right on going up until the moment it stopped, and this was hers, limping along like a horse suddenly gone lame, all because someone had chucked an obstacle in her path called Lilibet.

"So she's thinking about you, but you aren't thinking about her." Osla kept her voice level. "Why are you so edgy, then? And why have you been avoiding me since Christmas?"

"I wasn't—"

"Yes, you were."

A long pause.

"My family's got the bit in their teeth," he finally said. "Some guests at Christmas noticed the lay of the land—with Lilibet, I mean—and that's how my cousin George got wind of it." *George* as in the king of Greece, currently in exile from the throne. "Suddenly the whole family's buzzing. Uncle Dickie loves the idea, Cousin Marina won't let it go—she's written my mother. Everyone's harping on the possibility . . ."

"So?" Osla folded her arms. "They can't force you down the aisle because they want an alliance, Philip. This isn't the Middle Ages."

"I have obligations." He couldn't look her in the eye. "They're my family."

"Which family members would that be? The ones in exile from their own homeland? Or the ones allied with Hitler? You have told me for years that you feel you hardly have a family at all, and now that you might potentially make a match of it with the future queen of England, their wishes are suddenly paramount?"

"I have obligations," he repeated flatly.

"You have other obligations first, as you pointed out. There's a war on, *Lieutenant,* and fascists to fight. But what if we get to the other side of this war and your solemn, serious princess is still taking a dead set at you?"

A long pause. "Then my family will expect me to step forward."

Osla unfolded her arms, clasping her hands together to keep them from trembling. "And what will you do?"

Another long pause. Osla turned and took a seat by the wall, remembering the blackout when she and Philip had sat here all night kissing. She took some deep breaths, waiting for the tightness in her throat to subside. "Were you ever doing more than—marking time with me?"

"You know it's more than that!"

"Is it? You love me. I know you do. But did you ever mean it to last?" A brittle laugh. "You didn't, did you? What you said to me the night we met: *I'll lay odds you're hard to get over.*"

"I never promised you it was going to last." Philip dropped

down beside her, linking his hands between his knees. "You're too good for me by half—"

"That is a bunch of noble bloody rubbish. Another way of saying 'You're not good enough.' But I am, Philip. I'm of age, I'll have money of my own, I run in the same circles as you, and I've *always* been good enough. Yet I'm still just the one you telephone for a night out." She lifted her chin, refusing to look away. "It has been *four years*. Why did you never—"

"Be fair. I never took things far enough in the first place to raise your expectations."

"You mean because you never took me to bed, you think you're in the clear. Well—"

"Keep your voice down!"

"—there are other ways of *raising expectations,* Philip."

They were both shaking. Philip looked, Osla thought, like he wanted to give her a good slap. She wanted to claw his face bloody. But it wouldn't have taken much for them to fall into each other's arms, either. It never had. She tore her eyes away, staring at the tracks as another train rushed in. They both sat waiting as another flood of passengers jostled off, pushing for the stairs. Waited until the train pulled away and the platform was empty again.

"Maybe you should go home." Philip's voice was back under control. "We'll talk when I get more than a night off from the *Whelp*."

"And go back to how things were, is that what you're suggesting?"

"How they *are,* Os. You know how I feel about you. Nothing has changed."

"Sorry, Philip. Having already given you four years, I don't really feel like pouring more of my heart into you." The words scraped out of her throat like broken glass. "Not when I know you're ready to put on royal racing colors the minute Cousin Lilibet trots to the starting post."

"Don't talk about her like she's a horse," he flared. "She's got feelings, you know."

"*So do I.*" Osla tried to swallow around the spike in her throat. "Do you love her?"

"I was curled up around you at Christmastime—you think I'd bounce from that to falling for a girl barely out of the schoolroom?"

"I don't know. What would your family expect?" Pause. "*Could* you love her?"

The longest silence yet. Osla's heart contracted as if it were shrinking away from him.

"I think that might be a yes," she managed to say.

He looked at the ground between his feet, as if seeing something else. "The world she lives in . . . At Christmas I got to see them all behind the scenes a bit more. Her family's not like mine, scattered and quarreling. *Us four,* the king is always saying, so proud. Just a man and his wife and his two daughters—that's what they are, by themselves. Not grand."

"Not *grand*? A family with what, ten palaces?"

"You know what they do in those palaces? They drink tea and listen to the gramophone, and laugh while dogs flop about on everyone's shoes. Margaret reads a magazine while her mother talks horses and Lilibet and her father go walking . . . I could be part of that," Philip finished, low voiced.

That's the honey in the pot, Osla thought sickly. Not just a princess who was a suitable match for a prince . . . not even the fact that his relatives approved. Princess Elizabeth brought the one thing those without homes couldn't resist—the thing Osla herself wanted desperately. Lilibet came with a family ready-made, close-knit, and loving. A family, all tied up in a bow with the future queen of England, who was a *serious* girl rather than a silly deb.

An oasis in the desert, surely, for a boy raised without a home. A boy who'd grown into an ambitious man . . . Osla knew Philip so well; of course he was ambitious. What man in his lonely, bare-bones position would turn down such a chance—status, wealth, power, allied to a loving family *and* a girl he thought he might very well be able to love?

No one, Osla thought.

"I can't think about any of this yet," Philip went on. "Not until the war is done. There's not room for it. But Lilibet said she'd keep writing. She's never stopped." He looked at Osla. "*You* stopped."

The breath left Osla as if she'd been punched.

"I've told you things I never told anyone, Os. About Cape Matapan, lining up targets in the dark and watching them go down. Then I go off to sea again and you stop writing. So I think you're cooling off, you're backing away, and I should let you because you're right—I didn't get into things with you thinking it was something for the long run. So if you want to back off, it's only fair to let you. But I get home and you're in my arms at Christmas like nothing's happened, and you've got my head spinning all over again, but you won't tell me why you went off me, or even that you'll write again . . . I may have misled you, but we're pots and kettles here. You've misled me, too."

That's not my fault, Osla wanted to snarl. *I've* protected *you—I stayed away to keep London intelligence off your back*—but she couldn't say any of that. He waited for explanations, but the Official Secrets Act sat around her neck like a lead collar.

"At least with Lilibet," he said at last, "I know where I am."

"Do you know *who* you are with her?" Osla lashed back. "With me, you'd simply be Philip. With her you'd always be *the queen's husband*. Do you think you're built for that, playing Albert to her Victoria? I don't think you are. You'll be dead of boredom in three years."

Now he was the one who looked like he'd been hit.

The silence stretched, endless, taut, terrible. Somewhere distant, a clock chimed. Finally Osla rose, unpinned the naval insignia from her dress, and placed it in his palm. "Good luck with the *Whelp*." Avoiding his stricken gaze, she walked carefully, one step after the other, across the platform toward the ticket booth, where she could find out what the next train was back to Bletchley. Part of Osla hoped Philip would come after her—that the pull between them would defeat the promise of a family, and a royal one at that. But she knew he wouldn't.

She knew something else as well. If she put enough steps in line, one after the other, she would get there—to the ticket booth, to Bletchley, to the rest of her life—without crumbling into pieces. In the grand scheme of things, losing Philip wasn't remotely important. Not in a world where there were invasions of Europe being planned, where millions around the globe were dying. It didn't matter at all that she felt like she was being torn apart inside by white-hot pincers.

You'll get over it, Osla told herself. *There's a war on.*

Philip's voice came softly behind her: "Let me at least take you home, princess—"

Osla flinched like a lash had torn across her back. She turned in time to see Philip frozen midsentence, visibly realizing how ill advised that choice of endearments had been. She stood, spine straight, letting him get a good look at the rage in her eyes.

"I'm no princess, Philip," she said at last. "You've already got one."

CHAPTER 58

FROM *BLETCHLEY BLETHERINGS*, APRIL 1944

A thought, boffins and debs, and *BB* is aware it's a radical one: can we all perhaps retire the word *wog* from our vocabularies? *Such* an amusing term, *such* a joke, *such* an affectionate bit of slang to toss about in a moment of high-spirited fun . . . yet *BB* does not find the term particularly entertaining, and neither do those who hear it aimed at them, judging from their expressions.

Get off—" Beth waded into the scrum of children, grabbing a towheaded boy and a redheaded boy. They had Christopher Zarb on the ground in his own front yard and were pelting him with mud.

"He won't fight," the redhead jeered. "Just like his dad—"

Beth hauled off and smacked him on the back of the head. "Get out of here."

The boys ran. "My mum says you don't deserve to live in England if you won't fight for it," one yelled over his shoulder. "Stupid wogs . . ."

Christopher sat in the dirt, trying not to cry, brushing mud off his braces. Beth's heart squeezed. "Don't listen to them." She held out a hand, rather awkwardly, to her lover's son. "Come on, we'll get you cleaned up."

Sheila was inside laying out bread and marg for this month's Tea Party, but she swooped down on her muddied son. "Was it that Robbie Blaine again? The little bugger . . ."

"You take care of Christopher," Beth said, "I'll finish up here." She was early, the first one arrived. Harry came in as she was putting the kettle on, and he looked grim as Beth told him what had happened.

"Those little bastards have been after him for months. When I bang their heads together, their fathers come at me." Harry passed her a tea towel. "With luck, it'll slack off by next week."

"What happens then?"

A long pause. "I leave." He looked her in the eye. "I've enlisted, Beth."

A frozen, crystallized moment as they stood there in the cramped kitchen. Then Beth let out a short, incredulous laugh. "You aren't allowed."

"It is if you go for the Fleet Air Arm," Harry said quietly. "The naval air service. Anyone shot down in the Fleet Air Arm goes down at sea—no risk of capture, no risk to BP."

"Commander Travis wouldn't—"

"Travis gave permission to Keith Batey in Hut 6, back in June 'Forty-Two. Now me. I was going to tell you after the Tea Party, but—" Harry took a breath. "It's done, Beth."

"No." It came out reflexively, rushing through her throat in something very close to a whimper. She stood clutching the tea towel, suddenly terrified.

"I see you told her." Sheila stalked into the kitchen, pushing a strand of hair back into its string snood. "You talk to him, Beth. I've already worn my voice out. Maybe if he won't listen to his bloody wife, he'll listen to his bloody *mistress*." Glaring at Harry.

"Be fair," he said, attempting levity. "*Mistress* implies a kept woman, and nobody's keeping Beth anywhere she doesn't want to be."

The joke fell flat. Sheila turned around and began slamming cups about, leaving Beth to the attack. She crossed her arms, swallowing her fear. "How long have you been planning this?"

"January."

When she and Harry had quarreled over which was the worthier fight—the fight with a gun or the fight with a pencil. Neither of them had mentioned that quarrel since. Harry had been tender, pulling her into the cradle of his big body every time they came together, and she'd fallen into him gratefully, glad not to rehash the argument. She'd been *grateful,* and he'd been planning this all along. Beth gulped in a long breath, and with the air came rage.

"You idiot," she told Harry. "Your section needs you."

"Quite honestly, they don't. This isn't 'Forty-One, not enough people and everyone scrambling. It's not even 'Forty-Two, with the terrible shutout. You know how big my section is now? BP's turned into a well-oiled machine, thousands of cogs all doing their jobs. One cog won't matter."

"You aren't a *cog.* They can find more chess players and maths students, but they can't find another Harry Zarb." Her words scrambled, tumbled, pleaded. "They can't replace you."

"Yes, they can." His voice was gentle, and she hated it. "I'm not special, Beth. You could do my job better than me. So can women like Joan Clarke, who's one of the best brains in my section. That was the argument that clinched Travis—the ladies here have proved they are perfectly capable of handling the work. So let them do it, and let the men who want to join up go to the front while they can." Pause. "There's a big push soon. You know there is."

The Allied invasion. Everyone knew it was coming.

"You can't say one more body in that fight won't make a difference," Harry continued in that gentle voice. "Every one will count. Any number of qualified women can do my job. But those women can't join the Fleet Air Arm, which I can. And the Fleet Air Arm needs men."

"They don't need *you.*" But that argument wasn't working, so Beth switched tack. "What about your son? He needs both of you—"

"Sheila's parents have agreed to take up the slack."

"That will be a joy," Sheila muttered at the sink, banging cups. "You get to slag Krauts over the Atlantic, and I get to listen to my mother tell me I'm doing Christopher's braces up wrong—"

"If you go down in the middle of the ocean, he will be *fatherless.* She will be *widowed.*" Beth waved at Sheila. "Are you that selfish, Harry?"

"No." A glint entered his voice like a gleam off metal. "What's selfish is keeping myself bunked up in a safe, cushy job here in Bucks while every other able-bodied man in this country is expected to put his life on the line. They have children and wives, too—it doesn't exempt them from the danger. I have no right to keep myself safe for my family when they can't do the same, simply because they don't have my university degree and my easy out."

"Oh, don't be so everlastingly *noble,*" Beth snarled as Sheila snapped, "Christ, you're an ass."

Harry just looked at them both steadily, immovable as a granite pillar in the cramped kitchen. "I'm going," he said when they were finished. "I love that boy upstairs more than the world, and I love both of you, but I'm going."

To her own horror, Beth flew at him and began hitting him wherever she could reach. She couldn't stop. The panic was clawing its way out of her like a trapped bird. "Bastard," she jerked, realizing she was on the edge of tears, slamming at him with her fists. "You *bastard*—" Harry stood quietly, taking the blows. Sheila was the one who yanked her back.

"Stop that. People are looking."

At the door, Beth saw a cluster of newly arrived Mad Hatters hesitating uncertainly—Giles and Mab, the wide-eyed Glassborow twins. Beth turned away to hide her face as Harry awkwardly welcomed everyone inside. She wanted to keep pounding at him till he was bloody. She wrapped her arms around herself, hunching her shoulders, humiliated to have lost control so completely.

"Why were they arguing?" she heard Valerie Glassborow whisper to her twin as they went into the parlor.

"Does someone have to tell you what a ménage à trois is, child?" Giles asked, overhearing. "It's not going to be me . . ."

Beth seized her coat. "I'm not staying."

Harry followed her out into the spring twilight. "Beth—"

"You're a bloody mathematician, not a flier." She wrenched away before he could touch her arm. "You can do so much more here at BP, and you're still going to leave out of some—misplaced sense of nobility. And you're going to die in the middle of the Atlantic—" Beth felt tears rising up her throat at the thought of Harry's sinking under a glinting sea in a plane riddled by Luftwaffe fire. His complicated, questing brain turned to gray pudding, never to work out U-boat settings or theorize mathematical proofs again. The war had made a waste of so many men; why did it have to waste her beautiful, brilliant Harry?

Do you love me? Harry had asked her in January, and she hadn't known how to answer. Was this his way of finding out?

"I hate you," she whispered, aware she sounded like a child, too devastated to care. "Don't you dare write me when you leave, you walking-dead fool. Don't you *dare*."

NINE DAYS UNTIL THE ROYAL WEDDING

November 11, 1947

CHAPTER 59

Inside the Clock

It was only in the darkest, bleakest hour right before dawn that Beth could ever bring herself to contemplate the last name on her list for the position of Bletchley Park traitor.

Giles, a possibility. Peggy, another possibility. The rest of Dilly's section, suspects every one.

And finally . . . Harry.

Beth squeezed her eyes shut in the blackness of night, pushing down a fit of coughing. *Not Harry.*

But he had worked Knox's section from time to time, when they needed extra hands. She could even remember his arguing for greater aid to the Soviets, back in the days when they'd been losing millions to Hitler's eastern advance.

Harry, a traitor.

It can't have been Harry, Beth thought, defending him as she had a thousand times. It wasn't just a cry of *He wouldn't do that to me.* Harry had been in the Fleet Air Arm when the traitor wrecked Beth's life.

But what if he hadn't gone to the Fleet Air Arm? What if that had only been an excuse, and he'd gone . . . elsewhere? If he'd somehow monitored activity in ISK, or had someone monitoring it for him, when Beth finally cracked that fatal message of Dilly's abandoned cipher?

Far-fetched . . . but in three and a half years, Harry had never come to Clockwell. When the war ended, she'd pinned her hopes on seeing him come striding through the iron gates. He might not have been able to leave his regiment during the fight, but when the war was over, Harry would have come for her. Even if they'd quarreled before he left, *nothing* would have kept him away if he'd learned she was here.

They're going to perform surgery on me, Harry. Beth thought of her silent Go-playing partner, her one friend—taken away for surgery, not returned yet. A lobotomy, like Beth? Who knew? *They'll cut me open, and I don't know what they'll do after that. Come get me before . . .*

But he'd never come.

So . . . on one extreme, he was dead and had never learned what happened to Beth. On the other extreme, he was the traitor, and he'd put her here, and he didn't care if she died here.

Beth buried her head in her pillow and wept.

York

"Is this about my piece on Ascot hats?" Osla cradled the telephone between ear and shoulder, hooking up her stockings. She hadn't expected her boss from the *Tatler* to ring her here in York. "I winged it over your desk before I left London."

"Yes, I saw it—"

"Can I take a puck at turning it into a sort of upper-crust satire? It'll be an absolute screamer—"

"No, keep it straightforward. But this isn't about your piece, Miss Kendall."

Osla glanced at the time. If she was late checking out, she'd miss her morning train to Clockwell.

"You asked for a few days off. I think we'd better make your absence indefinite, until after the royal wedding."

She felt her jaw tightening. "Scandal rags still got the swithers?"

"Ringing round the clock for you. Take time away until things die down. It's not as if the world will fall apart if we don't have articles on Ascot hats."

Osla breathed through her nose. "When can I come back?"

"Well . . . you're getting married soon, so—"

"What's that got to do with it?" No one ever seemed to believe Osla wanted to work. Maybe fluffy, funny pieces on Ascot hats weren't exactly changing the world, but after translating so much tragedy at BP, Osla thought the world needed fluff and fun. She *loved* her job, damn it. "I have no intention of stopping after the wedding."

"Is your chap on board with that?"

Who cares? Osla wondered, reaching for her shoes. *I don't make a fuss who he fizzes the sheets with behind my back; he won't make a fuss about my job.* She issued her boss a few reassurances, rang off, then telephoned her fiancé. No answer, and she put down the handset with a guilty twinge of relief that she wouldn't have to talk to him, conjure up a story . . .

"You could do better, darling," her mother had told her upon meeting Osla's future husband. "Really you could."

No, I can't, Osla thought now, thumb running over her emerald ring. If Philip had taught her anything, it was not to trust passion. Far better to settle for reality: a job she loved and a friend she liked, even if he called her *kitten* and was probably gadding the weekend away with some tart from Whitstable.

Hauling her traveling case downstairs, Osla hailed the doorman. "If you'd be a lamb and call me a taxi—"

She stopped. Leaning against a well-maintained old Bentley parked opposite, looking smart in black trousers, enormous sunglasses, and a slouch-brimmed hat, was Mab.

THREE YEARS AGO

May 1944

CHAPTER 60

Letter from Osla to her Café de Paris Good Samaritan

Please tell me broken hearts aren't fatal. Please tell me this feeling won't kill me. Right now I wish it would. Float me a message in a bottle, Mr. Cornwell, and tell me it will be all right . . .

You could feel it, Osla thought, when something big was coming at Bletchley Park. Maybe no one traded details of their work, but you couldn't mistake the taut, febrile excitement in the canteen when waves of cryptanalysts sprinted in, bolted revolting platefuls of cheese and piccalilli without complaining, and sprinted out with pencils already in hand. You *felt* it. The temperature across BP rose like mercury in a thermometer.

The invasion was coming.

Not that other matters didn't intrude, however.

"Osla, do you see the traffic in your section on the Fleet Air Arm?" Beth spoke in a low rush, abruptly sitting down beside Osla in the canteen. "I need to know what planes go down. What the casualty rates are."

"Oh, Beth." Osla looked at her billet-mate, who had been pulling more shifts than ever since Harry left for training. Her complexion looked like ash. Osla pushed her plate over. "Eat my kippers. You're skinny as a hat rack."

"Just give me the numbers!"

Osla pushed a curl behind one ear. Her head ached, her hands were yellow from applying makeup to her legs after her last pair of stockings bit the dust, and oh, yes, she still woke up every morning thinking *Philip* and waiting for the accompanying stab of agony. So far the plan of utterly ignoring a broken heart on the theory that it wasn't important during wartime was not really working terribly well.

"I see some of the traffic about the Fleet Air Arm," she told Beth, who looked every bit as dead inside as Osla felt.

"Are the odds as bad as for the RAF?"

Osla chose her words carefully. "When they're shot down, they're . . . things are much more final than with the RAF. Because they can't bail out over land and make their way home."

"Tell me if you see anything about—"

"I'm not allowed, Beth. I can't."

"Yes, you can." Beth's voice scaled up. "We're not over an open telephone line, we're not out in public. We're inside BP. You can tell me."

"It's not your—"

"*Osla.*" Beth was getting looks across the crowded canteen now, hunched toward Osla with everything in her body saying *please.*

A pause, and Osla found herself nodding. "I'll look up the latest traffic." A minor breach in secrecy, but one everyone let slide—the huts were too full of women keeping anxious eyes on husbands and brothers at the front for there not to be a little discreet information trading. Osla couldn't stop herself from looking for the *Whelp,* now that it had sailed for the Pacific, no matter how many times she told herself it wasn't her business any longer.

Why couldn't hearts simply be reset, dialed back until they felt no more than the usual sympathy one felt for any man heading to war? Looking at Beth's reddened eyes, Osla thought her billet-mate might be wondering the same thing.

"Thank you," Beth said, low voiced. "I'm sorry to ask."

"Oh, plug it, if I can't bend a rule just a little for you of all people, what am I good for?" Osla felt a sudden rush of affection. All right, she didn't have Philip, but she had *friends*. More than the daytime friends like Sally Norton and the other translators; she had friends like Beth whom she would never have met if not for this war. Strange, quirky, brilliant Beth, who had recently confessed in a midnight heart-to-heart that she was deathly afraid of having no work like this once the war was done.

"I have to get back to my section," Beth said now, and in a blink was back to being crisp and calm. The workload was killing everyone else with this run-up toward the invasion, but for Beth it seemed to be revivifying. Osla envied her.

She worked on the week's issue of *Bletchley Bletherings,* then realized as soon as she got back to her block that it would have to be scrapped. There was much bigger news for *BB* than a lampoon of the Highland Reel Club.

"The date's been finalized," said their head, looking over the assembled naval section. "Sixth June. Last hours of the fifth, if the weather's good to us."

Osla felt her fingernails digging into her palms.

"All leave has been canceled," he went on. "Our focus is now on intercepts regarding positions of German mines in the channel. Good hunting, ladies."

Osla exhaled slowly. Maybe this was the purpose she'd been driving for the entire war, the time and place to finally prove herself. In three short weeks, amphibious vessels would be clawing through channel waters for Normandy.

Let's sweep their path.

She reached for her German dictionary. *Mine, mine-laying, mine ship . . .*

Time to buckle down.

CHAPTER 61

FROM *BLETCHLEY BLETHERINGS*, JUNE 1944

Cancel leave, cancel meals, cancel sleep. The day is set.

Bit by bit, Beth cracked the rose open.

"It's because the phrases are so short," she told Dilly. She conjured him up leaning against the desk opposite, poking his pipe. "There's so little to get a grip on. Probably because the Soviets were just trading dummy messages."

He nodded. "And?"

"I need a longer message." Beth gnawed her lip, ignoring the odd looks she was getting from the fellows at the nearest desk. "Did the Y-station get any more on this frequency?"

His eyes twinkled. "Why don't you check?"

Beth put in the request, laying aside the tight-furled cipher she'd come to think of as Rose. Ciphers and keys had been named after colors, animals—why not flowers? Shark and Dolphin were naval ciphers, she'd heard from some incautiously gossiping Hut 8 fellows . . . she diverted herself from the thought, because Hut 8 meant Harry, and the thought of Harry still speared Beth so sharply, all she could do was shy away from the wound.

She tackled Abwehr as soon as it came in. Just days till the invasion; all Bletchley Park was wound as tight as a clock spring. Everyone was turning up for shift early and going home late. "They're working you girls to death!" their landlady at Aspley Guise exclaimed.

It'll be worth it, Beth thought, *if we get our foothold on those beaches.* Beth's contribution to Operation Overlord was deception pure and simple. The most trusted double agents who had been tracked through Abwehr and turned against the Third Reich were all singing the same song back to Berlin: that the invasion would take place at Pas-de-Calais.

So far, every Abwehr message Beth cracked was saying that Berlin had swallowed it.

"How do you girls keep this pace up?" Giles groaned, sprawled in a tweed heap of limbs behind his desk. "You're all bally inhuman." Peggy and Beth looked at each other, shrugging. This was just going to be another Matapan. They'd done it before; they'd do it again.

But there were always a few hours before midnight when things slowed down, and every night Beth found herself heading back into the furls and byways of Rose. Word had come back from the request she'd filed for all traffic flagged by Dilly and all associated frequencies. "It was filed as low priority," the clerk said.

"I'll take it." A whole, lovely page to work with, not these frustrating scraps. "If the type of indicator on this machine is the same as the regular Enigma," she muttered, pencil flying, "it would *look* the same, but maybe . . ."

She had her foot in the door.

It was the fifth of June.

"NOW'S THE TIME to go back to your billet and get some sleep," Peter Twinn directed at sundown. "Starting midnight, it's all hands."

Most of ISK headed for the door, but Beth went back to her desk.

After midnight the invasion traffic would swallow everything—she'd rather work Rose than try to catch a few hours' restless sleep or try not to think about whether Harry was already in a plane headed for the channel. Surely he wasn't finished training yet, but she'd heard horror stories about pilots rushed into cockpits with just a handful of flight hours . . .

She gave a hard blink and banished Harry, reaching for the long Rose intercept. She got one wheel position, an R, and after evaluating a dizzying number of key-blocks, put a Z into the next. Beth looked at that for a while, then wondered if the message might have been wired to the key C-Z-R, for *czar*. It was supposedly a Russian intercept . . .

She poked her head next door, where ISK now had Typex machines set up. All the decodists had left; Beth hesitated a moment, then took a crack at the nearest machine. It took a while to figure out how to set it up, but eventually Beth got the wheels locked into CZR for a starting position, then sat down and began painstakingly typing the ciphered message in.

"What's that?" Peggy's voice sounded behind her, but Beth didn't turn around.

"Go away."

"Hang on, let me see . . ."

"Peggy, *go away*."

Heels clicked off, offended, and slowly the deciphered message unspooled. "Come on, you." All Beth wanted to see was if it came clear; she didn't care what it said—probably it *was* dummy traffic, the Russians experimenting with a captured machine. Beth just wanted to know that she'd broken it. If she could crack Rose, she could crack anything that would come at her in the invasion rush.

She was so used to seeing clumps of gibberish turn into clumps of German, it took her tired brain a moment to realize what she was seeing. It wasn't German; it was English. She raised her eyebrows, hesitated, then carried the sheet back to her desk, got the folder with the rest of the intercepts, and tried running them through on the CZR setting. Machine settings changed every midnight, but sometimes operators got sloppy . . .

Not this time. It all came out rubbish, so Beth abandoned the Typex machine and went back to the decrypted message. She began separating the five-letter clumps into words, but her eyes raced ahead of the pencil.

Beth stopped dead.

"I'M SORRY, COMMANDER Travis isn't in yet."

Beth stared at the middle-aged woman typing placidly behind her desk. The mansion was eerily quiet, half the offices deserted. "I need to speak with him. It's urgent."

"Everything's urgent today," the woman sighed. "He'll be in by midnight. Everyone's coming in at midnight."

Midnight? That was more than four hours away. Beth could hear her own heart thudding. She was clutching the folder of Rose messages to her chest like a shield. "I need to speak to him now," she repeated. It was all she'd been able to think when she read the cipher message in English.

"Well, he's probably getting a few hours of sleep. If you'll leave your folder—"

"No."

"Then I'm afraid I can't help you," the woman said, clearly out of patience.

"Listen, you dozy cow—"

"You listen, Miss Finch. Simmer down, or I'll have you tossed out on your ear."

Beth stumbled out, her mouth dry. She came to a halt between the stone griffons flanking the mansion's entryway, at an utter loss. The lawn stretched green and smooth down to the lake, but no codebreakers were playing rounders today in the long summer twilight. Men and women alike moved at a sharp clip between blocks, and the sky lowered gray and ominous. South of here, beaches designated Omaha, Utah, Sword, Juno, and Gold rippled with calm, unbloodied waves. They wouldn't stay unbloodied for long.

What am I supposed to do? Beth looked at her folder with the decrypted message and its horrifying revelations. She couldn't take it back to ISK—anyone might have seen it there, sitting on her desk while she tried to run the other Rose messages through the Typex. It was in English; anyone could have wandered by and read it—Peggy had come up behind her while she was putting it through the Typex machine. Had she seen? Had one of the others seen? What if—

Stop panicking, Beth told herself, but couldn't think where to go, what to do. She couldn't leave it unattended. She couldn't trust anyone in ISK. And when Travis came in, would he listen to her? The invasion launched in a matter of hours. Nothing would be more important, today and tomorrow, than that. Not even what she'd read in the decrypted message.

So keep it safe, she thought. *Until it can be dealt with.*

For now, "safe" was not Bletchley Park.

She thrust the folder under her cardigan and went through BP's gates at a flat sprint, heading for the nearest corner. She had never hitched a ride from a stranger in her life, but she hitched one now, flagging an ancient Vauxhall rumbling through town. "Sir, it's an emergency. Can you run me up the road to Courns Wood?"

CHAPTER 62

FROM *BLETCHLEY BLETHERINGS*, 5 JUNE 1944

"Take heed . . . how you awake our sleeping sword of war." Good old Shakespeare. It may be a different enemy today than in Henry V's era, but the sentiment remains the same as we look toward France.

Godspeed, boffins and debs.

"Waiting for the transport bus?" Giles was sauntering along with that fair-haired ISK colleague of Beth's—Peggy, Mab remembered, that was her name—and the two of them fell in beside Mab as she passed through Bletchley Park's gates.

"I was off at the usual time, but I'll return at midnight for the crush." Mab shifted her handbag from one arm to the other, trying to avoid Giles's gaze. She was still so embarrassed at having fallen apart in his bed, she could barely look at him.

He frowned. "You look like you haven't been sleeping, Queen Mab."

"I haven't." She'd cut down on the gin, and without its comforting haze she tossed and turned for hours before dropping off. Last night the dreams had all been of chasing Lucy through a choking maze of ash and rubble, and she'd wakened herself weeping.

"Well, that won't do," Peggy said briskly. "We need everyone fresh for tonight. Quite a thing, isn't it?" She nodded in the direction of the village. "We know the invasion is happening, and they don't have a clue."

"I'm not worrying about it until barges hit beachheads," Giles shrugged. "Have either of you seen Beth? I wanted to ask her to a concert or something after the imminent rush."

"She was at ISK when I last saw her." Peggy sounded irritated. "She bit my head off."

"I'm thinking maybe I've got a chance with her, now Harry's out of the picture . . ."

"She'll bite your head off too. I don't know how she's got any friends left." Looking at Mab. "I must say, you and Osla are more forgiving than I would be."

"What do you mean?" Mab frowned.

"You mean the Coventry raid?" Giles asked Peggy.

"Yes, I was—"

Mab stopped on the corner. "What about the Coventry raid?"

Peggy looked chagrined. To Mab, every detail of her face stood out in peculiar clarity: the fair flyaway hair, the thin intelligent face. "Have I put my foot in it? Look, I assumed after your husband's funeral, she would have apologized for . . ."

Mab's ears buzzed as though she stood inside a beehive. "For what?"

"Not warning you all to stay away from Coventry. I assumed she didn't, or else you'd never have gone. Beth broke an advance report about the raid—I was at the next desk." Peggy's eyebrows went up. Giles looked shocked. ". . . She didn't tell you?"

CHAPTER 63

Beth?" Mrs. Knox blinked in surprise, opening the door. "What on earth—child, you're white as a sheet."

"I'm sorry to disturb you." Beth felt the folder under her cardigan nearly burning through her blouse. "I need to get into Dilly's study."

Thank God Mrs. Knox was a woman accustomed to not asking questions. She led Beth inside, toward the library. It was nearly dark; when she switched on the lamp, the pool of yellow light threw shadows like gargoyles across the shelves of books. Beth looked at the cracked leather armchair where Dilly had so often sat, and nearly wept. *Dilly, why did you have to die?* It all would have been easy if he were alive. He'd have known what to do with the dynamite she'd decrypted.

But Dilly had been resting in his grave since last February, and Beth was on her own.

As soon as Mrs. Knox departed, Beth flung herself at Dilly's desk. He'd kept the key on his watch chain for as long as Beth had known him; where was it now? She gave a sob of relief when her frantic fingers sifted through the piles of old paper and found a familiar small brass key. She went to the panel in the wall and swung it out on its invisible hinge to reveal the safe. A turn of the key, and it opened—empty.

Slipping the folder of Rose-ciphered messages out of her cardigan, Beth hesitated. Most of them were still unbroken—she was tempted to take over Dilly's desk and see if she could crack any more. But time was slipping away, and she had to be back at BP by midnight. She looked at the first report, the only one she'd broken. The beginning was garbled and hadn't come out, but the message's middle lines in English were clear. She already had them memorized.

—possibility is intriguing, but for now we have our own methods. Please convey our thanks to your source inside ISK and assure our continued interest in any further information. The usual compensation.

There was some sort of code name as a signature, a word Beth didn't know. That wasn't the part that had frozen her to her marrow when she read it.

Your source inside ISK.

These weren't just dummy messages. Someone inside Bletchley Park had been passing information . . . and given the age of this traffic, they'd been doing it since '42.

"Did you suspect?" she whispered aloud, looking at Dilly's chair. But her simulacrum was silent tonight. Surely he hadn't realized—if the secrecy of Bletchley Park was compromised, the Rose cipher would have been assigned its own section, not left to a dying man in his private library. No, Dilly had only taken it on because Rose was different, interesting, an anomaly. His last puzzle.

My puzzle now, Beth thought, and locked the folder away, closing the wall panel over the safe. If something as secret as Enigma decrypts had to be taken off Park property, at least the Knox safe had already been approved as a secure location. Beth didn't dare take it back to Aspley Guise, and she couldn't leave it at ISK, either.

Someone there was a traitor.

Who? she thought in a twist of utter wretchedness—because they were precious to her, every single one. Peggy, who had taught her how to rod; Giles, who said she was the best cryptanalyst he'd ever seen and didn't sound resentful admitting it; Jean and Claire and Phyllida and all the rest of Dilly's team who had worked with her on the Matapan crisis . . . one of *them* was selling information from Bletchley Park?

The usual compensation.

Beth's stomach churned sickly.

She looked at the safe's key, then slipped it into her pocket. Dilly had often joked that he really should have more than one safe key; if he ever lost this one he'd be up the spout. The Rose file could sit there until Beth could bring it to Commander Travis, whenever that might be. *If he won't see me tonight, then he'll see me the hour the invasion is over, for better or worse. No later.* Beth didn't care if she had to hack her way into his office with a fire ax; he was going to give her a hearing.

"Finished, dear?" Mrs. Knox asked as Beth slipped out of the library.

"Yes. Please don't tell *anyone* I was here. I left something in the library . . . don't look for it."

"Of course not." Dilly's wife looked unfazed.

Beth hesitated, then reached out and gave Olive Knox a hard, brief hug. "Thank you."

Mrs. Knox's elderly man-of-all-work nodded at Beth as she came out to the front drive. "Where to, miss? I'm to give you a lift."

Beth was about to say *Bletchley Park,* but a familiar dull ache had bloomed low in her belly, and she felt a dampness on the back of her skirt—her monthly had begun. If she was going to be working a double shift starting midnight, then she'd need a sanitary towel. "Aspley Guise," Beth told the driver, and battled a wave of utter weariness. How much she hated being a woman sometimes: underpaid and underestimated and betrayed by your own body. She wanted to storm into BP and shout at the top of her lungs that they had a *traitor,* damn it, and everyone had better listen—but would they listen to a woman with blood on her skirt? So many men seemed to think women were crazy when they were bleeding.

She dragged herself up the stairs at Aspley Guise, fighting off the cold waves of suspicion as her mind turned from one ISK colleague to another—*It can't be you—Could it be you?—How could it be you!*—and let herself into her shared room. Osla was at the washstand scrubbing her face, and Boots looked up from his basket with a yawn. "Beth," Osla greeted her, "is something going on? I had a telephone call, something about Mab and Coventry . . ."

Beth was rummaging for her little bin of sanitary supplies, but she straightened with a sudden surge of nerves. "Coventry?"

"I couldn't really make sense of it—"

Mab stalked into the bedroom that she had once shared with the two of them, and not set foot in since her husband and daughter had died. Beth turned, barely in time to notice Mab's blazing eyes before her friend struck her savagely across the face.

CHAPTER 64

"You knew." Mab threw Beth back against the wall. The rage was choking her, rising in her throat.

"Mab—" Beth tried to fend her off, but Mab was head and shoulders taller, fueled by fury. She banged Beth into the mirror, setting it rocking, and Boots leaped out of his basket barking. Then Osla seized Mab by the shoulders and wrenched her away.

"Mab, *stop*. What's this about?"

Beth hunched frozen, arms about herself, Boots pressed to her ankles. Mab stood on the hooked rug, shuddering with anger. Osla poised between them, tiny and determined. For once, Mab felt no tangled confusion of anger and pain, looking at Osla. In Coventry, Osla had made a mistake—that mistake had let Lucy slip into the void, and Francis after her, but it had been a *mistake*.

Beth had made a choice.

"Tell her," Mab rasped, looking at Beth. "Tell her about Coventry."

"I don't have time for this," Beth begged, hands twisting. "I have to get to BP."

She made a move toward the corridor. Mab crossed to the bedroom door, slamming it shut and standing before it. "What is happening here?" Osla demanded.

Mab waited, but Beth stayed silent, huddled in on herself. "I was told Beth broke a report about the Coventry raid. The one that killed—" She couldn't force the names out. "She knew the attack was coming, hours before you and I left to meet Francis there with Lucy. She let us go without a word."

The accusation sank into the room like a stone in a pool, spreading ripples.

"Beth wouldn't—" Osla said, at the same time Beth whispered, "How did you find out?"

"Your friend *Peggy,* why does it matter? Is it *true*?"

Beth's head jerked up. "If I'd told you it would have compromised—"

"No, it wouldn't!" Mab cried. "We said goodbye to you at the BP canteen that same morning—no civilians in earshot, safe Park ground. You didn't have to give details. All you had to say was 'Please trust me and call off the visit.'" Mab would have telephoned Francis, asked him to meet them elsewhere. He'd be alive today. *Lucy* would be alive.

"I couldn't tell you," Beth repeated, pleading. "How could I put you ahead of everyone at Coventry who would have to sit the raid out, unknowing?"

"Because in a war, Beth, you save who you can. *Whenever* you can. You couldn't have safely warned Coventry, but you could have safely warned us."

"And you've done that before." Osla's voice was very quiet. "Autumn of 'Forty, you let us know when the German invasion was postponed."

Beth flinched. "That's why! I told you about the invasion, and I shouldn't have. I swore I wouldn't ever do it again. Besides, that's different—you knowing the invasion was canceled changed nothing. But if you knew about Coventry, you'd tell Francis not to come, then he might tell his neighbor, they might warn someone else, then before you know it—"

"We wouldn't have done that, Beth. Because we'd have lied

to Francis. We lie to everyone—just not each other." Osla was arrayed beside Mab now, arms folded like a shield. "Our knowing would have changed nothing, except that Francis and Lucy would still be alive."

"I didn't know that. I just hoped it would all turn out all right—"

"And my daughter *died,*" Mab spat. Perhaps she was being unfair to Beth, who had only tried to keep faith with an uncompromising oath. Even in the scarlet rush of rage, Mab knew that. But she didn't care. Beth had made a choice, and Mab's daughter was dead. Her husband was dead.

Beth was shaking her head stubbornly. "I took an oath."

"You expect us to break our oaths when it's convenient to you." Osla's ivory complexion had gone red. Mab realized, distantly, that she'd never seen Osla Kendall furious before. "You were just begging me to give you information on the Fleet Air Arm, because of Harry, and I *did it.*"

Beth's lips parted, but she didn't say anything.

"You sad little hypocrite," Osla said.

"I shouldn't have asked you." Beth's eyes were locked on the floor. "You should have told me no."

"I did it because our oath isn't as black and white as you're making it out to be, and we've all worked at BP long enough to know it. There are ways to share discreetly without ever, ever compromising secrecy."

"I couldn't think of a way—"

"You could have. But you didn't try. You told yourself it would be all right. And when it all went to hell, you still let me keep calling you a friend." Mab shivered with rage, thinking how much she had relied on Beth this past year. *Trusted* Beth, while blaming Osla.

"It was one raid!" Beth's voice rose. "Should I have warned you every time there was a raid over London, when you two were hopping up there every night you had free?"

"Everyone who goes to London knows it's a risk," Mab snapped. "London, Birmingham, Liverpool—they're constantly targeted; everyone who reads a newspaper knows that. You go to little places like Keswick or Coventry to be *safe*. You know we thought we were safe there—"

"You shouldn't have. You went to enough places that had been hit before. It finally happened and you're blaming me because you rolled the dice and lost. Coventry had been hit so badly already—"

"But no one anticipated it being targeted again. Not another big raid like that . . ."

Beth's hands twisted around each other. "I couldn't do it."

Mab lunged at Beth, or would have if Osla hadn't shoved her back. Mab inflated her lungs to shout, Boots circled barking and growling before his mistress—then a knock at the door froze them.

"Girls?" Their landlady's voice floated through. "Bletchley Park's transport pool sent a car for Miss Kendall and Mrs. Gray—it's waiting out front. You're being called in at once." Pause. "Is everything all right?"

"Quite all right," Osla called. Mab thought her voice scraped like a handful of pebbles.

They listened as their landlady's footsteps pattered away. Osla and Mab looked at each other, then at Beth.

"Let's go," Mab said. "I don't think there's anything more to say here."

Beth's lips trembled. "I've done nothing but what I thought was best."

"That's right. You did nothing, you Judas bitch." Mab yanked the door open. "Are you coming with us in the damned car or not?" Because even if she would rather have run Beth over than share a backseat with her, Bletchley Park was going to need her today.

But Beth sank down on the bed, laughing on a note that sawed across Mab's ears like nails. She was laughing but she was crying too, hands pressed to her temples, head shaking back and forth. Boots whined again, but she ignored the dog. "You have no idea," she said between the bubbles of laughter, as tears dripped down her chin. "No idea what's happening, none, none. My God. Dilly, why did you go, why did you have to go . . ."

"Girls," their landlady called from downstairs. "The car—"

They waited a moment, but Beth kept rocking, crying, bubbling with that strange bleak laughter. And finally, Mab and Osla had to leave her behind.

CHAPTER 65

Miss Kendall. Mrs. Gray." Commander Travis sat weary and upright behind his desk, his office crowded with blandly suited intelligence swots. "You've been asked here to provide corroborating information. We'll be quick; we've all more important things to do tonight." He leafed through a personnel folder, and even upside down, Osla had no trouble reading the name on it. Osla's roil of anger and exhaustion gave way to confusion—why, a matter of hours until the attack launched on Normandy and all Bletchley Park was plunged into madness, was Commander Travis nose-deep in a file on Beth?

"I understand you two ladies have billeted with Bethan Finch for the past four years," he said. "What can you tell us about her?"

Osla and Mab exchanged looks. Mab clearly had no idea what to say, either. However angry either of them were at Beth, outpourings about new grudges and old griefs were not relevant.

He clicked his tongue, impatient. "When did you last see her, and how would you describe her emotional state?"

"We saw her just before coming here," Mab said at last, voice crisp, "and she was completely hysterical."

A man behind Commander Travis made a *hmm* noise. "Would you agree with that, Miss Kendall?"

Osla didn't really want to, but yes—*hysterical* was an accurate way to describe Beth's laughing-crying jag. "I suppose so. She doesn't normally flip her wicket like that," Osla felt compelled to say. "She's very level."

"What did she say when was she hysterical?" That was one of the intelligence men. Osla recognized him—the smarmy fellow who had hinted she'd stolen files outside her hut. "Did she spout any wild theories? Talk about someone from her section?"

"No." Mab had drawn herself up cool and correct. You would have to know her very well, Osla thought, to know that she was still boiling with fury.

"Did she say anything about messages she'd broken?"

Osla pushed a curl behind one ear. "No."

"We understand she had a rather long-term liaison with a colleague in Hut 8." Pinstripes put a nasty edge on *liaison*. "A *married* colleague—Harry Zarb? The wog."

They both nodded reluctantly. No point denying it; everyone at BP knew.

"I understand he broke it off when he enlisted, and she became upset."

"The break came more from her than from him," Osla said.

Mab shrugged. "Yes, she was upset."

"She was already behaving erratically before this romantic disappointment, I believe? The death of her mentor Dilly Knox—did it make her unreliable? Unstable?"

Mab and Osla looked at each other. "That was part of her work, so it never came up."

Pinstripes bent over, murmuring. "We already had the other girls in, Miss Rock and what was the other one?"

"—Phyllida Something—"

"—and they said Miss Finch used to talk to Dilly after he was dead, as though he was still there in ISK working. Miss Rock said it gave her the shivers."

"Talking to people who aren't there—that's not the strangest thing you'll see in this place by a long shot," Osla began, but Commander Travis waved her off. He looked like a man who wanted nothing more than a few hours' sleep before the invasion, who had instead been dragged backward out of bed through a thornbush to be at this desk. *What is going on?* Osla thought in mounting unease. Beth couldn't possibly be in trouble over the Coventry raid; she'd get nothing but approval if her superiors knew she had kept the raid secret even at the risk of her friends' safety.

"I think we have more than enough evidence of worsening erratic behavior," Pinstripes said. "The real question—"

Commander Travis looked at Osla and Mab. "Did Bethan Finch ever violate the Official Secrets Act by repeating secret information outside Bletchley Park?"

Osla looked at Mab, who looked straight ahead and said, "Yes, she has. Once." Three women in a pitch-dark room, whispering classified information among themselves to feel safer in a cold, violent world.

Travis turned to Osla. "Miss Kendall, can you confirm this?"

An hour ago, Osla had flung the postponement of the German invasion in Beth's face. There was still the rock of anger in her middle about the Coventry raid, but she would never have chosen to tell Bletchley Park's higher-ups about Beth's single incident of indiscretion. She still wouldn't have. But now they were all staring at her cold-eyed, and Osla knew she couldn't lie. They might have very critical reasons to need the information—and if she lied, she could be charged with a crime. "Beth disclosed secret information once," Osla said reluctantly. "It was off BP grounds, but only to the two of us, in private, no possibility of eavesdroppers. She never did anything like that again."

"Irrelevant," Pinstripes snapped, and someone else began to lecture, "You two girls should have—" But Osla cut him off.

"Why is everyone getting hacked off about Beth and her moods?" Something here smelled *off,* all this information suddenly cascading down over Travis's desk at once. *On Mab and me, too,* Osla thought. "Beth's one of the best people we've got—now is not the time to put her out on the tiles."

"Thank you, Miss Kendall, Mrs. Gray." Travis cut her off. "You may return to your posts. I imagine you'll both be needed."

Osla tried again. "Sir, this frankly looks like someone trying to nobble Beth. I don't think—"

"Just don't think, you silly deb," one of the MI-5 swots snapped.

Osla's eyes stung, but she would have kept arguing. Only it wasn't going to do any good. Travis was pivoting in his chair, saying, "Can we close this matter, gentlemen? We've heard from the girl's billet-mates; we've called in her section colleagues and her mother. You may have noticed that there is considerably more to do tonight than deal with one broken-down—"

The office door swung shut, cutting off his voice. Osla drew breath, puzzled and angry and full of foreboding, but a buzzing sounded overhead, outside. She looked at Mab, and they both bolted for the entrance hall and out the door. They stood, faces turned toward the rainy black sky, as codebreakers began spilling out of the mansion and blocks. Osla's ears pounded as the shadows passed overhead under the clouds: hundreds and hundreds of RAF bombers towing gliders behind them, winging toward the channel.

"It's started," someone whispered, and then they were all shouting. "It's started—it's started!"

Nothing for it now. Osla ran for her block, Mab ran back into the mansion, and everything was forgotten except the fact that the invasion had at long last begun.

CHAPTER 66

Beth had no idea how long it took to pull herself together. When she stopped hiccupping and laughing and weeping, she lifted her swollen face from Boots's neck and looked at Dilly Knox standing in the corner. He wasn't really there, but it soothed her to pretend he was. "I know," she said. "I have to go." No time to go to pieces, no time to grieve for her broken friendships, no time for anything.

She scrubbed her eyes, fixed herself up with a sanitary towel, then put Boots on his lead and took him with her—who knew how long the invasion would keep her chained to her desk at ISK. Dear God, how was she going to work a double shift breaking Abwehr intercepts, knowing someone she trusted—maybe someone in the *room*—was selling information?

Put that away, she told herself, heading out under a dark, rain-lowering sky. Lock it in its own separate iron safe behind a wall panel, like the one in Dilly's library.

She hoped to flag a ride to Bletchley Park, but no cars passed by. Beth was nearly howling with frustration by the time the transport bus arrived, full of codebreakers she didn't know. How much had changed since she'd been recruited! The sleek triple-shifted operation of thousands merging seamlessly in and out of the new concrete blocks was nothing like the cheerful, frantic, slapdash days of the green huts. She climbed off the transport bus at the gates, determined to make her report to Commander Travis before losing herself in Abwehr until the invasion was over. Right now, the knots and byways of Abwehr looked like a haven. Beth hurried forward, fumbling for her pass.

"This is her." A big jowly man in a checked suit stepped forward, gripping her shoulder in a massive hand. "The Finch girl." He nodded at a shorter fellow in pinstripes smoking a Pall Mall by the guard station.

"What do you want?" Beth tried to tug away but it was like trying to move out from under a boulder. At her feet, Boots was whining. "I don't know you—"

"We know you, missy." The man in pinstripes sauntered over. "You've been talking about things you shouldn't. Or maybe you're just not right in the head. That's for other people to figure out, fortunately." He clipped her pass out of her hand and tossed it to the gate guard. "This pass is revoked, orders of Commander Travis. Bethan Finch is not to be allowed back inside Bletchley Park's grounds."

"*What?*" Beth's voice scaled up. "No, I have to see Commander Travis—"

"Afraid that's not possible, missy. He's a very busy man right now."

"It's important. I have documents—" She remembered to whisper, aware of the passing flood of codebreakers making their way through the gates. Showing their passes, slipping through, looking sideways at the little knot of disturbance. "There is information being passed out of the Park. It's very important—"

"Oh, I see. An informant? A spy?" The pin-striped man chuckled. "That's what they said you'd say."

"Who said?" What in God's name had been happening over the last few hours? It had still been daylight when she left ISK with her Rose decrypts, no one giving her a second look—now she was being escorted from the premises?

A gesture to the jowly man gripping Beth's shoulder. "Take her."

Boots barked wildly, towed by the lead around Beth's wrist as she was frog-marched toward a long black Bentley. "Just ten minutes with Commander Travis—"

They ignored her completely. Pinstripes leaned in to the driver. "You have the address for Clockwell Sanitarium?"

"Yes, not the first time I've driven a cracked-up boffin to the loony bin."

Beth heard the word *sanitarium* and went mad. She clawed the jowly man's hand off her shoulder, drawing blood from his knuckles, and turned to sprint for the gates. But Boots was still barking and wheeling on his lead, and she stumbled over him, going down hard on the road. The jowly man was on her then, picking her up bodily and carrying her to the car. The lead fell off her wrist as she thrashed and shouted. Every Bletchley Park codebreaker within fifty yards was staring.

"Don't mind her," Pinstripes called briskly. "She's had a bit of a crack-up, and now she's going for a rest." Beth realized with a splinter's clarity how it looked: the shiny, official car; the shiny, official men; the wild-haired woman with her swollen eyes, her crumpled clothes, her snarls and howls.

She threw herself at Jowls again as he slid into the car after her, but he captured her wrists, muttering, "So you're one of *those* . . ."

"Please," Beth babbled to the driver, "you can't take me to a *sanitarium,* I haven't had a crack-up, I have evidence of an informer—"

But the driver didn't respond, and Beth's eyes were drawn to the flash of silver as Jowls drew something out of his coat. She twisted frantically as the car started up, staring out the back window, gulping in a breath to shriek—and then she felt the prick of a needle through her sleeve.

The last thing she saw before everything went dark was the woolly gray shape of her dog, blundering up and down the shadowed road, dragging his lead behind him, as the Bentley pulled away.

SHE WOKE SLOWLY, to the smell of cigarettes and rain. Her entire body felt heavy, her skull stuffed with wool, her mouth dry.

The backseat was shadowed with gray light, empty besides herself. It was barely dawn, the Bentley parked on a barren hillside clouded with morning mist and spiky gorse. She couldn't see Jowls or Pinstripes—just the driver in the front seat. He'd cracked one window open enough to tap his cigarette outside.

"You're awake." He looked around: a blocky man, nondescript, middle-aged. A complete stranger. "We're out of petrol, if you're wondering where the other blokes are. They hoofed it to the station a few miles ahead to get a jerry can. MI-5 gets all the petrol coupons they need, you know. I said I'd sit with you."

Beth glanced groggily at the door handle, wondering if she could make a run for it.

"Don't try," he said, seeing her glance. "The needle stick you've had, you'll be moving like you're dipped in treacle. Besides, we're in the middle of the Yorkshire moors; nothing about but gorse and the odd sheep."

Yorkshire. They must have been driving all night. What was the place they had mentioned—Clockwell Sanitarium? *What is that? Where's my dog?* Her senses still felt dulled; the terror wasn't slicing her to pieces the way it had at Bletchley Park's gates. "Who are you?"

"Just the driver." He took another drag off his cigarette. "Driving for these London fellows doesn't pay as much as it should, so I'm not averse to making the odd shilling on the side . . . and before we left BP, someone paid me five quid to give you something, assuming I could get you alone."

"Who?"

"Not saying is part of the five quid."

"*I'll* pay you," Beth said desperately. "If you let me out, I'll—"

"No chance, duck. Five quid to pass on a message no one else will ever see is one thing. Letting you go is trouble I don't need. You want the message or not?"

Beth swallowed. "Yes."

He poked a folded sheet of paper across the seat divider. Beth shook as she read the terse, typewritten words.

`I saw the report you broke in ISK. I want to know what you did with it, and the others. Tell the driver yes and I'll find a way for you to send word from Clockwell. Once I've had a bonfire in the grate, I'll see you're released.`

`Say YES.`

`If you don't, you'll rot in a madhouse the rest of your life. Osla and Mab testified against you. Your mother testified against you. No one will save you.`

`Give me what I want.`

Beth looked up. "Who gave you this?"

But the driver only snatched the paper back. "Yes or no?"

"Do you even know what you're asking? It is a *traitor* who paid you off."

A snort. "What I heard was you took something that didn't

belong to you, that's all. You're on the way to a loony bin, and you're saying I should believe your story over that?"

"When the others come back with the petrol, I'll tell them—"

"Go ahead." The driver held the typed message out the window, set it on fire with his cigarette, and watched it flare up brightly before dropping it into the road. "I'll deny everything. I've driven for them for five years, and you're a crazy bint with veins full of sedative. So, yes or no? I get another five quid when I give your answer back."

To the informer. Whoever that was, they'd done a fine job of sewing her up, Beth thought bitterly. It wasn't hard to seed doubt about a codebreaker cracking up. As far as BP was concerned, she was a potential risk that had been plugged; they'd forget about her and plunge into the chaos of the Normandy landings. Distantly, Beth wondered how that invasion was progressing. Allied soldiers might be battling through waves on those distant beaches already, and she wasn't at her desk—she'd never sit at that desk again. For an instant, that hurt more than the knowledge she was headed to a madhouse.

You took it from me, she thought to the traitor in a flash of murderous fury. In one day, she'd been stripped of everything: her job, her friends, her oath, her home, her dog, her freedom.

Not everything, Dilly Knox said. *You're the cleverest of my Fillies.*

"So?" The driver looked impatient. "Yes or no?"

Beth doubled over with a sudden gasp, clutching at her lower belly. Reaching under her skirt to her soaked sanitary towel, she brought her hand out covered in blood. "My monthly—"

Like most men, the driver went completely to pieces when confronted with a woman's private functions. He fumbled for a handkerchief, for water, for anything that would get the blood off her fingers. It was the easiest thing in the world for Beth to reach into her knicker pocket with her unbloodied hand, take out the little key to Dilly's library safe, and slip it into her mouth.

The brass clicked between her teeth, metallic as blood. She took a shuddering breath, and then she swallowed it. It took some doing, forcing the metal edges past her own reflex to gag, but she got it down.

"Look, give me an answer." The driver eyed her as she cleaned the menstrual blood from her fingers, looking sorry that he'd ever taken that five quid. "Our friends will be back with the petrol soon. Yes or no?"

Beth leaned back in her seat and closed her eyes. "No."

She didn't say a word when the others returned, or when the car started up again. She didn't say a word for hours, until the Bentley rolled through the gates of a high, forbidding wall up to a stately gray stone house. Where Beth Finch was escorted through a blaze of summer roses to the front doors of the sanitarium, and heard the whirring gears of a great clock rise to a scream in her ears as the madhouse gates closed behind her.

CHAPTER 67

German intercepts decrypted at Bletchley Park during Normandy invasion

From: 11th U/B Flotilla

Immediate readiness. There are indications that the invasion has begun.

From: GRUPPE WEST

MOST IMMEDIATE. Off LE HAVRE 6 battleships and about 20 destroyers.

From: Seeko NORMANDY

MOST IMMEDIATE. MARCOUF reports: a great many landing craft approaching, protected by battleships and cruisers.

```
To: KARL

Endeavor to reach CHERBOURG. Attack enemy
formations as long as ammunition lasts.
```

The prime minister's voice poured through the telephone into Osla's ear like weary gravel. "News?" She could imagine him pacing his study, staring at the eastern wall toward Normandy. "Well?"

"In a jiff, sir." Osla had been at her desk for too many hours to feel a thrill at talking to the prime minister. She handed the telephone off to her superior and went back to translating, mind feeling as if it had been sanded. She read nothing she translated; it flowed into her eyes, through her pencil, and out again without leaving a trace. Thirty hours later she staggered home.

And found that Beth's half of the room had been cleared out. Her blouses and dresses were missing from the wardrobe; her drawers stood empty. There wasn't so much as a hairpin to indicate Beth Finch had lived here. Even Boots was gone.

Osla sat down on her bed. She had never in her life been so knackered, too tired even to crawl into bed. A familiar clack of heels sounded on the stairs, and Mab came into the room. "Beth's gone," Osla greeted her. "Maybe she went back to her family, or—"

"She's gone to a sanitarium," said Mab. "The gate guards told me—she completely crocked up."

Osla stared. "You're chaffing me. Beth would never break down like . . ." But right here in this room when they were all last together, Beth had had a fit of hysterics. Laughing and crying on that high-pitched note like a nail gouging slate. Osla rubbed her aching temples. "Did *we* do this? Land her in the basket—even if she deserved it—when she was exhausted and keyed up for the invasion?"

"I don't know." Mab sat down on Beth's stripped bed, looking as wrung out as Osla. "I shouldn't have shouted at her. Given the invasion, I should have left it till later."

"And who told Travis Beth broke her oath?" The timing of all of this . . .

"London intelligence monitors all of us informally, to make sure no one's talking. I've heard them talking about it at the mansion," said Mab. "Someone must have heard something about Beth, that's all."

They sat in silence for a while. Osla's head ached. "The invasion," she said eventually. "Did you hear anything at the mansion?"

"The Germans swallowed our Pas-de-Calais deception hook, line, and sinker."

"Well, isn't that just topping."

Another silence as they sat hoping that far away in the bloody sand and surf of Normandy, the death knell of Hitler's Reich was sounding across the beachheads.

"I'm leaving Bletchley," Mab said. "Not yet, but soon. They're sending a few ladies to the Admiralty in London. In the middle of all the fuss today, someone remembered to tell me I'd been chosen. Your friend Sally Norton, too. 'To facilitate cooperation between Bletchley Park and the naval high-ups' . . . I think they want us to flash our legs at the admirals so they won't fuss about how the naval information from BP is obtained."

No Mab at BP. No Beth, either. Harry already gone, Sally going . . . "Take care, Mab," Osla said, wondering if maybe they could at least *part* friends, of a sort anyway. She stretched out a hand.

Mab jerked away, her face hard. "I don't want your good wishes, Os."

"Well, I won't bother you with them." Osla's anger flared through the exhaustion. "You East End bitch."

Mab looked at her, weary and contemptuous. "Crawl back to Mayfair, you stupid deb."

Osla had never slapped anyone in her life. She slapped Mab now, and walked out of the room.

"Are you all right, dear?" Their landlady again, mounting the stairs with an armload of towels.

"Yes, quite." Continuing downstairs, insides churning. That contemptuous *stupid deb,* from Mab of all people . . .

But that's all you are. Osla halted at the foot of the stairs. She was never going to be anything else, no matter how hard she tried. So why bother trying?

She remembered meeting Mab on the train to Bletchley Park: two bright-eyed girls with their suitcases and questions, wondering what the mysterious Station X had in store. Girls who wanted to serve their country, make friends, read books . . . girls who were, above all, determined. Mab to get a husband, Osla to prove herself.

Be careful what you wish for, Osla wanted to tell those laughing girls in the train compartment. *Oh, be careful!*

She supposed she'd better choke down some tea, then make up a new post-invasion *Bletchley Bletherings* and head back on shift. She might be a silly socialite without friends, lover, or home, but she still had work to do: making people laugh, and translating horrors. Plenty of that would be needed, surely, in the months to come.

Another long, slogging year and more, as it turned out. There were some bright points—billeting with the effervescent Glassborow twins after Mab moved out; going to hear Glenn Miller with Giles; getting the news that Hut 6 had broken the message for Germany's unconditional surrender; sitting on the back of one of the Trafalgar Square lions on V-E Day getting sauced on Bollinger with a couple of American GIs. Writing message-in-the-bottle letters to J. P. E. C. Cornwell, wherever he might be; finally telling the Mad Hatters she'd been writing *Bletchley Bletherings* all along and relishing their groans and laughter. And oh, the day Valerie Glassborow was on duty to hear the word come in that Japan surrendered, and the news spread—Osla found herself on the lawn flinging rolls of loo paper into the trees with mad abandon, watching the white loops unroll against the sky and crying for happiness.

But that was the epilogue, she thought later. The real Bletchley Park ended for Osla on D-Day. The day three friends last spoke to each other; the day Mab Gray received a transfer to London; the day Beth Finch disappeared into the blue.

NINE DAYS UNTIL THE ROYAL WEDDING

November 11, 1947

CHAPTER 68

Inside the Clock

Even the inmates of Clockwell had celebrated V-E Day and V-J Day. Hitler's suicide, the German surrender . . . happy tears had been shed among staff and inmates alike. And then a few short months later, news came of the great bombs that brought Japan to her knees, and cheap wine was doled out in paper cups so everyone could toast to victory and peace.

To Bletchley Park, Beth had toasted silently. *Without BP, there would be no victory* or *peace.*

She had wondered then—and she wondered now, wandering the rose garden looking to see if her Go partner was back yet from surgery—what became of Bletchley Park after the war was finally over. She imagined the Typex machines falling silent, the huts emptying. No more rounders played on the lawn, no more canteen kidneys on toast at three in the morning, no more Mad Hatter Tea Parties of bread and marg and library books by the lake. Where would they all go, that collection of strange and remarkable people assembled by wartime desperation? *Go back to your old lives,* Beth imagined everyone being told. *Go back to your old lives, and never speak of this to anyone.*

Had Bletchley Park fallen into ruin, once the gates closed behind the last codebreaker? Would anyone ever know what had happened there?

I'll know, Beth thought, fighting off a fit of coughing, brass key to Dilly's safe nestled in its customary hiding place in her shoe. *If I'm locked here until I'm a hundred and three, I'll remember what happened at BP. They can take everything else, but never that.*

She thought she knew who the traitor was, too. Something else that couldn't be taken away.

She'd had three and a half years, after all, to ponder the question. Three and a half years to hide her key and sift her memory. Over the last few days, in the agony of waiting for Osla and Mab to respond to her cipher message, she'd kept herself occupied by weighing every possibility over again, even the names that hurt. And her conclusion was the same.

It came down to one very simple question: who had told Mab that Beth cracked the report about the Coventry raid?

Because the timing had been too neat, too pat. The one piece of information that would turn her billet-mates against her, delay her, and strip her of supporters who might defend her against accusations of instability—who had dropped that perfectly timed nugget?

Beth remembered herself whispering, *How did you find out?* Mab spitting, *Your friend* Peggy.

Peggy, who had been on shift in ISK the afternoon Beth cracked Rose. *What's that?* as Beth hammered at the Typex. *Let me see.*

Peggy, go away.

Heels clicking off into the distance . . .

"It was you," Beth whispered. Sometimes she had doubts, but most of the time she was certain.

The traitor was Margaret Rock.

CHAPTER 69

Mab nearly didn't make it to the Grand Hotel in time to catch Osla before she headed for Clockwell. She was packing her traveling case when the front door banged downstairs; there was the usual clamor from Eddie and Lucy, and then Mab's husband came into the bedroom. He was smiling at the twins, who were hanging off him like monkeys, but his jaw tightened as he looked at Mab.

Not another quarrel, she thought. *I do not have time!*

His eyes stopped on her traveling case. "Going somewhere?" he asked in the Australian drawl that persisted even after five years in England.

"An impromptu hen weekend with old friends," Mab said brightly. "Don't look so downcast, Mike. You'll have the nursemaid to help with the babies."

His voice was level. "I was hoping we could finish last night's conversation."

"I don't remember," she lied. "I was very tired."

"Not too tired to climb on me rather than finish the discussion. Which is usually how you get out of any conversation you don't want to have with me."

"I'd have thought you'd be happy to have a wife who doesn't get headaches at bedtime." Mab slammed her traveling case shut. "I've left a sausage and tomato pie for supper, and a syrup tart for pudding—"

"Stop, Mab."

"There's leftover casserole if—"

"I don't care about supper. *Talk* to me."

She looked at her husband, standing there in his shirtsleeves, capably juggling little Lucy in his arms as Eddie clung to his trouser leg. Mike was so good with babies—something she hadn't anticipated when she chose him. It had been in the giddy week after V-E Day; all London was celebrating, and Mab had been sorting boxes of naval decrypts at the Admiralty when one of the secretaries came in with her baby on her hip, saying that her mum was sick, asking if she could keep him on shift this once. "Hold him, Mab . . ." And Mab had stretched out her arms in an utter trance. She was still sleepwalking through her days and enduring her nights filled with bad dreams, just as she had been since Coventry. But in the mad furor following Germany's surrender, when all Britain was finally asking the question "What now?," Mab asked it too as she looked at the little boy gurgling in her arms, and the answer came with a desire that bordered on violence: *I want a baby.*

So she had put away her black wool for wine-red silk that swished around her legs like sin incarnate and set out to net a second husband. A very different hunt than her first—as the widowed Mrs. Gray, she already had a bank account and a home; all she needed in a second husband was kindness, a wish for children, and as little resemblance to Francis Gray as possible. Enter Lieutenant Mike Sharpe, six and a half feet of suntanned former RAF pilot who had jostled her in the crush at the Savoy one night and said in an Australian lilt, "Hello, gorgeous."

You'll do, Mab had thought more or less on the spot.

"I want to hang up my wings somewhere foggy and cool, never

go back to ruddy Canberra, and go back to engineering," Mike had said when she asked what he was going to do now that the war was over. That was all the confirmation she needed; Mab fell into bed with him the same night and they were married within a week. The war was over and everyone was falling in love, and Mike had been no exception. He'd been in love, and Mab had been in love with the idea of satin-cheeked babies with those blue, blue eyes.

The eyes now looking back at her from both her children.

"You never talk to me unless it's the weather or the kids or what's for supper," Mike said now. "I never have the faintest goddamned idea what's going on in that head of yours. And if I dare to ask, you either start talking about Eddie and Lucy, or you climb in my lap and screw my brains out—"

"Don't be obscene," she said coldly.

"—to stop me from ever, even by accident, getting to know you better. And it's a pretty good tactic, strategically speaking, but it's wearing a little thin." He paused, visibly holding on to his temper. Mike usually made for a very calm husband, not in an opaque way like Francis, who had been like a well to the center of the earth, but in what Mab had learned was a very Australian way: endlessly laconic, but once that relaxed ease gave way to anger, it came on like a shark moving through deep water. "I know you had a bad war, but you're still frozen there. And I'm bloody tired of sitting back and hoping you'll defrost."

Mab averted her eyes, feeling like a coward. "You don't understand—"

"You never give me the chance to."

Fair, Mab thought. The day she recited her wedding vows for the second time, she had been pierced by a huge irrational terror that if she let this man into herself the way she'd let Francis in, the world would smash her into pieces all over again. It was inviting trouble, opening your heart that way. She couldn't do it. She *refused* to do it. And there wasn't any reason to do it, because as far as Mab could see, most men weren't like Francis; they didn't expect soul-searing intimacy with their wives. They expected to bump along together, a husband in his sphere and a wife in hers, amiable, contented. So she'd locked Francis and the woman she'd been with him away in a vault—and for the most part, she'd assumed everything with Mike was fine.

But recently, these little quarrels had started flaring.

"I'm sorry you find me so disappointing." Her voice was stiff as she heaved the traveling case off the bed. "Considering that I don't nag, I'm not extravagant, I keep a good house, and I gave you two beautiful children—"

"Yes, yes, you're a good wife. You tick it off like you're checking a list. Good meals, tidy house, loving mother, check, check, check—"

"What's wrong with that?" she fired back. She was *proud* of being a good wife, damn it. If you married a good man like Mike, he deserved full value for what he was giving. Mab knew she gave good value. He had no reason to complain, *none*.

"I'd like to know if you love me at all," he said. "Or if you'd have settled for any half-baked bastard who'd give you babies."

Mab's breath left her as if she'd been kicked. He regarded her steadily, not backing down.

"Excuse me," she said finally. "I need to leave."

"Are you coming back?"

"If that's your way of asking if I am having an affair—"

"You're the last woman on earth to have an affair. You'd have to let someone *in,* to do that." He blew out a breath. "Don't leave. Talk to me—this is important, Mab."

No, she wanted to shout, *it's not more important than the job in front of me! I have to visit a lunatic in an insane asylum to verify if there's a traitor loose in the country. A traitor who sold wartime military secrets from a place so secret, I'm not even allowed to* dream *about it. That's what's more important here, darling!*

But there was no version of that she could voice. What a thing it was to have so many secrets inside a marriage. Her husband shared her table and her bed and her body, and he had no idea how many lies Mab had had to tell him over the years.

The children started to fuss, aware of the tension in the room. Mab swooped her son up and squeezed him tight. "Your mum has to go away for a few days, Eddie." She wondered if men felt like this going off to war. *I don't want to leave, but there's a fight to be won, and I have to do it.* She passed Eddie to his father and buried her nose in Lucy's soft dark hair. Little Lucy didn't have curls like her older sister had had, and Mab was glad. This Lucy might have shared the same name in tribute, but she was entirely herself, not a copy or a replacement. "We'll talk when I get back, Mike." Mab stroked Lucy's chubby wrist. "I promise."

"Will we?" Mike followed Mab downstairs, his voice angry but his hands gentle as he walked the twins down the steps, one clinging to each leg. "It's not a hen party you're going to, is it? I know when you're fibbing, Mab."

"You aren't always forthcoming, either." Mab turned the argument round so she wouldn't have to answer it. "You're all stories about working on the airfields now, but I don't think I've heard you say more than two words about your war years."

"I don't particularly like reliving the bit where I got shot down over Kent and invalided out with a bum leg." Mike let the twins' hands go so they could toddle over to their toy box. "Now, your turn."

Mab kissed his cheek instead. He turned his head and caught her mouth on his, pulling her against him. Mab kissed him back with all the anger she had, the heat of him igniting her effortlessly—that part of things had always been easy between them, fire to spare. But there wasn't time, and she pulled away and reapplied her lipstick before the hall mirror. "I'll see you in a few days."

"Where are you going?" His voice was dreadfully quiet as she opened the door. "Why can't you tell me? State secret?"

Yes, thought Mab, slamming the door behind her. *It is.* And she put the whole mess that was her second marriage behind her in the Bentley's rearview mirror, driving to the Grand Hotel to wait for Osla.

"Get in," Mab greeted her old friend unceremoniously, enjoying Osla's astonished expression. "You navigate to the asylum, I'll drive."

CHAPTER 70

"There you are!" Beth sat down at the Go board, summoning a smile. "I've been looking for you. Fancy a game?"

The woman stared at her blankly. She had a bandage about her head; her hair had been shaved from the crown of her skull.

Beth kept the smile pinned in place, laying out the black and white pieces. "You first."

The sharp-eyed woman just sat there, looking at the board as if she'd never seen one before.

It's just drugs, Beth told herself. Every patient was dozy after surgery. Most surgeries here were minor things . . . Beth reached out, touching the woman's hand, then nearly jumped out of her skin as a nurse spoke behind her.

"Visitor for you in the rose garden, Miss Liddell."

Osla? Beth nearly overturned her chair, forgetting about her Go partner for an instant. *Or Mab?* Oh, God, one of them had come at last . . .

But it was a man standing beside the stone bench at the center of the dormant rose garden. A tall man in an expensive overcoat, his back to Beth, smoking a cigarette. The smoke smelled foreign but somehow familiar.

Gitane cigarettes.

Giles Talbot turned, a smile fixed in place, but the smile disappeared as he took in her appearance. He stared at Beth with something more than horror . . . with guilt. Beth stared at him as the matron droned about visitation rules, and connections clicked in her brain like a lobster sliding into place under her pencil.

"It's you," she said when the matron departed. "You." Not Peggy, after all.

He managed a rueful smile. "Hullo, Beth."

She looked at her old friend. His suit was expensive, and his red hair gleamed; he was a long way from the rumpled academic she'd met at Bletchley Park. *Giles.* All this time it had been Giles, not Peggy. Beth could feel fury boiling beneath her skin. If he touched her, his fingers would blacken.

"It's safe to talk." He stubbed out his cigarette, not quite meeting her eyes. "One never trusts visiting rooms; anyone could be listening." There was no one in earshot here; the day was too cold for many inmates to venture outside. "But a garden . . . I think we can talk freely."

"What is there to say?" Beth answered.

"Look, I really am sorry. I never meant to land you in this mess. I just—panicked. Had to get you out of the way before you had a word with Travis about that report."

So he'd been the one to spot it on her desk as she was trying to break the other Rose messages. "I thought it was Peggy," Beth heard herself saying. "She told Mab about the Coventry raid."

"I told *her.* She was annoyed at you already because you bit her head off in ISK. I was going to tip Mab off about Coventry, but I thought it would look better coming from someone else, so I primed Peggy to carp about you instead. Wasn't sure it would work, but she brought it up without any nudging once I steered the conversation round."

"Clever," said Beth. It really was. "Why are you here, Giles? Why now?"

"I never thought things would go on this long. Time to bring an end to this little standoff."

That was ominous, but Beth was filled with too much rage to make room for fear. "I'm limited to family visitors only. Who are you supposed to be, my brother?"

"I got them to bend the rules for an old friend. And that's right, isn't it?" He smiled. "We really are old friends."

"Friends don't lock up their friends in asylums."

"Come now, it's not a bad place. I made sure of that. Top-quality care, gentle handling—"

"Yes, I'm very *gently* bundled into a straitjacket whenever I complain about anything." Beth spat out the words. "You *traitor.*"

He brushed a bit of pollen off his sleeve. "I'm no traitor."

"You broke the Official Secrets Act."

"I am a patriot—"

Beth laughed.

"I am patriotic enough to commit treason in my country's best interests." His voice was low, fierce. "Grow up, Beth. Countries are high, shining ideals, but governments are made of selfish, greedy men. Can you honestly say our fellows at the top always know what they're doing?" The words spilled from him in a torrent. Beth wondered if he was relieved, finally, to have an audience for all these carefully marshaled arguments. "How often did we watch them bungle information we gave them? Misuse it or ignore it or withhold it from allies who were dying for need of it?"

"I don't know." Beth leaned forward, lowering her voice too. "What was *done* with the information was never my business. My job was to decrypt it and pass it on."

"Such a little worker bee. Well, let me tell you that isn't enough for some of us." He bent forward, his nose almost touching hers. An outsider would think they were lovers, Beth thought—a man and woman swaying toward each other among the roses, eyes locked in passionate, unblinking communion. Only that passion was hatred, not love. "Maybe you can close your eyes to where your work goes and let the Official Secrets Act dictate your conscience. I can't. If I see information that should be passed to our allies rather than dying in a Whitehall desk drawer because the cabinet doesn't want to share its toys, I don't make excuses. I act. I knew what the consequences were, I knew what my own people could do to me, and I acted anyway. Because it was the right thing to do, if we were going to defeat Hitler and his rancid ideology."

"It wasn't our job to decide what the right thing was."

"It's every thinking human being's job, especially in war, and don't tell me differently. Letting a wrong happen because the rules forbid you from acting—that was the defense of a good many Germans, after the war. *I was following orders.* But it didn't save them from the noose when the war crimes trials started. I looked at my superiors and I knew they were doing wrong, so I moved against them. I got myself a Moscow contact, and I passed information that saved thousands of Allied lives in the USSR."

"Passed information or sold it?" she asked, mocking.

"They pay me, but I don't ask for it. I'd have done it for nothing."

"So you're still a patriot. Just a richer one." Looking at his fine coat, his air of success. "All from smuggling decrypted messages?"

"And gathering gossip. Women love to talk. Confide in a female and—here's the key—tell her you're in love with someone else. Either she's relieved because she knows you're not about to lay it on, or she takes it as a challenge and starts to flirt. Either way, she starts talking."

Beth shook her head. "I still can't believe no one ever caught you."

"Osla just about did." He sounded unconcerned. "I nipped

into Hut 4 when everyone was out goggling over a visiting admiral, and she nearly caught me copying some files out."

Beth remembered something. "Were you the one who reported her taking files out of Hut 3 later?"

A shrug. "She kept sniffing about, checking things—I didn't want anyone believing her."

"Brave of you," said Beth. "Throwing another friend under the train."

"You know nothing about brave." Giles moved even closer. "You'd never have the courage to do what I did, you prim little rule follower. You couldn't make a choice that bleak and live with the consequences."

"But you're not exactly living with the consequences, are you?" Beth whispered back. "I am. You're walking around free, and I'm locked up for a nervous breakdown I never had. You stole my life, because I found you out." She drew back, looking him right in the eye. "How does your conscience square that?"

He flinched almost invisibly. *There,* Beth thought. *That's the weak spot.* Her old friend really didn't think he'd done wrong in selling intelligence . . . but he *knew* he'd done wrong getting her locked up.

"I didn't mean this to happen—"

"But it did. The road to hell, Giles—what's that paved with again?"

"You're the one responsible." He withdrew, pacing quickly around the stone bench. "You can get out of here whenever you want. Just give me those decrypts."

Beth thought of Dilly's safe, the key she'd been hiding in her shoe for the past three and a half years. Triumph warmed her in a sudden savage glow. Giles had sewn her up so neatly, but he'd missed her bolt to Courns Wood.

"I know you hid them somewhere," he rushed on. "Did you get anything else out of the other messages? Did any of them mention my name?"

Beth didn't answer.

"Never mind. Tell me where they are, and I'll see you out of here."

"What gives you that authority?" she replied. "Why would you have any right to dictate my future?"

"I'm MI-5 now, Beth. Recruited after the war. I'm not the contact on file here at Clockwell, handling your case, but my bosses won't think it odd if I start taking an interest in you, considering we used to be friends. I can volunteer to take your case, put in a report that you've got your mind and your self-control back. You'll be released."

To be free. Fresh air, buttered toast, a bed that smelled of starched linen and not of old piss stains . . . Beth bit the inside of her cheek. It was an illusion and she wasn't going to be tricked by it.

"Do something for me," she heard herself saying. Her hand crept up, fidgeted with the ragged ends of her hair. "Please?"

"Anything." He bent down, took her hands. "I want to help you."

"Every night, tell yourself what you told me. How you're a patriot, not a traitor. How you're the *hero* of this story, not the villain." Beth smiled. "Then remember that you got an innocent woman locked in a madhouse to save your own skin, and ask yourself: how goddamned heroic is *that*?"

He said nothing. His face had gone white.

"By the way," Beth added, "how long have you been selling MI-5 secrets to Moscow? I'm guessing since your first week on the job."

He turned even whiter. Beth sat down on the bench, thinking, *Checkmate.* It had just been a guess.

"I don't know what you're talking about," he said at last.

She smiled contemptuously.

"How—" he began, and stopped.

We won the war and no harm came to BP—even with your meddling, Beth thought. *But who knows what damage you might cause now, interfering in MI-5 business?*

"The Soviets aren't our allies anymore. How do you justify that, Giles? Selling to our *enemy*. Are you calling this patriotism, or is it just cold hard cash now?" Raising her eyebrows. "Or maybe it's self-preservation. You give them what they want or they turn you in? Are you only now realizing the hold they've got on you, as long as they want it?"

"It won't be forever." His face hardened like a stubborn child's. "Just a few bits and pieces, then I'm done."

"Is that what they're telling you? Or what you're telling yourself?"

He seized her hand, a gesture that would have looked friendly to any nurse watching from a distance, but he bent her little finger back almost to the wrist. A spike of pain drove up Beth's arm, and she cried out in surprise.

"I was trying to do this nicely," he whispered. "But if you're going to be stupid, I'm done dancing around. Give me what I want."

"No." Beth tried to yank free.

"Yes. Because if you don't, you'll be a drooling idiot forever. The new head physician has reviewed the case of Alice Liddell, and he has a suggestion to improve your moodiness and your occasional fits of violence. Oh, and your promiscuity—apparently you propositioned an orderly in a closet recently. Can't have promiscuous acts among the patients; it wouldn't be good for the place's reputation." Giles leaned closer. "Do you know what a lobotomy is?"

The pain was still screaming down Beth's arm.

"It's a neurological procedure favored in America. Surgical severance of the connections between the prefrontal cortex and the rest of the brain."

Beth's skin crawled as if a rat had run over her nerves.

"They shave your scalp and drill into your skull, then shove a metal spatula in there and hack until the links are severed." His voice was brutal. "You're awake the whole time. The nurses encourage you to sing songs, recite poetry, answer questions. The procedure is over when you're no longer able to speak."

Horror slithered down her spine. Beth saw herself on an operating table, her head in a vise, singing *When Cunningham won at Matapan by the grace of God and Beth.* Struggling to find the next line. Falling silent—

Like her Go partner.

"After the operation, you'll be in a state they call *surgically induced childhood.*" His words rolled over Beth in waves. "Sounds spiffing, doesn't it? Didn't we all adore being children? But it might not be much fun the second time around, once you get past toilet training. Ideally you'll remain in an infantile state, and they'll guide you into a more docile, accepting personality. Results vary, of course. You might end up a vegetable pissing her sheets for the next fifty years."

Beth managed to wrench away. Her whole arm was numb; she stood clutching it and trembling.

"You're telling yourself I'm lying. I'm not." He looked down at her, biting his lip as though he were the one in pain. "Dr. Seton is very enthusiastic about the procedure. He's already begun lobotomizing some of his other patients; perhaps you've noticed. He really shouldn't have told me you were on the list, considering

I'm not the MI-5 contact on record in your case, but I can be very persuasive."

Beth collapsed back onto the bench, breath coming in gasps. Holes drilled in her skull. Toilet training. She could imagine herself sitting on this bench, smiling vacantly, remembering something about keys and roses, but having no idea what it all meant. Sitting on this bench for the next fifty years.

You're lying, she thought. But she no longer believed it.

"MI-5 won't contest your doctor's recommendation, Beth." Giles dropped onto the bench beside her. "Maybe you'll end up fine, a little fuzzy around the edges. But maybe you'll be a shell with a head full of mashed turnip." His voice rose. "So give me what I want, or you'll find yourself strapped to a table as they go at your skull with a drill."

Beth screamed. She clapped both hands over her mouth in time to contain it, but it went on and on inside her head. Her head, her brain. She was nothing without her mind. She'd survived here for more than three years because of her *mind.*

"I didn't suggest this, I'll have you know. I didn't even know the procedure existed. But I'll let it happen." He leaned closer. "You want to know why I'm finally here talking to you? Because I'm tired of worrying if you've figured out it was me. I'm on my way up, I'll have a family soon, and I'm done worrying if you might be a threat to all that. So tell me what I want to know. Either you walk out of this place with no proof against me, or you stay here forever unable to *remember* what proof you had. Either way, I'm free."

He stood. "Think about it. Because I hate the thought of anyone cutting into that admirable brain of yours, but my God, I'm tired of living on the edge."

He waited.

Beth flung herself on him. She couldn't stop, couldn't think, couldn't reason, just flew at Giles and tried to tear him to pieces. She would have clawed his eyes out of his sockets, but he threw her away like a rag doll before the orderlies could even descend.

"Your surgery is scheduled for the afternoon after the royal wedding." He stepped back, straightening his tie. "I'll ring here that morning. Tell the doctors you wish to see me—I'll speak to the MI-5 chap handling your file, get the surgery stopped, and volunteer to take your case. Say nothing, and the surgery goes forward." Pause. "I like you, Beth. I always have. So don't make me do this."

CHAPTER 71

Since when can you drive?" Osla asked Mab as they motored out of York.

"My husband taught me." Mab took a sharp bend with confident speed. "He's Australian; grew up eight hundred miles from anything important and four hundred miles from anything at all, so he learned to drive in the cradle."

Osla slanted a glance at her. "What did you tell him about this day trip?"

"Visit to an old friend. The best lies have the most truth."

"*That's* certainly true."

They exchanged guarded glances as the Bentley halted at a four-way stop. *Maybe we can get through this day without flashing any more claws,* Osla thought.

"You didn't used to wear trousers," Mab said with a glance at Osla's sleek red slacks. "They made you look squat. This prolonged rationing is such a blessing for some people . . ."

"You're not in *Casablanca,*" Osla shot back, "so stop wearing your hat over one eye like a third-rate Ingrid Bergman."

Mab glared. As they climbed up into the high moors, Osla outlined the route to Clockwell. "About a two-hour drive."

"And when we get there?" Mab steered the Bentley round a bend. "How are we getting in?"

Osla outlined her plan. "The matron on telephone duty shouldn't have told me so much, but I detoured her onto a nice long gossip about the royal wedding, and there's really nothing most women won't tell you right now in exchange for royal wedding gossip. I let it slip that the bridal bouquet would be myrtle and lilies, and I tell you, that woman was *mine*."

"Is the bridal bouquet going to be myrtle and lilies?"

"How the blithering hell should I know? I made it up. As for getting admitted to visiting hours without identification—" Osla ticked through the last details. "If they double down on us, we start up the waterworks. We're *so distressed* to be coming here, doctor, please, we've come *all this way*." Osla dabbed an imaginary handkerchief. "It's amazing what men, even doctors, will do to get weeping women off their hands."

"You can cry on command?"

"Of course. Frightfully useful."

A pall fell over the car, maybe just a cloud sliding across the sun. "What do you think will happen?" Osla heard herself ask.

Mab stared straight ahead. "We'll realize Beth's mad as a hatter and be off the hook."

"That's what you *hope* will happen. Rather beastly of you, too," Osla couldn't help adding.

"I'm a beastly person, Os. That's been made abundantly clear lately. By you, by my—" She stopped, jaw set.

"In some ways, I'm glad you're beastly." Osla curled her feet beneath her. "If Beth's not mad and not lying, we're going to have to put things right. I'd much rather have a cast-iron bitch on my side for that fight than a fainting ninny."

"Get your shoes off the seat!"

Osla ignored her. "Who do you think the traitor is?"

"Maybe it's you," Mab suggested.

"Do shut up. The traitor—"

"Look here, do we have to go on saying *the traitor*? I feel like I'm in an Agatha Christie novel, and not in a good way."

"I'm floored at all points here trying to imagine a *good* way to be in an Agatha Christie novel."

"You're the corpse in chapter one," Mab suggested, smirking.

The car was winding further into the fells. "You're very nearly enjoying this," Osla observed. "That must have been quite the up-and-downer with your husband, if you're on the verge of enjoying a drive to a lunatic asylum with *me,* darling."

That got her a withering look.

"Just the glare, no quip? You're losing your touch, Queen Mab." Maybe Osla could enjoy this moment too, just a bit. "If I call the traitor the *informer* instead, will you keep glaring?"

"I will allow *informer*."

"Topping of you. What if the informer is . . . someone we know?"

"If Beth knew them," Mab replied grimly, "we probably do, too. Odds are it's a woman."

"How do you figure that?"

"There were more of us at BP. And people don't suspect women."

"Don't talk slush!" Osla snorted. "We can't walk off alone with a man without being called fast, we can't check into a hotel without suspicion we're there for hanky-panky—"

"People suspect women of hanky-panky," Mab corrected. "But they never suspect women of espionage. No one thinks women can keep secrets."

"What are the three fastest means of communication?" Osla quoted the old joke, then she and Mab chanted the answer together: "*Telegraph, telephone, tell a woman!*"

"You have no idea how I hate that joke," Mab said.

"Darling, I have a *very* good idea."

They fell silent. The car scraped past an elderly farm truck trundling along an exposed spine of country road, mud splatting across the windscreen. “Why did you settle in Yorkshire of all places?” Osla asked.

“Because my husband got a job here, and because it was far away from London and Bletchley,” Mab said shortly. “Because it had no memories at all.”

Osla twisted the big emerald around her finger. “You said you had a family now . . .” Oh, blast, she couldn’t ask if Mab had children, given the phantom that was little Lucy, hovering between them—it would drive the knife in to the hilt.

“I have twins,” Mab said unexpectedly. “Eighteen months old.” The flash of love through her face was the first softening Osla had seen since clapping eyes on her yesterday.

“I’m happy for you,” Osla said honestly. “What are their names?”

“Edward—Eddie—and Lucy.”

Osla felt the phantom glide of a little girl’s wrist wrenching out of her grip. “Mab . . .”

“Don’t.”

Osla looked straight ahead to the road twisting down the slope. “Go on hating me,” she said. “I hope it helps.”

“I don’t hate you, Os.” Mab’s eyes were invisible behind her huge sunglasses. “I try not to feel much of anything these days—love *or* hate. I love Eddie and Lucy, because you can’t help loving your children, and that’s how it should be. But it’s easier if I don’t feel much of anything for anyone else.”

“Easier to do what?”

“Endure.”

They motored on in silence.

CHAPTER 72

Twelfth November. Nine days before Beth's surgery, for which she'd been receiving increasing examinations; eight days before the royal wedding, which the nurses blathered about endlessly. "They say the bridesmaids are wearing white, but with the princess wearing white . . ." Chattering and chattering as Beth sat with her Go partner, desperately trying to engage the woman.

"Just one move. The black stone." Nothing. "Would you rather try chess?" Beth laid out the chessboard. "Remember when you first taught me how to turn a pawn into a queen?"

Nothing. The woman who had played chess like a grand master now sat utterly still, utterly vacant, occasionally shitting herself. Her eyes were blank as shaded windows. *It can't end this way,* Beth screamed inside. *Not for you, and not for me either. It can't!*

But then it came:

"Special treat for you, Miss Liddell," the matron cooed.

A vise for my head. Then the whine of a drill, the wet shoving sound of a surgical tool cutting through her brain . . .

Had they moved the procedure up?

Panic hit Beth in a wave, and the chessboard upended in a scatter of black and white pieces as she tried to run.

CHAPTER 73

Only a two-hour drive to the asylum, but everything had gone wrong. A road was washed out and they had to detour for hours; a tire blew, then a torrential downpour of rain hit. "That snaffles it," Osla had seethed. "Visiting hours will be done by the time we arrive." She and Mab had ended up spending a resentful night at a drab hotel two miles from Clockwell and making their way through the asylum gates the following morning.

Mab steered the Bentley through the grounds and parked in the indicated lot. There was no trouble about their names or any request for identification when Mab and Osla strode in with their most confident swing of hips and handbags. "Here to see our sister Alice Liddell—Mrs. Riley and Mrs. Chadwick." Giving the names of Beth's married sisters.

The matron at the front desk rose. "I'll show you to her. We do ask, of course, that you not mention your sister's upcoming surgery during the visit."

Osla's heart began to thud. "What surgery?" This place had looked so friendly when they rolled up: a mellow stone country house with two extended wings, surrounded by rambling gardens. Now the bright winter light streaming through the windows looked glaring, a spotlight to cut down anyone who passed through it.

"The surgery was discussed with her parents, as her next of kin. It's a procedure that has had tremendous success improving the temperament of moody or emotionally distressed patients. Simple surgical severance of the connections between the—"

"In English, please," Mab said. Osla gripped the edge of the desk, pulse beating ominously.

"It's a new wave in advanced treatment of the mentally impaired. Much more common in America, but our new chief physician is versed in the latest techniques." The matron smiled. "It's called a lobotomy."

"What's a lobotomy?" The word gave Osla the shivers.

"A harmless procedure, I assure you. Your sister will be much the better for it." Twinkle. "Now, come with me."

THE GARDEN WAS dry and dead, but white-smocked, empty-eyed women still wandered through it. "Patients have the grounds in the afternoon for exercise . . ." Osla ignored the matron. They'd been brought to wait beside the stone benches in the center of the rosebushes, and she was about to see Beth, on whom she hadn't laid eyes in three and a half years. At her side, she could see Mab blinking too rapidly for calm, though she was the picture of elegance with her smartly slanted hat.

"No—" A raspy voice startled Osla, the edge of desperation so sharp it raised her hackles. "I don't want a *treat,* I know where you're taking me—"

"You silly girl, your sisters are here." A nurse's exasperated voice approached through the roses. "Don't you want to see them?"

Beth stumbled into the center of the rose garden and stopped dead.

Osla and Mab froze, too. This was *Beth*? Their old billet-mate who had transformed herself from a beaten-down spinster in a moth-colored jumper to a star codebreaker with a Veronica

Lake wave? This woman looked like a haunted-house apparition, stripped down to bones and tendons and raw, raging will. Beth's nails were bitten bloody, her blond hair chopped at her shoulders, where she fidgeted constantly with its ragged ends. She started violently at every sound, yet Osla didn't think she looked afraid. She looked too maddened to know what fear was: a writhing mess held barely upright by fury.

"She had a bout of pneumonia this spring," the matron said a touch defensively, seeing their horror. "That's why she's so thin . . . I'll leave you, shall I? Visits last one hour."

She bustled off. Beth stood staring at the pair of them, and Osla's nose prickled at the smell of sweat, fear, infrequent washing. "I—" Beth began, her voice raspier than it had once been, and stopped. "Don't look at me, I'm not used to being looked at, well, doctors look, they look all the time, and the inmates are always watching but the doctors and inmates don't expect you to behave logically. You need me to be logical, or else you're going to walk out thinking I belong here, and I don't—" She ran out of breath, speaking in a monotone almost too fast to follow.

"Beth." Somehow, Osla found herself sitting on the bench, crossing her ankles and indicating the seat opposite for Beth as if they were sitting down to tea. *Back straight, girls!* she could hear her old finishing-school teachers cry. *There's no social disaster that can't be remedied with good manners!* "We're here, and we're listening." Osla kept her voice as calm as possible.

Beth gulped again. Mab took the seat beside Osla, and Osla could read the flicker of her eyes like newsprint. *Insane?* Mab was wondering. *Or terrified?*

Osla leaned forward. There was no one close enough to eavesdrop; she could finally ask. "Who is the traitor?" And the word didn't sound this time like something from a melodrama. It sounded like truth.

"Giles Talbot," Beth said, and horror drenched Osla in an icy flood. *No,* she thought, *it can't be Giles, it* can't—but the words were spilling from Beth in a torrent.

She looked mostly at the roses as she spoke, and her recitation had a clipped haste, as though she'd imagined this moment too long not to rush delivering it. At last she fell silent. Osla looked at Mab and knew they were both picturing irrepressible redheaded Giles with a ludicrously decked-out top hat and a plate of bread and marg. Giles, who had apparently been *here* just yesterday, threatening Beth.

Osla looked down at her clenched hands. Whatever she'd been expecting Beth to say, it wasn't this.

"He was always angling for gossip." Mab disordered the carefully set waves of her hair with a rake of one hand. "Not trying to charm it out of you, just being . . . cozy."

"He liked to tell a woman he was in love with someone else," Beth said. "It made them feel safe or it made them feel competitive, but either way they'd talk."

"He once told me he was head over heels for you." Mab looked at Beth, startled.

"He once told me he was head over heels for you," Osla managed to say, looking at Mab.

"We all trusted him," said Beth.

"He's the goods, all right." Osla heard her voice come out very small as she looked down at the emerald on her finger. "He's also my fiancé."

MIDWAY THROUGH '44, going with Giles to see the Glenn Miller band near Bletchley Park. Jitterbugging to "Chattanooga Choo-Choo," taking nips from Giles's flask, trying to banish the memory of dancing with Philip, trying to banish the bloody *heartbreak.* Letting Giles kiss her when the music swung into "In the Mood."

"I know what I'm in the mood for," Giles had murmured in her ear—he'd been chaffing her, trying to get a hint what she'd been translating in Hut 4, but she hadn't given him a word, and when marvelous, unbeatable Glenn Miller changed the tune, so did Giles. "Come on, Os. You've got someone you'd like to forget. Why not give it a try with me?" And Osla, a little sauced and wholly heartsick, had thought, *Why the hell not?* Because what had being good ever got her, except here, heartbroken and wretched?

So they nipped off to Giles's car and climbed in the backseat and it was all finished four minutes later, and Osla felt no different except to think all the fuss about It had clearly been a lot of sound and fury, signifying nothing—like the whole idea of romance to begin with. *This is all you get,* she thought. *This is all there is.*

Giles hadn't seemed to expect much, just gave her a comradely smack on the flank and then drove her home. He'd gone on being exactly the same: a good friend, an occasional date, even a roll in the hay now and then after the war. Funny, exasperating Giles, who had slouched toward her at exactly the right moment earlier this year—the moment she was on her beam ends, thinking she might as well marry just to get on with life—and said, "Let's give it a go, Os. Romance is for bad novels, but marriage is for pals—pals like us. What do you say?"

Once again, she'd thought, *Why the hell not?* and let him park an emerald on her finger.

And here she was, listening to an old enemy tell her that her future husband was a traitor to the crown.

"Your *fiancé*?" Beth had gone so white she looked ready to faint. "He told me just yesterday that he'd have a family soon. He didn't say—" She broke off, ripping at her nails. "Did you tell him I'd sent you a message? Did you tell him you were coming *here*?"

"No." And why hadn't she? Osla couldn't help wondering in the midst of her shock. Giles knew about Beth and Bletchley Park; it was one of the appeals of marrying him—that she wouldn't have to tell whoppers about her war years. Osla could have asked his advice when she deciphered Beth's Vigenère square. Why hadn't she?

Something instinctive had sealed her mouth like a lock.

"You don't believe me." Beth's voice was bleak as she looked at Osla. "You believe him."

Osla opened her mouth, not even knowing what she was going to say, but memories were slotting themselves into place with the sudden click of keys turning in locks. "June 'Forty-Two, when I was hauled into Commander Travis's office about those missing files," she said slowly. "Travis said someone reported me—"

"Giles," said Beth. "He told me. He said you nearly caught him, more than once—something about the Hut 4 box files."

Osla thought of that whisk of coat disappearing just out of sight. *I knew it was something fishy* . . . But the realization brought no pleasure.

Mab took up the thread. "There was a night, after I was transferred to the mansion, when Giles kept pouring drinks into me at the Recreation Hut. I was a bloody mess . . . I had a set of keys that locked up the file cabinets. He said I'd turned them in to the watchman after leaving the Recreation Hut, but I didn't remember . . ."

"He had himself a rummage through the mansion's files when you were drunk." Beth's voice was hard. "He turned the keys in, but not before having a good poke-around."

Mab went white too, and Osla could tell she was parsing what kinds of reports would have been accessible with those keys. Her chin lifted, and Osla saw her paleness was fury. "He used me," she clipped. "He used me, he stole from me, then he *comforted* me."

And he turned us against Beth, Osla thought. Something stabbed her stomach again—this time it was shame.

She looked at Beth: twitchy, wary, desperate, raw. Had she stayed entirely sane, after more than three years in a place like this?

Even if she was not entirely *sane,* she was still not *wrong.*

"I believe you," Osla said.

"You—" Beth's raspy new voice was barely a whisper. "You do?"

Mab nodded, too.

"We'll get you out." Osla checked for listeners. Their allotted hour was slipping away. "I'm going straight to London to report this. Once the wheels start to turn—"

"Too long. They're operating on me the day after the royal wedding. They will cut into my *brain*—" Beth shivered violently. "Please—you can't let them do that to me. Get me out now."

She managed to hold her gaze steady this time, not sliding sideways. Osla and Mab exchanged glances.

"I have a plan," Beth whispered. "I spent three and a half years watching the routines here. Tell me, did you get here by car or train . . ."

And their heads came together, among the dying roses.

CHAPTER 74

Osla was being charming and Mab was being terrifying, and between the two of them, Beth dared to hope she might get out.

Mab had collared two orderlies, the head matron, and a doctor doing his rounds. "I have serious concerns about my sister's health." Arms folded, scarlet fingernails drumming. "If we can discuss your therapies . . ."

Osla had gathered every nurse in sight and most of the inmates, and was chattering like a breathless Mayfair magpie. ". . . two hundred pounds of rose petals in the abbey alone. She'll be wearing an absolutely topping tiara of the queen's for her 'something borrowed.'" Leaning forward confidentially, making the women lean in. "You mustn't tell anyone, because Mr. Hartnell swore me to secrecy at my dress fitting, but the queen will be wearing lilac silk, a real fizzer—"

"How did you get invitations to the royal wedding?" one of the matrons breathed.

"My husband rubs shoulders with some useful London people. We saw Prince Philip once. An absolute *dream* . . ."

No one was paying attention to Beth, lingering close but not too close to the locked gardening shed.

"Perhaps increased outdoor activity?" Mab was suggesting to the doctor. He was visibly writhing to please her. "My sister always loved working in the garden. If that would help with these mood swings you describe . . ."

"Gauloises, anyone?" Osla passed her cigarette case around, throwing smiles like diamond chips. "There's simply nothing like French cigarettes, French knickers, or French *men*! Now, the princess's bridesmaids . . ."

"What kind of gardening tools do you have for the patients?" Mab steered her entourage around to the shed. "I'm sure my sister would improve if she could get her hands in the ground. Let me see what you have . . ."

The head matron unlocked the shed. Hanging inside was that set of keys that opened the small access doors where the gardeners trundled wheelbarrows of dead leaves off-grounds. The shed that had never once in the three and a half years Beth had been watching it been left unattended, not for so much as a cigarette break.

"They say Princess Margaret will be in white organza, but I think she'll switch at the last minute to make a splash—" Osla broke off, patting her forehead. "Goodness, is anyone else warm?"

Glances at the cloudy sky. "It's November, ma'am . . ."

The shed was open; Mab stepped inside to frown at the tools. "You could use more spades and trowels. I'll speak to my husband about a donation. Tell me, what other supplies could the institution use . . ."

"Really, it seems quite warm . . . ?" Osla's voice trailed upward uncertainly. She rose, frowning—and toppled over in a heap on the grass.

"*DOCTOR!*" Beth screamed.

("Scream *loud,* Beth—we need every single head spinning in that moment to look at Osla.")

The doctor jerked away from Mab and came at a trot. The nurses and even the inmates clustered around Osla, who lay on the ground with her limbs twitching, head rolled back.

("The doctors here have seen epileptic fits. Can't you just pretend you saw a spider?")

("It will work, Beth.")

"Nurse, it's some kind of seizure. Hold her head—"

Osla twitched gently, not overdoing it. *You're good,* Beth thought, hope beginning to hammer at her ribs.

("As soon as the distraction's under way, Mab moves.")

With every eye on Osla, Beth watched Mab's hand move to the key hook inside the shed.

("The keys aren't labeled, but it will be one of the smaller ones. I don't know which; grab them all. Are you sure you can get them off the ring without being seen?")

("It may have been a long time since I was pocketing lipsticks from Selfridges, but I've still got a fast swipe.")

Beth saw her arm move in a quick yank, and then Mab was shutting the shed doors and pushing into the crowd around Osla. "My sister has always been prone to these little spells. Give her some air . . ."

Osla's eyelids fluttered. Mab helped her sit up; there were blushes, apologies. *Oh, how too too embarrassing, doctor . . .* One of the nurses, Beth saw from the corner of her eye, was hastily locking up the shed, not bothering to look inside.

Doctors and orderlies fought to help Osla up, and she drooped gracefully against all the solicitous male arms. "Time to get my sister home," Mab announced, and brushed through the crowd toward the house, a stream of nurses and patients moving with her. She and Beth managed to reach the door at the same time, jostling each other. Beth felt the three small keys press into her palm.

("After that, Beth, it's up to you.")

DON'T RUSH IT, Beth thought.

Wait for Mab and Osla to be escorted out. Wait for the commotion from Osla's fit to die down, for the common room to settle. Wait for the nurses to fall back into their usual rounds. Wait.

But what if the grounds crew goes back into the shed, and they see—

Beth squashed the panic. She'd waited for three and a half years; she wasn't going to ruin everything now out of haste.

Drifting slowly out of the common room, as if returning to her cell. Drifting down the passage instead, whisking behind a curtain. The matrons at the front desk weren't supposed to leave the entrance unattended, but they did, all the time. The patients were so quiet; there wasn't any real risk—and besides, there were the walls outside to contain them if they wandered into the grounds. Matron Rowe, on the desk today, couldn't go forty minutes without a cigarette . . . sure enough, she whisked round the corner after fifteen patient minutes of waiting. Beth slipped outside, barely breathing.

Down the stone steps. Beth remembered mounting those steps the day she came here, feeling like Alice fallen down the rabbit hole. *I am not Alice any longer,* thought the former Miss Liddell. *I am no longer trapped inside the clock.*

Drifting, not running, around the women's wing toward the back of the house, crouching under the windows. The access door came into sight, and Beth checked the clock tower. Ten thirty—the orderlies made rounds of the wall on the hour.

She flung herself at the gate, fumbling the trio of keys out of her sleeve. First key didn't fit. She yanked it out, panting, fumbled with the second key, dropped it—

"What are you doing here?"

An orderly stood staring at her, stopped buttoning his coat over his uniform. Ginger-haired, scrawny, clearly off duty and headed out. He was the one Beth had serviced in a linen closet, trying to learn what a lobotomy was. The one who had ruffled her hair afterward.

"You shouldn't be out," he began, coming toward her, and Beth didn't hesitate. She threw the useless key at his head, and as he flinched, she flung herself on him. He yelled in surprise, trying to fend her off, but she darted her head forward like a viper and sank her teeth into his cheek. The man yelped like he'd been scalded, and Beth forced her hand over his mouth, trying to contain the shout. He fell heavily, and Beth felt the impact along her entire left side as she fell with him, but her teeth only sank deeper. She heard herself making a mad keening noise. All the helpless rage of the last three and a half years boiled up her throat and roared when it met the coppery tang of the man's blood in her mouth. She tasted more than blood; she tasted the chalky flavor of sedative tablets and the antiseptic tang of nurses' fingers thrusting into her mouth to force her jaws apart. She tasted shame and despair and the urge to wind a bedsheet round her throat and hang herself. She tasted bleak stony hatred for Giles and a blunter, smaller venom for the nurses and orderlies who bullied the inmates; she tasted the metal of the drill that would have cut her skull open and the tensile snapping of her brain's strands as her codebreaking mind was mutilated. "Let go," the orderly squealed into her ear, faces locked together as if they were dancing cheek to cheek. "Let go, you mad bitch—"

"*No,*" Beth snarled through her teeth clamped into his face, and managed to get her fingers into his hair to yank his head against the ground. She banged his head once, twice, and he went slack. She banged one more time to be sure.

Beth's ears buzzed. Her jaws ached as she released her teeth, and she wiped an unsteady hand across her mouth, feeling blood smear. She looked at the unconscious man below her, his cheek torn open. She didn't know if it had been his head hitting the ground or if he had fainted, but he was out cold. She checked his pulse. Strong.

He was too heavy to move, and she had no way to hide him. She'd have to take her chances it would be a while before he was found.

She got to her feet, shaking, and staggered back to the access door. Her hands trembled too much at first to fit the second key to the lock. Her mouth was still coppery with blood. The second key didn't fit. *Please,* Beth prayed, fitting the third.

It turned.

She was through the door in a flash, wedging it shut and locking it from the outside: outside the walls, for the first time in three and a half years. The path led down a grassy slope, toward a road she'd never seen. Beth flew down it, legs pumping. She'd told them where to wait; if they weren't there . . .

Please, she prayed again.

There was Osla, perched on the long hood of a forest-green Bentley, hair ruffling in the cold breeze. Mab slouched behind the wheel, lighting a cigarette, saying, ". . . been trying to stop, but the week you stage an asylum breakout is *not* the week to quit smoking." They looked up, hearing her footsteps, and Beth saw them both flinch at the blood on her mouth. They tried to hide it, but she saw. For an instant her step faltered.

Osla slid off the hood and threw open the door. "Coming?"

Beth crawled into the backseat, lying flat. She was suddenly dizzy, inhaling scents she hadn't smelled in years: leather upholstery, Osla's Soir de Paris, Mab's Chanel No. 5 . . . and her own smell, fear and ammonia and sweat. *I want a bath.* Mab started the car up, and they were swinging round. "Don't speed," Beth said. "We don't want to attract attention."

"Hide under this," Osla ordered, shoving a car rug over the partition.

Beth squirmed under it, but she couldn't resist a peek through the rear window as they turned off the asylum road. Just a big gray stone house behind a tangle of dead roses and high walls, receding into the distance. Sleeping Beauty's crumbling castle. The air coming through the open window was freezing cold, fragrant with bracken. Free air . . .

"Lie down," Mab hissed, mashing the pedal.

Beth lay down, head spinning. Mab and Osla were arguing, low voiced.

"—once they realize we aren't Beth's sisters—"

"—they have no blinking idea what our real names even *are*—"

The question burst out of Beth from under the blanket. "Can you tell me what happened to Boots?"

A startled pause. Beth shrank, dreading the answer. "He was returned to Aspley Guise after you were taken away," Osla said. "Our landlady kept him. She mentioned him in her last Christmas card."

Beth squeezed her eyes shut. Her dog was alive, safe. That seemed like the best omen in the world.

Mab spoke up then. "Where are we *going,* Beth?"

Beth opened her mouth and closed it again. The first real decision she had been offered in three and a half years. The Bentley rocketed over the moor as Beth Finch shut her tear-filled eyes with a sob of joy.

Alice escaped the looking glass, Giles. And now she's coming for you.

CHAPTER 75

"Why did Giles get mixed up with Soviets?" Mab wondered, changing gears. The Bentley was speeding past Blackpool now, well south of York, even further from Clockwell. "We had more than a few at BP who flirted pink on the political side, but Giles didn't seem to have an ideological bone in his body."

"He thought BP wasn't doing enough to help our allies." Beth was sitting up in the backseat now, wearing a print dress from Mab's traveling case; it sagged off her gaunt frame. Osla had pressed a comb on her too, and some scent: *Not to put too fine of a point on it, darling, but you look like a dog's dinner.* "He saw an opportunity to help the Soviets win their war, so he did. In his eyes"—she spat the words—"he was a *patriot*."

"The PM *was* stingy about sharing our findings with the Soviets," Osla pointed out. "I used to get in a wax about that, too."

"Yes, but you didn't betray your country," Beth said.

Would I feel quite so defensive of my country if it had locked me *up in a madhouse?* Mab wondered. Because Giles might have planted the seeds, but it was BP's obsession with secrecy that made Beth's imprisonment possible . . . then again, Beth had always had that peculiar rigid streak. It didn't matter that her country had betrayed her; she'd taken an oath to it, and she would uphold that oath until she died. Maybe that streak of unbending iron in her soul was what had kept her from crumbling, surrounded by lunatics.

"We could contact Commander Travis first," Osla began. "He's living in Surrey now. He knows us, and with his connections, contact with MI-5 would—"

"No." Beth cut her off. "No Travis, no MI-5. Not yet."

Mab took her eyes off the road long enough to stare. "We need to regularize your position as soon as possible. We've already risked charges, breaking you out—"

"You put me there to begin with," Beth flared.

The undercurrent that had been running through the Bentley snapped taut.

"Beth." Osla reached to touch Beth's hand where it rested on the backseat partition, then apparently thought better of it. "We didn't know they were thinking of sending you to a sanitarium. If we'd known that when we were questioned—"

"I lost three and a half years of my life because you two were angry at me." Beth's fingers flexed and opened, flexed and opened. "Have I been punished enough to suit you? Do you have any *idea* what it was like in Clockwell?"

"Of course I don't." Mab stamped on the brakes as they came to a four-way stop, harder than necessary so they all jolted in their seats. "And I'd never have wished it on you in a thousand years, no matter how much bad blood we had between us. All I'm saying is that if you want to sling blame, that goes both ways—so I suggest we don't, because it *doesn't matter*. The person guilty of a crime here, a real crime, is Giles Talbot, and Osla and I are here to help you deal with him. So why can't we go to the authorities immediately?"

Beth drew something from her pocket and swung it between two fingers: a small brass key. "Because I still need to break the Rose Code."

CHAPTER 76

It was past ten by the time they motored through Buckinghamshire, the Bentley creeping along pitch-black country roads. They had all fallen silent some thirty miles back—at about the time, Beth knew, when they drew closest to Bletchley Park.

"I haven't seen it since I left for the Admiralty in autumn of 'Forty-Four," Mab said abruptly. "It was still buzzing along like clockwork . . . we had *thousands* of workers by that point. Remember the early days, when everything felt so ramshackle and you knew every face at shift change?"

"I was let go September 'Forty-Five," Osla said. "That cool little form: '*Owing to the cessation of hostilities, etc. etc., please bugger off and never talk about what you did here or you'll be hanged, drawn, and quartered.*'" A sigh. "The clear-out was starting even before I left. They sent a party of us back to the old Hut 4, made us crawl over every board. People used to jam bits of decrypts into the cracks in the walls when drafts were blowing; we had to find every scrap and burn them."

Part of Beth yearned to stop by Bletchley Park's gates, and part of her was glad it was too dangerous to risk being seen so near her hometown. She didn't know if she could bear to see BP empty and abandoned. *We did such things there, and no one will ever know.*

They made the turnoff in silence and parked, unfolding stiffly from the car. Beth didn't know when she had ever been so tired: this morning she'd wakened in her cell; by noon she was out; they had driven all afternoon and through the evening across most of England. Had all of that really happened in one day?

Mab rang at the door of the darkened house for a long time; at last there was the creak of hinges. "What's this about?" came the alarmed voice of Dilly Knox's widow. "Has there been an accident?"

"No accident." Beth came forward, seeing the older woman's eyes widen. "I'm very sorry to disturb you, Mrs. Knox, but it's an emergency. Three and a half years ago, I locked something in your husband's safe. I've come to retrieve it."

BETH COULD FEEL Dilly so strongly as she came into the library, she nearly broke down in tears. *I didn't fail you,* she thought, moving past his battered wing chair. *I didn't give in.* Osla and Mab stood back, watching as Beth went to the wall and opened the panel.

A deep breath, looking at the safe door and inserting the key. Beth felt the quiet *click* at the base of her heart as well as in her ears. She heard the intake of breath from the others as she reached inside and took out the Rose file.

"That's it?" Osla whispered.

Beth took the file to Dilly's big oak desk and spread out the pages. The sight of the familiar five-letter blocks of Enigma brought a wave of memory that nearly knocked her off her feet. It made some feline, sleeping part of her brain uncoil, stretching and hungry. She laid out the pages, starting with the single message she'd broken and run through the Typex on her very last day at the Park, and realized her hands weren't fumbling anymore but moving with swift precision. "Come look," she ordered, and the others obeyed, reading over her shoulder the words she'd had memorized for years.

Osla was the first to see the problem. "We," she said succinctly, "are utterly graveled."

"It doesn't name him." Mab looked ready to spit nails. "Did *he* realize that?"

"He didn't know what I had." Beth tapped the words: *your source inside ISK.* "Without a name, it's not proof enough to take him down."

"But he moved against you as soon as you found this out. He got you locked up so you couldn't bring this to Travis." Mab picked up the decrypt. "That proves it's him."

"He can say the source inside ISK was *me.* That I was the one about to move against *him.* If he flips it round, it doesn't sound any less plausible than our version. And he's the one with a respected career, not a twitching woman escaped from a madhouse."

"But the accusation would taint him." Osla nibbled a varnished fingernail. "That's the kind of thing that destroys careers. Especially after I cram his emerald down his throat and start ballyhooing his guilt to every influential connection I've got, and I have got *heaps.*"

"He might lose his post. He might live under a cloud. But I'd still go back to Clockwell and face having my brain scrambled." Beth looked up, certainty hardening. "We need more before we go to MI-5—*I* need more. I want something with his name on it, something he can't lie his way out of. One of these"—she fanned the undecrypted messages out on the desk—"might have that." *I hope.* "I need to crack them, and I need to do it now."

Mab's fingers drummed. "How long before he realizes you've escaped?"

"The asylum will notify MI-5 that I'm gone. But Giles wasn't their contact on file; someone else is handling my case. So even though MI-5 will be casting their nets for me, Giles won't be told I—"

"He'll find out," Mab stated. "You know he'll have your name flagged—any changes, any unexpected developments. Your handler will tell him you're gone, and then what? He sits around waiting, gives you all the time you need to break this cipher?"

"Maybe he *won't* find out." Osla looked thoughtful. "Just after Giles and I became engaged, I asked him if he could make inquiries at work, find out what had become of Beth—"

"You did?" Beth asked, surprised.

"You think I've gone three and a half years without once thinking of you? Of course I wanted to know. Giles did some digging, but they wouldn't tell him anything. Something about 'conflicting interests,' given that he'd been your friend," Osla quoted. "So, if he told you he could get reassigned to your case anytime he wanted, I think he was talking slush. He might have charmed the Clockwell doctors into giving him information about you, but it didn't work on his superiors at MI-5. They didn't tell him anything then, and I don't think they'll tell him you've escaped now—no matter what alerts he's tried to put in place."

"Giles was lying to one of us." Beth gnawed her lip. "What if it was you?"

"I don't think so. When he lies, it's to make himself look better—and he didn't like telling me he'd been dismissed like a schoolboy. He wants everyone to see him as a man who can pull strings, get anything."

"It's still a risk," Mab said. "Taking time to crack the rest of these messages—"

"We have no choice. If we go to MI-5 now, without better evidence, he *will* squirm out of it." Beth took a deep breath. "My surgery is scheduled for the day after the royal wedding. Giles said he'd telephone Clockwell that morning. If we count on MI-5 keeping him out of the loop until then—"

"One week." Osla looked at the other two. "The morning after the wedding, we go to MI-5 with whatever we've got."

Seven days to crack Rose and pin Giles Talbot to the wall. Beth had only broken the one message, and that had taken her months. The sheer cliff of the task loomed in front of her.

They all jumped at the knock on the library door. Mrs. Knox came in, balancing a tray against her dressing-gowned hip. "Tea," she said, yawning. "And I've opened up some bedrooms upstairs. Have at it, my dears, whatever it is. I'm going back to bed. Don't tell me a thing."

SIX DAYS UNTIL THE ROYAL WEDDING

November 14, 1947

CHAPTER 77

"Is she making any headway?" Osla asked.

"Hard to say." Mab shook her head. Watching Beth work over the last two days had been fascinating and not a little disturbing. She'd taken over Dilly's big oak desk, drawing up cardboard strips called rods and haphazard lists of cribs; she broke endless pencils and drank endless pots of coffee. She held long conversations with her former mentor as though he were actually sitting there—"What if . . ." "I tried that, Dilly . . ." "Did you ever try . . ."—and then fell into hours of abstracted silence.

"Is *this* how the boffins did it during the war?" Mab couldn't help asking dubiously. She'd worked so many stages of the intelligence chain at BP, but she'd never been part of the stage where human brains made the critical initial breaks. As Mab watched, Beth scribbled something, scratched it out, swigged all the coffee in her cup, and started over. She'd been going nearly thirty-six hours.

"I can see why the intelligence swots thought BP people were all loons," Osla said, then winced at that particular choice of words. But Beth hadn't noticed. Mab wasn't certain if Beth would notice if the house exploded. Her frayed hair had been pushed behind her ears, she had a flare of color in her cheeks, and her eyes glittered like shards of glass. Frankly, she didn't look *sane*.

Is she actually doing anything*?* Mab wondered. *Or are we watching a madwoman shuffle paper?*

"Sometimes it takes months." Beth spoke as if reading Mab's mind, not looking up from some chain of letters she was diagramming.

"Well, we haven't got months," said Mab. "Even if you get the wheel settings, how can you decrypt it without an Enigma machine or a Typex?"

"The machines were all shipped out of BP at the end of the war," Osla mused. "Broken up for scrap?"

"With thousands of Enigmas and Typexes and bombes, you'd think at least some would have survived." But Mab wasn't sure how they'd find out. You couldn't just go round asking where top-secret decoding machines were kept.

"I wonder if my uncle Dickie can turn something up. He's in India now, but maybe his old Admiralty aides . . ." Osla turned with a flip of her skirt, heading for the hall telephone.

Beth looked up so abruptly Mab started. It took her a while to focus on Mab's face. "Coffee?"

"Coming right up, Your Highness," Mab said a little sourly, but she supposed there wasn't any other way she could help. She couldn't decrypt Rose; she had no powerful relations who could pull strings; she might as well make the coffee. *What am I even doing here?* Mab wondered, heading for Courns Wood's kitchens.

"If that girl doesn't need more coffee," Mrs. Knox said from the kitchen sink, "I'll eat my apron."

The woman certainly knew codebreakers. "She does."

"Fresh pot already brewing. Help me with the washing-up?"

Mab tied a tea towel around her blue-sprigged cotton dress. "You put your feet up and let me do it, Mrs. Knox. It's the least we can do, after invading your home."

"I like hearing the place lively again." Mrs. Knox dried a teacup, looking pensive. "It's been nearly five years since my husband died."

"I only met him in passing . . . I worked in another section. But I've heard he was a great man."

"He was. A great man, but maddening. Most great men are. The way he went through tobacco and pens . . . and dear me, the water bill for all those long hot baths when he was working through some problem!" Mrs. Knox shook her head, smiling. "I miss him."

A memory of Francis pierced Mab, his lathering up at the mirror in the Keswick hotel. She blinked it away with a hard swallow. "Do you have more soap?"

"I'm afraid that little sliver is it. I'll be that happy when soap isn't rationed anymore." Dilly's wife scrutinized Mab, curious. "I keep thinking I've seen you before, Mrs. Sharpe. Did we meet at one of the Bletchley Park revues?"

"Perhaps. I—I was Mrs. Gray, then."

"Ah." Gently, Mrs. Knox took a cup from Mab's hand. "My condolences, dear. I'm glad you've found happiness again."

Mab stared into the water. *Eddie,* she thought. *Lucy.* But under the fierce wave of love for her babies welled an ocean of flat, blank *nothing.* She just didn't choose to admit it was there, most of the time.

"Dilly was my second love, you know." Mrs. Knox's voice was thoughtful. "I had a fiancé—he died in France, in the *first* war. My goodness, so long ago. When I got the telegram . . . I've never been so certain I was going to die. But one doesn't, of course. I thought for a while that I'd never let myself grow so fond of anyone again. But one can't really do that either. Being cut off from life is like being dead. It would have cut me off from a certain very absentminded papyri-translating professor with a gift for codebreaking and a mania for long baths. That would have been a great pity."

"Yes," Mab made herself say, voice brittle. "There, that's the last cup. I'll see what's keeping Osla . . ." Escaping into the corridor, Mab stood a moment, rubbing her hands up and down the towel over her dress, and then she saw Osla slumped against the telephone. Mab stiffened. "What is it?"

Osla looked up, smile grim. "I'm dithering about whether I should ring Giles. Feed him a line or two why I'm away longer than planned . . . I can't bear the thought of hearing his voice." Her finger traced the telephone cord, emerald engagement ring glinting. "I've made a perfect mug of myself, trusting him."

"You're not the only one." Mab thought of the night she ended up drunk in his bed. "Thank God I didn't sleep with him."

"Lucky you. He's a thumping bore between the sheets."

Mab's lips twitched. Osla's did too, and for a moment they were on the verge of laughter. Then Osla said, "No use putting it off," and picked up the telephone, and Mab went into the library, where Beth was pacing.

"You look like a gothic heroine about to pitch herself down a well," Mab observed, but Beth just shook her head.

"It's no good. I'll never crack it in time. I'm too rusty—"

Mab cut her off. "Ring Harry."

Beth flinched. "What?"

"You don't want to ring Harry," Mab said impatiently. "Because you haven't seen him in three and a half years and you don't know what you still mean to him and you don't want to face any of that yet, but we need another brain. Someone to help break those messages and not turn you in." Mab folded her arms. "Ring Harry."

Beth didn't have time to answer before Osla stamped into the library, face flushed with fury. "If this doesn't just take the biscuit," she snarled. "An invitation's come for Giles and me, and I've got to run up to London. Mrs. Knox," she said as Dilly's widow came in with the coffeepot, "can the others impose on you a little longer?"

"By all means, dear. I haven't had this much excitement since V-E Day." Mrs. Knox began passing mugs tranquilly.

"Who on earth called you up to London?" Mab asked Osla.

"Would you believe the palace?"

FIVE DAYS UNTIL THE ROYAL WEDDING

November 15, 1947

CHAPTER 78

"Your Royal Highness."

Dimly, Osla was aware of Giles's bowing, the other guests' fluttering through the private drawing room where they had all been ushered. Osla had no idea who the others were; she kept thinking of them as *the camouflage*. Especially as she made the appropriate half curtsy and straightened, taking in the smoke-blue dress, the string of pearls, the serene shield of a face . . . and the steady blue eyes, level with Osla's own.

"How do you do," murmured Princess Elizabeth.

Osla had a flash of memory, running to meet Philip at the train station, face tilted up toward his, realizing she'd forgotten how blue *his* eyes were. *They will have beautiful blue-eyed children.*

"Delighted to meet you, Miss Kendall." Pert, pretty Princess Margaret in buttercream yellow, giving a bold glance up and down the dress Osla's mother had brought back from Paris: ribbed silk in deep lavender, a huge skirt, a wide sash with impressionist flower swirls like a band of Monet's water lilies about the waist. "Smart frock. Dior?"

Just be chummy, Osla reminded herself, as everyone was ushered to a table glittering with silver gilt and crystal, and she and Princess Elizabeth sank down opposite each other in a mutual billow of crinoline and unblinking gazes. *That's what this whole luncheon is about.* Someone in the palace had clearly had enough of those scandal-rag tidbits about Philip's former girlfriend and decided on a little preemptive strategy: Osla and her fiancé, cozy with the princesses over lunch, everyone friends, then a nice mention in the papers the next day. Osla couldn't decide if she wanted to laugh or rage at the bally timing of it all. On one hand, she'd rather have eaten nails than choke down an elaborate lunch with her traitorous fiancé and *anyone,* let alone her former boyfriend's royal wife-to-be. On the other hand, Giles would think any stiffness on Osla's part was Buckingham Palace jitters and not because she'd rumbled his game.

"And if he's at the palace, he's not thinking about Beth," Mab had pointed out. "Watch him, Os. If he seems worried . . ."

He didn't—he looked utterly chuffed to be here at Buck Place, and Osla felt cautiously optimistic that Beth's guess was right: he hadn't been notified of her escape. "You look smashing," he whispered into Osla's ear as the first course was served. "How'd I get so lucky bagging a filly like you?"

Because you took a dead set at me when I'd have said yes to the bloody postman, Osla thought. She'd been giving his seemingly casual proposal a great deal of thought since learning what her fiancé really was. He might have had a First from Cambridge, but Giles didn't run in the crowds she did . . . crowds he'd been very eager to enter. *Social climber,* Osla thought, giving Giles her biggest smile over the turtle soup. *I was never a friend to you, just a rung in the ladder.* She was very glad Philip wasn't at lunch today. Unlike her fiancé from hell, he'd have twigged her real mood in two seconds flat. Not just her anger, but what lay underneath it: a shiver of fear, to be sitting beside a man who would have a woman lobotomized because she wouldn't give him what he wanted. A man capable of *anything.* A man she was engaged to marry.

The future queen took her first spoonful from the shallow Coalport dish, and everyone followed suit. "I hope I may present my personal felicitations for your upcoming marriage, ma'am," Osla said, taking the bull by the horns. "I wish you every happiness."

A faint softening in the future queen's eyes. "Thank you."

"Such a fuss over one day," Princess Margaret said airily. "Quite makes me want to run off to the registry office when my time comes. I don't think Philip would be averse either. He's always been one for informality, Miss Kendall—but of course, you know that. I shan't tell you the childhood nickname he had for me; it's quite unflattering." A gleam in Princess Margaret's eye. "What did he nickname you?"

Osla would rather have been strapped to a rack than say that Philip had once called her *princess*. Giles saved her by launching on a self-deprecating story about school nicknames. A few of the other men laughed; Princess Elizabeth addressed an elderly lady at her side. Turtle soup was replaced by roast partridge and potatoes. Princess Elizabeth came back to Osla with a polite comment about the weather; Osla replied and took a different bull by the horns. "The newspaper coverage of the wedding has been quite unrelenting. It must be a relief to know the scrutiny will return to its usual level soon."

I'm not here to throw a spanner in your wedding plans, she wanted to say, preferably embroidered on a banner in three-foot letters. *Can I skip dessert and go home? I've got a traitor to collar, and he's sitting here blithering on about his school days!*

One of the other ladies was asking Giles if there was a date set for their wedding. "June," he said with a smile, pressing his knee to Osla's under the table. Osla wished she could jab her silver-gilt dessert fork into his leg. "We'll be quite unfashionable, with the new fashion for winter weddings, ma'am." An ingratiating smile to the future queen; Osla distinctly saw Princess Elizabeth's jaw tighten as she yawned without so much as parting her lips. You had to respect a woman who could yawn with her mouth closed.

"A June wedding!" Princess Margaret knocked back her wine. "Too, too original!"

Some mention was made of Princess Elizabeth's wartime service, and Osla fell gratefully on the change of subject as the partridge was replaced by fluffy crepes doused in apricot jam. "I understand you were with the ATS during the last year of the war, ma'am. What a lark, working with engines and automobiles."

"I enjoyed it." A spark lit the princess's blue eyes. "You can do a lot if you're properly trained."

"Yes, you can," Osla said, thinking of Hut 4.

Princess Elizabeth tilted her head. "Did you serve, Miss Kendall?"

"I did, ma'am." Biting into a crepe. "I would have been thoroughly ashamed not to do my part."

"Not one of the women's branches, I believe?"

"I wish I could say more, ma'am"—swallowing her crepe—"but I'm afraid your superiors would disapprove."

The future queen looked startled. Osla smiled sweetly. *Mark the occasion: the very first time I ever enjoyed BP's song-and-dance of secrecy: over lunch at a very different BP.*

Princess Margaret had another glass of wine in hand when luncheon broke up, and she drew Osla to the window as if to point out the gardens. "I'm the one who wanted to invite you, you know. Lilibet wasn't keen at all." Her eyes glittered with mischief. "Come on, spill. What's Philip like when you get him . . . *alone*?"

Osla blinked, innocent. Princess Elizabeth glanced over at them, then went back to nodding as Giles told her yet another story.

"Maybe Philip's no great shakes, considering you've moved on." Margaret looked at Giles. "Your fiancé's rather nice."

"He's a crashing bore." Strange how a traitor could also be a real yawner.

The princess laughed. "So ditch him! One understands the need for a wedding date, but afterward—"

"I quite agree," Osla said.

Margaret grinned. "You aren't so milk and water as you seem! I didn't think you could be. Philip hates dishrags."

"He will be very happy with your sister, I'm sure."

"If other people don't muck it up for him . . . Mummy wasn't keen." Margaret scrutinized Osla. "Look, you know him. Is he up for this? Can he do it?"

Osla remembered her own words to Philip, that last meeting in Euston station: *Do you think you're built for that, playing Albert to her Victoria? I don't think you are.* The look on his face afterward . . . looking at Margaret now, Osla realized she could complicate Philip's entry to this family quite efficiently, with just a few drips of poison. "You can trust him," Osla said. "He's not perfect, and you shouldn't expect it. But he's nearly an orphan—like me—and family is everything to people like us."

"What about country?" Margaret asked, arch. "Mummy called him 'the Hun,' you know."

"In his own words, he's near committed murder on behalf of the British Empire." Smiling at Margaret's startled expression. "Perhaps someday, if he really trusts you, he'll tell you about his experiences at Matapan."

Family *was* everything, Osla thought. And maybe—yearning to get back to Courns Wood—she had more family than she thought.

"THAT WENT SWIMMINGLY!" Giles was gleeful as they were ushered out. "I can already see tomorrow's write-up: *The princesses lunched privately with special friends, including Mr. Giles Talbot and his fiancée, Miss Osla Kendall . . .*"

Osla dug in her handbag for her gloves, hoping Giles wouldn't want to take her out for a night of cocktails. Oh, God, if he tried to wheedle her between his sheets she was going to absolutely *heave.*

"Excuse me, Miss Kendall." A footman caught up to them halfway down the burnished hall outside, bowing. "If you will come back with me? Your gloves . . ."

But there were no gloves when Osla left Giles and returned to the drawing room. Only Philip, standing hands in pockets by the window.

"Hullo," he said with a crooked smile.

Her stomach was suddenly in ropes. "Hullo." She wasn't entirely sure what to call him: he'd be elevated to a dukedom on the morning of his wedding but hadn't received that title yet; he'd renounced Greek citizenship to marry England's princess, so he was no longer Philip of Greece.

Philip nodded the footman out, motioning for the door to be left cracked. A private meeting, then, Osla thought, but not *private.* "I wanted a hello, since I couldn't join you at lunch. How was it?"

"I'm sure you've been filled in." Something told Osla Philip had already spoken to his fiancée. "I hope no one thinks I had anything to do with those scandal-rag pieces."

"I know you, Os. Never your style."

They gazed at each other. Philip looked strange out of uniform, his bright hair no longer picking up the glint of gold braid but shining over a civilian suit. His eyes landed on her emerald ring. "I thought you hated green."

She did. Since the Café de Paris bombing, after which her nightmares were studded by flashes of her blood-drenched green gown. *Ozma of Oz . . . we'll get you back to the Emerald City, right as rain.* "I've learned to tolerate it," Osla said. "Like a lot of other things."

"Margaret thinks your fiancé's a prat."

"Margaret talks too much."

"She also relayed what you said about me." Pause. "Thank you. You could have said a good deal to her . . . it would have made its way to her sister and— Well, you could have made things difficult between my fiancée and me. I wouldn't even have blamed you, considering how things ended."

An ocean of words hovered visibly at his lips. *I didn't behave as I should have,* perhaps. Or *I let myself care more than I should have, and you were hurt.* It all remained unsaid. Philip was more contained than Osla remembered: the future consort, already weighing every remark. She felt a moment's regret for the boisterous wartime lieutenant who laughed and spoke on quicksilver impulse.

"You look well." Philip studied her. "I'd like to see you happy, too. Is Giles Talbot the one to do that?"

"I don't think you're quite entitled to an opinion on my future husband," she said evenly.

"That's fair."

"Don't think I'm eating my heart out, Philip." The twinges of regret could ache sometimes, even now, but Osla's heart was no longer in smithereens. It wasn't heartache now, it was . . . "What pains me," she said slowly, finding her way, "is that I've never quite been allowed to leave you behind. When can I be Osla Kendall again, not Prince Philip's old girlfriend?" She answered her own question. "I know it will happen eventually. You'll become our future queen's husband, there will be little blue-eyed princes and princesses, and I'll have a husband and children of my own, and people will forget. I just wish it would come sooner—the day my name becomes mine again, not just something to remind people of someone more important."

His mouth quirked. "I might know something about how that feels."

He might, at that. He'd chosen a woman who outranked him, who always would. *If you'd married me,* Osla thought, *you'd be a naval lieutenant—maybe a captain by now—free to sail the world, and I'd always be* the prince's wife. *You'll marry her, and you'll probably never sail into battle again, and you'll always be* the queen's husband.

"You can do it, you know," Osla said. "What I said at the train station, that you could never play Albert to Princess Elizabeth's Victoria—you can do it, Philip. I know you can. She'll need someone like you, and so does England—someone who doesn't take loyalty for granted." Unlike Giles, who had been born into the nation Philip had chosen and fought for, yet had thrown *his* loyalty away.

"Thank you," he said simply. "She . . . makes me happy."

"I'm glad you found your place in the world, then."

"What's your place, Os?"

"I'm going to be the wittiest, most successful satirist at the *Tatler,*" Osla said. "With a syndicated column before I'm thirty." She said it flippantly but realized it was exactly what she wanted. Maybe she hadn't let herself realize that, because it seemed like wanting the moon . . . But Osla decided right now that she was getting a column, and it was going to be a ripping good column, too.

"Shall I ring someone at the *Tatler*?" Philip asked. "I could put in a word for you."

"No, I'm going to get it for myself," Osla decided. As soon as she'd wrapped up this business of catching a traitor, that is.

"I look forward to reading your work." Philip hesitated. "Friends, Os? I don't want to lose you."

"You won't."

"Then take this." Holding out a slip of paper. "My private line here at the palace."

"Is a bit of Mayfair crumpet like me allowed to ring a duke at Buck Place?" Osla gibed.

"You're no Mayfair crumpet, and you know it." Philip hesitated. "Maybe you can't tell me, but I know you did more during the war than type reports."

That knocked Osla for a wicket. "*What?*"

"People who have been to war, suffered for it in some way . . . you see the marks. The damage. I knew fellows who couldn't stand loud noises after Matapan, fellows who got the tremors after we were dive-bombed in the Mediterranean. I don't know what you did, Os—I didn't think about it much at the time—but afterward, when I looked back, I realized . . . well, from the pattern of your flinches, it can't have just been typing." Slanting a brow. "Though you were very good at selling it that way."

Osla stared at him, nearly breathless.

"Tell me one thing," Philip said. "Whatever it was, were you good at it?"

"I was blinking *great* at it," she said.

"There you are. So no more 'silly deb' business, eh?"

She grinned. "As the royal consort, you *might* get permission to find out what I did. Possibly. Ask MI-5."

"I will." Philip checked the time. "I've got to go. Look, don't be afraid to ring if you ever need anything. One of my people will answer it, day or night."

"You have *people* now?" she teased. He grinned back, coming to kiss her cheek, and she smelled an unfamiliar cologne. "Good to see you, Philip."

When Osla was escorted back to Giles, waiting between a mirror and a hideous mid-Victorian still-life, he was good humored. "You were gone an awfully long time for a pair of gloves, kitten. Should I be jealous?"

She beamed at Giles, disarming him before she dumped the

goods on him. "You're the one who's been tipping off the scandal rags about me, aren't you?" A shot in the dark, but a reasonable one.

He had the grace to looked chagrined. "Just once or twice. The things journos pay for tips . . ."

Excellent, Osla thought. She could row with him all the way back to Knightsbridge, and he'd be far too busy scrambling for apologies to even think about inviting her out to cocktails, or, God forbid, to bed. Far too busy to think about Beth, either. "You utter *rotter,* Giles Talbot!" Osla shouted, working up some tears as she stamped down the endless palace hall. That shiver of fear his presence gave her subsided in a wash of relief. She could get out of his sight and back to Beth, Mab, and Courns Wood by nightfall. Back to the people who mattered.

CHAPTER 79

"I hear you need a boffin."

Beth's head jerked up. Harry stood leaning against the library door, old jacket thrown over one shoulder. His black hair was shorter—he would no longer be forgetting the barber for weeks at a time because of triple-shift binges breaking U-boat codes. She'd forgot how big he was. "You're here," she said, heart thudding.

His gaze went over her, and she winced at the horror that flashed briefly across his eyes. She was clean scrubbed now—a long soak in Mrs. Knox's bathtub had washed away the asylum smell—but there wasn't any hiding her skeletal thinness, her ragged hair and nails. "Harry," she said, hearing the rasp in her own voice now, the perpetual hoarseness from years of daily vomiting.

"Mrs. Knox let me in." He looked like he had a river of words begging to be released, but he kept his voice careful, quiet. Like a man trying not to spook a wild animal. "Mab and Osla, are they—"

"Mab's making coffee, Osla was called to London." Harry had a fellowship at his old college in Cambridge now. Mab had tracked him down yesterday. Beth felt her hand stealing up to worry at her hair and made it stop.

"My college owed me some days." Harry took a step forward. "Beth—"

"How is Sheila?" Beth blurted out. She wanted to know why

he'd never come to Clockwell. She also didn't know if she could bear to hear the answer. "And Christopher?"

Harry pulled himself visibly back from some ledge. "Christopher's—he's well. My father's come round a bit about us never darkening his doorstep; he sent Christopher to a specialist to have his ankle operated on. He walks quite a bit better now. Sheila's over the moon."

"That's good." Beth took a deep breath. "Did Mab tell you about Giles?"

"Yes." Harry said something flat and filthy about Giles Talbot. "This cipher message you broke—how is it the Soviets were talking about Giles, in English, via an Enigma machine when they don't use Enigma for their own traffic?"

Beth had thought about that. "Probably a captured German army machine. Maybe they were communicating with his handler in England, asking more about its uses and operation. Who knows?"

Harry pulled up a chair. "How can I help?"

She pushed the Rose messages across the desk.

He leafed through the sheets of Enigma traffic, a smile touching the corner of his mouth, and Beth's heart plucked. "This takes me back." He inhaled the smell of the decrypt paper. "I'm working theoretical mathematics now, the Poincaré conjecture—stuff I missed when I was at BP. Pure research, no lives at stake. But sometimes I look round my office and I miss the night shifts, the chicory coffee, the morning rush on the U-boat traffic . . ."

"Working elbow-to-elbow in Knox's section, everybody climbing over each other when the dispatch riders came in . . ." Beth could have had another year of that, if she'd worked to the end of the war. Yet another thing Giles had taken from her. She shook the anger off; there was no time for it. "We don't have much in the way of cribs . . ." She walked Harry through how she'd broken the first Rose message. He fell into the work without another word; she fell into it too with another steadying inhale.

"I looked for you as soon as I was demobbed." He spoke perhaps an hour later, quiet words dropping into the stillness. "Your mother told me you'd died in an institution. She wouldn't even tell me where you were buried."

Beth squeezed her eyes shut. *Ah, Mother.*

"You never talked about her—I didn't know enough to disbelieve her." A ragged pause. "I loved you, and I left you in that place—"

"Harry," Beth broke in desperately. "Let's stay focused, shall we? I can't . . ."

She trailed off. He blew out an uneven breath. "All right."

Beth looked at the cipher message before her, not seeing it for a moment. *I loved you.* Past tense.

Well, three and a half years was a long time.

She went back into the spirals of Rose, with something of an effort. Another hour limped by, working a potential crib that went nowhere. Beth sat back, eyes burning. "Why can't I do this?" she heard herself whisper. "I've been going at it three days now, and there's nothing. I can't *see* it, the way I used to."

"You will."

"What if I don't?" The words came out more despairing than she'd intended. "What if I can't do it anymore?"

The thing that terrified her most—being locked out. That headlong rush of falling down the spiral into Wonderland, the world of letters and patterns that she'd walked in with such starry-eyed enchantment. Now she was banging on Wonderland's gates until her fists bled, and everything remained locked. "How much of my mind did I leave inside those walls?" In the asylum, she had felt like the sanest one there. Now she was out, and she felt like a caged lunatic on display at a circus.

Harry's big hand extended across the desk. Beth hesitated, then slid her bitten-raw fingertips into his palm. "Beth, you didn't leave any part of your mind in that place." His gaze was steady. "You can still do this."

Her eyes blurred. He was warm, he was sane, and he believed in her. "Just—don't treat me like I'm made of glass, Harry. I don't have time to be broken right now." Later, when Giles was caught, she'd let herself shiver and sob, feel all the damage the asylum had inflicted on her. Not now.

He squeezed her hand fiercely. "Then let's get back to work."

ANOTHER HOUR LATER, Harry was reading through boxing chains as Beth tried to follow a Dilly-esque thought about crabs and turnovers—and they both looked up as heels clattered in the corridor. "We're absolutely dished," Osla called, stamping into the library in her Buckingham Palace finery. "I've had no luck—*Harry*!"

"Hullo, gorgeous." Harry rose, picking Osla up and out of her tiny patent-leather sling-backs. "I thought you'd be a duchess by now."

"Even worse, darling. I'm engaged to a traitor, hadn't you heard?" Osla turned to Beth as Harry set her back into her shoes, and Mab came into the room drying her hands on a tea towel. "I tapped all my godfather's people in London, discreetly. No luck figuring out where we might turn up an Enigma machine."

"Forget the Enigma machine for now. We still need a good break before we've got anything to feed into one." Beth tugged at her frayed hair. "And we're not getting there fast enough."

"We need more brains on this." Harry considered, fingers drumming. "I'll ring the Prof; he's in Cambridge on a sabbatical year. And my cousin Maurice, he worked on ciphers in Block F and he's at the Crédit Lyonnais in London now—if they could come and put a few days in—"

"We can't tell anyone about this," Beth protested, panic beginning to lick through her veins. "We can't trust—"

"We can." Harry's voice was quiet but very sure. "Beth, not many people have friends with intelligence work clearance and the absolute ability to keep secrets, but we do. Christ, do we ever. And we have a traitor loose and only a matter of days to catch him. Let's put out the call to the ones we can trust."

"We trusted Giles," Osla pointed out.

"We have to trust that he's the only bad apple in our acquaintance. We *were* picked. We *were* vetted. Overall, we have to trust that the process worked. Or else BP would never have thrived."

A long pause. "What do we tell them?" Beth said, gnawing her thumbnail.

"That it's BP business," Mab said. "They'll drop everything and come running, just like us. They spent an entire war doing that. It's in their blood."

"I'll make up some more beds," said Mrs. Knox, behind Mab. "Though I'll wager there won't be much sleeping. Goodness, how exciting." Off she went, waving off help, and the others looked at one another.

"Assemble the Mad Hatters." Osla headed for the telephone. "Invitations are being issued for one last absolutely topping Tea Party."

CHAPTER 80

Knock knock. "Mr. Turing," Mab greeted the dark-haired, round-shouldered man she'd seen ramble through BP followed by admiring whispers. "Thank you for coming at such short notice. Take this . . ." Folding his hand instantly round a cup of coffee. She'd learned something these last few days about dealing with cryptanalysts: point them at the coffee, point them at the problem, then get out of the way. "Work's over there, in Dilly's library."

The Prof ambled to a seat opposite Beth and Harry, and Beth pushed over the stack of increasingly dog-eared messages. "Let's see . . ." He began humming tunelessly, and Mab had to stop herself from snapping *Stop that!* She wasn't going to snap at Alan bloody Turing just because she was missing her family and felt like biting someone's head off. Mab had rung home that morning to say she'd be away another few days; the conversation with Mike had contained a lot of thorny silences and questions she'd had no choice but to evade. *Think about that later,* she advised herself.

Knock knock. "One of Dilly's team?" Mab guessed, assessing the rosy-cheeked woman in the corridor.

"Phyllida Kent. Look, I'm happy to help, but I need some sort of authorization or proof that what you're doing here is on the up—"

"We're working on that. Come in, have a go . . ."

Knock knock. A brisk blond broom handle of a woman in a home-knit jumper came straight in and kissed Mrs. Knox on the cheek. Mab barely knew her except that she'd been another of Dilly's team. *I thought she was the traitor,* Beth had said. *Thank God she's not, because she's as good a codebreaker as me.* "Peggy Rock, came as soon as I could. What have you got, and why do I need to get us authorization to investigate it?"

"We're calling it Rose." Harry pulled out a chair for her at what Mab was already thinking of as Boffin Island—the desk and two tables all pushed together, covered in decrypts, pencils, and rods. Like Puffin Island off the coast of Wales, where Mike had taken Mab on their honeymoon, but covered in weird cryptanalysts instead of weird birds.

"Hullo, you," Peggy greeted Beth. "I thought you'd had a breakdown."

"Frame-up," Beth said succinctly.

"Bastard." Peggy surveyed everything, hearing the rest of Harry's succinct explanation. "All right, let me work up some official cover for all this through my office. Semi-sanctioned operation investigating remaindered code for purposes of research and security, maybe." That, Mab thought, ought to satisfy any of the BP volunteers who wanted something more concrete than Beth's word that they were working for legitimate purposes. "I'll talk to my superior at GCHQ—Government Communications Headquarters," Peggy expanded when Beth looked blank. "Where I work now. The name's changed from the GC & CS days, but it's the same stuff. Codebreaking when we're *not* at war."

"Is there any chance you could you get your hands on an Enigma machine through your office?" Mab broke in. "Surely they can't all have been destroyed after the war."

Peggy reversed for the telephone. "Let me ring a chap . . ."

It really was the most extraordinary thing, Mab thought. BP

men and women came and went from Courns Wood—some of them Mad Hatters she had known like family, some vague acquaintances from night shifts or the canteen, every one vouched for. Peggy got them some mysterious authorizations, worked forty-eight hours round the clock, then departed looking elusive. The Prof came and went with an absent expression, two hours here, four hours there, whenever he could make the journey from Cambridge. A bespectacled fellow of Worcester College dropped in from Oxford and had a pencil in hand before "Asa, absolutely ripping—does everyone know Asa from Hut 6?" was fully out of Osla's mouth. Harry's cousin Maurice came, a cadaverous-looking man in the most expensive suit Mab had ever seen, then a fellow named Cohen with a Glasgow accent . . .

No one said Giles's name. No one discussed his treachery. No one had to be warned to say nothing when they departed. "I've missed this," Phyllida sighed when she finally had to leave.

Yes, Mab thought. *I've missed it, too.*

Though the work still had its stresses. "Beth," Mab said, noticing her former billet-mate had snapped two pencils in the last half hour, "take five minutes. I'm going to trim your hair."

"Why?" Beth blinked.

"Because you need a spot of tending if you're going to get your focus back." Cryptanalysts, Mab had learned, needed a certain amount of care if they were to perform at their peak. Thinking of Mrs. Knox and her wry indulgence of Dilly's quirks—and the way she kept supplying her sudden influx of visitors with coffee—Mab shooed Beth into the washroom, borrowed a pair of scissors, and began smartening up that butchered blond hair while Beth slowly blinked her way back into the world around her.

"Why are you bothering?" Beth asked as Mab flicked a side part into place. "You hate me, even if you *did* break me out of the asylum."

"I don't entirely hate you anymore, Beth." That surprised Mab, and she worked through it as she did her best to clip that Veronica Lake wave back into shape. After what Beth had endured at the asylum, it felt like only a heart of stone could condemn her to unrelenting hatred. "When I look at you, I prickle. And I don't think I'll ever understand you. But no woman should walk around looking like she backed into a threshing machine." And Beth went back to work, swinging her neatened hair in a pleased sort of way, and in another hour she'd broken out a wheel setting on one of the messages.

"We're in luck." Peggy Rock blew back into the library with a wooden case in her arms. Mab felt her neck tingle. She'd never laid eyes on an Enigma machine before, only the much bulkier Typex. This had the same rows of keys, the same set of wheels on one side, but it was sleeker, more compact . . . more dangerous.

"How?" Harry's cousin Maurice breathed.

"Let's just say not all the machines were destroyed after the war," Peggy said with GCHQ caginess. "There's an underground bunker; never mind where. My superior pulled strings to get me a machine on loan from the bunker. He's ex-BP, which helps."

"Is there any chance that bunker has a bombe machine as well?" Harry asked as Peggy shut the wooden case into Dilly's wall safe. "It could cut days off the process."

"You think I can magic up a bombe machine as easy as an Enigma? Something twice as big as a wardrobe?"

"Yes," Beth, Osla, and Mab said in unison. Osla added, "I'll eat my knickers if you haven't already asked."

Peggy gave her closed-lipped smile. A bombe—Mab hated the beasts, but she wasn't able to *do* much here at Courns Wood except refill the coffee. If they could get their hands on a machine . . .

"I *may* have made inquiries with my GCHQ superior. There *may* be a few surviving bombes in storage, and there *may* be one on loan to a computational research project based in London." Peggy dropped the hypothetical, seeing their impatient looks. "It's in a repair lab at the moment, and there's no way to get it out, but we just might be able to get to it. The lab's closed up the last few days before the royal wedding. I could get us in, but we'd only have up until the wedding to work in privacy."

Mab could see Beth hunching into herself at the thought of leaving Dilly's library. But she still nodded. "It would help."

"One more thing," Peggy added. "If it's in a repair lab, there's no guarantee what shape the machine will be in."

"RAF engineers did bombe maintenance during the war," the fellow named Cohen volunteered in his Glasgow burr. "I used to talk to them in the BP canteen. Let me see . . ." Disappearing toward the telephone.

"We need more than a technician," Harry argued. "We'll need someone to operate the ruddy thing."

Mab felt a grin hook itself nearly behind her ears. "I can."

Some muffled wrangling from the corridor, and eventually Cohen swung back in. "Alfred's in Inverness now and David's on a jaunt to Penzance, but there's another laddie who can join us tomorrow night."

"Have him meet us in London," said Peggy. By morning they were all piling into assorted cars and waving goodbye to Mrs. Knox, Beth and the Enigma machine hidden under a blanket in the back of Mab's Bentley. Their makeshift, miniature Bletchley Park was on the move.

KNOCK KNOCK.

Now the new arrivals had to come to a back door at the end of a complex of ugly warehouses clustered on the outskirts of London. The repair lab was echoingly empty, comprehensively locked; someone anonymous came to the rear entrance and spoke briefly with Peggy, and then they were setting up shop all over again in a big maintenance bay littered with tools and old tea mugs. "Let me guess," Mab asked Peggy as Beth and the others began dragging tables together, unpacking the Rose files. "We dinnae need to know what strings you pulled to make this happen."

Peggy looked bland, unpacking the Enigma machine. "We never leave the machines unattended, and *no one* comes in who isn't vouched for."

Knock knock, came the rapping knuckles again, and Peggy let in Osla, staggering under a load of sandwiches, biscuits, and cigarettes. "Sustenance, darlings." She laid out food, placed a sandwich actually in Beth's hand because otherwise she wouldn't eat, and came to where Mab was working on their prize: the bombe on loan from its mysterious bunker, towering in one corner like a pagan altar. "How's it coming?"

"The drums are a mess." Mab shook out her fingers, sore and pinched from hours of teasing coiled wires apart with her eyebrow tweezers. "Where's that bloody technician?"

"Delayed, apparently. Let me see about getting some more hands to help with the wiring, in the meantime . . ."

Knock knock. "Val Glassborow," Mab said gratefully as Peggy ushered in a familiar face a few hours later.

"Val Middleton now. You're lucky I was in town for the royal wedding." She brushed back a lot of glossy brown hair, sliding past Beth and the boffins hunched over their cipher messages. "Peggy gave me the gist; where do you want me?"

"Grab a drum, darling," Osla called from where she sat with a drum in her own lap. The Bletchley Park bubble had snapped into place around the drafty maintenance bay, and there was a ticking clock hanging over their heads as urgent as any they had slaved under at the Park.

Knock knock. Long after sundown, Peggy ushered in the last arrival. ". . . sorry I'm late," a man's voice floated from the corridor. "Had to find a mate to take the kids." The Australian drawl penetrated Mab's ears belatedly, she was concentrating so hard on the drum before her. She frowned, straightening, just as a man's voice said, "Mab?"

In the doorway, kit bag in hand, was her husband.

"HUT 6," MAB said. "Then Hut 11 and 11A, then the mansion."

"I worked Eastcote, Wavendon, the outstations," Mike said. "After I was shot down, they heard I was an engineer, slapped the Official Secrets Act in front of me, and set me to fixing bombes." He shook his head. "And you were one of the operators? I thought they were all Wrens."

"I was a fill-in because I was tall. Then I became a regular."

The two of them were working alone by the bombe. Osla had taken Valerie, the tweezers, and a heap of drums to the other side of the room, tactfully giving Mab and her husband some privacy. Mab sat tweezing wires apart and Mike was up to his elbows in the cabinet's back wiring, stripped down to shirtsleeves and braces. Mab could hardly look her husband in the eye.

Mike had worked for Bletchley Park? Her own husband?

"How did we not run into each other?" He smiled, doing a delicate bit of work with narrow pliers. "I was called to BP now and then. It's how I got to know Cohen, one of those three-in-the-morning canteen friendships. If I'd seen you, I'd have noticed."

"When did you come, 'Forty-Four? Thousands at BP by then. We didn't cross paths, that's all." It was perfectly possible—likely, even.

"So this is what had you flying south in such a hurry." Mike swiped his forehead on his elbow. "A lot just straightened out in my mind."

"I don't like the lying," Mab said, just to be clear. "But I don't have a choice."

He nodded. "It's what you do."

"When you're us," she agreed.

"Did *he* know?" Mike looked at her. "Francis."

"Yes." She focused on the drum, prising two crumpled wires apart. "He wasn't BP, but he was in the same world."

"Did that make it easier?"

"We—didn't really have enough time to figure it out."

"While we're telling truth . . ." Mike wore that guarded expression he had whenever the name Francis Gray came up. "When I look at you, I think how lucky I am. When you look at me, you think how I'm not him."

Mab looked down at the drum in her lap.

Her husband's voice was steady. "Am I wrong?"

"Yes." She tweezed two wires apart. "I don't think of him when I look at you—because I've tried to block him out altogether. It hurts less."

"I think you blocked us both in the same go."

Francis: stocky and endlessly calm; holding her against him; rarely laughing. Mike: tall and exuberant; holding their babies; rarely without a grin. "Maybe I did," Mab said, eyes filling until she could barely see the drum's wires.

"I liked his poetry." Mike reached for a spanner. "Read his book when I was in the RAF. Maybe we didn't have the same war, and he wasn't a flier, but I could tell he *got* it. War."

"Yes, he did." Her tears spilled over. Not a flood, just a trickle of pure pain for the man with the little girl in his arms, standing in the wreckage of Coventry with both their lives stretching before them.

"I don't mind hearing about him . . ." Mike's voice upturned at the end, the rest hanging unspoken: *I just want you to talk to me.*

"I'll tell you more about him someday." Mab wiped her eyes. "Right now, I'd rather hear about you. What was the work like, fixing bombes?"

Her husband took the diversion, turned it over with his laconic Australian smile. "Forty-eight hours sometimes trying to run down a fault, some Wren at your shoulder going into spasms. How was your work?"

"Tedious. Exciting. Stressful. Dull. A bit of everything." Mab managed a smile. "Shall I tell you about the night all the Wrens and I stripped down and worked in our underwear?"

"Crikey, yes . . ."

Hours later, Mab and her husband rose, looked around the maintenance bay, and realized everyone but Beth had left.

It was midnight, the day before the royal wedding, and the bombe machine stood ready.

CHAPTER 81

"Tomorrow," Mab said, eyes gleaming, "or rather, later today, we'll be seeing what happens when we plug her up."

She and her husband left arm in arm, grubby from machine oil. The last to go, Beth realized. One by one the exhausted Mad Hatters had gone home to their unsuspecting families, crawled off to neglected flats for a few hours' sleep, or gone with Osla, who was putting the rest up in her Knightsbridge digs.

"You're sleeping here?" Harry had asked Beth, pulling on his jacket. He'd been first to leave this evening, just after Mike Sharpe had arrived.

"I made a nest of blankets in the supply closet. Peggy doesn't want the machines left alone." Besides, Beth had no desire to head outside, even on London's outskirts, while Giles was in this city. "Are you going back to Cambridge?"

"I'll stay and see it through. Christopher knows his dad has important work right now." Harry smiled. "Sheila sends her love."

Beth remembered something she hadn't thought of until now. "Did Sheila's flier survive the war?"

"He did, actually. Nice chap; I've met him. Sheila spends every Tuesday and Thursday with him at his flat in Romford." Harry had nodded good night and headed out . . . and now everyone had gone and Beth was alone in the echoing space, looking up at the impassive bronze face of the bombe. "You'd better be useful," she said aloud.

Feed me something useful first, it answered.

She wandered back to Boffin Island and leafed through the stack of messages again. "Come on, Rose. Open up." Beth remembered why she'd called this cipher Rose to begin with: the way it furled in on itself, overlapping and secretive. It had taken her months to break Abwehr, and they didn't have months for Rose. Or even days.

A knock came at the outer door hours later as Beth dozed over the decrypts. She roused with a start. Harry's voice drifted: "*It's me.*"

"What are you doing back already?" Letting him in.

"Bringing you a friend." Harry set a covered basket on the floor, raising the lid. Boots popped his square gray head over the rim.

"Oh . . ." Beth crashed to her knees and swept up her dog. He wriggled and snuffled, trying to caper on his short legs, and her shoulders heaved. She wasn't sure how much time passed, as she held her dog and told him she loved him, before she could look up at Harry through swimming eyes. "You brought him for me."

"Your landlady's glad to hear you're well. I swore her to secrecy, of course." Harry picked up the basket. "Good night again, Beth."

"Stay." The word fell out of her mouth before she could think about it.

He stopped, a vast shadowy shape against the door.

"Or maybe you don't want to," Beth rushed on. "All this week, you won't really—look at me."

Harry dropped the basket, returned in one long stride, and sank down to the floor beside her, reaching out slowly. His big hand warmed the side of her throat. "I didn't know if you could bear to look at *me,*" he said quietly.

"Why?"

"Because I *left you there*." His voice was even, but his hand slid into her hair and tightened. "When your mother threw me out of her kitchen, I stumbled home and wept for you, when I should have been hunting up Commander Travis or Mab or Osla. I believed your gorgon of a mother, and you stayed there *rotting*—"

"Stop talking." Beth linked her hands around his neck, heart drumming. "Do you want me? Do you love me? If the answer to either—I don't even need both!—is yes, then please *do* something about it."

Harry buried his face in her collarbone, shoulders shaking. For a moment she thought he might be crying, but he was laughing. "Yes, ma'am," he said, slipping the first button of her dress loose, then the next. She helped him with the rest, wanting to climb inside him and never come out. He rose, picked her up, tripped over Boots, then walked into the little supply closet without taking his mouth away from hers. He kicked the door shut, opened it a moment later, pushed Boots out with a "Sorry, chap," and they pitched over onto the makeshift nest of blankets.

Three and a half years, Beth thought—but it was like they'd never been apart. Harry's weight over hers; his hand catching her wrists and pinning them over her head; her toes locking around his knees as her back arched. Lying in the dark afterward, breast to breast, palm to palm, just breathing.

"You've got that look." Harry rose to let Boots in. The schnauzer stamped around their twined feet, chuffing, then curled up on the floor with an outraged expression. "What are you thinking about?"

"Rods and lobsters," Beth said sleepily.

"Thought so." Harry's chest vibrated with laughter as he tugged a blanket around them both. "Christ, but I love you."

"PUT ON A scarf," Osla told Beth at dawn when the rest of the Mad Hatters returned. "I can practically count the kisses, you hussy!" Beth, leaning over the stack of Rose, hair skewered back above her kiss-blotched neck with a pencil, barely heard a word. She'd been back at work since three in the morning, Boots was snoring on her feet, and she was deep down the spiral.

All through the day and into the winter twilight, Beth had the feeling that she'd wedged a fingernail round the edge of Wonderland's gate. Rose was fighting, but she had it firmly in her grip, spiraling down toward its calyx. *I beat the Italian naval Enigma,* Beth told it. *I beat the Spy Enigma. You're no match for me, Rose.* It wasn't a match for Harry, either—Harry, who had gone to work right alongside her at three, periodically leaning over to drop a kiss on the nape of her neck. Or the Prof, or Peggy, or the Hut 6 fellow named Asa who'd rejoined them from Oxford when Cohen and Maurice had to return to their own offices.

We're going to pry you open tonight, Beth thought calmly.

"We've got enough," Harry said eventually, long past suppertime. No one had departed for meals or sleep—they were too close, and they were almost out of time. "The bombe can make a start with this." *It has to,* he didn't have to say. The hours were slipping away like grains of sand in an hourglass.

Mab peered at the mess of tables and letter pairs, rod squares and diagrams. "Can anyone make a bombe menu?" Beth looked at her blankly. "For God's sake, the way they compartmentalized our jobs is just massively unhelpful."

"Too, too frightfully shortsighted of them, darling," Osla drawled. "Not to realize our pressing need for operational understanding if a treason case ever popped up."

"I did menus at BP . . ." Asa was already turning Beth's work into a tidy diagram. Mab took it with a nod, and everyone gathered round. Mab's Australian husband watched with an enormous grin as his wife handled the complicated mass of plugs and wires like a snake charmer funneling vipers into baskets. Valerie Middleton was wide-eyed. "So that's how it works . . ."

"Stand clear," Mab ordered, and threw the machine into life.

The drums began to whir and rotate, their mechanical thrum filling the room and sending a bolt of excitement down Beth's spine. "Looks so primitive now," the Prof said, standing beside Harry. "Compared to the machines I've worked on since . . ."

The drums kept rotating and the mechanical whir kept rising. Mab's eyebrows rose along with it. "Well, get back to the other messages," she said, shooing the others. "Average time to a complete job is about three hours with a three-wheel army key like this and I'll be doing multiple runs. Even when and if it breaks, we've no guarantees this message has what we need."

Beth wrenched her eyes away from the hypnotic whirl, reaching for one of the other messages.

She couldn't say how many hours passed, how many runs Mab did on the bombe machine as the others paced. At some point Beth looked up to see that the machine was still, drums frozen in a silence that left her ears ringing, and that Mab was running some sort of complex check on the Enigma machine, which until now had sat neglected. "Got to test the stops," she muttered. "Find the *Ringstellung* . . . the Hut 6 Machine Room did this part, but I wasn't there very long . . ." Everyone stood poised in suspense.

At last Mab looked up, swiped her dark hair out of her eyes. Grinned. "Job up, strip down."

They were all cheering, voices echoing through the maintenance bay. Valerie pushed her way behind the Enigma machine, setting the wheels as Mab read off the positions. It was long past midnight, Beth realized as she rubbed one foot along Boots's back—in fact, it might be near dawn. Harry wrapped his arms around her from behind; she could feel his heart banging away in his chest. Asa stood polishing his spectacles, Peggy jabbed a pin into the pale knot of her hair, Osla bounced on her toes. The Prof shifted from foot to foot. Mab leaned against one side of the bombe and her husband against the other, both muttering encouragement as Val laboriously hammered out the encrypted Rose message.

"Give it here!" Osla snatched the cipher text almost before it emerged from the machine. It came out in English, Beth could see at a glance, but the BP translator in Osla had snapped on duty anyway: she'd taken her place in the chain, separating the five-letter clusters into words with a few pencil strokes. Beth couldn't stay back any longer; she rushed to look over Osla's left shoulder, vaguely aware Mab had rushed to Osla's right, and everyone else crowded behind.

Everyone's lips moved silently as they read the broken Rose.

Beth spoke with quiet satisfaction, seeing Giles Talbot's face under his red hair. "We've got him."

CHAPTER 82

Giles, darling." Osla kept her trill of greeting through the telephone perfectly natural. She was in a telephone box outside the repair lab; jammed into the box beside her, Mab gave a terse nod of approval. "Did I wake you?"

"Of course you did." Giles's sleepy voice came down the line. At the sound, Beth's eyes got that unsettling feral glitter that prickled every nerve Osla had. No one was ever going to look at Beth Finch, since the madhouse, and think she was just a little mouse of a thing. "It's six in the morning."

Osla made a *shoo* gesture at the Mad Hatters, clustered around the telephone box. They gave her some room and she launched into it. "Don't you dare get in a flap, Giles. I'm still furious with you for talking to the papers."

"I said I was sorry." His tone was wheedling. "You aren't giving me the old heave-ho, are you?"

"I should, you know." Osla made sure to sound pettish. "But I refuse to go to the wedding today without an escort, so consider yourself forgiven. I'll swing by your flat in a few hours—"

"Nonsense, I'll pick you up."

"You don't need to—"

"Darling, it's the least I can do."

Osla let it go. Push too hard to come to his door, he might get suspicious. "Bright and early," she said, naming the hour.

"I'm your man, kitten."

That's the last time you'll ever call me kitten, *you rat bastard.* Osla rang off, looking at the Mad Hatters. "Step two accomplished."

Step one, of course, had been to ring MI-5 regardless of the hour—but lines were busy, phones rang unanswered, or harried-sounding voices insisted on taking messages rather than listening to a word. Peggy had no luck with her GCHQ connections either: "My superior's out, and I'm not bringing this to anyone but him." Osla hadn't been surprised. No one in all of Britain—intelligence services, law enforcement, or constabulary forces combined—was going to have an ear free, not with the wedding of the century barreling down. "We go to London and sit on Giles ourselves until the wedding's over and we can present him to MI-5 with our evidence," Beth stated.

"Why sit on him? As long as he's not suspicious, he's not going anywhere."

"What if he decides to ring the asylum a day early and finds out I'm gone? If we can't get him arrested till after the wedding, I want him locked down."

They swept the maintenance bay one last time and piled out after giving the sheeted bombe a final pat. "I wonder when they'll notice it's suddenly in much better condition," Mike remarked. Some of the Mad Hatters were returning home now that their part was done—the Prof ambling back to Cambridge, Asa to Oxford, Valerie muttering, "*I have no idea what I'm going to tell my husband, absolutely none.*" Peggy was packing the Enigma machine straight back to GCHQ, swearing she'd keep the lines ringing there until she had someone at MI-5 listening.

Five of them crammed into Mab's Bentley and turned toward London: Mike driving (and wasn't he scrummy, Osla thought—he and Mab were going to have the tallest children in the *world*),

Mab beside him with Boots, Harry squashed in the back with Beth, Osla, and the file of decrypted Rose.

"Reminds me of hitching rides to London with half-sauced RAF pilots," Osla said, trying to extract her elbow from Harry's ear. "Squished together like sardines, barreling round blind turns absolutely pipped. Amazing we survived the war at all."

"I was supposed to be hosting a royal wedding listening party today," Mab observed. "I learned how to fold napkins into swans."

For some reason that struck Osla as funny. Perhaps it was lack of sleep, or perhaps it was euphoria because today Giles Talbot was going down. Soon everyone was howling with laughter as the Bentley barreled toward the heart of London.

Where it hit the traffic that had come in for the wedding, and stopped dead.

"TWENTY MINUTES BEFORE Giles nips round!" Osla hurled the door of her flat open, sprinting straight through to the bedroom. It had taken literally *hours* to crawl through the city toward Knightsbridge; they'd abandoned the Bentley and run the last six blocks. Beth now collapsed with Boots under her arm, scarlet as a telephone box, and Mab was doubled over wheezing. "Now will you cut down on the bloody cigarettes?" Mike demanded, limping in last due to his old knee wound.

Osla had already hurled off her crumpled skirt and was shimmying into the tube of silver satin she'd set aside for the royal wedding. Giles would knock; Osla would answer the door looking abbey-ready; she'd ask him in for a cigarette—*My nerves are all a-jangle, darling*—and as soon as the door was shut, Harry and Mike would pin him. Giles Talbot was going to spend the rest of the day and night here, the Mad Hatters sitting on him until they could escort him and the Rose file to MI-5.

Osla flew out, tugging on her long white gloves, pushing diamond clips into her hair. "Is it too early for a drink?" The sound of cheers and noise from the streets below made their way through the windows. Osla slung a few ropes of pearls about her neck, took the flask Harry offered, and swigged. They were all waiting for the knock. Harry prowled back and forth like a black-maned lion; Beth ripped at her nails; Mab was on the telephone trying to get through to someone at MI-5, GCHQ, anywhere. Mike massaged his knee, remarking, "Can I pound this bugger?"

"I get first crack," Harry growled.

"*I* get first crack," Beth protested. "I'm the one he locked in a loony bin."

The minutes ticked by. Mab turned on the radio, and they heard the commentators: "*At Kensington Palace, His Royal Highness the Duke of Edinburgh*"—so that was Philip's new title, Osla thought—"*with the Marquess of Milford Haven, his best man, checked the time for the start of his drive . . .*"

"Giles is late." Mab and Osla exchanged glances. "He's never late."

"Traffic?"

Osla didn't dare take that chance. "Mike, stay here. Nab him if he turns up." Osla, Mab, Beth, and Harry headed for the door. Osla ditched the silver fox stole she'd have worn if she really were going to the wedding, yanking on J. P. E. C. Cornwell's trusty old overcoat as she ran for the stairs. Surely Giles couldn't have smelled a trap . . .

His flat was just a few scant miles from Osla's, but the way lay right through the heart of the city, and they hadn't a hope of a taxi. People were flooding off the sidewalks and spilling into the street; here and there an automobile inched along, horn blaring, but the crowd was a relentless river flooding inexorably toward the abbey. Harry forced a path through the crush, Beth at his elbow, Mab and Osla bringing up the rear. Overhead the sky lowered, gray and cloudy. Osla's heart thundered.

Is he making a run for it?

Over an hour, forcing a path through the crowds. By Buckingham Palace, people lined fifty deep along the street, holding up mirrors to get a better look. Banners flapped, pennants waved, and a great heaving cheer went through the crowd as a horse-drawn carriage emerged from the gates and began rolling toward the abbey: the queen and Princess Margaret. Osla caught a flash of white flowers in the bridesmaid's dark hair, then the carriage was gone. The crowd surged, and Harry shouted back to form a chain, dragging them bodily through.

Off the main thoroughfare at last, into the residential streets, where people still buffeted past toward the abbey. Giles's building—a stitch stabbed Osla's side like a stiletto, but she took the stairs two at a time. How many times had she come here after a date, chatting companionably? *Rot,* she thought, knocking her gloved knuckles against the door, hoping her breathlessness sounded like excitement. "Giles, darling, don't faff about. What's keeping you?"

No answer.

"I'm breaking it down," Harry said, forcing the knob—but the door swung open, unlocked.

The room inside had been ransacked. Every drawer stood open, clothes lay on the floor, a rattle of change spilled near the door as if money had been counted too hastily.

Beth gave a wordless snarl, barely human.

I cannot have tipped him off, Osla thought frantically, going over her telephone call. She would *swear* Giles had heard nothing in her voice to cause alarm. If she'd made the mistake that ended up ruining this operation . . .

"He was coming to meet you." Harry picked up the gloves

lying atop the pristine hat by the door—a gentleman's finishing touch to a formal wedding ensemble. "It can't have been our call that spooked him. What made him—"

Mab held up a newspaper lying beside a tea mug. The newspaper's front page was all wedding news, but it was folded to the back pages—a picture of Beth's unsmiling face. "'*Reward offered for news of the woman in this photograph. Contact the following number, as her family is concerned*' . . . That's an MI-5 number, or I'll eat my hat. '*Recently spotted in Buckinghamshire*'—bloody hell, do you suppose one of Dilly's neighbors saw—"

"Who cares who spotted her? Giles knows Beth's done a bunk." Osla's mouth had a sour taste. "And he'd know if she got all the way to Bucks, she could find BP friends. People who would believe her."

Beth stood silent, shaking, furious.

"All right, so he's rabbited," said Mab. "Wherever he goes to ground, MI-5 will track him down. We stick to the plan, present our evidence, let them bring him in."

"It could be tomorrow morning by the time they're putting things in motion. What if he uses the wedding confusion to train it out of London, head for the channel? If he leaves the *country* . . ."

They all looked at each other.

"He can't have got far yet." Osla touched the teakettle on the stove. "Still warm. He'll never get a car through these crowds, so he'll be on foot. Probably making for the next train out of the city." Osla knew the trains here like the back of her hand. "Victoria station is nearest."

That would take them into the thick of the crush again, but there was no help for it. Mab rang Osla's flat, telling Mike to meet them at Victoria as Osla hurtled down the stairs. The others pressed behind, back out to the main thoroughfare, where they were met by a wall of screams. All London was going wild. A gilt-decked coach pulled by two swiftly trotting white horses was rolling past, and Osla caught a flash of white lace in the window: Philip's royal bride.

"This way," Osla shouted, hauling her silver satin train over one arm and taking off for Victoria through the brick wall of wedding revelry.

CHAPTER 83

He will get away. The words slid through Beth's blood like poison. She didn't trust that MI-5 could find him if he disappeared from London. Who knew what Moscow connections might help him vanish overseas? Perhaps the fear was irrational, but she couldn't shake the thought: if he got away now, he might get away for good.

"He could take the Chatham main line all the way to Dover." Mab's eyes flew over the train schedule. "Disappear across the channel—"

"There's a train leaving twenty minutes sooner than that for Brighton, he might grab the first ride out of London—"

"Check them both—"

Mike and Mab charged toward the Brighton line like a couple of long-legged greyhounds. Harry went for the Chatham line, Osla shoving behind in her silver satin and diamonds, Beth bringing up the rear. Victoria station was more of a madhouse than Clockwell during a full moon. Women in wedding-day best poured off trains with flowers and pennants, men passed flasks to toast the royal pair, children shrieked with excitement. The crowd heaved out toward the stairs like a boat wallowing in heavy seas, Beth and her friends seemingly the only ones fighting their way in and not out. Beth couldn't breathe around the scream locked in her lungs. *He won't get away—he* will not *get away . . .*

Osla halted, diamond roses coming loose from her hair as she craned her neck. She looked like a royal bridesmaid who had been cut out of the wedding party and run mad—*mad, mad, mad;* the word chimed through Beth's mind. They fought their way through to the last platform, Harry checking every bench, Beth pushing into the gents' loo, looking for that flash of red hair. "Hey there—" a startled man protested, dribbling piss over his shoes. Back out, toward the station's entrance. The most recent train had emptied, passengers squeezing toward the surface; the crush thinned. Beth's eyes hunted. Nothing.

"Too late." The words pushed out through her stone-stiff lips.

"That son of a *bitch,*" Osla snarled.

The nearest ticket booth had the radio turned all the way up. Over the squeal of train wheels came the sound of the broadcast from the abbey: "*Philip, wilt thou have this woman for thy wedded wife?*"

"We are not too late," Osla said fiercely, a tiny diamond-decked lioness yanking Beth along. Over the pushing throng, Beth saw Mab and Mike coming toward them, no sign of a red-haired man dragging between them. The sob built in Beth's throat.

"Elizabeth Alexandra Mary, wilt though have this man . . ."

Then the crowd eddied, and Beth saw him.

A split-second glimpse of a man in an impeccable overcoat and trilby, fingers drumming on the handle of his overnight case as he looked down the track, and then an excited family in Sunday best pushed across the platform and hid him from view.

But he was there.

"Giles," Beth whispered, and then she was making for him. "Giles." Shoving a man twice her size out of her path, knocking over a display of wedding-day pennants. "*Giles.*"

He couldn't have heard her, but his head jerked up, as though he felt her coming. Beth saw shock ripple across his face. For all his fear at seeing her escape in the paper, fear sufficient to send him running for the nearest train, he'd surely never thought she was so close: Beth Finch, the woman he'd wronged, no longer confined behind walls and straitjackets but mere feet away, aiming at him like a sword thrust. And behind her the others: Osla, Mab, Harry, Mike, catching sight of their enemy and closing in like hounds.

Be afraid, Beth thought, feeling her hair blow across her face from the whirling gust of another train as she advanced on him. *Be afraid now, traitor.*

Giles dropped his bag and ran.

Beth sprinted after him, and Osla was only half a step behind, silver satin billowing in her wake.

A party of schoolchildren cut off Mike and Harry, slowing them down, but Mab's tall shape broke forward ahead of the crush. Beth saw the cry that escaped Giles the moment he registered Mab's unmistakable Valkyrie head. He broke left; Mab made a grab for his elbow and tweaked his gabardine sleeve, but he stumbled and kept moving, sliding through the clumps of passengers disgorging from the newest train. He was making for the stairs leading aboveground.

Mab and Osla and Beth were all running together now, Harry and Mike somewhere behind, but the crowd was too thick and they'd all sprinted themselves breathless getting to the station. Mab's breath was coming in cigarette rasps—Osla with her shorter stride was falling back—Beth tried to put on a burst of speed but her lungs were still weak from asylum pneumonia—and Giles was pulling ahead with a bound onto the first stairs. If he lost himself in the vast crowds outside—

Beth saw Osla swing toward a man leaning against the station wall, reading a heavy leather-bound book. Osla wrenched it out of his hands and hurled it like she was bowling a ball in a Bletchley Park rounders game.

The book hit Giles square on the shoulder, and he stumbled on the steps. That was all Mab needed, catching up in three leaping strides of her endless legs, seizing him by the elbow, and swinging him back round into the station with a snarl that bared every tooth in her head.

Giles ripped his arm free with a shout, but momentum sent him stumbling headlong toward Beth. Everything seemed to slow in that instant, enough for her to gather her limbs and launch herself into his chest. Beth bore him to the ground with a scream of fury that scraped her throat like a handful of knives and spun every head within fifty yards.

In the sudden stunned hush, Beth heard tinny voices from the ticket-booth radio: the Westminster Abbey choir, voices lifted in joyous clarion song. The royal couple were married.

Underneath her, Beth could feel Giles shuddering. She looked into his face inches under her own, and a wave of disgust and fury lashed her as she realized he was crying. "I'm sorry," he whispered.

"I don't—want—your *sorry,*" Beth spat, lungs still fighting for air. "You cut-price—second-rate—*asinine* little traitor."

"I'm not—"

"That's exactly what you are." Osla limped up, panting, one shoe missing, and sat down in a billow of silver satin on Giles's tangled legs. "Don't even think about getting up. And by the way"—twisting off her emerald—"the engagement's off. Never liked green stones, anyway."

"Shall I spike him?" Mab placed one smart-heeled boot on Giles's forehead, glaring down. He lay without struggling, tears slipping down his cheeks in tired gusts. Whispers were rising from the puzzled onlookers.

"Here now, what's going on?" A policeman, red faced, indignant, the most welcome sight on earth. "Brawling on Her Highness's wedding day, now, I won't stand for that, not in Victoria station."

Mab tried to explain, Harry's voice sounded, and then people were shoving, voices rising. A railway conductor tried to haul Mab away from where she was still half standing on Giles, and Mike promptly clocked him. The man went down like a sack of turnips. Osla was gesticulating at the policeman, who shouted her down, and Beth was the only one to hear Giles's terrified whisper.

"What's going to happen to me?"

Beth looked down into his eyes. The man who'd stolen years of her life. Betrayer of her friends; betrayer of the future queen who was even now signing her bridal registry; betrayer of the stalwart stammering king who had walked her down the aisle. Betrayer of Churchill, who beamed beside the new prime minister in the abbey—Churchill, who had limped into Bletchley Park and told them the war couldn't be won without them.

Betrayer of Bletchley Park, all that it was, all that Beth loved.

She pushed herself unsteadily away from Giles, not wanting to touch him. "Whatever happens to you," she rasped, "it won't be enough."

"You are all under arrest," the policeman trumpeted, and the world went right on sliding into madness.

CHAPTER 84

I missed the wedding of the century, Osla thought, contemplating her cell bars. *Oh well!*

The police had ended up arresting Giles, Osla, Mab, Beth, Harry, Mike, the man with the leather-bound book, and two ticket collectors. Now here they all were in a drunk tank, who knew where, with threats from the policeman that they could all bloody well stay there overnight or until the wedding celebrations were over, whichever came first. Somewhere further along the corridor Osla had seen Mab and Mike go into one cell, Beth and Harry and Giles into another. Giles was protesting, but not very clearly. Somehow in the scuffle before handcuffs came out, he'd tripped over Harry's boot, crashed to the ground, and come up with a dislocated jaw. Sad, that. Osla smiled, contemplating the wreck of her silver satin Dior, hearing the rattle of bars. *We did it,* she thought.

Well, almost. Giles Talbot couldn't talk his way out of this cell before Peggy Rock got through to someone at her GCHQ offices and rallied assistance—or, failing that, before Osla played her trump card. "If it's not too too inconvenient, sir," she'd already drawled to the sergeant, sliding a discreet pound note into his palm, "could I just bip out to the desk and make the teensiest 'phone call before you release anyone in our party?" Blinking her lashes, playing up the Mayfair vowels: clearly a female with the kind of family you didn't want descending wrathfully on your doorstep to rescue their lost princess.

"Witless bloody debs," the sergeant had muttered, but Osla just grinned. The phrase had lost its sting. Could a witless deb have helped catch a traitor to the crown? No. And the important people—her BP family, the consort of their future queen, and a highly secret portion of MI-5—knew, or would soon know, what she'd done. If the rest of the world continued to rate her low, well, that was their loss. Osla Kendall had proved herself to everyone who mattered.

"You're definitely not my wife," a voice commented from the other side of the cell bars. Osla looked up to see a tall officer in Rifle Brigade uniform.

"I don't think I'm your wife either," Osla replied. "Unless I'm suffering from spectacular amnesia."

The officer turned to the sergeant. "Why exactly did I get called to the clink for some woman I'm not married to?" His voice sounded familiar . . .

The sergeant handed Osla's overcoat over. "Your name was in the label, Major Cornwell. That desk clerk should have verified—" Commotion further along the corridor made the sergeant break off. "A moment, I'll be back . . ."

He hurried off, and Osla looked at the worn-out overcoat she'd been hauling about since the Café de Paris. Looked at the man holding it: dark haired, a major's insignia on his uniform, a Military Cross . . . "You're J. P. E. C. Cornwell." Her Good Samaritan with the low voice, so soothing in the aftermath of the explosion: *Sit down, Ozma, and let me see if you're hurt* . . . Osla scrambled up, coming to the bars. "What do all those initials stand for? I've been wanting to know for *years.*"

"John Percival Edwin Charles Cornwell," he said, still looking bemused, throwing a half salute. "Major, Rifle Brigade. First in Egypt, then with the partisans in Czechoslovakia—"

Osla reached through the grill, took hold of her Good Samaritan's collar, drew his head down, and kissed him warmly on the mouth through the bars of her cell. She smelled heather and smoke—that wonderful scent that had long since faded out of his overcoat. "I've owed you that since you pulled me out of the rubble of the Café de Paris," she said, drawing back with a grin. "For God's sake, tell me: who's Ozma of Oz?"

"L. Frank Baum's lost princess. My favorite book." He gave her a slow, thoughtful look. "Pleased to meet you, Osla Kendall. May I say, you have very nice handwriting."

"Oh, blast. You actually got my message-in-a-bottle letters?" Osla had assumed those missives had dropped into limbo, considering the lack of response. She'd never written anything about BP, but still . . .

"They sat in a heap with my old landlady until I finally came back to London. I wrote you back then, but that Buckinghamshire address was defunct." He regarded her with a nearly invisible smile. "Did you ever get over that chap who broke your heart?"

Osla waved a hand. "He's last year's news, darling."

"Good. You sounded very low for a while there."

"I'm really quite a fizzing sort, normally. You're just always running into me when I'm in a blue funk. Heartbroken, or recently bombed, or incarcerated . . ."

"Yes, why are you in jail, exactly?"

"'Fraid I can't say. Official Secrets Act."

Major John Cornwell rubbed a hand through his dark hair, looking bemused again, but the sergeant's voice interrupted. "You're free to go, sir. Sorry for the inconvenience. And you, Miss Kendall, have been cleared to make your telephone call."

"*Don't* go anywhere," Osla told J. P. E. C. Cornwell with a sparkling smile, breezing past him for the front desk. Where her trump card hit the table as she rang a number by heart:

"A message for Prince Philip, please—yes, the Duke of Edinburgh. I'm aware he's at his wedding breakfast." She lowered her voice and murmured for a long moment, as every policeman within earshot gaped. "No, I can't give any further details. But he gave me this number for any moment of dire need, and that need is now."

CHAPTER 85

*****SECRET: INTENDED RECIPIENT EYES ONLY*****

AS PER PENALTY OF PROSECUTION UNDER
OFFICIAL SECRETS ACTS 1911 AND 1920

21 December 1947

Our red-haired chap has been very talkative. After we've finished picking his brain, I recommend our Kiloran Bay facility in Scotland—significantly more secure, if more bleak, than the sanitarium which failed to hold Miss Finch.

One final thought . . . there are hints that our red-haired chap is not the only compromised individual in our circles. Once the current matter is finished, I suggest we divert our efforts toward this new information. Time to settle accounts.

"It looks dead," Mab said.

"Deader than Manderley after the fire," Osla agreed.

Beth gazed across the weed-choked lake at Bletchley Park's mansion. The green copper dome and elaborate brickwork thrust against the gray winter sky, and a few people came in and out—but BP had changed. The long block buildings and old green huts were shuttered for Christmas, the grounds all but empty, but it was more than that. Beth shivered in her smart new tartan coat and scarlet scarf, bending down to rub Boots's head. She was suddenly glad she hadn't come alone.

"It's not usually this empty. The space is rented out now, for training courses and so forth." Osla's breath puffed in the cold; in her full-skirted ivory coat edged in silvery mink, complete with mink hood sitting on her dark hair, she looked like a Christmas tree fairy. "If it weren't two days before Christmas, this place would be bustling."

"Not with our kind of bustle." Mab looked at the mansion. "Remember the day we arrived, and you called it Lavatory Gothic?"

Beth still couldn't say a word. The mansion's double doors, which she'd pushed open in the dead of a rainy night with Matapan's decrypted battle plans in her fist . . . the lakeshore where the Mad Hatters had discussed so many books . . . the Cottage, out of sight from here, whitewashed and homely. Mentally she opened the door to see Dilly Knox at his desk. *Have you got a pencil? We're breaking codes . . .*

Tears blurred her eyes. "Let's go."

Neither Osla nor Mab argued. They turned, meandering back toward the gates, which were no longer manned by stern guards. A faint sprinkling of snow frosted the ground.

"So we're all done with our debriefings." Mab stalked along in forest-green trousers and a long jade-green coat, a fedora like a man's slanted across her brow. "MI-5 isn't going to call us in again, surely."

"Doubtful, darling," Osla said. "Did either of you find out just why the Russians were discussing Giles via Enigma traffic in the first place? I asked during my interview, but the chap got dreadfully snippy."

"Peggy told me after her debriefing," Beth said. "My guess

was right. The Reds captured a German Enigma machine during one of those back-and-forths across Soviet territory. They passed a few messages through Giles's contact in London, trying it out—Giles was hoping they'd adopt it for their own coded traffic. Our Y-stations were monitoring Soviet radio chatter, so it was flagged and Dilly saw it."

"What do you think happened to Giles?" Mab stared at the lake, and Beth knew she was remembering when she and Osla first clapped eyes on him: wading out in his drawers, grinning and friendly.

"I don't think we're ever going to know," Beth said, indifferent.

"What's more, I don't give a toss," Osla pronounced. "As long as he's gone."

They wandered clear of BP, not looking back. "Are we all going to the station?" Osla asked at last. "I'm nipping back to London, Mab's off to York. *Don't* tell me you're going to the village to see your family, Beth."

"No." The Finch family was in an uproar: first Beth's escape from Clockwell, then her official release, then the news that her father had left Mrs. Finch out of the blue. He'd moved to a tiny flat and was refusing to come home; the house would apparently have to be sold; Mother had taken shrieking to her bed; none of Beth's siblings wanted her to live with them . . . Beth had already decided the entire matter could be worked out without her. "I'm waiting here. Harry's driving over from Cambridge."

Osla cocked her head. "You and Harry . . . is that still on? Don't you want something more, I don't know, *usual*?"

Marriage, Beth supposed she meant. Children, a house, a man's shoes to line up with hers. Beth shook her head but smiled. "It's what I want, and it's very much still on."

"Well, where are you going to live? You can bunk with me in Knightsbridge as long as you like, you know."

Bless Osla, Beth thought, but *no.* Three and a half years in the asylum; what she craved now was space to herself. Space to process what had happened to her, let the bad dreams come, get through it and out the other side. Harry understood that without a word needing to be said—he'd wangled her a clerk's job at Scopelli's Music Shop in Cambridge, and a room too: *Mr. Scopelli says you can use the old bomb-shelter bedroom in the back, until you get digs of your own.* Beth imagined mornings alone with Boots and a cup of tea, listening to Bach partitas; afternoons quietly working the counter; Sunday mornings in chapel, thinking of codes as hymns soared. Harry bringing lunch from his college every day, staying the night when his family could spare him . . . She smiled again. For now, that sounded fine.

"I still think MI-5 owes you compensation," Mab said tartly. "Locked up unfairly and still managing to bring a traitor to their door? A little cash to rent you a flat is the least they could do."

"There might be something, eventually." Beth knew she wasn't going to work at the music shop forever. *If you want the sort of job that uses our skills, come to GCHQ with me,* Peggy had said after their final debrief. *Even without a war, Britain needs people like us. They'd leap for joy to get you.*

Yes, Beth thought. Her work was a drug she had no desire to ever purge from her blood; she wanted to go back to it . . . just not quite yet. She was no longer trapped inside the clock, but she didn't feel like she'd entirely caught up with time outside it, either.

"To tide you over until those chintzy MI-5 snakes cough up"—Osla took out her cigarette case and extracted a flash of green from among the Gauloises—"here. Pawn it."

Beth looked at the ring with its emerald the size of a halfpenny. "You're sure?"

"I thought about throwing it in Giles's face when we were arrested," Osla mused. "But really, why should *he* get it back? And outside novels, who really tosses emerald rings around like seashells, anyway? I'd far rather it went to rent you a flat."

Or maybe, Beth thought, it could pay for treatment for her Go-playing friend still locked in Clockwell. To see if anything might be done for her. "Thank you, Os."

"Give me one of those cigarettes?" Mab asked before Osla put away the case. "And a light . . . ooh, what's that?" Examining Osla's silver lighter. "*JPECC*?"

"The Honorable John Percival Edwin Charles Cornwell," Osla said, lighting two Gauloises.

"How the *hell* do you walk into jail with a traitor and walk out again with a lord?"

"He's not a lord, yet. His father's the seventh Baron Cornwell, that's all. They have an absolutely topping place in Hampshire. I'm visiting over New Year's, once I've negotiated my new post with my *Tatler* editor." Osla passed Mab's cigarette over. "Christmas in York for you, my queen?"

"I'll be back in time to bundle Lucy and Eddie up for their first snowball fight. You wouldn't believe how excited Mike gets about snow. It's an Australian thing." Mab turned her wedding ring around her finger. "It'll be good to be home."

"Funny thing about homes." Osla looked thoughtful, taking a deep draw off her cigarette. "I was always thinking I didn't have one, not really. Houses, hotels, places to stay, but no home. No real family. Not really belonging anywhere." She looked back at Bletchley Park. "But there's this place."

"This place is dead," Beth pointed out.

"We still belong here. All of us. Look how everyone answered the call, even people we barely knew like Asa and the Prof, Cohen and Harry's cousin Maurice. All hurrying out to Courns Wood without a question asked. That's a kind of family." Osla smiled, a few snowflakes catching in her dark lashes. "Not exactly the sort of family I was always dreaming about, but it still counts."

They stood in the softly falling snow, putting off the moment of departure. *Osla returning to London,* Beth thought, *me to Cambridge, Mab all the way back to York.* Despite Osla's talk of family, what were the chances they'd ever meet up again without the work of Bletchley Park to draw them together? The three of them had nothing in common besides BP. In the normal course of life, they would never have crossed paths at all.

"Thank you," Beth blurted. "Both of you. Breaking me out of the asylum, hiding me . . ." It had to be said, they had to be thanked. What if she never got the chance after today?

"I don't need thanks." Mab took a last drag on her cigarette. "Duty, honor, oaths—they are not just for soldiers. Not just for men."

"I want to thank you anyway." Beth took a deep breath, eyes blurring. "And—and I'm sorry. Coventry. Not warning you . . ."

She couldn't hold their eyes. She looked away, back toward Bletchley Park.

"Bloody hell, Beth." Mab dropped her cigarette, grinding it out under one high-heeled boot. "There are things I don't want to forgive you for, you *or* Os, and maybe I won't ever be able to completely. But that doesn't mean we don't—" She stopped. Looked up, brows slanted at their most ferocious angle.

The rushed three-way hug was fierce, spiky, awkward. Beth felt the silkiness of Osla's mink against her cheek, inhaled Mab's familiar perfume.

"Look—" Mab scowled as they pulled apart. "Trains run all the way to York. Don't be strangers, you two."

"We could pick a book, start up the Mad Hatters again." Osla swiped at her eyes. "Meet at Bettys, have a Tea Party with actual scones and jam . . ."

Beth pushed her wave of hair behind one ear. "I've been reading the *Principia Mathematica*." She found Isaac Newton flat going, but sometimes she caught a glimpse of intriguing spirals round the edges of the complicated exercises Harry showed her. Spirals of numbers rather than letters.

"Oh, darling, don't make us do maths," Osla groaned. "What about *The Road to Oz*? I've been devouring Baum."

"Too fantastical," Mab complained. "There's a new Hercule Poirot coming out—"

"We never did agree about books," Osla said.

"We never agreed about anything," Mab snorted, and checked her watch. "I'm going to miss my train."

A final nod, and then Beth stood before the gates with Boots whuffling about the frozen ground, watching the ivory coat and the jade-green coat swing up the road.

"Osla!" she called suddenly, almost shouting. "Mab!"

They turned in unison, those two smart brunettes who had stalked with such style into the Finch kitchen and Beth's life in 1940. Beth filled her lungs: "'*These have knelled your fall and ruin . . .*'"

Osla caught on first. "'*. . . but your ears were far away . . .*'"

Mab picked it up. "'*. . . English lassies rustling papers . . .*'"

They finished in a triumphant shout: "'*. . . through the sodden Bletchley day!*'"

And for the last time in decades, Bletchley Park resounded with the laughter of codebreakers.

EPILOGUE

Duchess of Cambridge Reopens Bletchley Park

June 2014

Job's up, strip down!" The replicated bombe machine stops, and the Duchess of Cambridge smiles at its demonstrator during her tour of Bletchley Park, Britain's now-famous codebreaking center. During the Second World War, this stately home thrummed with top-secret activity as thousands of men and women worked to crack the unbreakable Axis military codes—a feat that according to many historians shortened the war by at least two years.

The former Kate Middleton, stunning in military-style navy-and-white skirt and blouse by Alexander McQueen, officially reopens Bletchley Park after a yearlong restoration project that has restored the mansion and its surrounding huts to their wartime appearance. The site deteriorated into near-dereliction after the war but now hosts hundreds of thousands of visitors every year. The duchess has a personal reason for visiting BP: her grandmother Valerie Middleton, née Glassborow, was employed in Hut 16. Retracing her grandmother's footsteps, the duchess met with veteran codebreakers such as Mrs. Mab Sharpe, who works part-time at BP as a bombe machine demonstrator. Mrs. Sharpe—a gray-haired, unbent five foot eleven at age ninety-six—instructed her old colleague's granddaughter in the art of intercepting and decoding a Morse code message.

"What an incredible story," the duchess said. "I was aware of it when I was a young girl, and often asked Granny about it, but she was very quiet and never said anything."

"We didn't talk in those days, ma'am. We still don't." Asked if women like herself were ever called to put their talents to use after the war, Mrs. Sharpe gave a noncommittal smile. "Oh, no . . . it's enough to see the work appreciated today."

It's not a view shared by all Bletchley Park veterans, even now that the term of secrecy has officially expired. Mrs. Sharpe, surrounded by six-foot children, grandchildren, and great-grandchildren, appears happy to reminisce with Bletchley Park visitors. Other veterans have refused to release their stories until after their deaths—view the spate of posthumous memoirs, such as *Bletchley Bletherings* by Lady Cornwell, née Osla Kendall, the award-winning satirist and *Tatler* columnist whose droll, touching account of her time as a Hut 4 translator was not published until after her death in 1974. And other veterans consider the oath of secrecy binding in perpetuity. Miss Beth Finch, retired GCHQ, is known to have served as one of Bletchley Park's few female cryptanalysts, but the white-haired ninety-eight-year-old in her rose-pink cardigan politely refuses to discuss her war work: "That would be a violation of my oath."

The code of secrecy upheld by Bletchley Park's workers is fully as remarkable as their codebreaking achievements. In an age of instantaneous social media, jaws drop at the idea that thousands of men and women were simply handed the most incendiary secret of the war and kept it, to a man (or a woman). Churchill famously referred to them as "the geese who laid the golden eggs, but never cackled."

Despite the bustle of Bletchley Park today—the camera flashes of the royal visit, the millions of visitors come to marvel at the bombe machines—something of that golden silence still holds over these grounds in a hush of honored and unspoken secrets. There are stories here still untold, without a doubt: stories locked in steel-trap codebreaker minds, behind steel-trap codebreaker lips.

Bletchley Park's walls have been renovated. If only they could speak . . .

But some codes will never be broken.

About the author

2 Meet Kate Quinn

About the book

3 Author's Note

20 Reading Group Guide

23 Further Reading & Entertainment

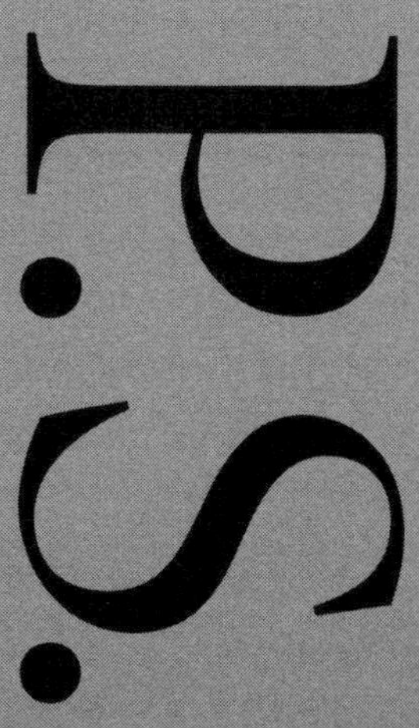

Insights,
Interviews
& More . . .

About the author

Meet Kate Quinn

Laura Jucha Photography © 2018

KATE QUINN is a *New York Times* and *USA Today* bestselling author of historical fiction. A native of Southern California, she attended Boston University, where she earned bachelor's and master's degrees in classical voice. A lifelong history buff, she has written four novels in the Empress of Rome Saga and two books set in the Italian Renaissance before turning to the twentieth century with *The Alice Network, The Huntress,* and *The Rose Code.* All have been translated into multiple languages. She and her husband now live in California with three black rescue dogs.

Author's Note

"The biggest bloody lunatic asylum in Britain."

A gate guard described Bletchley Park in those words—and to the bemused eyes of many, wartime BP more resembled a madhouse or a wacky university campus than a top-secret decryption facility. Codebreakers pitching tea mugs into the lake after fits of rumination; codebreakers cycling to work in gas masks to avoid hay fever; codebreakers playing rounders among the trees, sunbathing nude on the side lawn, and prank-riding laundry bins into unlocked loos—BP's reputation for eccentricity was inevitable, given its tendency to recruit nerds and oddballs. The staff had an extraordinarily relaxed attitude toward weird personalities; square pegs weren't required to fit into round holes, and in consequence worked spectacularly well at their nearly impossible job. Without the achievements of the people who so thoroughly cracked the supposedly uncrackable Enigma codes used by the Axis powers, the war might very well have have been lost. At the very least, it would have dragged on much longer and cost many, many more lives.

Before war was even declared, a handful of Oxford and Cambridge men were recruited into intelligence and set to work on Enigma, building on the genius work of Polish cryptanalysts Marian Rejewski, Jerzy Różycki, and ▸

Author's Note ***(continued)***

Henryk Zygalski—brilliant men whose earlier Enigma breakthroughs made Bletchley Park's success possible. The early BP cryptanalysts recruited trusted friends and acquaintances from college tutorial groups and university connections, eventually branching out to women's colleges and secretarial pools as a scattershot organization flung across a few prefabricated huts grew into an intelligence factory employing thousands. Churchill relied heavily on Park intelligence to guide his public policy; he visited the grounds in September 1941, where he commended the codebreakers on their silence as well as their work. There was certainly some information-passing within the Park—wartime diaries and memoirs record that BP workers weren't above discreetly trading news to keep an eye on friends and loved ones—but security to the outside was watertight: the Axis powers never found out how thoroughly Britain was reading their mail.

The burden of secrecy took its toll: illness, burnout, and breakdowns were common among BP staff. To combat the stress, a thriving social life grew up—off-duty codebreakers may not have had a Mad Hatters literary society reading books like *Gone with the Wind* (a bestseller of the time known for sparking controversial discussions even in the forties) or an anonymous weekly humor column, but they played in amateur dramatics, competed in chess tournaments, put on musical revues, practiced Highland dancing, and much more. The codebreakers worked hard and played hard, and veterans remember finding an open-mindedness at BP that was sorely lacking in ordinary life. Women enjoyed a level of equality with male coworkers that they were unlikely to get on the outside for years or decades; homosexual members tended to be tacitly acknowledged and accepted; people who would today be diagnosed with autism spectrum disorder could work without being forced to mask their neurodivergence. BP might have appalled military personnel with its casual attitudes to dress, language, and first-naming, but it was in many ways a haven of acceptance.

Osla Kendall is lightly fictionalized from the real-life Osla Benning, a beautiful, effervescent, Canadian-born heiress and Hut 4 translator who was Prince Philip's long-term wartime girlfriend. I have renamed my Osla out of respect for Osla Benning's still-living children; the real Osla was not at the famous bombing of the Café de Paris, was already married by the time her ex-boyfriend married Princess Elizabeth, and spent her life as a diplomatic wife rather than a columnist. But I have remained faithful to the broad strokes of her life in bringing my Osla to the page: lonely daughter to a frequently married society mother (who did maintain a suite at Claridge's), irrepressible firebrand who finagled her way back to England on a purloined air ▸

Author's Note ***(continued)***

ticket rather than sit out the war in Canada; polished debutante who gleefully got her hands dirty building Hurricanes before her fluent German landed her at Bletchley Park. She was introduced to Prince Philip at the beginning of the war by her friend (and fellow goddaughter of Lord Mountbatten) Sarah Norton, and the two promptly became inseparable. Philip and Osla bonded over similar privileged but lonely childhoods and a mutual penchant for pranks and fun; he gave her his naval insignia, took her out whenever he was in town, and wrote to her when at sea. The two drifted apart toward the end of the war, around the same time a young Princess Elizabeth appears to have caught Philip's eye at a Christmas weekend following her fundraising *Aladdin* performance at Windsor (a performance he nearly missed after a bout of the flu while holed up at Claridge's!).

No one can know whether Osla's oath of secrecy might have contributed to her estrangement with Philip, or if his German connections might have caused difficulties for Osla at BP, but there was certainly doubt about Philip of Greece's familial background in the early days. Post-Philip, Osla Benning had a short-lived engagement to a cad whose emerald ring she removed with a flippant "Never liked green stones, anyway!" before marrying John Patrick Edward Chandos Henniker-Major, a Rifle Brigade officer with a Military Cross won fighting beside Czechoslovakian partisans. He would eventually join the Foreign Office and become the eighth Baron Henniker, and he and Osla did indeed dine with Princess Elizabeth and Princess Margaret before the royal wedding in some vague idea that Osla would give the royal bride tips on handling her husband-to-be. (No word on how or if *that* was discussed over the canapés!) Lord Henniker remarked wryly that the tabloids frequently tried to dig up dirt on the lifelong friendship between his wife and the Duke of Edinburgh, who stood as godfather to Osla's eldest son. Anyone interested in the real Osla should read *The Road to Station X,* the memoir by her friend Sarah Baring (née Norton) of their time together at Bletchley Park, from which I repurposed many of Osla Benning's droll one-liners and high-wire pranks for Osla Kendall.

Beth Finch is a fictional composite of two very real women. One is nameless, a codebreaker who supposedly suffered a nervous breakdown after her love affair with a married BP colleague collapsed—the woman was sent to an asylum in fear that she would divulge secret information in her broken state. The other contributor to Beth's character and achievements is Mavis Lever, one of Bletchley Park's stars. Mavis was recruited in her teens and became one of "Dilly's Fillies"; all of Beth's codebreaking achievements—the breaking of "Today's the day minus ▸

Author's Note ***(continued)***

three," which would lead to the Cape Matapan victory; the all-L's crib; the cracking of Abwehr Enigma—are pulled from records of Mavis Lever's feats as one of Bletchley Park's few female cryptanalysts. I dramatized Mavis's achievements with a fictional character because I did not wish to imply that one of BP's greatest legends went to an asylum when in the real historic record she married a Hut 6 codebreaker as brilliant as herself and served BP until the war ended. I was not able to discover what became of the nameless codebreaker confined to an asylum. Clockwell and the Kiloran Bay facility are both fictional, but institutions of that type certainly existed, functioning as dumping grounds for inconvenient women as well as mentally ill ones. Sadly, many lobotomies were performed on the mentally ill during this period—the procedure was eventually outlawed as medically barbaric, but not before thousands of patients were maimed. The most famous victim of the surgery is probably JFK's intellectually disabled sister, Rosemary Kennedy: subjected to a prefrontal lobotomy at twenty-three in an attempt to calm her emotional outbursts, she spent the remaining sixty years of her life institutionalized, reduced to the mental capacity of a toddler.

Mab is fictional, representing the many women who served as BP's worker bees. Such women came from all walks of life, from shopgirls to lords' daughters, and served as decodists, filers, and bombe machine operators, among many other jobs. Some found the work boring and some found it fascinating—but overall, their reminiscences speak fondly of the relaxed and egalitarian attitude at Bletchley Park. BP did not employ many women at the top levels of management and cryptanalysis, and women workers tended to be paid less than their male counterparts, but it was still a place where women's voices were valued, and many missed its camaraderie and purpose once the war was over. Mab's two husbands are both fictional as well; Francis Gray is modeled after Great War poets like Wilfred Owen and Siegfried Sassoon, who immortalized the horror of trench warfare and lost innocence in verse, and Mike Sharpe is a tip of the hat to the hardworking RAF engineers who kept the bombe machines humming. The idea that a husband and wife could both work at Bletchley Park without realizing it at the time or telling each other afterward might seem like a soap opera twist, but it really happened, and more than once. Sometimes a couple only made the realization after decades of marriage!

Harry is based on two real-life Bletchley Park codebreakers: Maurice Zarb, a Hut 4 recruit of Maltese, Arab, and Egyptian descent who came to BP via a prominent London banking family (I included him as Harry's cousin so as not to erase a real man from BP history), and Keith Batey, a brilliant ▸

Author's Note *(continued)*

Hut 6 mathematician who worked with Mavis Lever, fell in love with her over the rods and cribs, and married her. Keith, like Harry and indeed many male cryptanalysts, suffered keen guilt over not being able to enlist on the front lines, and wangled permission to join the Fleet Air Arm, where he served briefly before returning to codebreaking. Bletchley Park men were frequently subjected to social shaming, both from strangers and from their own unwitting family members, for their apparent refusal to join the fight—shaming they could not refute, since they could divulge no details of their service.

Most of the other Bletchley Park people mentioned here are real: Margaret Rock, Sarah Norton, Miss Senyard, Commanders Denniston and Travis, Asa Briggs, Michael Cohen, Olive Knox, Ian Fleming (of later James Bond fame, who liaised with BP from the naval intelligence division), and Valerie Glassborow, who would become Kate Middleton's grandmother. Alan Turing, one of the great brains of the twentieth century, was the shining light of Hut 8 and would make history later with his contributions in the field of computer science and artificial intelligence. He was prosecuted for homosexuality and sentenced to chemical castration in the fifties, a hideous miscarriage of justice for which the British government has since issued an apology. Turing died of cyanide poisoning not long after, probably self-inflicted. Dilly Knox was one of the Park's eccentric geniuses, notorious for his absentmindedness, his Alice-in-Wonderland approach to codebreaking, and his habit of recruiting only women for his team. He did not have the mania for keeping his codebreakers in ignorance that prevailed in the other huts, stating, "Such action cripples the activities of the cryptographer who depends on cribs," and so his ladies tended to be better informed about the nature of their work than their colleagues. Cancer forced Knox's retirement midwar, but he worked at home until the end, reportedly on Soviet ciphers. The key to his library wall safe at Courns Wood was never found after his death, which gave me the idea to speculate what that safe could possibly have held.

Unlikely as it may seem, there really was a traitor at Bletchley Park who passed information to the Soviet Union during the war. John Cairncross worked in Hut 4 and then MI-6, and served as the basis for Giles Talbot: a red-haired individualist who became convinced that Britain was not sharing enough information with its Russian allies and took it upon himself to smuggle hundreds of decrypts out of BP to his Soviet contact. Such an activity was relatively easy, as Osla points out in *The Rose Code,* because the guardhouse effected no searches of departing shift workers (indeed, there would have been almost no way to efficiently search thousands of departing workers every ▸

Author's Note ***(continued)***

day for tiny slips of paper). Cairncross's spy activities were not exposed until years later when he was living abroad; thus he was never prosecuted. To the end of his life he maintained that he was a patriot and not a traitor; he claimed his actions saved thousands of Russian lives and denied ever passing intelligence to the USSR after the war. He was far from the only Soviet mole in MI-5, MI-6, and the Foreign Office: the ring known as the Cambridge Five (a group of Englishmen recruited during their university days) was uncovered in the highest reaches of British intelligence during the sixties. Some escaped to the Soviet Union and lived out the rest of their lives, others made deals; none were prosecuted. It has long been posited that there were more Soviet moles beyond Cairncross and the others—Giles Talbot was created to fill that unknown void. In my imagination, his discovery at the end of *The Rose Code* prompts the investigation that will eventually unearth the Cambridge Five. The Russians used their own methods of encryption during the war but definitely experimented with using captured Enigma machines, even finding ways to make them more secure postwar.

As always, I have taken some liberties with the historical record in order to serve the story. There may be some inaccuracies in the depictions of Osla, Mab, and Beth's earliest shift work; Bletchley Park was still in its infancy in

1940, protocols changed constantly, and the day-to-day operating procedures of those early days in the huts proved very difficult to research. Osla's indexing/filing section of Hut 4 was possibly not known as the Debutantes' Den until 1942; the arrival of the Glassborow twins to Bletchley Park was moved up somewhat; Bettys in York didn't lose their apostrophe until the sixties; the chemist in Bletchley village wasn't a Boots; and although the bombe operators did receive a compressed lecture about how and why the machine functioned, that lecture wasn't approved until later in the machines' usage than depicted here. Mab as a civilian would probably not have worked long-term as a bombe machine operator since the bombes were serviced by Wrens (though they did need to be tall, hence my supposition that a tall civilian woman might have been called upon to fill in).

The real Osla did build airplanes at the Hawker Siddeley factory, though they may not have begun accepting women as early as I have depicted here, and she didn't come to BP until 1941, arriving with Sarah Norton, with whom she billeted at Aspley Guise throughout her service. Osla and Philip's romance is necessarily fictionalized, since we don't know private details of their intimate moments. I have attempted wherever possible to use Philip's real words (his stiff-upper-lip "I just had to get on with it" response to his own ▸

Author's Note *(continued)*

pain over his mother's incarceration and his shattered family; his diary-entry accounts of what the Cape Matapan battle and other naval engagements were like), but he was a self-contained man even when young, and Osla was even more bound by secrecy, so my imagination has had to put words in their mouths. I've done so with a respectful attempt to depict the heady first love of two young people destined to find happiness with others, who nevertheless must have shared something very genuine and important considering that they remained friends throughout their lives.

The heavy air raid on the town of Coventry in late 1944 is fictional, though the town's devastation during an earlier raid (inspiring the German verb *coventrieren*) is true and became the foundation for one of Bletchley Park's great real-life mysteries: the claim that Hut 6 broke the warning about that raid, but Churchill sacrificed the town to protect the safety of the code. To this day, some veterans insist the message break's timing was fishy, while others insist news of the raid simply wasn't cracked in time to effect a warning. I come down on the latter side of the argument, but when the time came to enact my own fictional drama of a raid being known in advance and no warning given, I placed it all at Coventry as a nod to the existing urban legend.

There is no evidence that the brilliant Margaret Rock, who enjoyed a long, illustrious, exceedingly secret career at GCHQ after Bletchley Park, knew about the hidden bunker where a stash of undestroyed Enigma machines and bombes were stored for a rainy day . . . but there was such a bunker until 1959, and it's entirely possible that the machines were lent out to aid the postwar boom of computer science projects funded by many universities and corporations. Turing was involved with one such project in Manchester, and another was funded by Birkbeck College in London—but even if the Birkbeck College project borrowed a bombe from GCHQ's bunker and had to send that machine to a maintenance lab, it was in all probability not used in an illicit off-the-books meeting of Bletchley Park codebreakers trying to catch a traitor on the eve of the royal wedding!

And yet . . . if there had ever been a dire need for BP's brilliant personnel to dust off their skills postwar, I have no doubt that such a secret would have been flawlessly kept. Bletchley Park is at last receiving credit for its wartime achievements; the doors have been thrown open and matters that would have been unthinkable to whisper in 1941 are now discussed openly under the official Twitter handle @bletchleypark. But does that mean BP and those who worked there have shared all their secrets? Not by a long shot. There are undoubtedly stories—ciphers broken, off-the-books meetings convened, ▸

Author's Note ***(continued)***

betrayals covered up—that have been taken to the grave.

I owe heartfelt thanks to many people who helped in the writing and researching of this novel: My mother, Kelly, this book's first reader and invaluable critic. My husband, who has served with shipmates working in similar fields to the Bletchley Park women and advised me on portraying its stresses accurately, as well as the toll it takes on deployed personnel. My marvelous critique partners Stephanie Dray, Anna Ferrell, Lea Nolan, Sophie Perinot, and Stephanie Thornton, whose criticism helped whip this ungainly manuscript into shape—I would be lost without you all. My fellow historical fiction author Meghan Masterson, who named Francis Gray's book of war poetry. My agent Kevan Lyon and editor Tessa Woodward; thank you for cheering this book every step of the way. Above all, I give my fervent thanks to Kerry Howard, Bletchley Park historian and author in her own right, who fact-checked every page of this manuscript and saved my bacon in flagging its historical errors prepublication—if any inaccuracies remain after her meticulous work, it's entirely my own fault.

Thanks to historians, experts, and the indefatigable Bletchley Park Trust, BP's legacy is preserved today in countless podcasts, articles, and nonfiction books, which do honor not only to the work done there but to the

Park's veterans. Donations, grants, and the unceasing labor of both scholars and volunteers have made Bletchley Park a superb historic visitors' site—if you can manage a trip there, I highly recommend it, as the house, gardens, and surviving huts make for a fascinating walk into the past. Other sites mentioned in this book still make marvelous side trips today. Keswick, where Mab and Francis honeymoon, is beautiful if the weather is fine, and Surprise View over Derwentwater offers an astounding panorama of Lake District scenery. London is a dazzling mix of modernity and history, a far cry from its wartime, Blitz-cratered, blackout-curtained self, and Veeraswamy, where Mab and Francis had their first date, is still in business—the UK's oldest Indian restaurant. Coventry has been rebuilt, although the roofless cathedral still stands in a poignant memorial to the attack that nearly destroyed it. York is sumptuous and historic—be sure to drop by Bettys (no apostrophe), which to this day offers up an unbeatable cream tea.

Author's Note *(continued)*

Bletchley Park

British bombe machine

Kate Quinn

Enigma machine

Reading Group Guide

1. Did you come to *The Rose Code* with any preconceptions about the Bletchley Park codebreakers? Or were their achievements and history completely new to you?

2. Very little physical danger threatens Bletchley Park throughout the war, but the strain of secrecy imposes a different kind of pressure on its workers. Discuss the impact of lying to friends and loved ones about work, keeping quiet when being taunted about the lack of wartime contribution, and being unable to seek outside help for the stresses of codebreaking. How do you think you would function under such pressure? Do you think you could keep such a secret, not just during the war but for the rest of your life?

3. Fun-loving Osla struggles continually to do something important with her life and skills, but is dismissed over and over again as just a silly girl. How have such stereotypes changed for modern women? How have they remained the same?

4. Self-made Mab sees a gentlemanly husband as her ticket out of East End poverty—not just for herself, but for Lucy. How do her goals shift over time, and why?

5. Shy Beth flowers from a bullied spinster to a star cryptanalyst. How did your opinion of her change throughout the book?

6. Books and literary discussions provide a welcome distraction for Mab, Osla, Beth, and the rest of the Mad Hatters throughout the war. How do book clubs and a love for reading remain important in troubled times?

7. Osla's romance with Prince Philip is doomed to failure, given his ultimate fate as consort to the future Queen Elizabeth II. Did you root for them anyway? What about the other couples—Mab and Francis, Beth and Harry?

8. Dilly Knox, Alan Turing, Margaret Rock, Valerie Glassborow—Bletchley Park was stocked with many eccentric and interesting real-life figures from history. Which was your favorite and why?

9. Beth makes the decision not to warn Mab and Osla about the coming air raid on Coventry. Was she right to uphold her oath, or should she have found a way to warn her friends? Could you have forgiven her if you experienced what Mab and Osla did?

10. The traitor argues that giving information to the Russians was ▶

Reading Group Guide ***(continued)***

an act of patriotism, not treachery, because the Russians were Britain's allies during World War II, the prime minister wasn't sharing enough information with them, and passing intelligence saved Allied lives and ultimately helped defeat Hitler. Do you agree or disagree?

11. In the final confrontation, the Mad Hatters are able to unmask the traitor and turn them over to MI-5 for justice. Were you satisfied with their fate, or did you hope for something different?

12. The codebreaking process had many stages, from cryptanalysis (Beth's job), to machine decoding (Mab's job), to translation (Osla's job), not to mention registraton, filing, and analysis. Do you think you could have been a codebreaker? What job do you think you would have been given, if recruited to Bletchley Park?

Further Reading & Entertainment

NONFICTION

The Road to Station X by Sarah Baring
Dilly: The Man Who Broke Enigmas by Mavis Batey
Secret Days by Asa Briggs
Debs at War by Anne de Courcy
The Bletchley Girls by Tessa Dunlop
My Secret Life in Hut Six by Mair and Gethin Russell-Jones
Bletchley Park People by Marion Hill
Codebreakers: The Inside Story of Bletchley Park by F. H. Hinsley and Alan Stripp
Dear Codebreaker by Kerry Howard
The Secret Lives of Codebreakers by Sinclair McKay
1939: The Last Season of Peace by Angela Lambert
Stalin's Englishman by Andrew Lownie
We Kept the Secret by Gwendoline Page
Enigma by Hugh Sebag-Montefiore
The Debs of Bletchley Park by Michael Smith
The Secrets of Station X by Michael Smith
Cracking the Luftwaffe Codes by Gwen Watkins
The Hut Six Story by Gordon Welchman
Enigma Variations by Irene Young

Further Reading & Entertainment

(continued)

FICTION

In Farleigh Field by Rhys Bowen
Princess Elizabeth's Spy by Susan Elia MacNeal
Enigma by Robert Harris
The Amber Shadows by Lucy Ribchester

ON-SCREEN

The Bletchley Circle
The Bletchley Circle: San Francisco
Enigma
The Imitation Game